VAULT
JUL 5
VAULTCOMICS.COM

PUBLISHER
DAMIAN A. WASSEL

EDITOR IN CHIEF
ADRIAN F. WASSEL

ART DIRECTOR
NATHAN C. GOODEN

VP BRANDING/DESIGN
TIM DANIEL

DIRECTOR OF MARKETING
KIM McLEAN

PRINCIPAL
DAMIAN A. WASSEL, SR.

WRITTEN BY
TIM DANIEL

ILLUSTRATED BY
PATRICIO DELPECHE

LETTERED BY
DERON BENNETT
FOR ANDWORLD DESIGN

VAULT PRESENTS

FISSURE

CHAPTER ONE

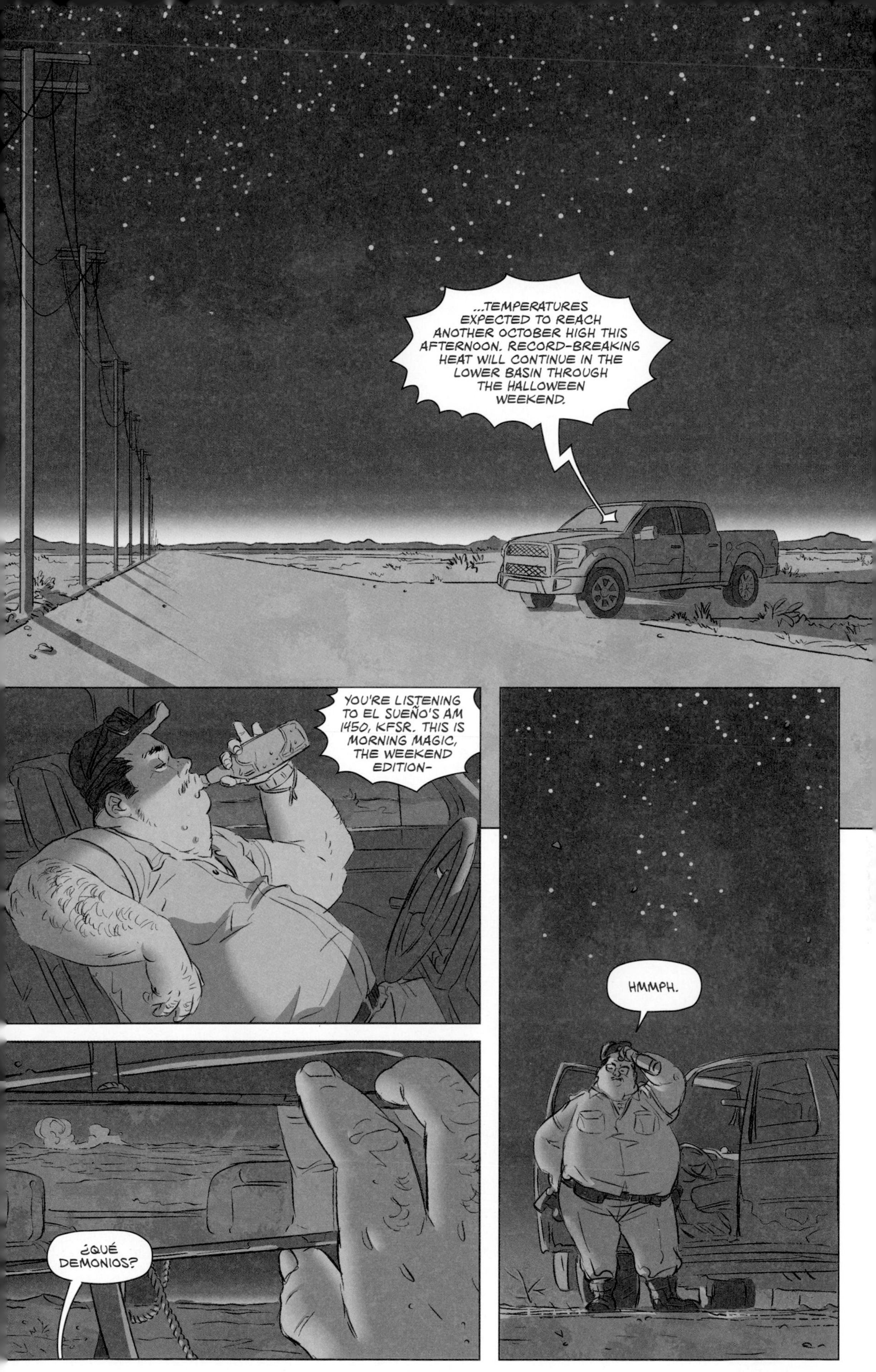
...TEMPERATURES EXPECTED TO REACH ANOTHER OCTOBER HIGH THIS AFTERNOON. RECORD-BREAKING HEAT WILL CONTINUE IN THE LOWER BASIN THROUGH THE HALLOWEEN WEEKEND.
YOU'RE LISTENING TO EL SUEÑO'S AM 1450, KFSR. THIS IS MORNING MAGIC, THE WEEKEND EDITION-
¿QUÉ DEMONIOS?
HMMPH.

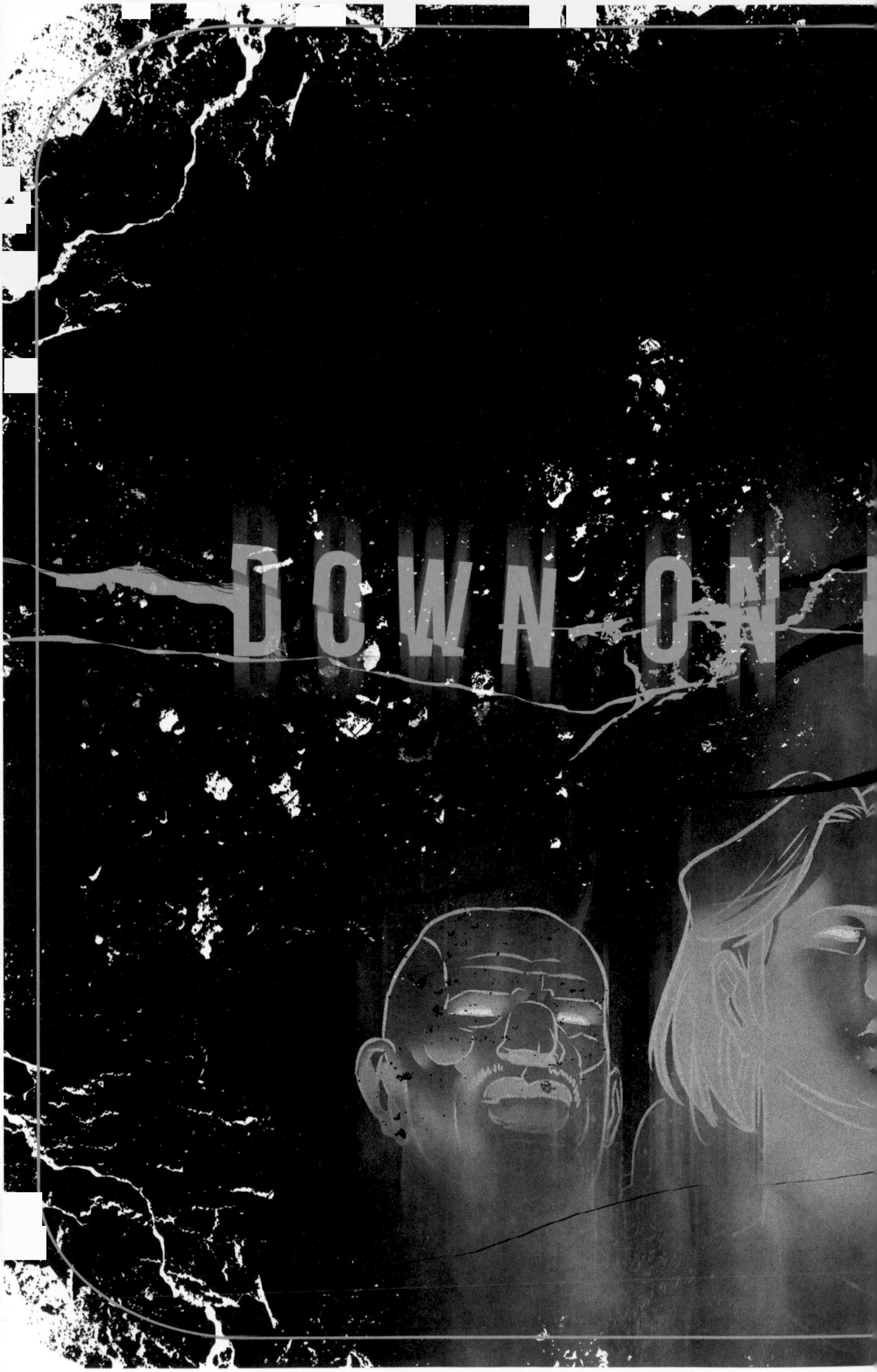
DOWN ON

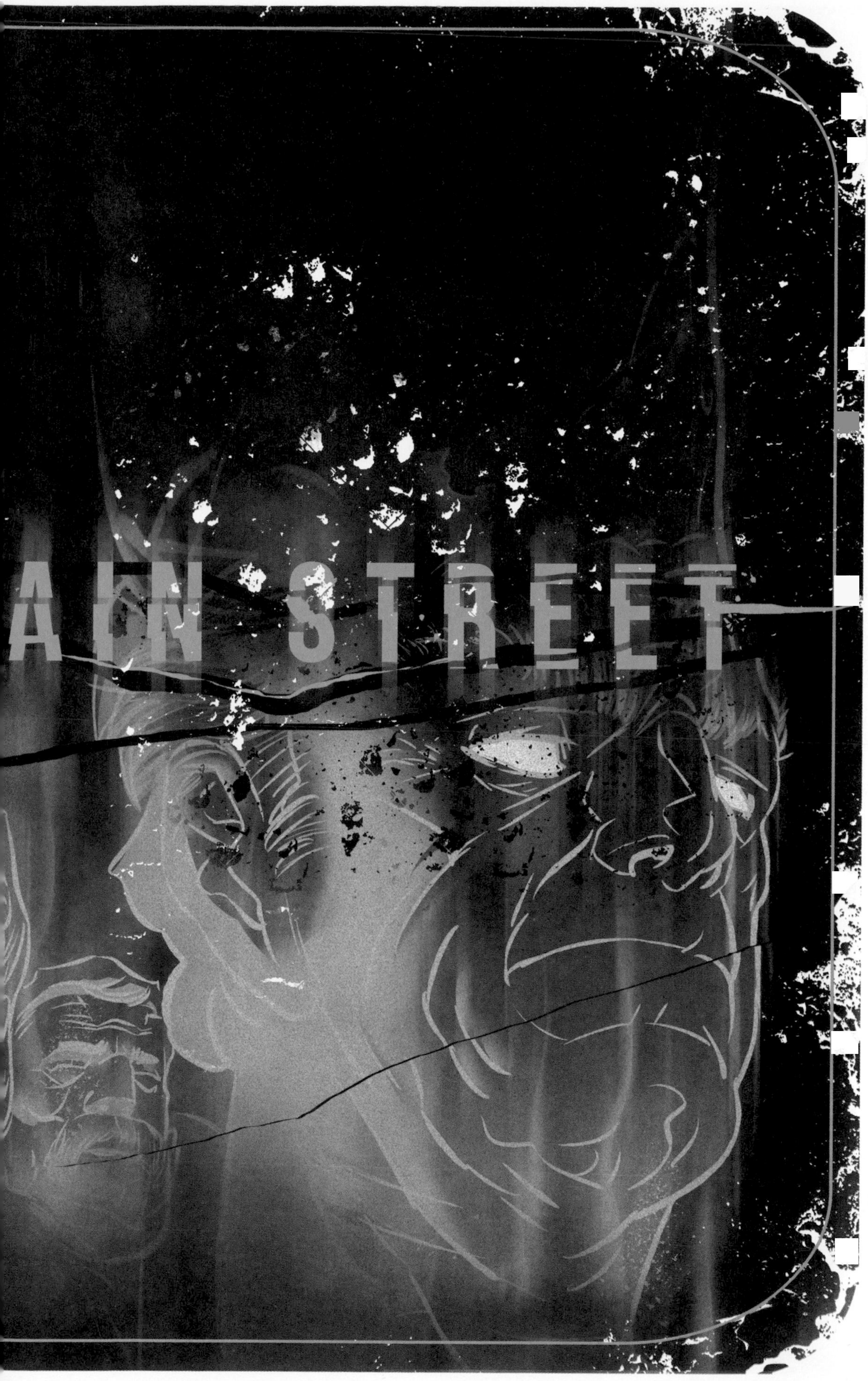
AIN STREET

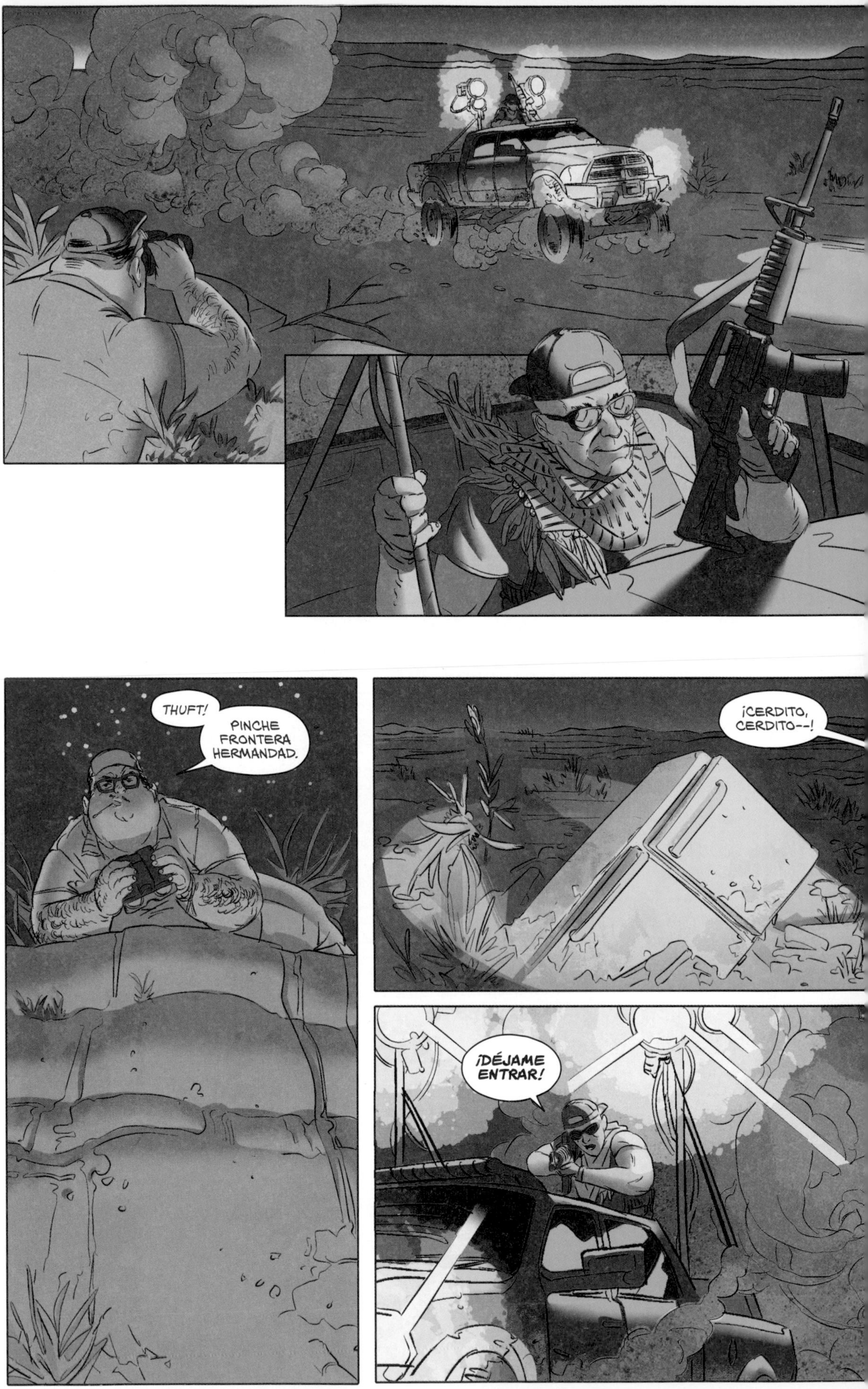
THUFT!
PINCHE FRONTERA HERMANDAD.
¡CERDITO, CERDITO--!
¡DÉJAME ENTRAR!

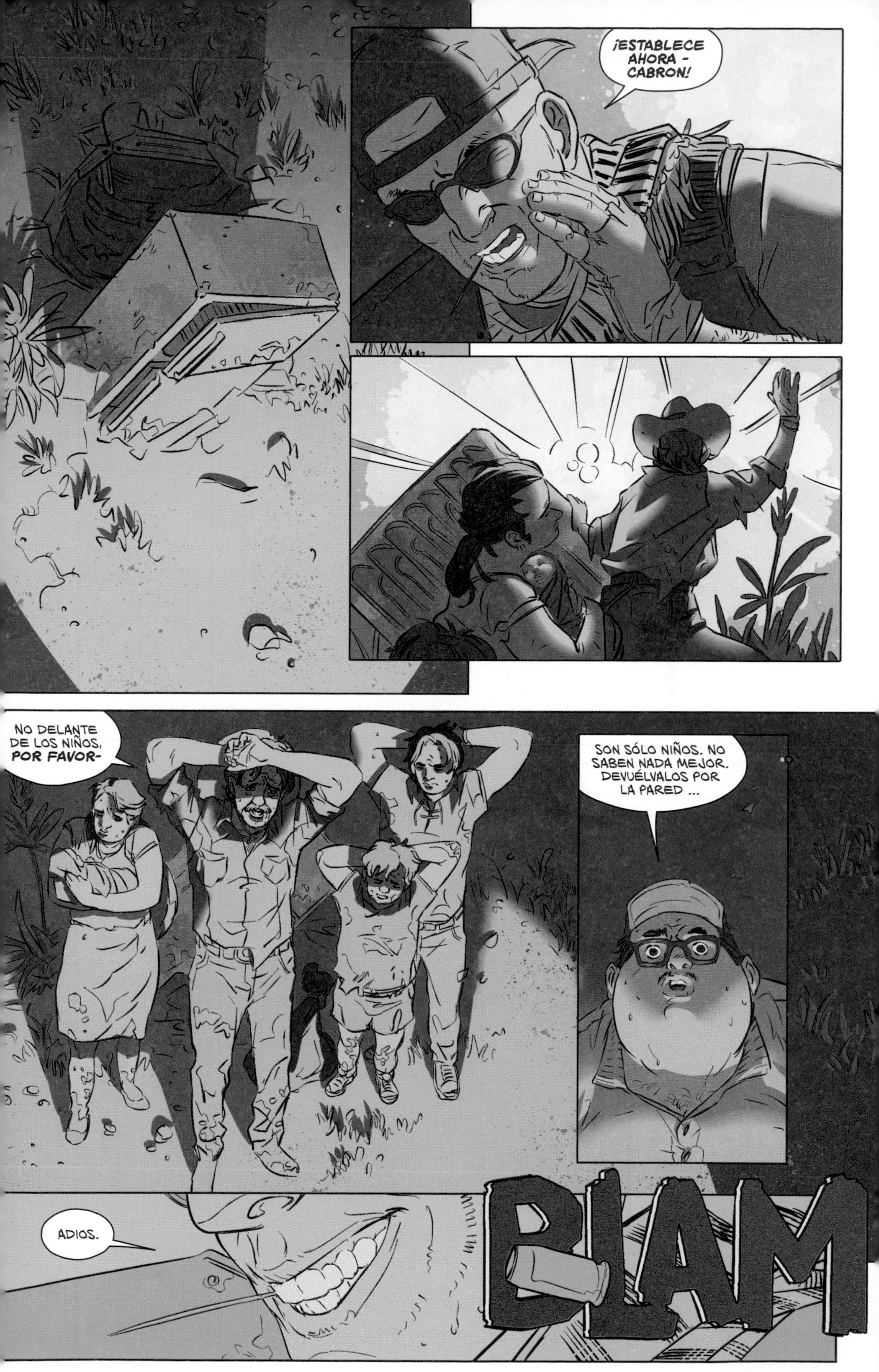
¡ESTABLECE AHORA - CABRON!
NO DELANTE DE LOS NIÑOS, **POR FAVOR-**
SON SÓLO NIÑOS. NO SABEN NADA MEJOR. DEVUÉLVALOS POR LA PARED ...
ADIOS.
BLAM

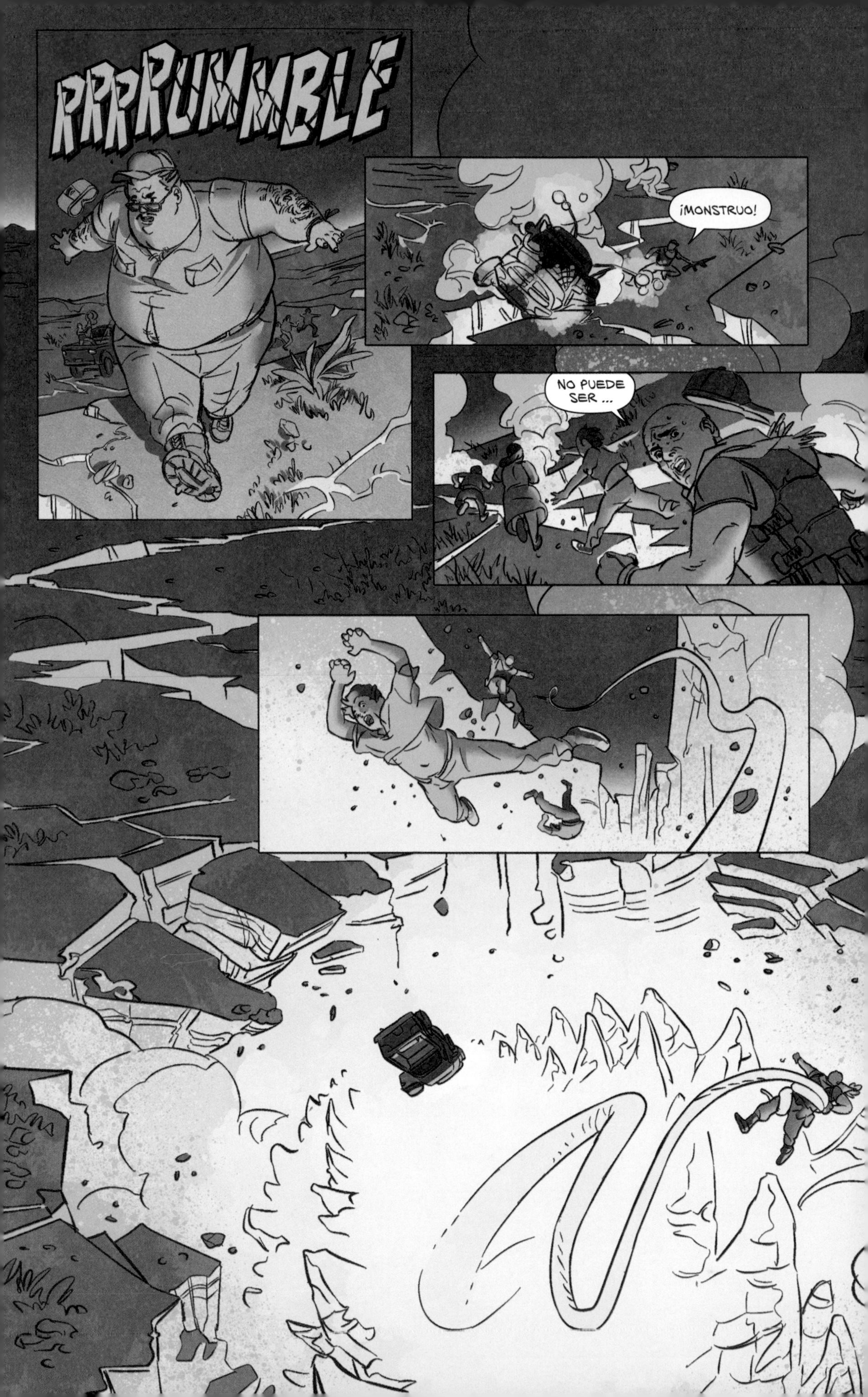
RRRRUMMMBLE
¡MONSTRUO!
NO PUEDE SER ...

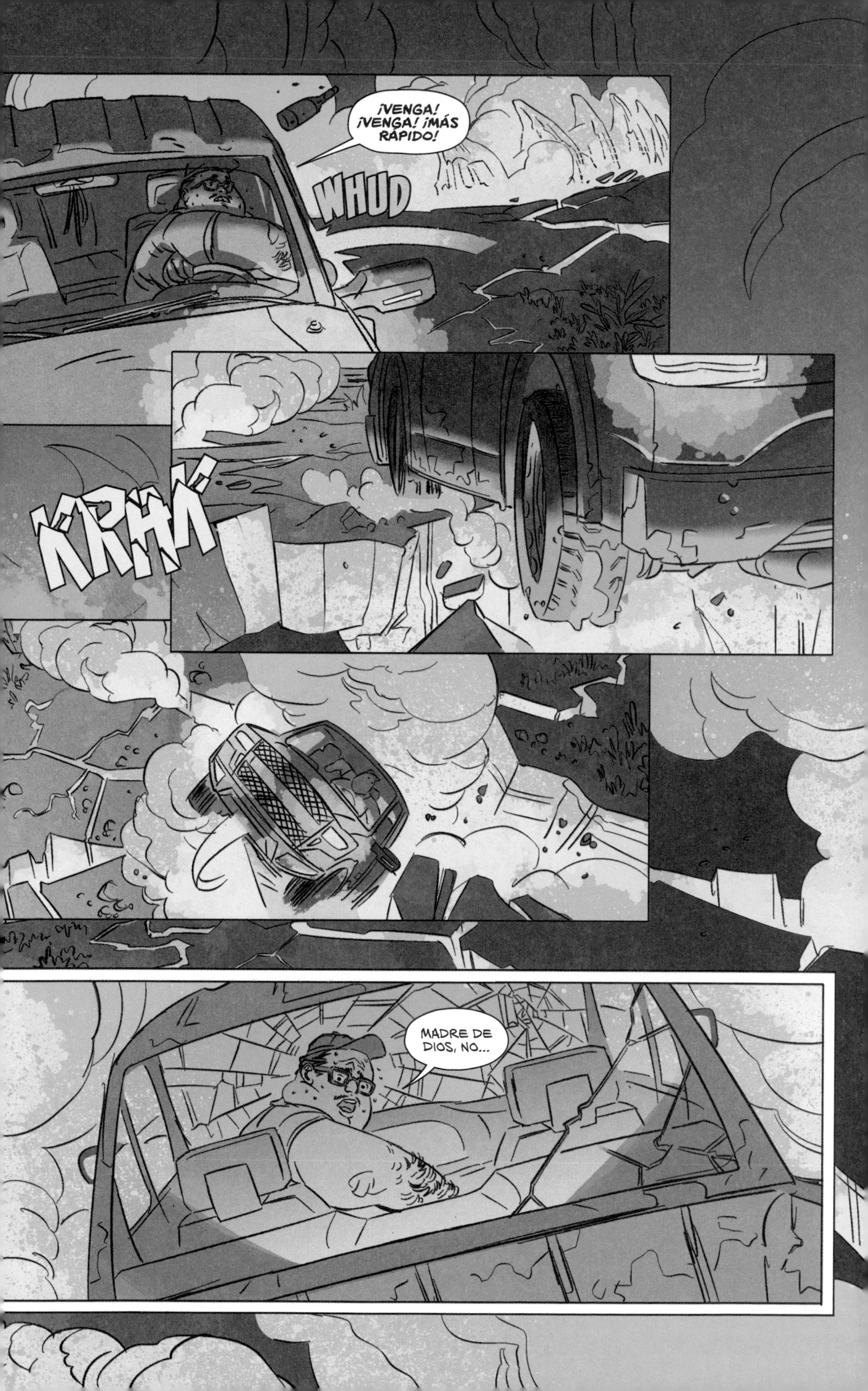
¡VENGA! ¡VENGA! ¡MÁS RÁPIDO!
WHUD
KRAK
MADRE DE DIOS, NO...

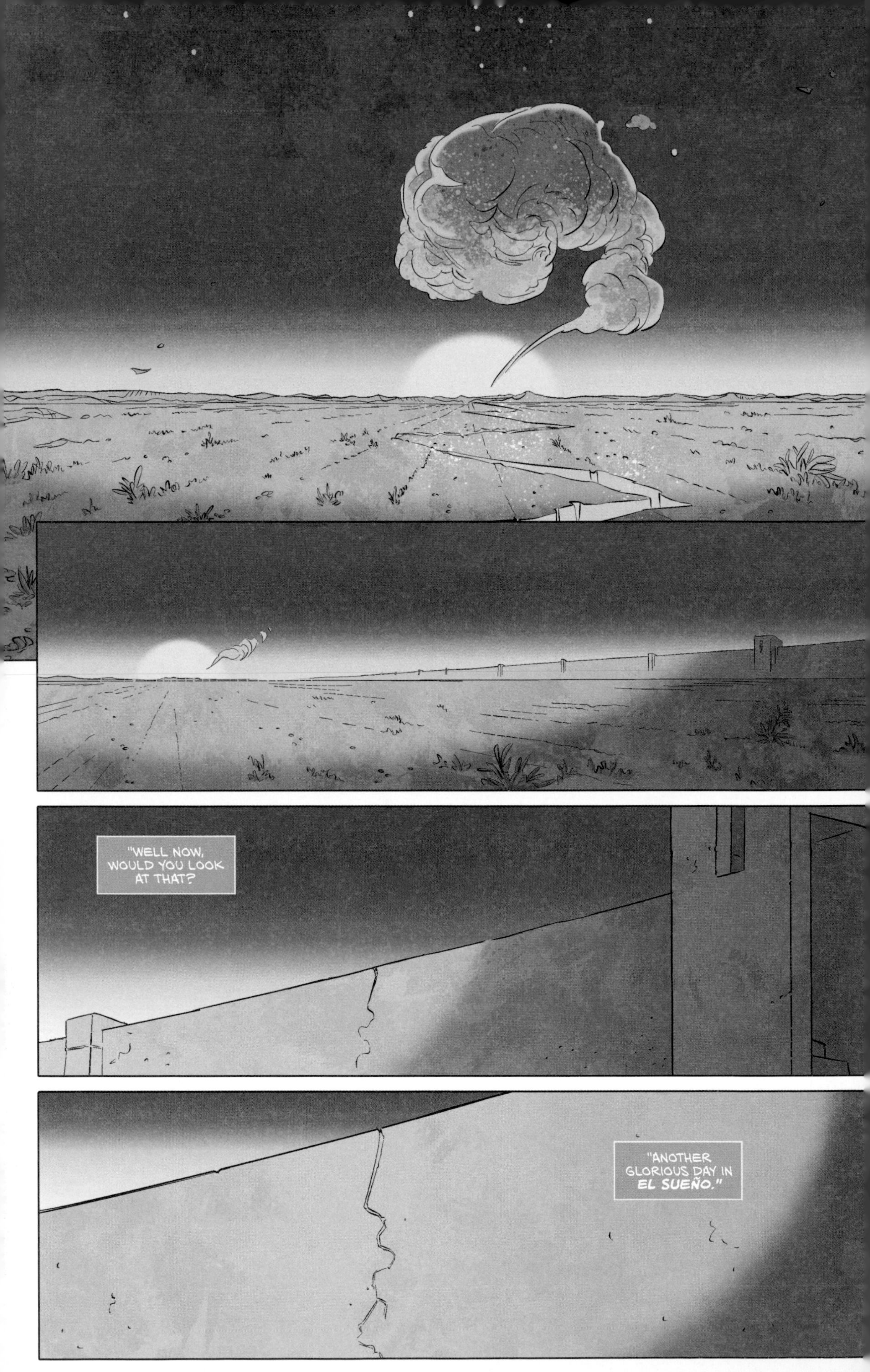
"WELL NOW, WOULD YOU LOOK AT THAT?
"ANOTHER GLORIOUS DAY IN EL SUEÑO."

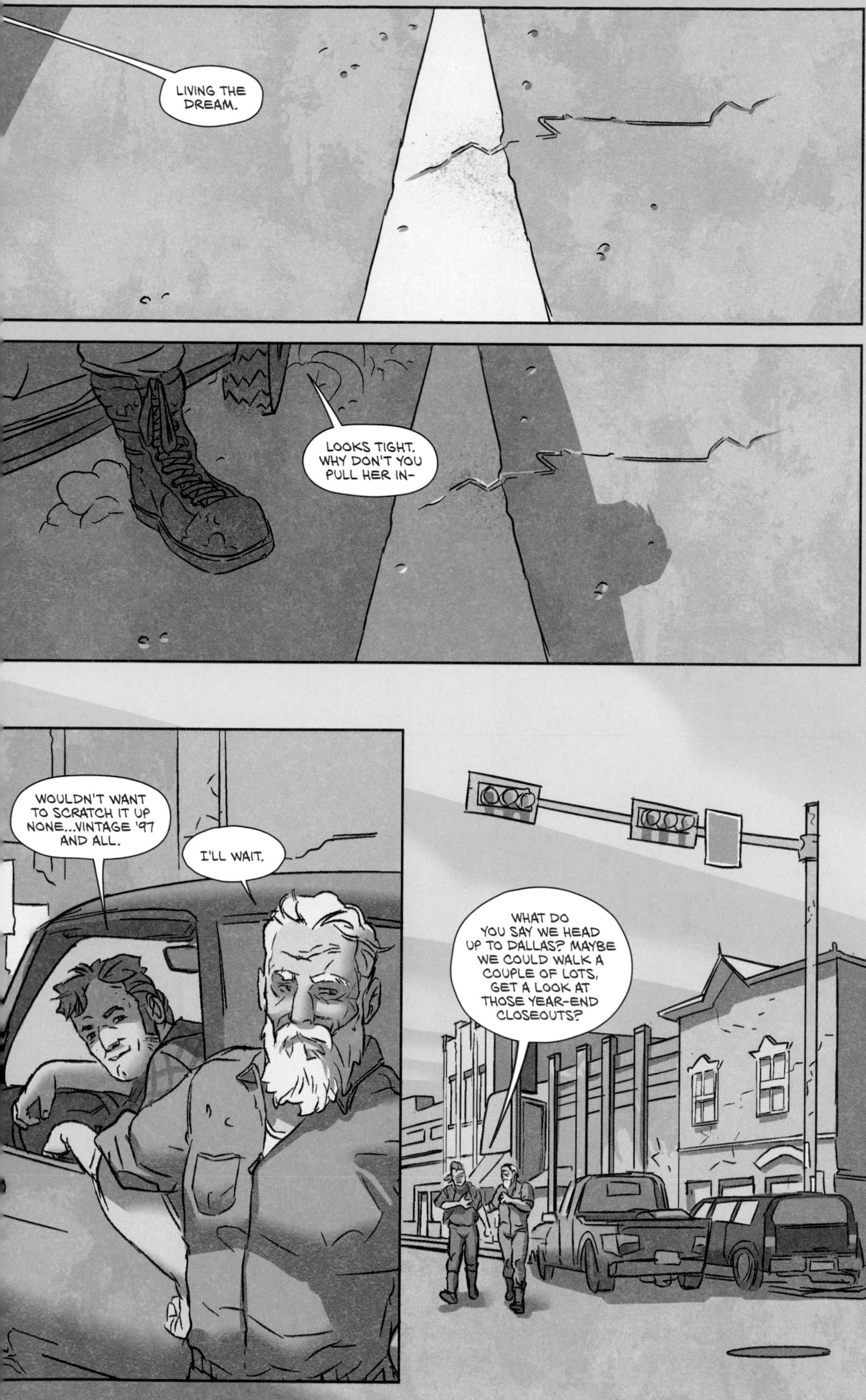
LIVING THE DREAM.
LOOKS TIGHT. WHY DON'T YOU PULL HER IN-
WOULDN'T WANT TO SCRATCH IT UP NONE...VINTAGE '97 AND ALL.
I'LL WAIT.
WHAT DO YOU SAY WE HEAD UP TO DALLAS? MAYBE WE COULD WALK A COUPLE OF LOTS, GET A LOOK AT THOSE YEAR-END CLOSEOUTS?

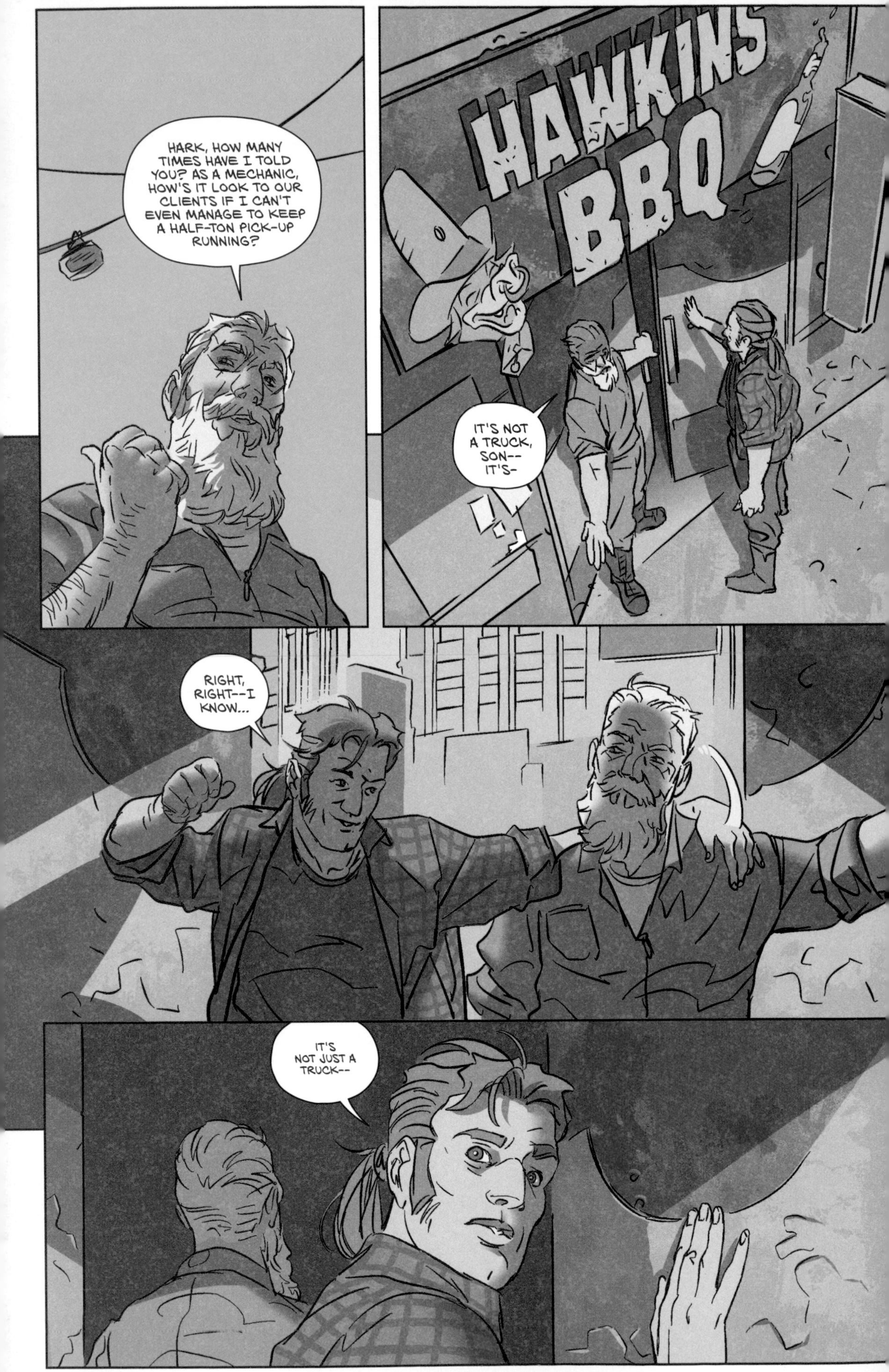
HARK, HOW MANY TIMES HAVE I TOLD YOU? AS A MECHANIC, HOW'S IT LOOK TO OUR CLIENTS IF I CAN'T EVEN MANAGE TO KEEP A HALF-TON PICK-UP RUNNING?
HAWKINS BBQ
IT'S NOT A TRUCK, SON-- IT'S-
RIGHT, RIGHT--I KNOW...
IT'S NOT JUST A TRUCK--

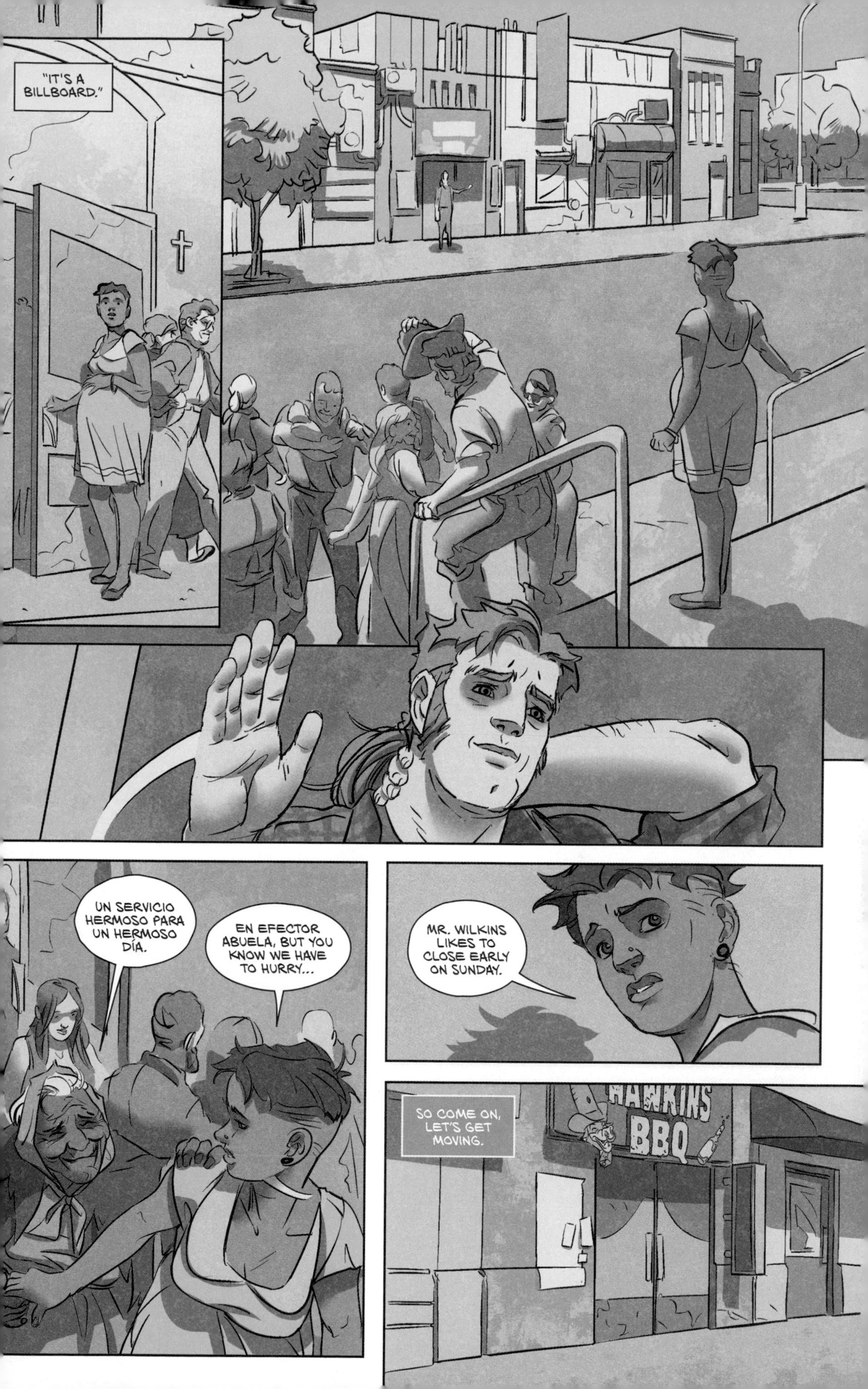
"IT'S A BILLBOARD."
UN SERVICIO HERMOSO PARA UN HERMOSO DÍA.
EN EFECTOR ABUELA, BUT YOU KNOW WE HAVE TO HURRY...
MR. WILKINS LIKES TO CLOSE EARLY ON SUNDAY.
SO COME ON, LET'S GET MOVING.
HAWKINS BBQ

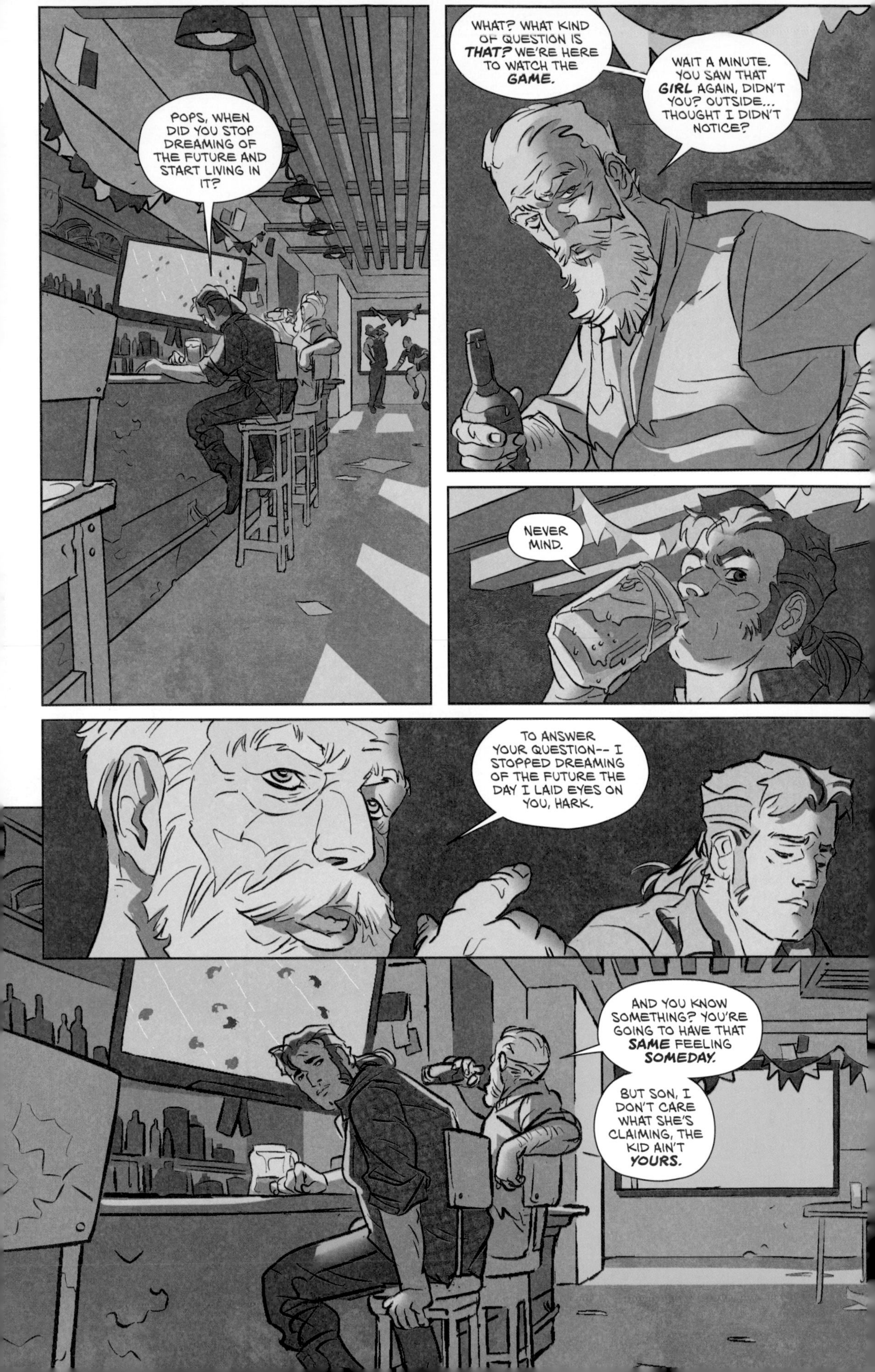
POPS, WHEN DID YOU STOP DREAMING OF THE FUTURE AND START LIVING IN IT?
WHAT? WHAT KIND OF QUESTION IS **THAT?** WE'RE HERE TO WATCH THE **GAME.**
WAIT A MINUTE. YOU SAW THAT **GIRL** AGAIN, DIDN'T YOU? OUTSIDE... THOUGHT I DIDN'T NOTICE?
NEVER MIND.
TO ANSWER YOUR QUESTION-- I STOPPED DREAMING OF THE FUTURE THE DAY I LAID EYES ON YOU, HARK.
AND YOU KNOW SOMETHING? YOU'RE GOING TO HAVE THAT **SAME** FEELING **SOMEDAY.**
BUT SON, I DON'T CARE WHAT SHE'S CLAIMING, THE KID AIN'T **YOURS.**

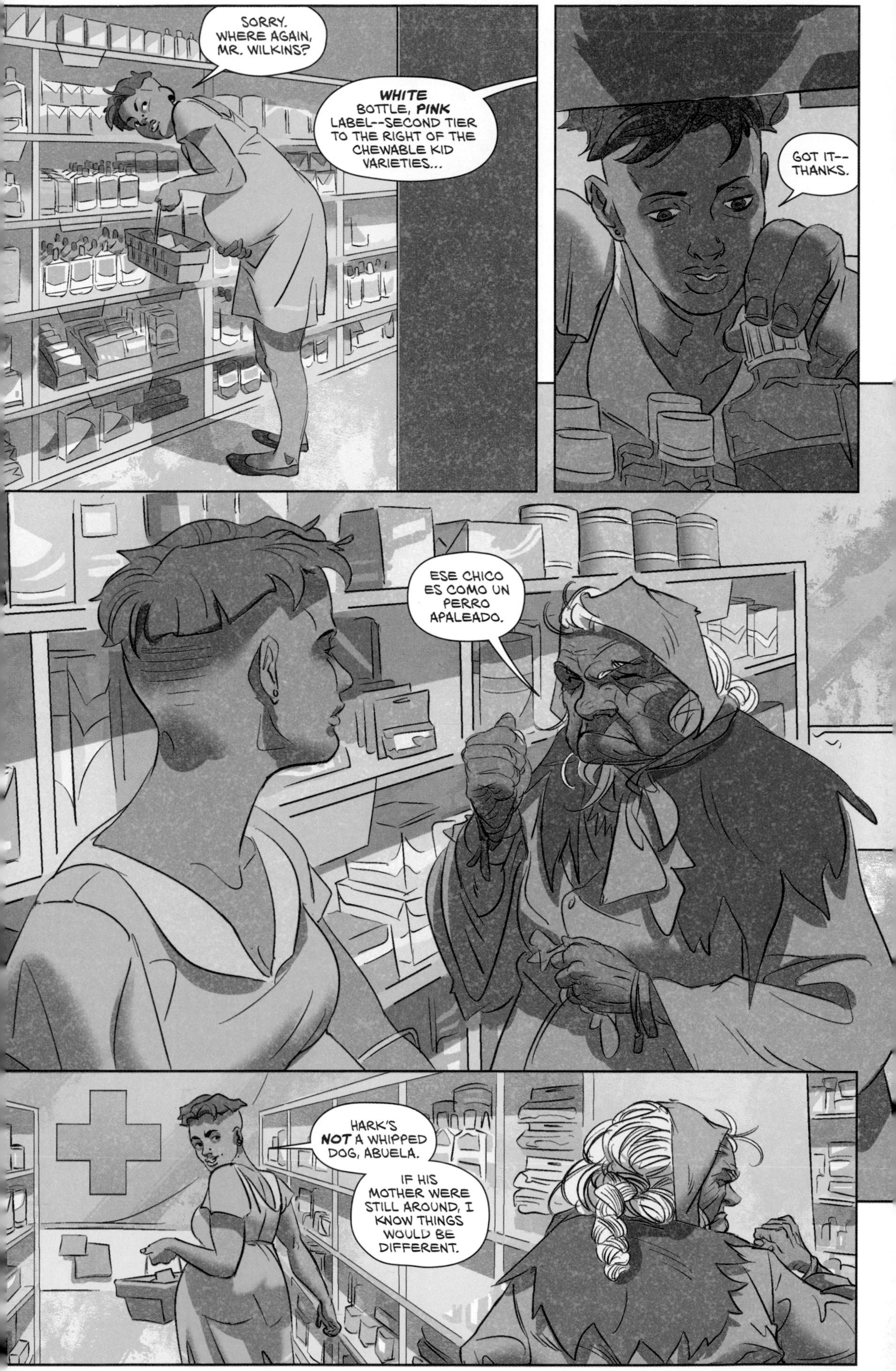
SORRY. WHERE AGAIN, MR. WILKINS?
WHITE BOTTLE, **PINK** LABEL--SECOND TIER TO THE RIGHT OF THE CHEWABLE KID VARIETIES...
GOT IT--THANKS.
ESE CHICO ES COMO UN PERRO APALEADO.
HARK'S **NOT** A WHIPPED DOG, ABUELA.
IF HIS MOTHER WERE STILL AROUND, I KNOW THINGS WOULD BE DIFFERENT.

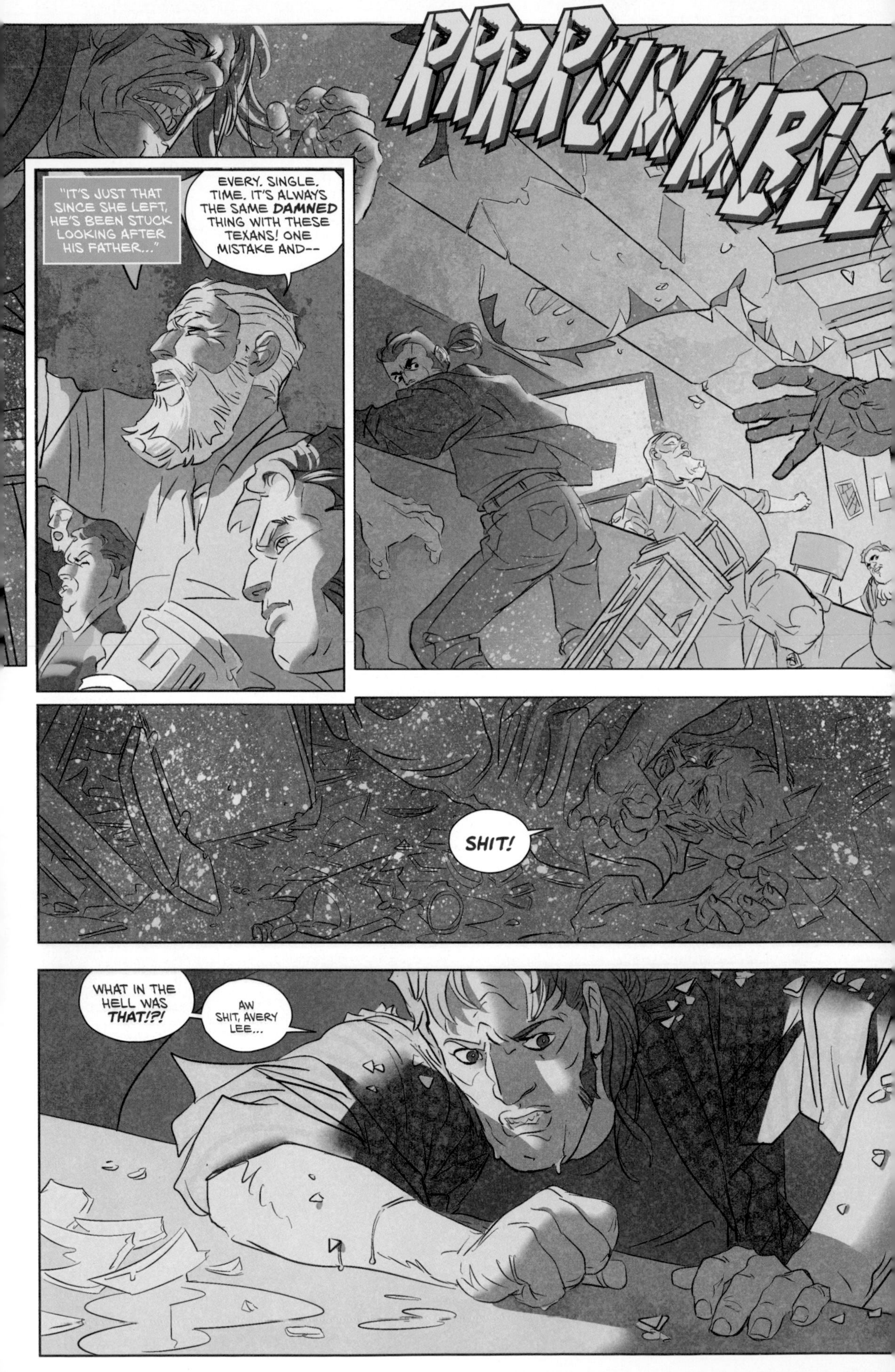
"IT'S JUST THAT SINCE SHE LEFT, HE'S BEEN STUCK LOOKING AFTER HIS FATHER..."
EVERY. SINGLE. TIME. IT'S ALWAYS THE SAME **DAMNED** THING WITH THESE TEXANS! ONE MISTAKE AND--
SHIT!
WHAT IN THE HELL WAS ***THAT!?!***
AW SHIT, AVERY LEE...

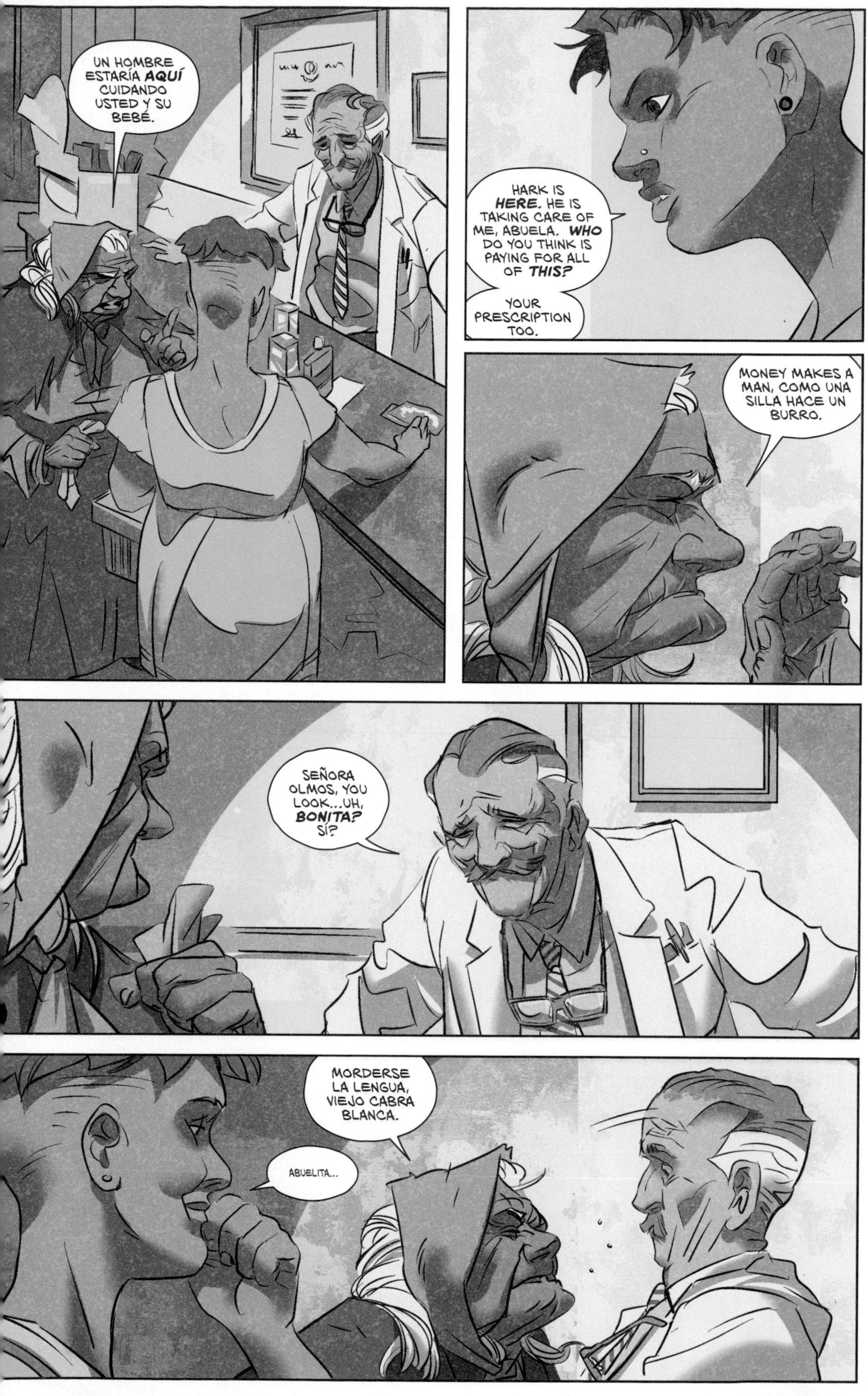
UN HOMBRE ESTARÍA **AQUÍ** CUIDANDO USTED Y SU BEBÉ.
HARK IS **HERE.** HE IS TAKING CARE OF ME, ABUELA. **WHO** DO YOU THINK IS PAYING FOR ALL OF **THIS?**
YOUR PRESCRIPTION TOO.
MONEY MAKES A MAN, COMO UNA SILLA HACE UN BURRO.
SEÑORA OLMOS, YOU LOOK...UH, **BONITA?** SÍ?
MORDERSE LA LENGUA, VIEJO CABRA BLANCA.
ABUELITA...

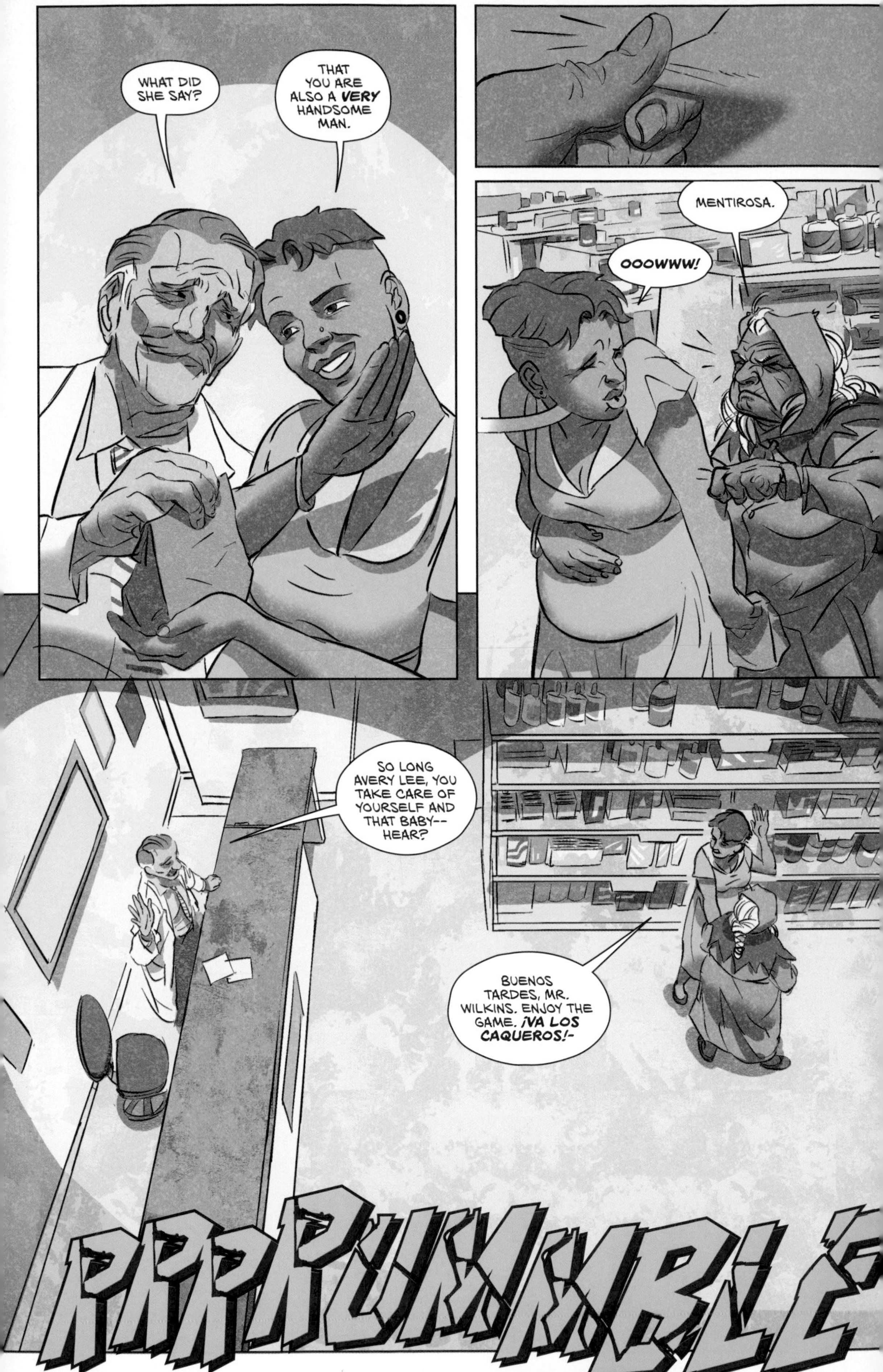
WHAT DID SHE SAY?
THAT YOU ARE ALSO A **VERY** HANDSOME MAN.
MENTIROSA.
OOOWWW!
SO LONG AVERY LEE, YOU TAKE CARE OF YOURSELF AND THAT BABY-- HEAR?
BUENOS TARDES, MR. WILKINS. ENJOY THE GAME. **¡VA LOS CAQUEROS!-**
PRRRUMMMBLE

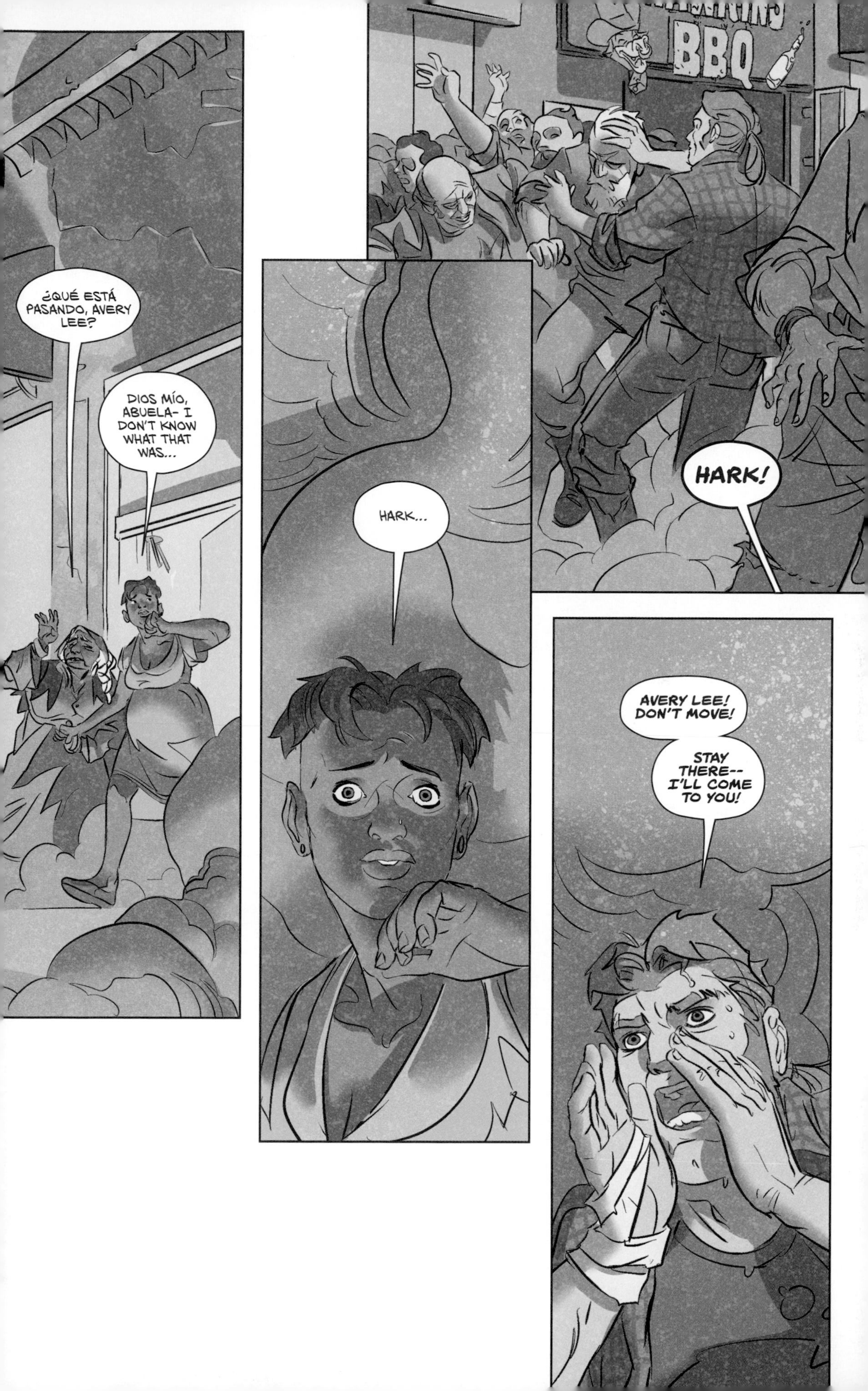
¿QUÉ ESTÁ PASANDO, AVERY LEE?
DIOS MÍO, ABUELA- I DON'T KNOW WHAT THAT WAS...
BBQ
HARK!
HARK...
AVERY LEE! DON'T MOVE!
STAY THERE-- I'LL COME TO YOU!

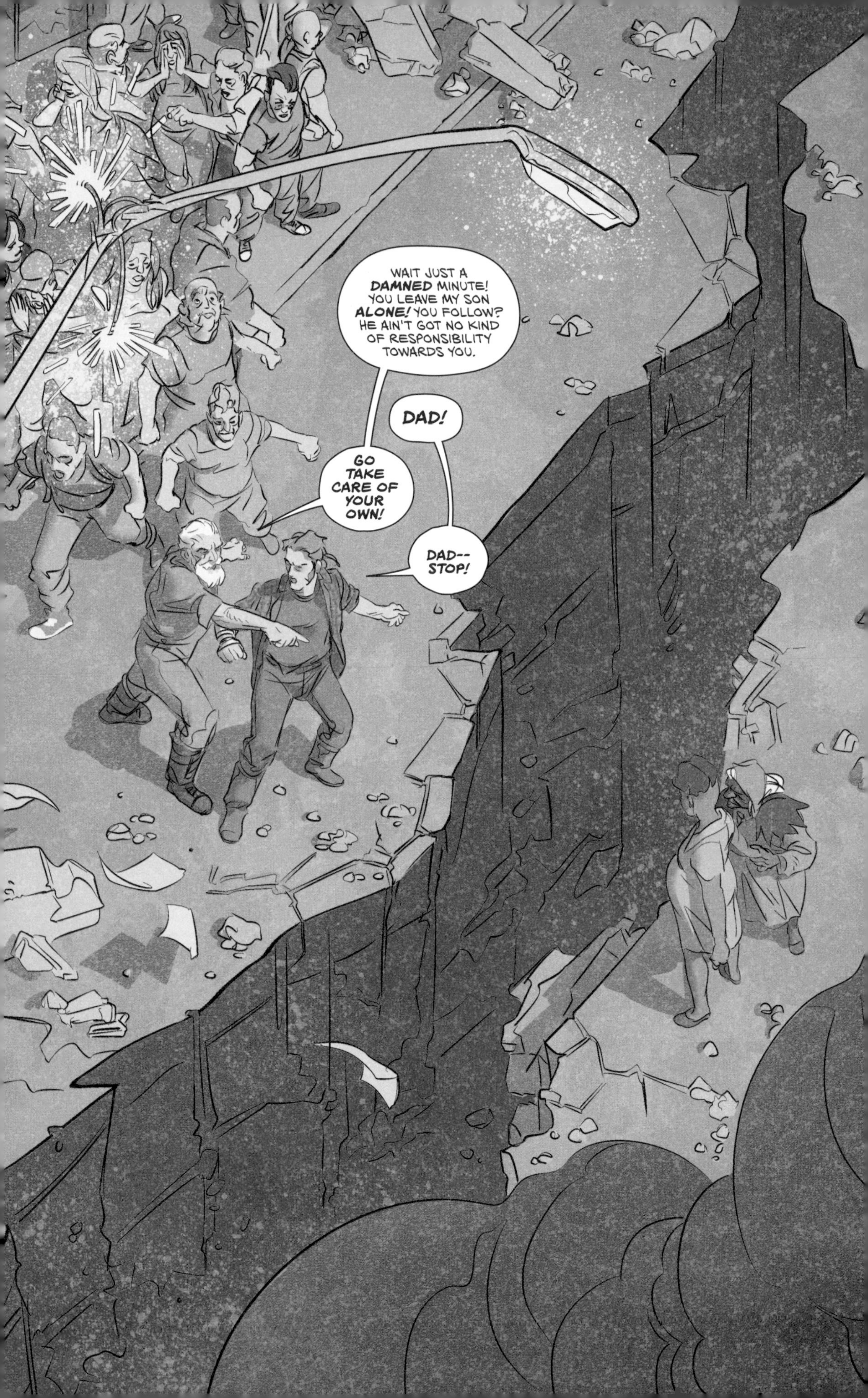
WAIT JUST A DAMNED MINUTE! YOU LEAVE MY SON ALONE! YOU FOLLOW? HE AIN'T GOT NO KIND OF RESPONSIBILITY TOWARDS YOU.
GO TAKE CARE OF YOUR OWN!
DAD!
DAD-- STOP!

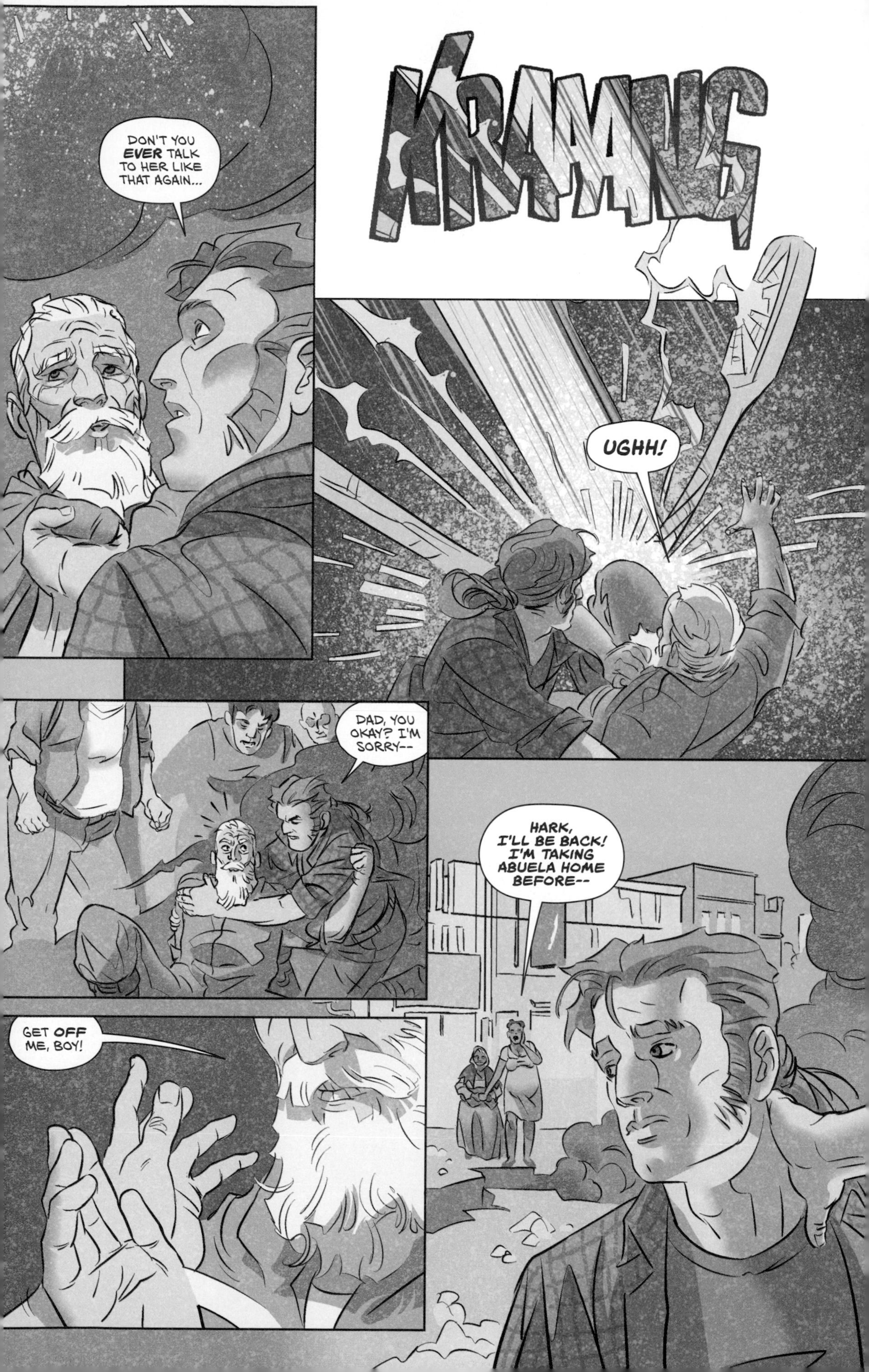
DON'T YOU EVER TALK TO HER LIKE THAT AGAIN...
KRAAANG
UGHH!
DAD, YOU OKAY? I'M SORRY--
HARK, I'LL BE BACK! I'M TAKING ABUELA HOME BEFORE--
GET OFF ME, BOY!

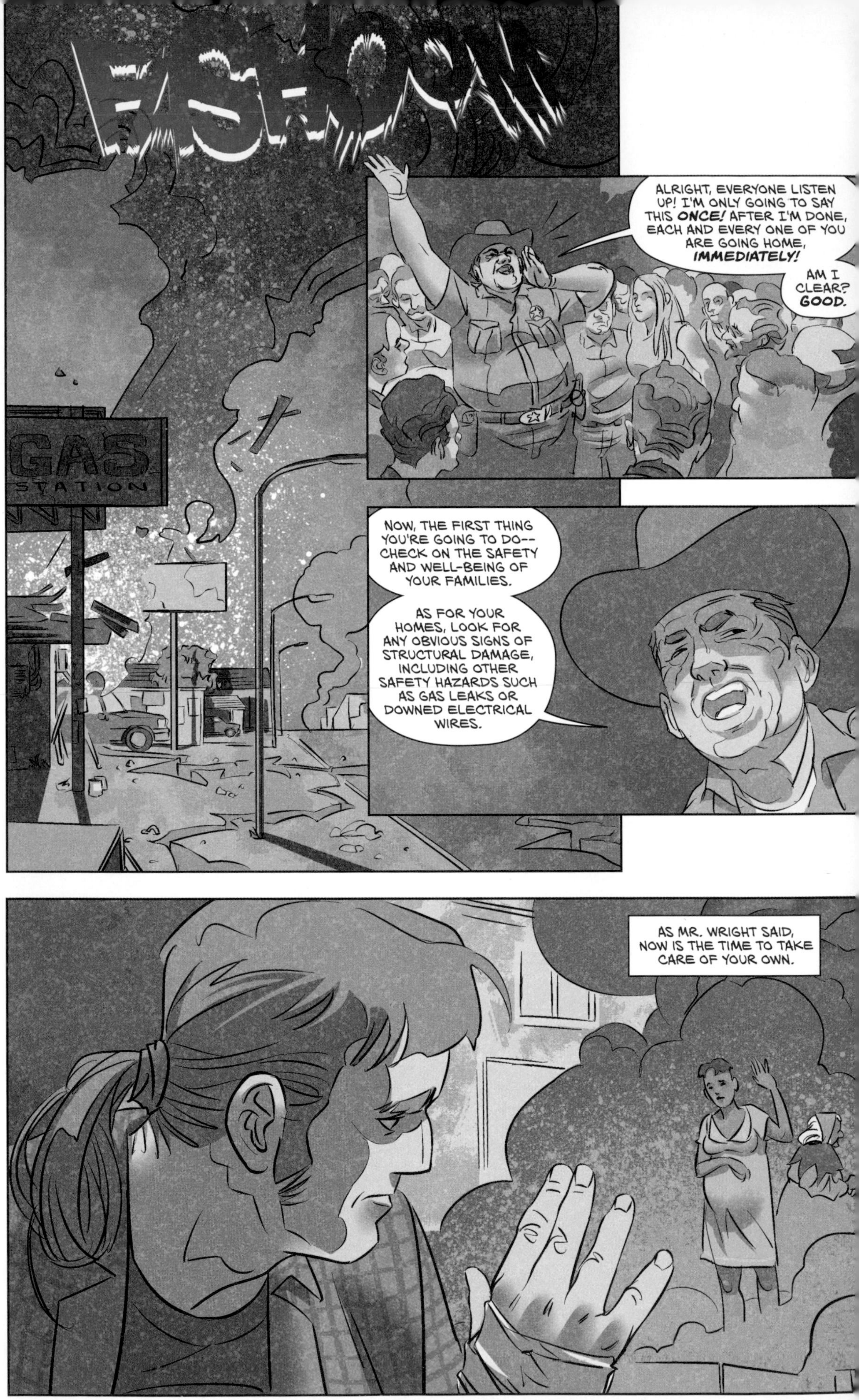
ALRIGHT, EVERYONE LISTEN UP! I'M ONLY GOING TO SAY THIS ONCE! AFTER I'M DONE, EACH AND EVERY ONE OF YOU ARE GOING HOME, IMMEDIATELY!
AM I CLEAR? GOOD.
NOW, THE FIRST THING YOU'RE GOING TO DO-- CHECK ON THE SAFETY AND WELL-BEING OF YOUR FAMILIES.
AS FOR YOUR HOMES, LOOK FOR ANY OBVIOUS SIGNS OF STRUCTURAL DAMAGE, INCLUDING OTHER SAFETY HAZARDS SUCH AS GAS LEAKS OR DOWNED ELECTRICAL WIRES.
GAS STATION
AS MR. WRIGHT SAID, NOW IS THE TIME TO TAKE CARE OF YOUR OWN.

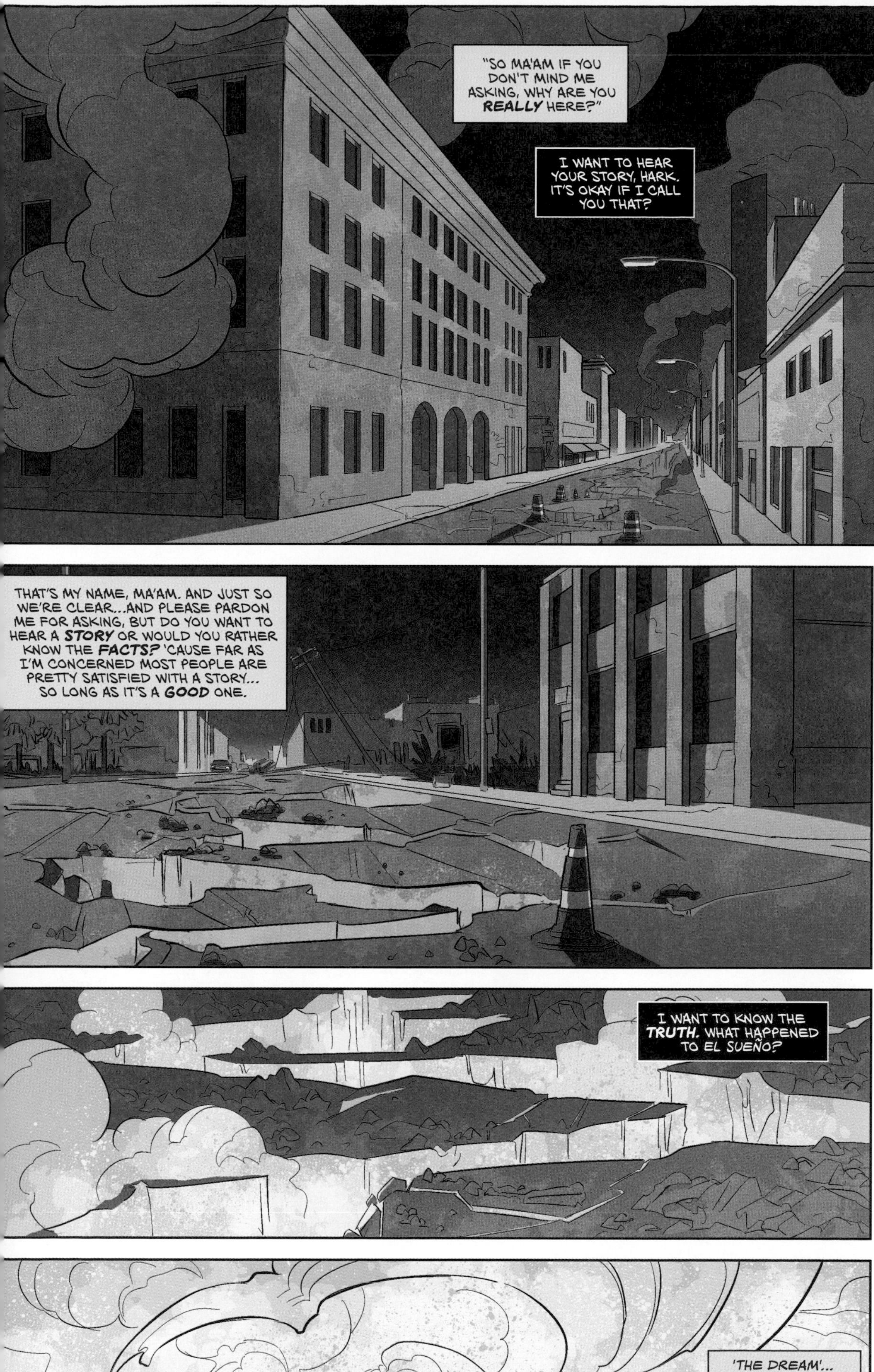
"SO MA'AM IF YOU DON'T MIND ME ASKING, WHY ARE YOU **REALLY** HERE?"
I WANT TO HEAR YOUR STORY, HARK. IT'S OKAY IF I CALL YOU THAT?
THAT'S MY NAME, MA'AM. AND JUST SO WE'RE CLEAR...AND PLEASE PARDON ME FOR ASKING, BUT DO YOU WANT TO HEAR A **STORY** OR WOULD YOU RATHER KNOW THE **FACTS?** 'CAUSE FAR AS I'M CONCERNED MOST PEOPLE ARE PRETTY SATISFIED WITH A STORY... SO LONG AS IT'S A **GOOD** ONE.
I WANT TO KNOW THE **TRUTH.** WHAT HAPPENED TO EL SUEÑO?
'THE DREAM'... IT'S **LONG** GONE.

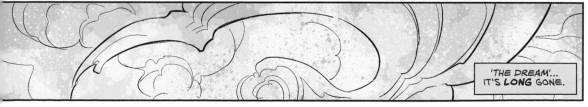

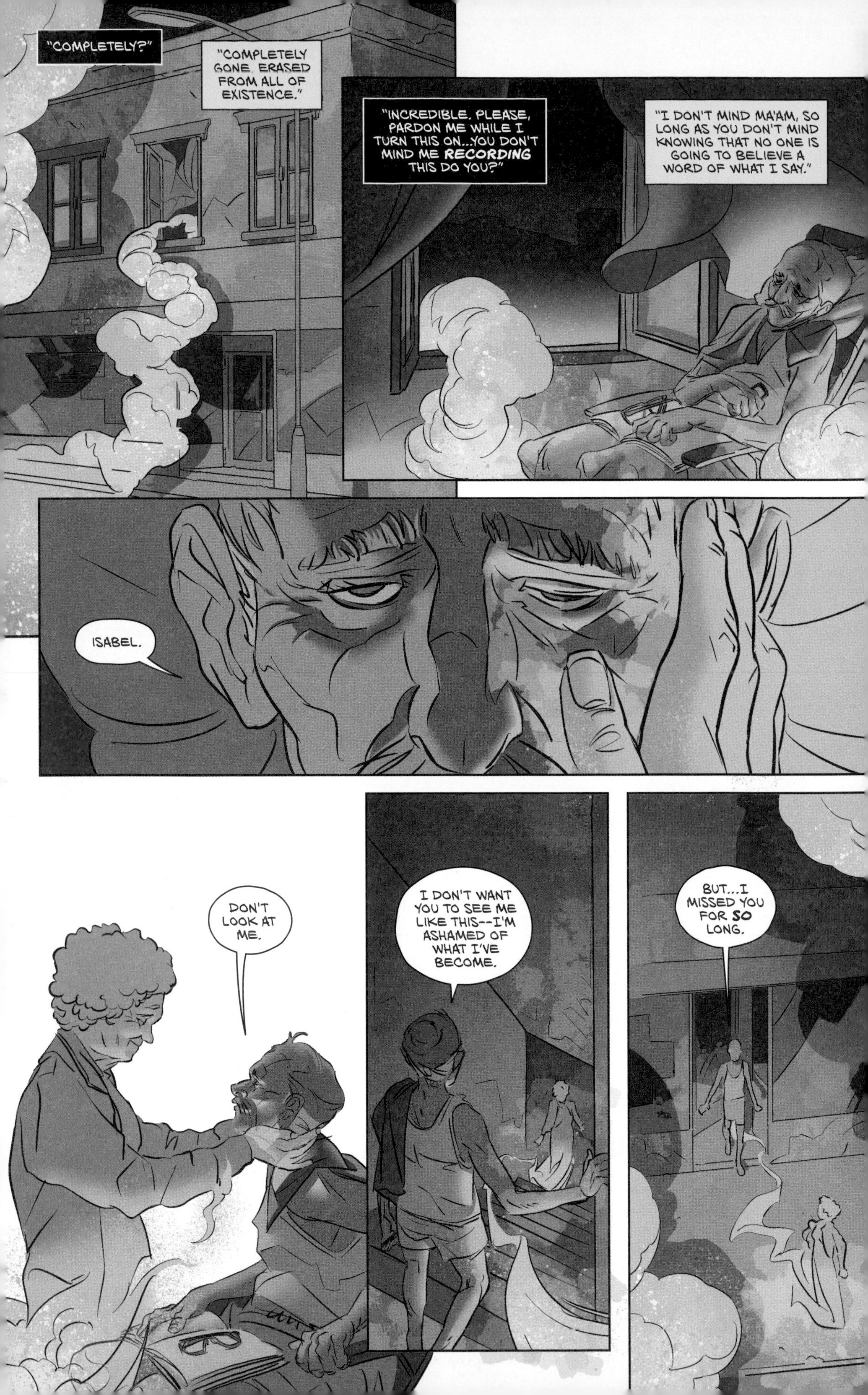
"COMPLETELY?"
"COMPLETELY GONE. ERASED FROM ALL OF EXISTENCE."
"INCREDIBLE. PLEASE, PARDON ME WHILE I TURN THIS ON...YOU DON'T MIND ME RECORDING THIS DO YOU?"
"I DON'T MIND MA'AM, SO LONG AS YOU DON'T MIND KNOWING THAT NO ONE IS GOING TO BELIEVE A WORD OF WHAT I SAY."
ISABEL.
DON'T LOOK AT ME.
I DON'T WANT YOU TO SEE ME LIKE THIS--I'M ASHAMED OF WHAT I'VE BECOME.
BUT...I MISSED YOU FOR SO LONG.

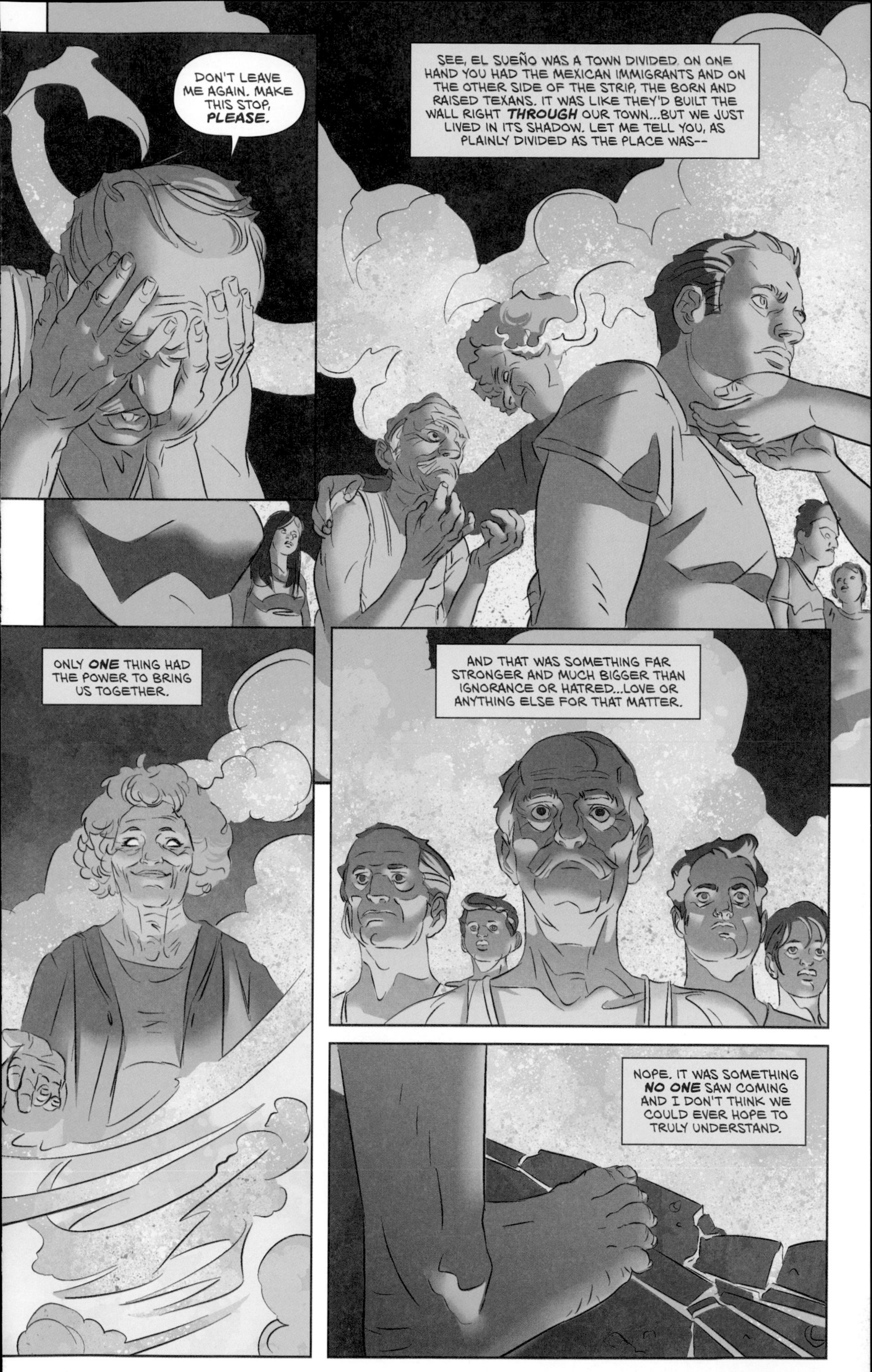
DON'T LEAVE ME AGAIN. MAKE THIS STOP, **PLEASE.**
SEE, EL SUEÑO WAS A TOWN DIVIDED. ON ONE HAND YOU HAD THE MEXICAN IMMIGRANTS AND ON THE OTHER SIDE OF THE STRIP, THE BORN AND RAISED TEXANS. IT WAS LIKE THEY'D BUILT THE WALL RIGHT **THROUGH** OUR TOWN...BUT WE JUST LIVED IN ITS SHADOW. LET ME TELL YOU, AS PLAINLY DIVIDED AS THE PLACE WAS--
ONLY **ONE** THING HAD THE POWER TO BRING US TOGETHER.
AND THAT WAS SOMETHING FAR STRONGER AND MUCH BIGGER THAN IGNORANCE OR HATRED...LOVE OR ANYTHING ELSE FOR THAT MATTER.
NOPE. IT WAS SOMETHING **NO ONE** SAW COMING AND I DON'T THINK WE COULD EVER HOPE TO TRULY UNDERSTAND.

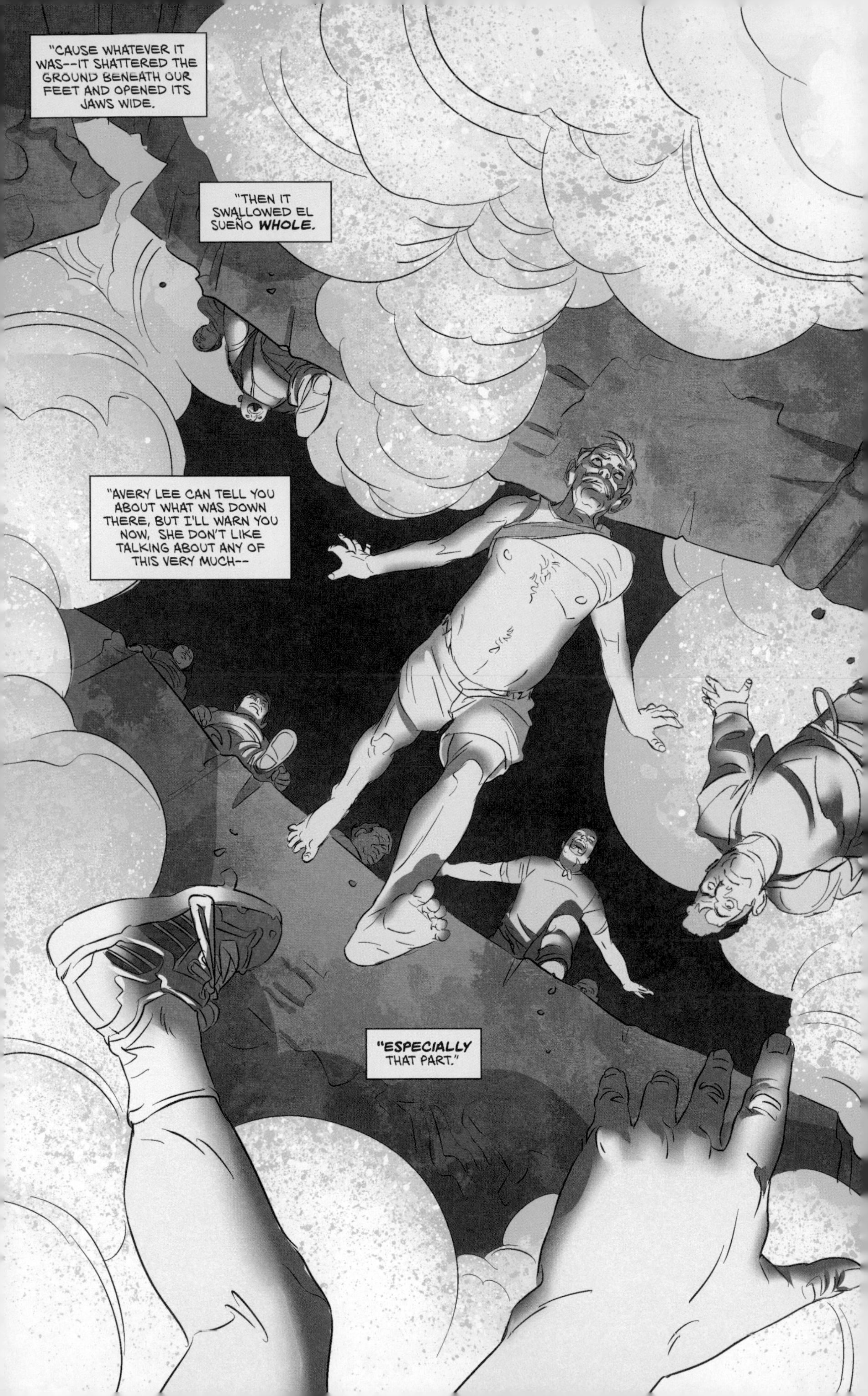
"CAUSE WHATEVER IT WAS--IT SHATTERED THE GROUND BENEATH OUR FEET AND OPENED ITS JAWS WIDE.
"THEN IT SWALLOWED EL SUEÑO **WHOLE.**
"AVERY LEE CAN TELL YOU ABOUT WHAT WAS DOWN THERE, BUT I'LL WARN YOU NOW, SHE DON'T LIKE TALKING ABOUT ANY OF THIS VERY MUCH--
"**ESPECIALLY** THAT PART."

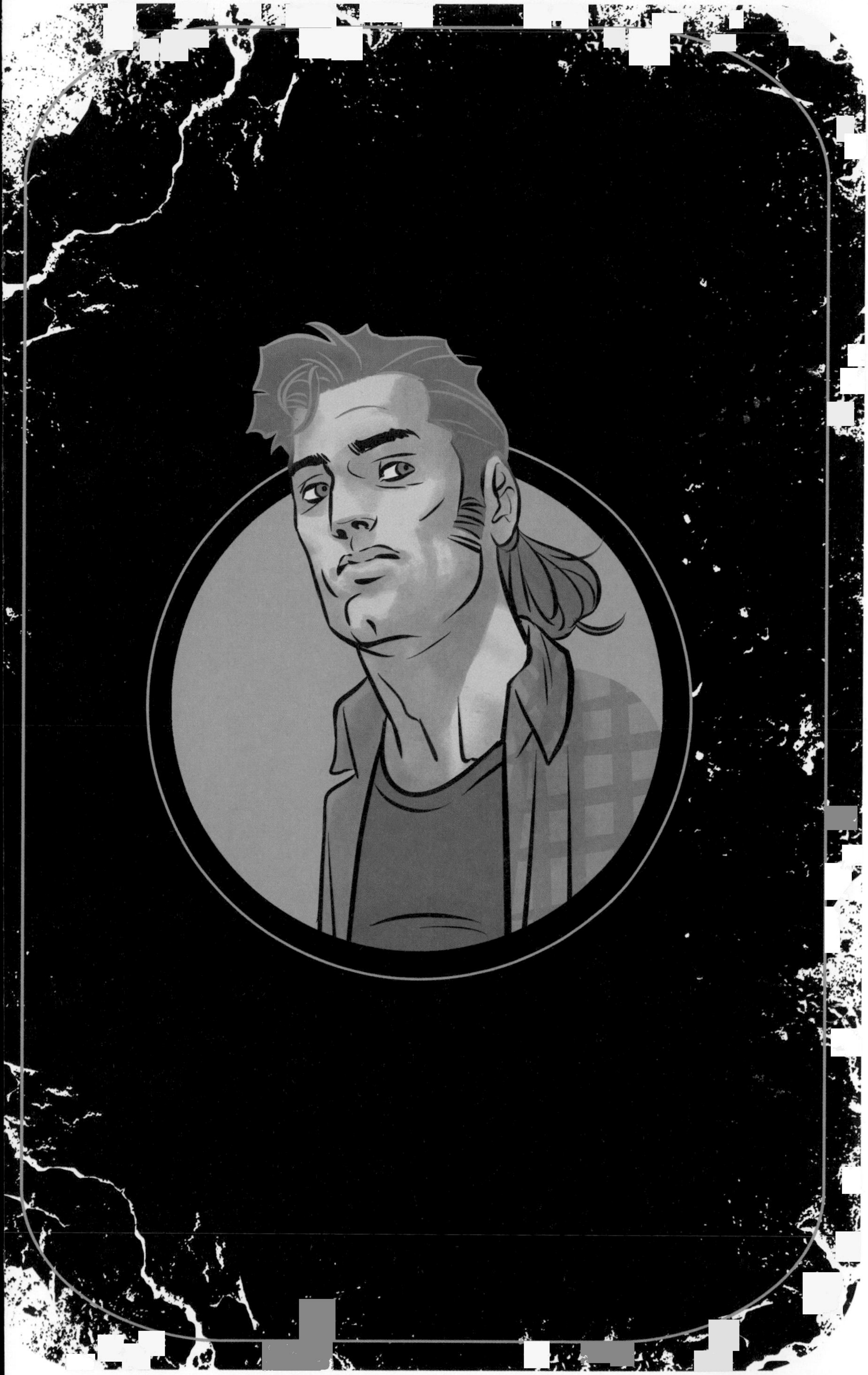

CHAPTER TWO

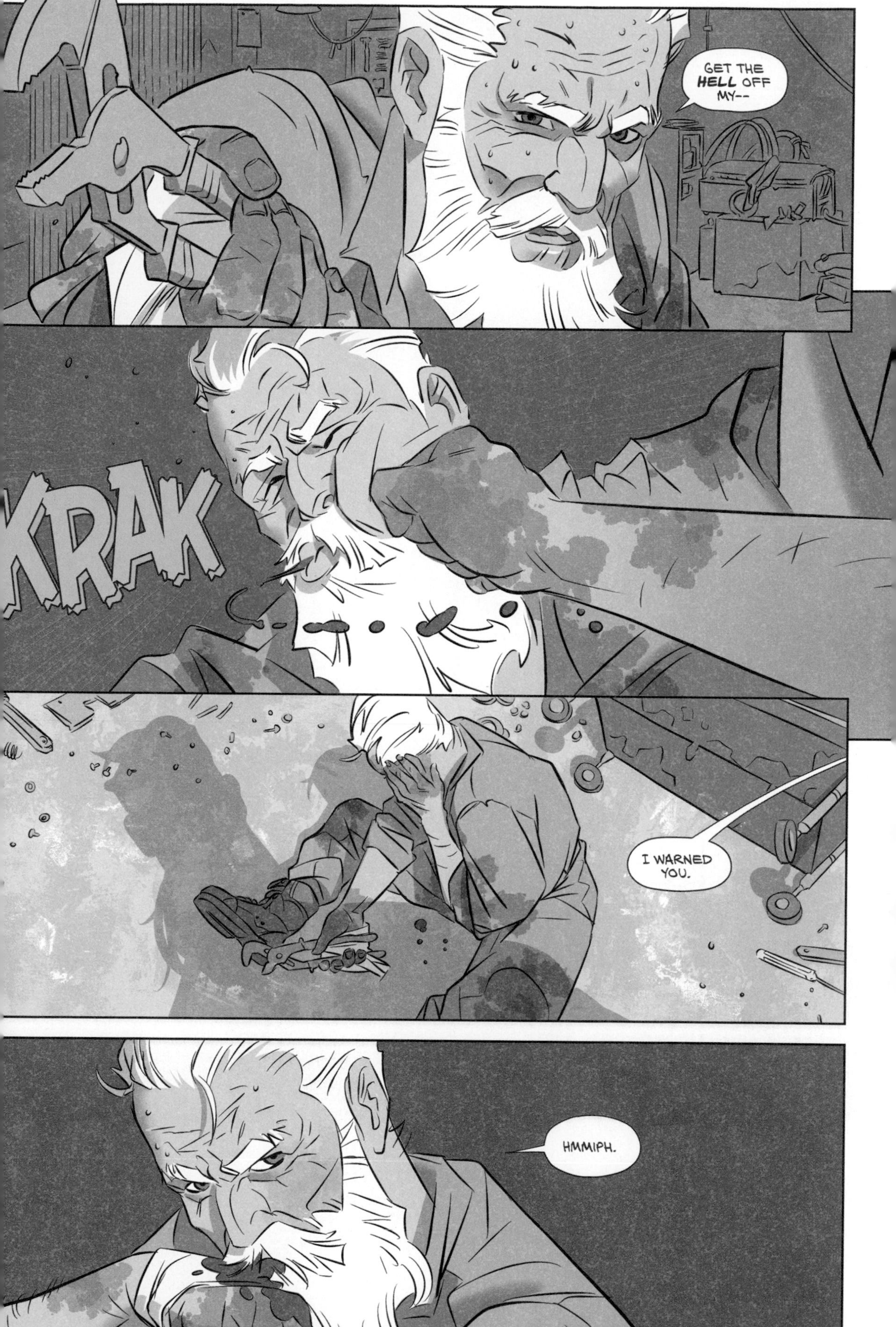
GET THE **HELL** OFF MY--
KRAK
I WARNED YOU.
HMMIPH.

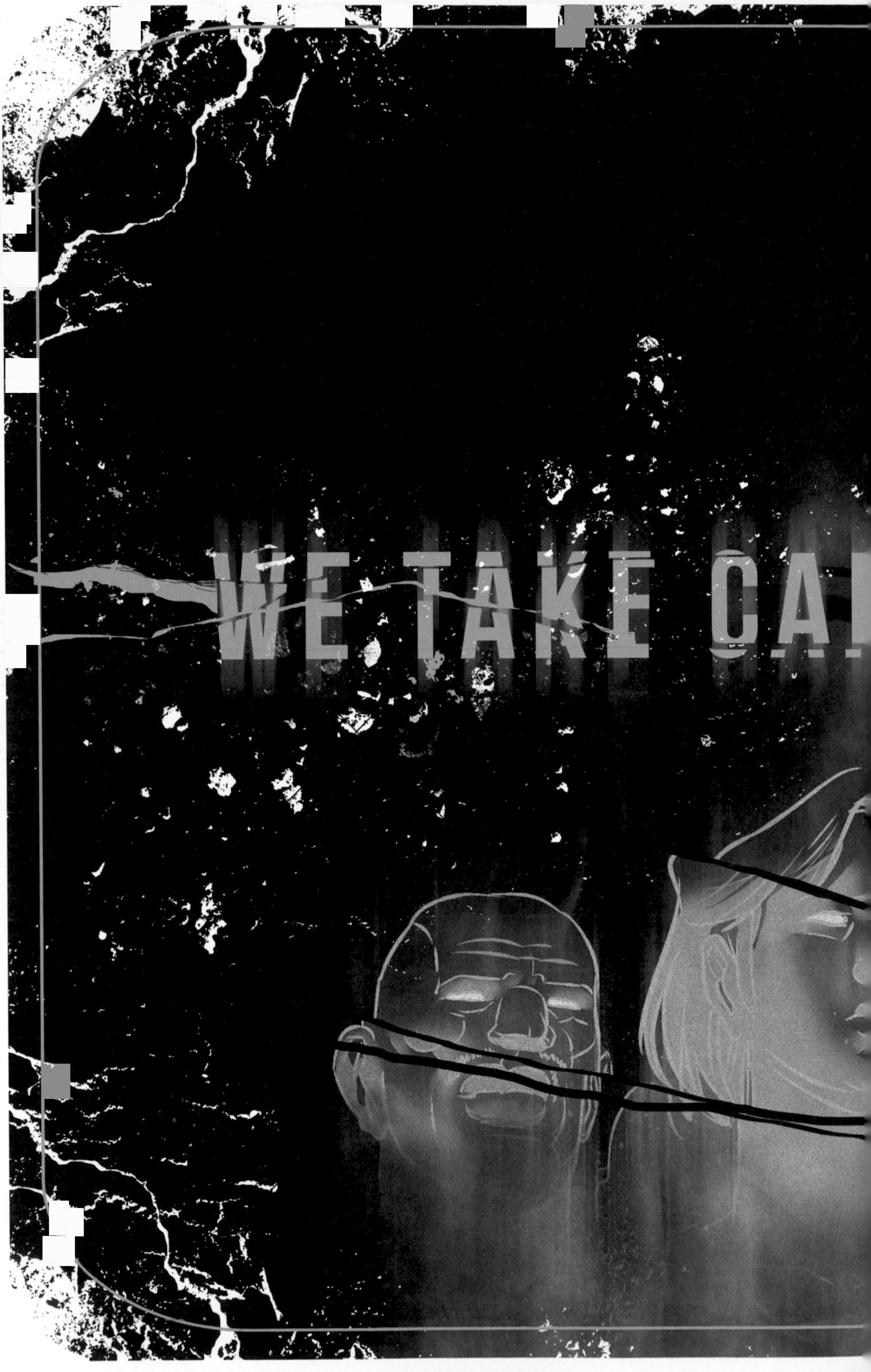
WE TAKE CA

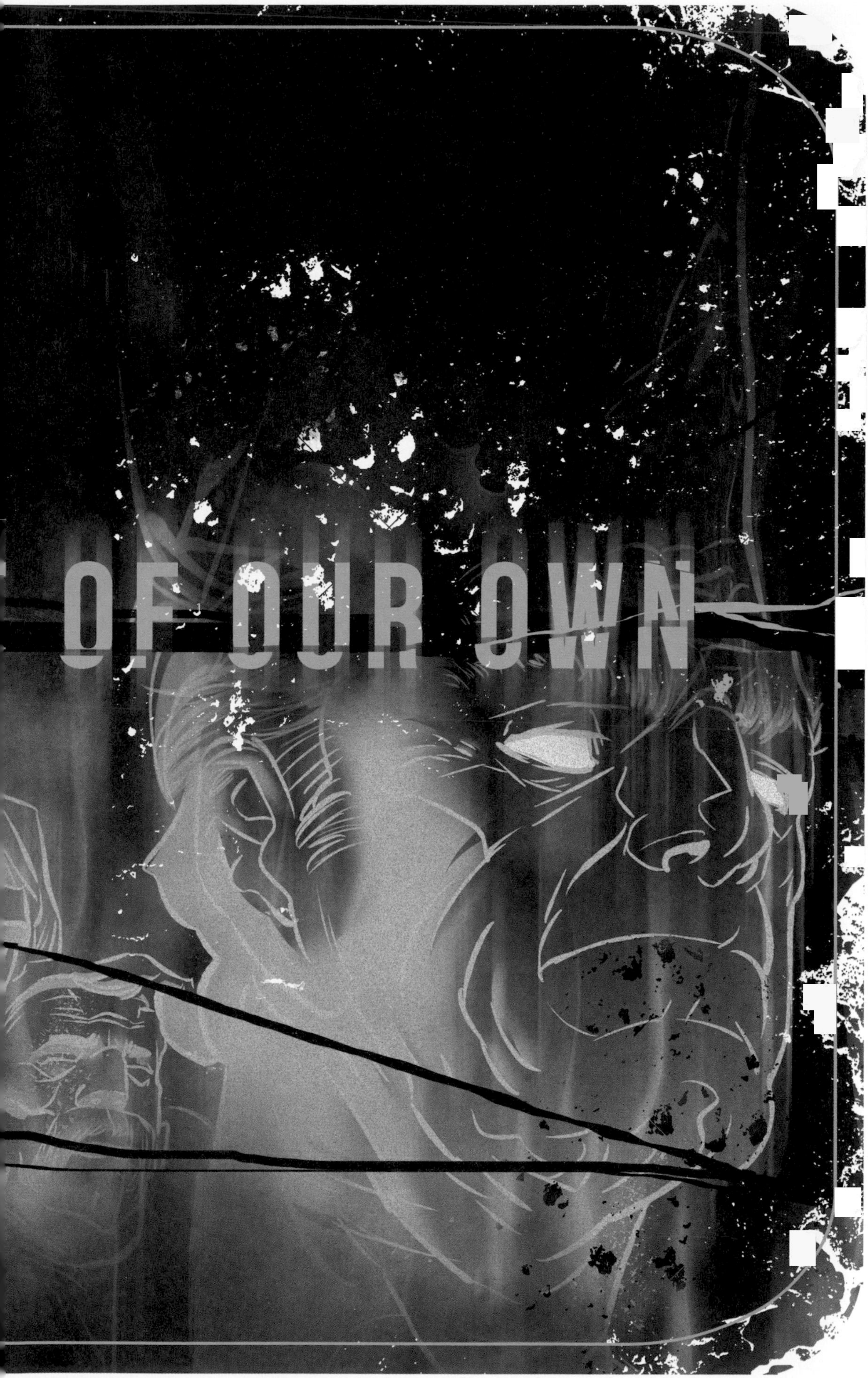
OF OUR OWN

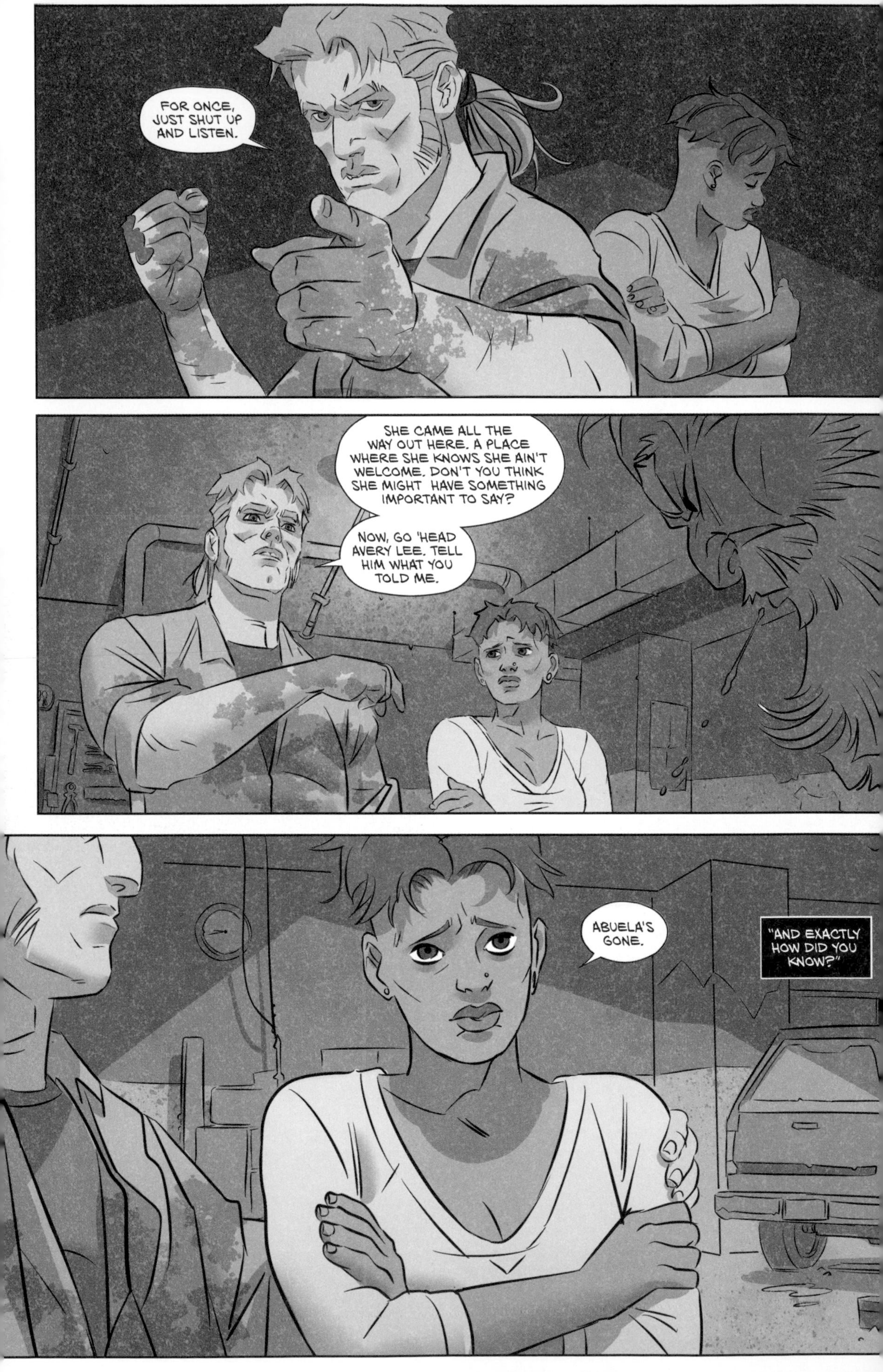
FOR ONCE, JUST SHUT UP AND LISTEN.
SHE CAME ALL THE WAY OUT HERE. A PLACE WHERE SHE KNOWS SHE AIN'T WELCOME. DON'T YOU THINK SHE MIGHT HAVE SOMETHING IMPORTANT TO SAY?
NOW, GO 'HEAD AVERY LEE. TELL HIM WHAT YOU TOLD ME.
ABUELA'S GONE.
"AND EXACTLY HOW DID YOU KNOW?"

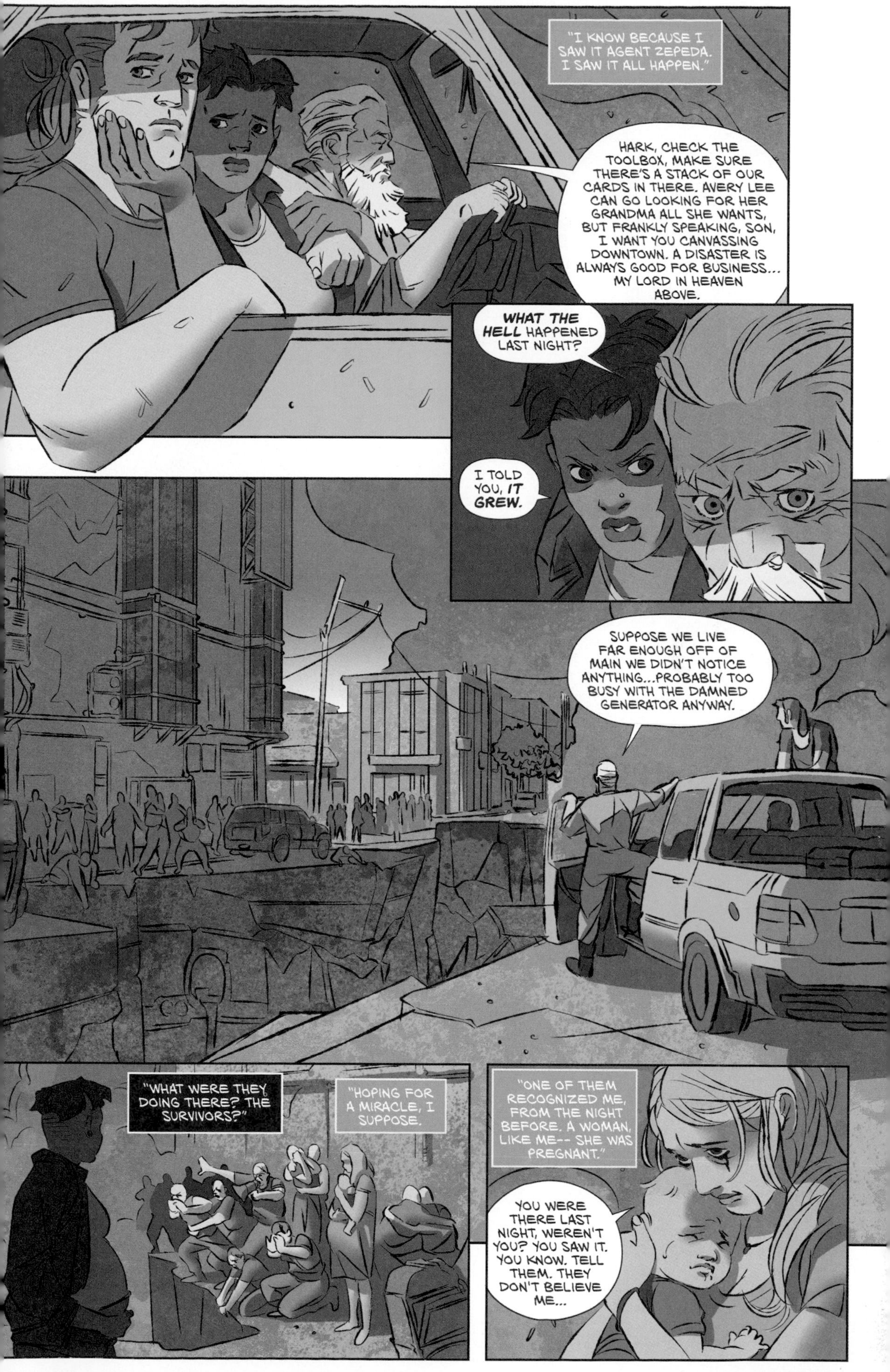
"I KNOW BECAUSE I SAW IT AGENT ZEPEDA. I SAW IT ALL HAPPEN."
HARK, CHECK THE TOOLBOX, MAKE SURE THERE'S A STACK OF OUR CARDS IN THERE. AVERY LEE CAN GO LOOKING FOR HER GRANDMA ALL SHE WANTS, BUT FRANKLY SPEAKING, SON, I WANT YOU CANVASSING DOWNTOWN. A DISASTER IS ALWAYS GOOD FOR BUSINESS... MY LORD IN HEAVEN ABOVE.
WHAT THE HELL HAPPENED LAST NIGHT?
I TOLD YOU, IT GREW.
SUPPOSE WE LIVE FAR ENOUGH OFF OF MAIN WE DIDN'T NOTICE ANYTHING...PROBABLY TOO BUSY WITH THE DAMNED GENERATOR ANYWAY.
"WHAT WERE THEY DOING THERE? THE SURVIVORS?"
"HOPING FOR A MIRACLE, I SUPPOSE.
"ONE OF THEM RECOGNIZED ME, FROM THE NIGHT BEFORE. A WOMAN, LIKE ME-- SHE WAS PREGNANT."
YOU WERE THERE LAST NIGHT, WEREN'T YOU? YOU SAW IT. YOU KNOW. TELL THEM. THEY DON'T BELIEVE ME...

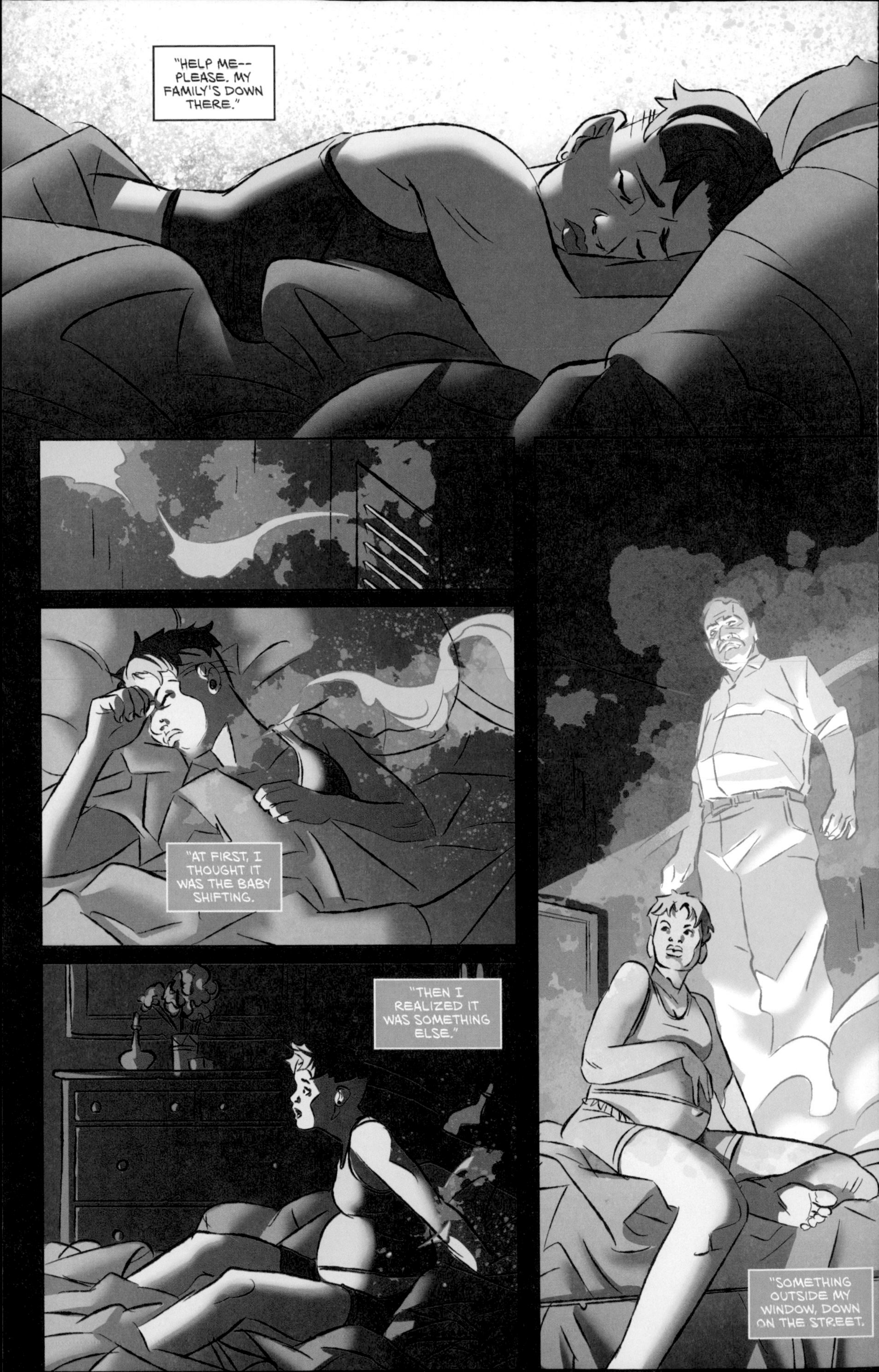
"HELP ME--PLEASE. MY FAMILY'S DOWN THERE."
"AT FIRST, I THOUGHT IT WAS THE BABY SHIFTING.
"THEN I REALIZED IT WAS SOMETHING ELSE."
"SOMETHING OUTSIDE MY WINDOW, DOWN ON THE STREET.

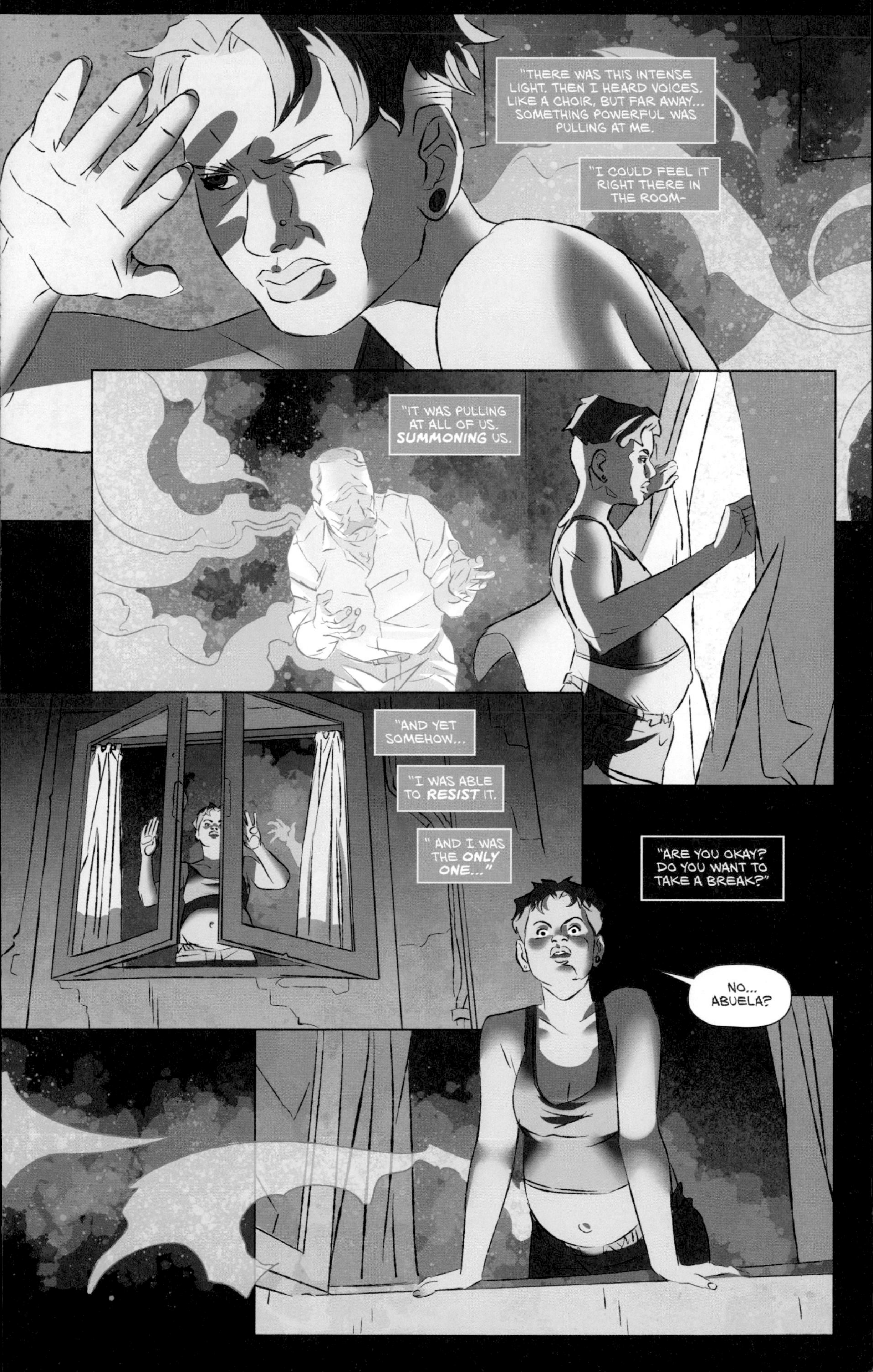
"THERE WAS THIS INTENSE LIGHT. THEN I HEARD VOICES. LIKE A CHOIR, BUT FAR AWAY... SOMETHING POWERFUL WAS PULLING AT ME.
"I COULD FEEL IT RIGHT THERE IN THE ROOM-
"IT WAS PULLING AT ALL OF US. SUMMONING US.
"AND YET SOMEHOW...
"I WAS ABLE TO RESIST IT.
" AND I WAS THE ONLY ONE..."
"ARE YOU OKAY? DO YOU WANT TO TAKE A BREAK?"
NO... ABUELA?

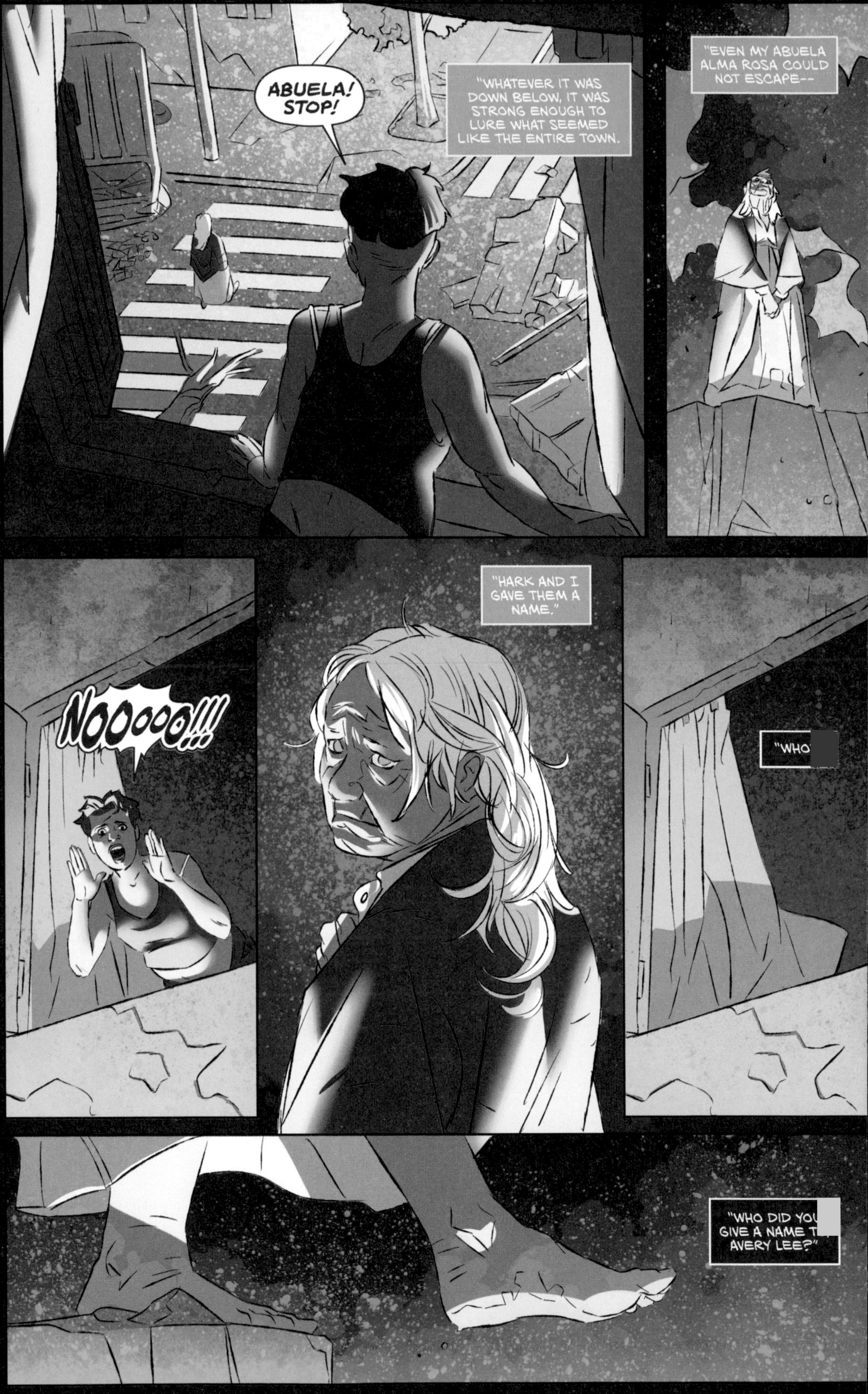
ABUELA! STOP!
"WHATEVER IT WAS DOWN BELOW, IT WAS STRONG ENOUGH TO LURE WHAT SEEMED LIKE THE ENTIRE TOWN.
"EVEN MY ABUELA ALMA ROSA COULD NOT ESCAPE--
NOOOOO!!!
"HARK AND I GAVE THEM A NAME."
"WHO[redacted]
"WHO DID YOU GIVE A NAME T AVERY LEE?"

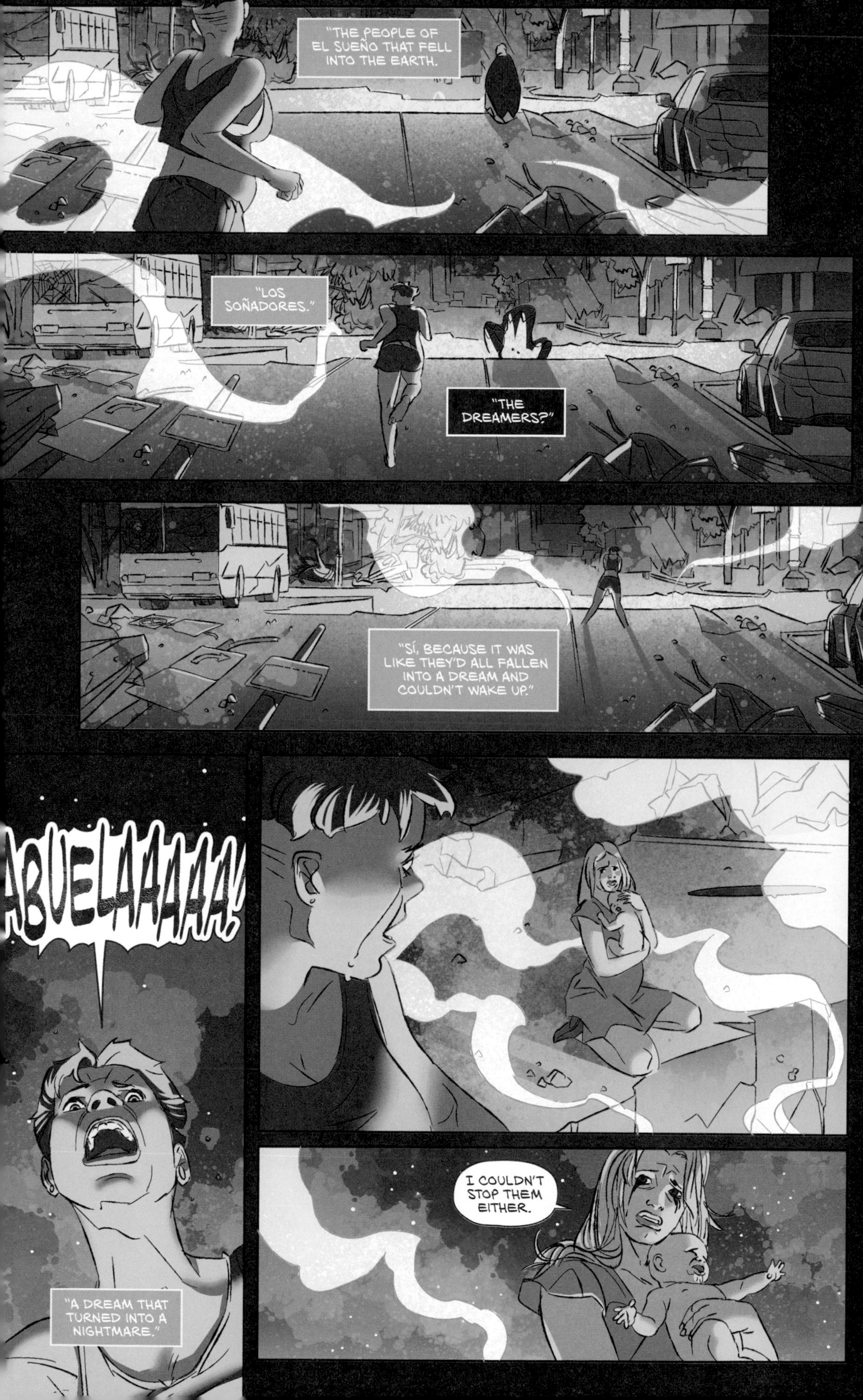
"THE PEOPLE OF EL SUEÑO THAT FELL INTO THE EARTH.
"LOS SOÑADORES."
"THE DREAMERS?"
"SÍ, BECAUSE IT WAS LIKE THEY'D ALL FALLEN INTO A DREAM AND COULDN'T WAKE UP."
ABUELAAAAA!
"A DREAM THAT TURNED INTO A NIGHTMARE."
I COULDN'T STOP THEM EITHER.

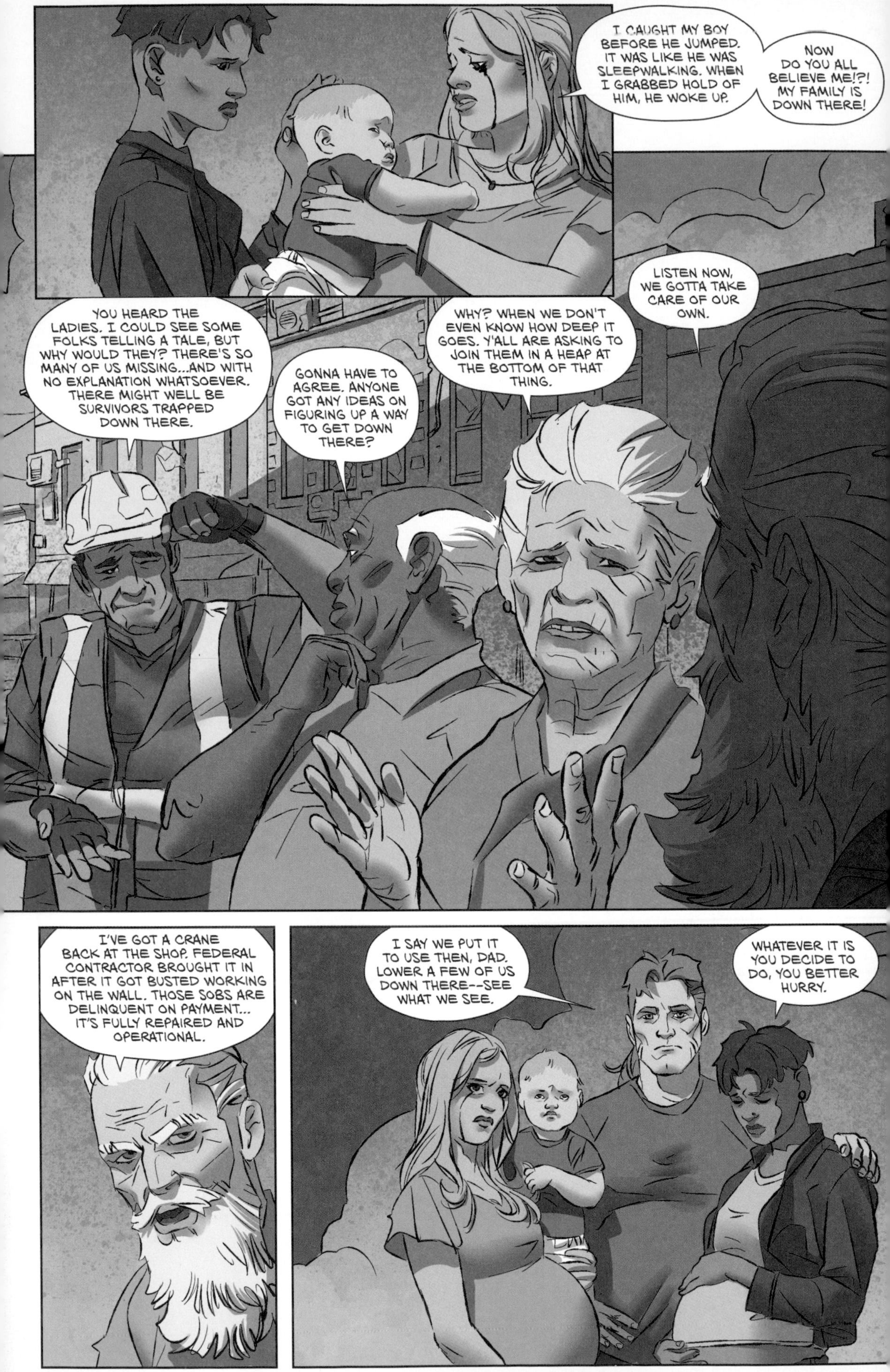

I CAUGHT MY BOY BEFORE HE JUMPED. IT WAS LIKE HE WAS SLEEPWALKING. WHEN I GRABBED HOLD OF HIM, HE WOKE UP.
NOW DO YOU ALL BELIEVE ME!?! MY FAMILY IS DOWN THERE!
YOU HEARD THE LADIES. I COULD SEE SOME FOLKS TELLING A TALE, BUT WHY WOULD THEY? THERE'S SO MANY OF US MISSING...AND WITH NO EXPLANATION WHATSOEVER. THERE MIGHT WELL BE SURVIVORS TRAPPED DOWN THERE.
GONNA HAVE TO AGREE. ANYONE GOT ANY IDEAS ON FIGURING UP A WAY TO GET DOWN THERE?
WHY? WHEN WE DON'T EVEN KNOW HOW DEEP IT GOES. Y'ALL ARE ASKING TO JOIN THEM IN A HEAP AT THE BOTTOM OF THAT THING.
LISTEN NOW, WE GOTTA TAKE CARE OF OUR OWN.
I'VE GOT A CRANE BACK AT THE SHOP. FEDERAL CONTRACTOR BROUGHT IT IN AFTER IT GOT BUSTED WORKING ON THE WALL. THOSE SOBS ARE DELINQUENT ON PAYMENT... IT'S FULLY REPAIRED AND OPERATIONAL.
I SAY WE PUT IT TO USE THEN, DAD. LOWER A FEW OF US DOWN THERE--SEE WHAT WE SEE.
WHATEVER IT IS YOU DECIDE TO DO, YOU BETTER HURRY.

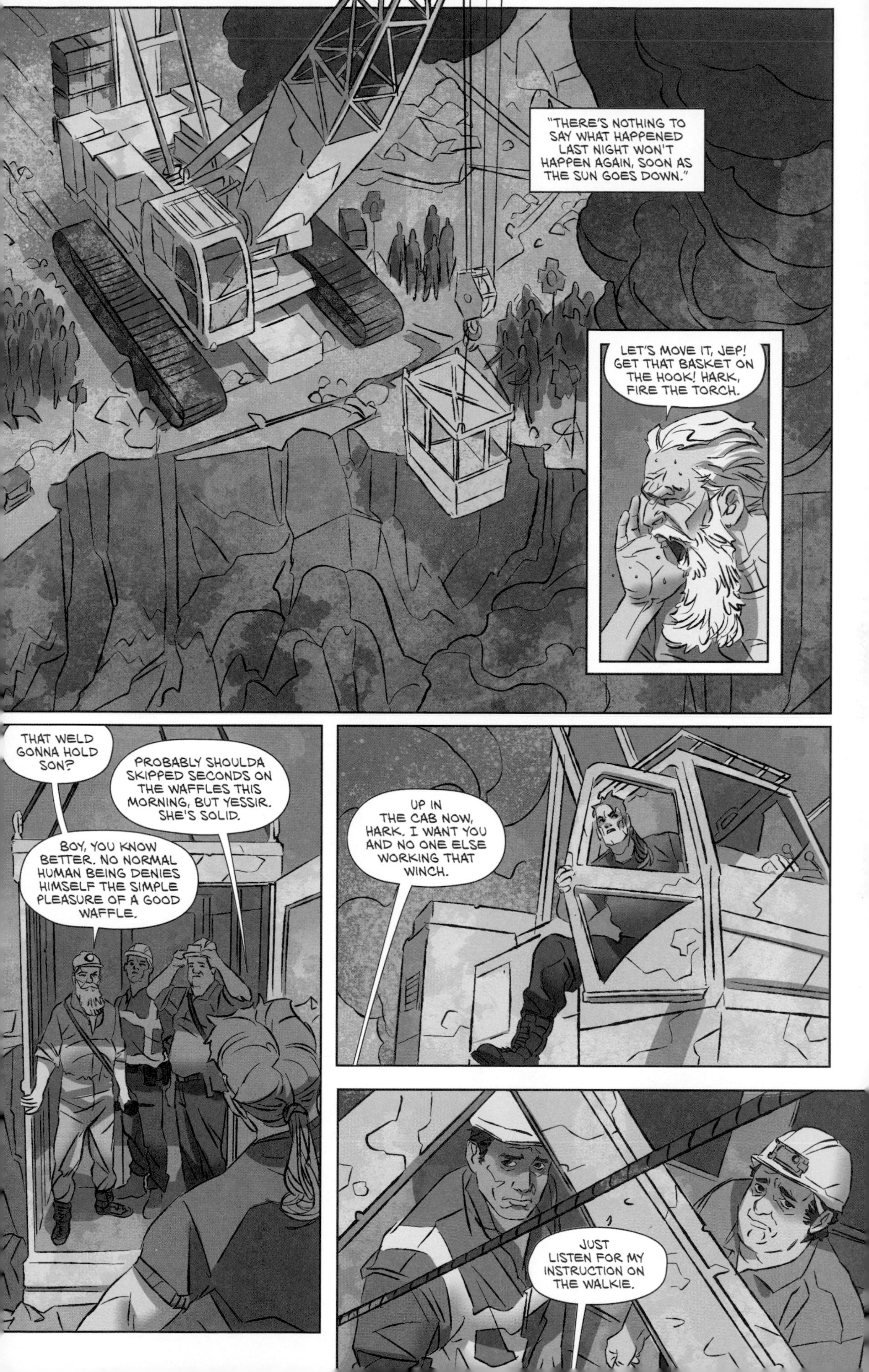
"THERE'S NOTHING TO SAY WHAT HAPPENED LAST NIGHT WON'T HAPPEN AGAIN, SOON AS THE SUN GOES DOWN."
LET'S MOVE IT, JEP! GET THAT BASKET ON THE HOOK! HARK, FIRE THE TORCH.
THAT WELD GONNA HOLD SON?
PROBABLY SHOULDA SKIPPED SECONDS ON THE WAFFLES THIS MORNING, BUT YESSIR. SHE'S SOLID.
BOY, YOU KNOW BETTER. NO NORMAL HUMAN BEING DENIES HIMSELF THE SIMPLE PLEASURE OF A GOOD WAFFLE.
UP IN THE CAB NOW, HARK. I WANT YOU AND NO ONE ELSE WORKING THAT WINCH.
JUST LISTEN FOR MY INSTRUCTION ON THE WALKIE.

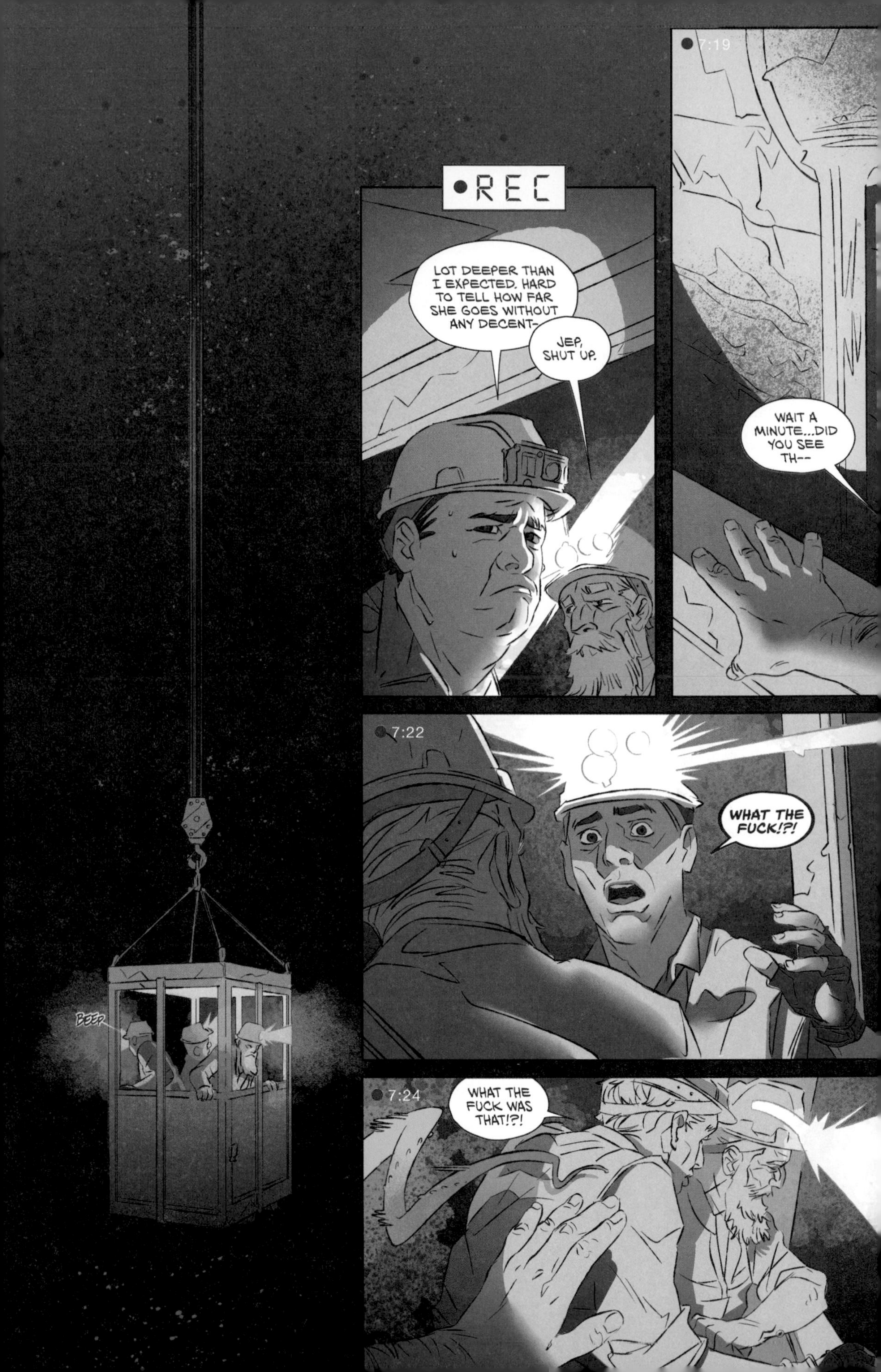
BEEP
•REC
LOT DEEPER THAN I EXPECTED. HARD TO TELL HOW FAR SHE GOES WITHOUT ANY DECENT-
JEP, SHUT UP.
7:19
WAIT A MINUTE...DID YOU SEE TH--
7:22
WHAT THE FUCK!?!
7:24
WHAT THE FUCK WAS THAT!?!

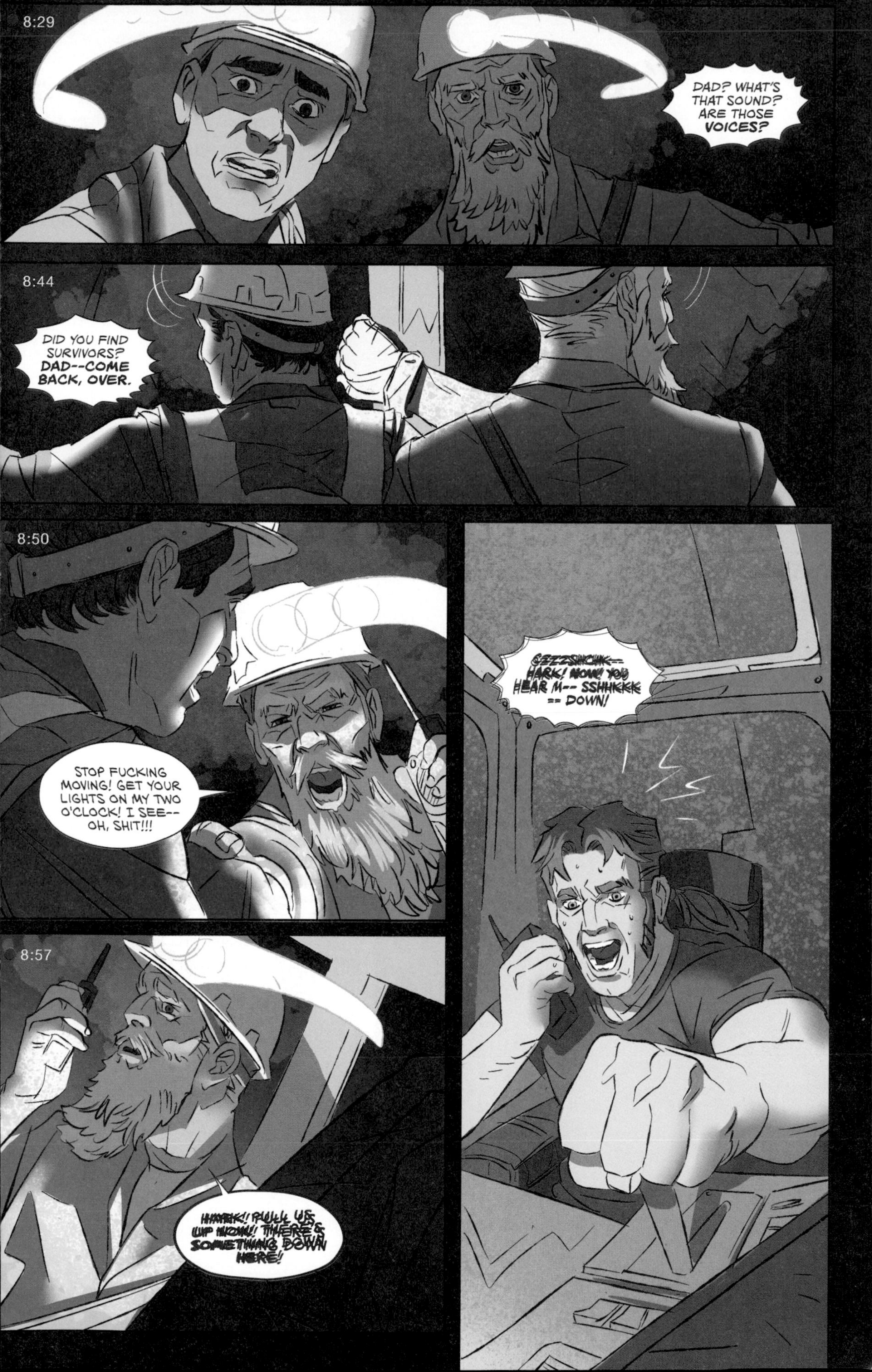

8:29
DAD? WHAT'S THAT SOUND? ARE THOSE VOICES?
8:44
DID YOU FIND SURVIVORS? DAD--COME BACK, OVER.
8:50
STOP FUCKING MOVING! GET YOUR LIGHTS ON MY TWO O'CLOCK! I SEE-- OH, SHIT!!!
CZZZSHCHK-- HARK! NOW! YOU HEAR M-- SSHHKKK == DOWN!
8:57
HHARK!! PULL US UP NOW! THERE'S SOMETHING DOWN HERE!

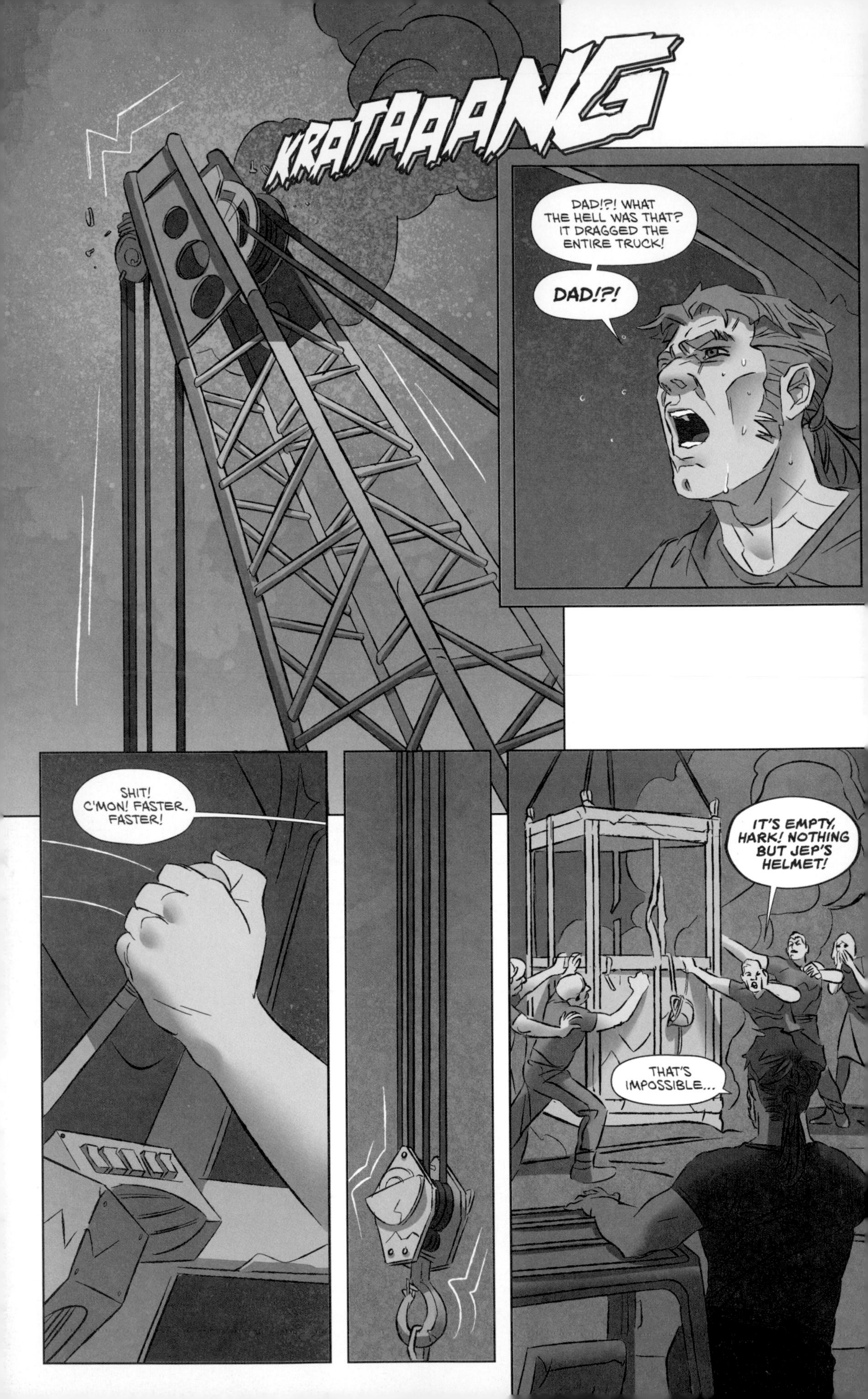
KRATAAAANG
DAD!?! WHAT THE HELL WAS THAT? IT DRAGGED THE ENTIRE TRUCK!
DAD!?!
SHIT! C'MON! FASTER. FASTER!
IT'S EMPTY, HARK! NOTHING BUT JEP'S HELMET!
THAT'S IMPOSSIBLE...

OUTTA THE WAY. HE HAD HIS BOY'S CAMERA STRAPPED TO IT-- WAS RECORDING THE **WHOLE THING.**

HE'S A STRONG MAN, HARK...

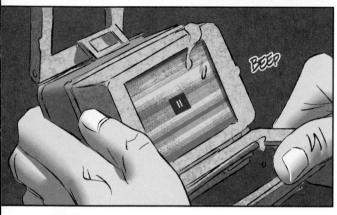

BEEP

▼ MODE

◀◀ REWIND   ❙❙ PAUSE   ▶ PLAY   FORWARD ▶▶

11:55

--YOUR LIGHTS ON MY TWO O'CLOCK!

12:08

I SEE... OH SHIT!!!

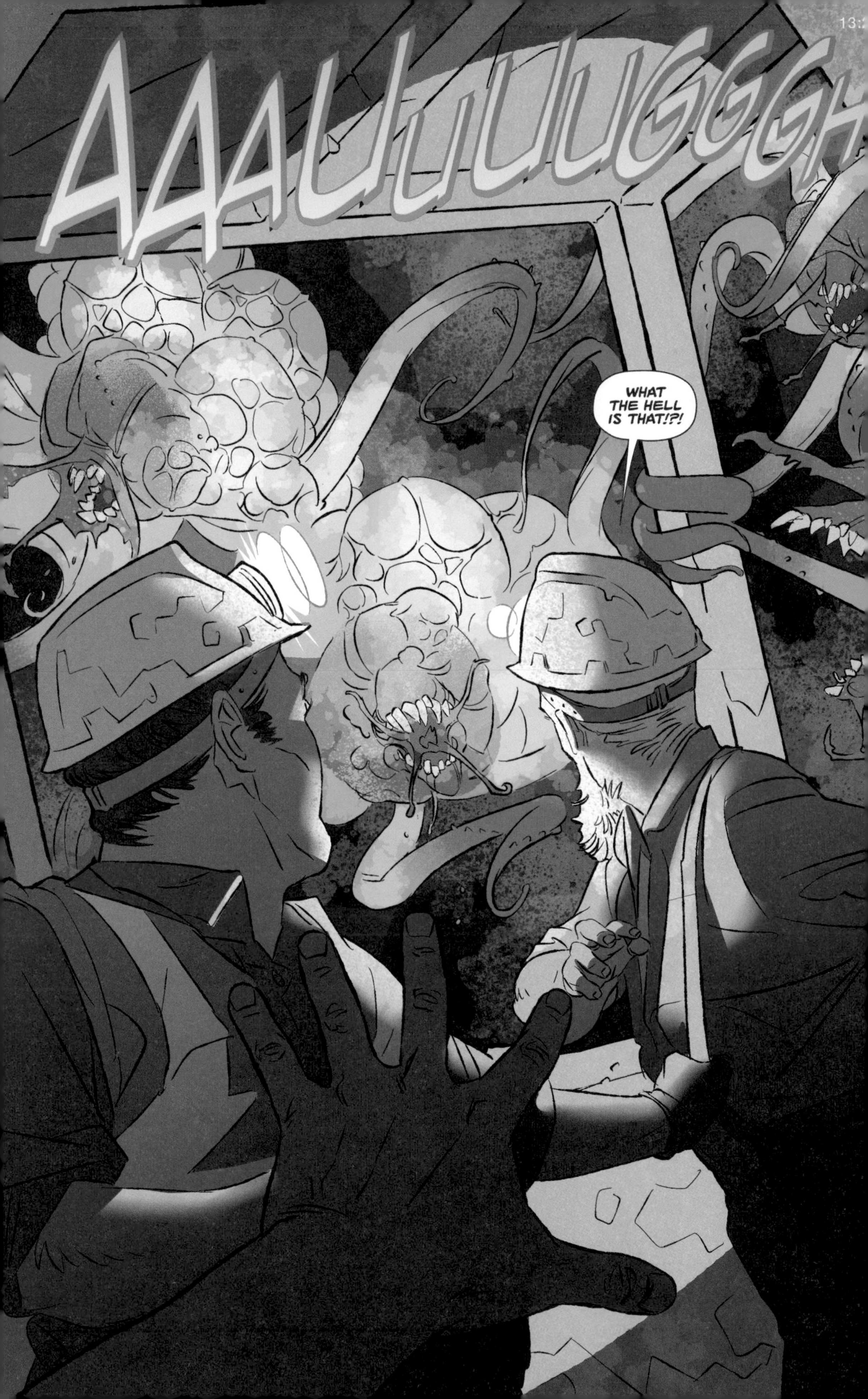
AAAUUUUGGGH
WHAT THE HELL IS THAT!?!

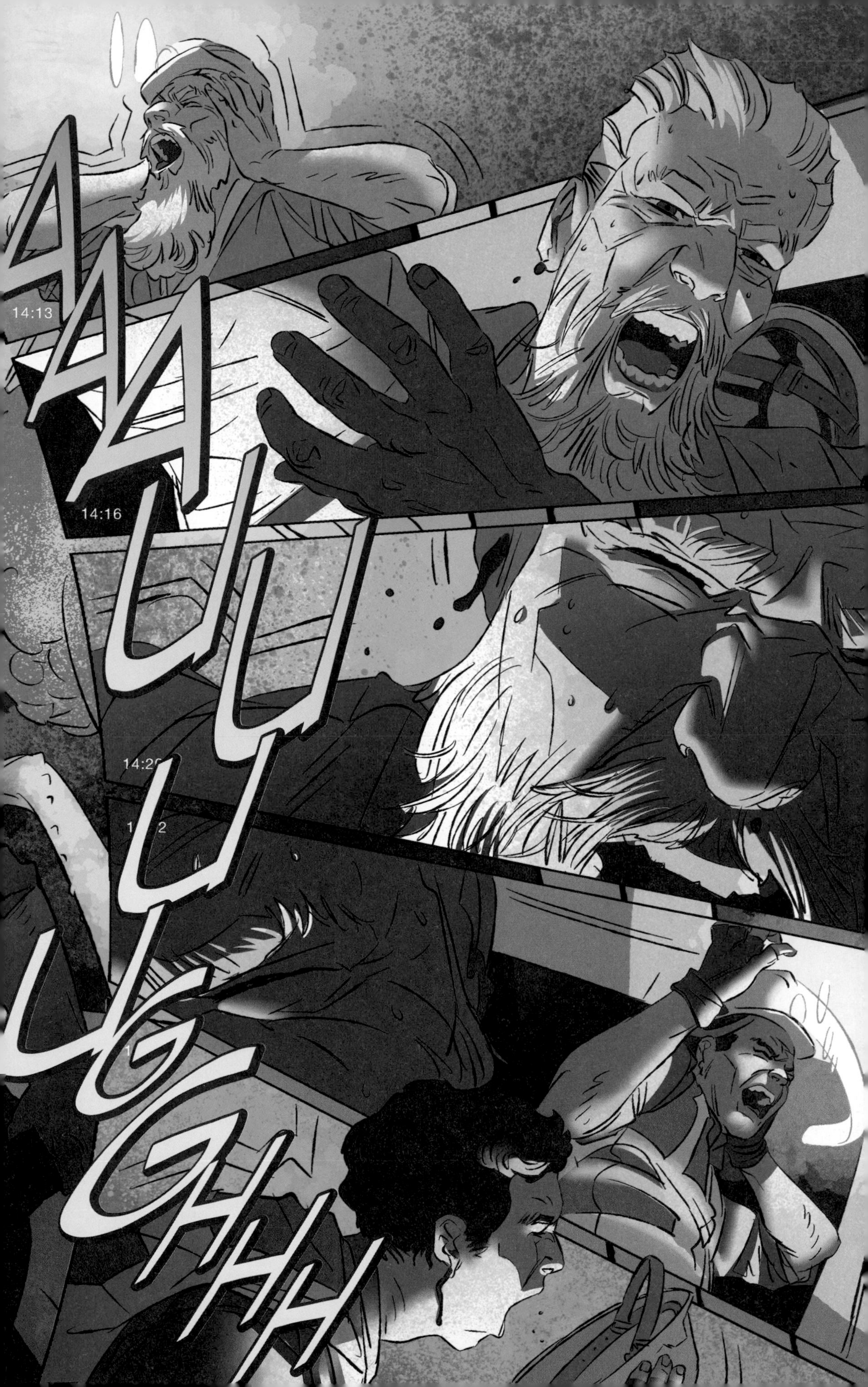
!!
14:13
14:16
AAAUUUUGGHHH

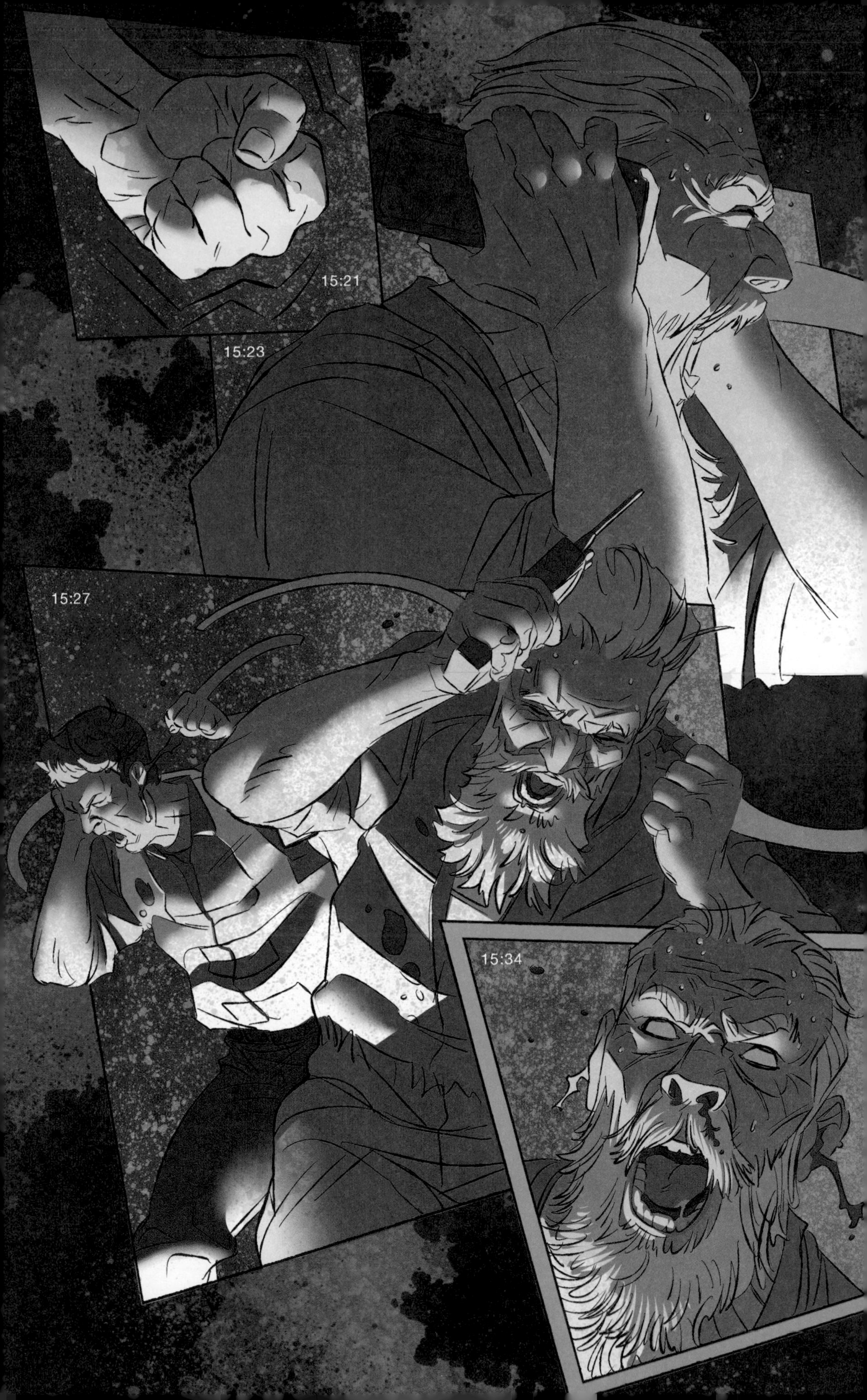
15:21
15:23
15:27
15:34

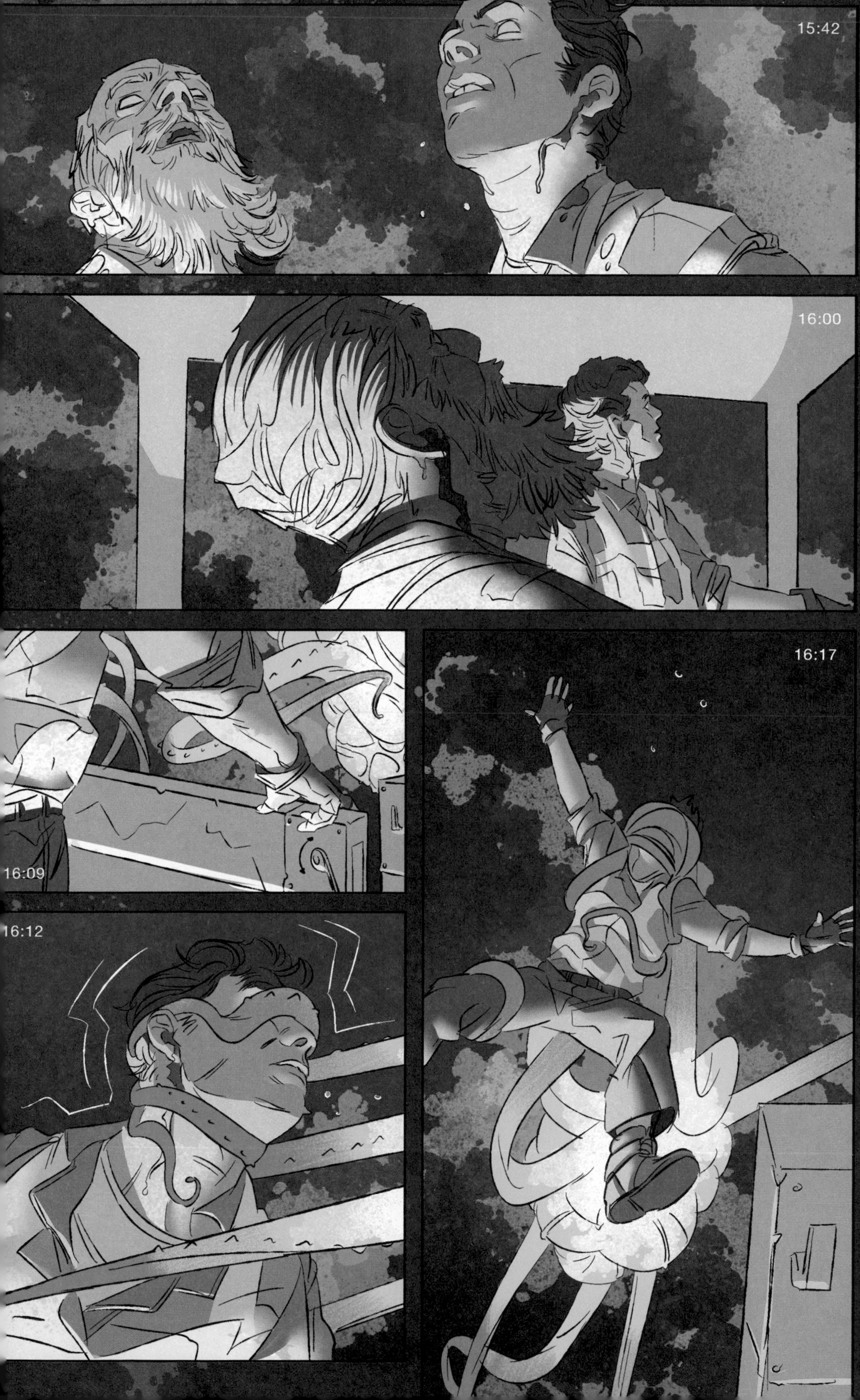
15:42
16:00
16:09
16:17
16:12

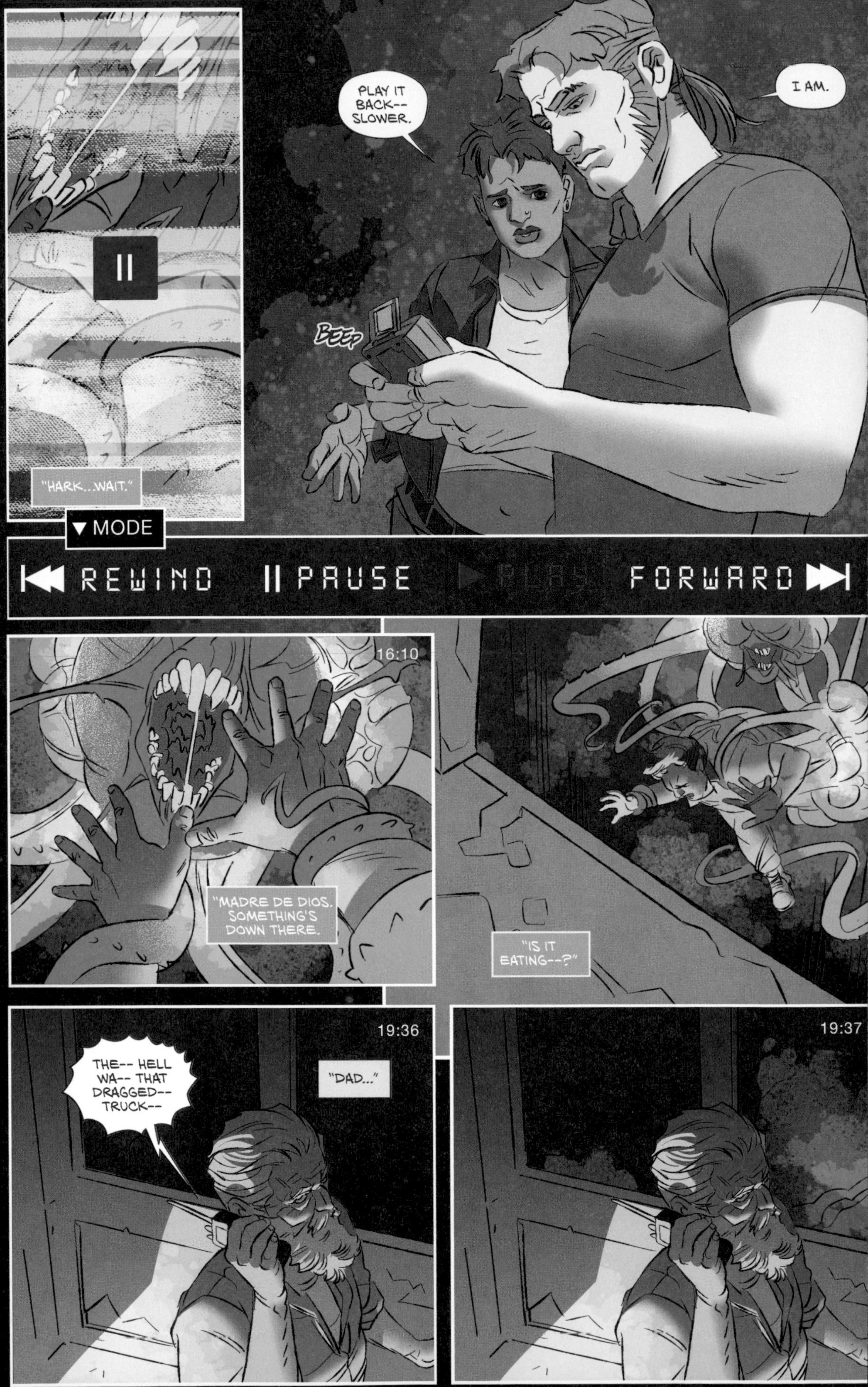
PLAY IT BACK-- SLOWER.
I AM.
BEEP
"HARK...WAIT."
▼MODE
REWIND
PAUSE
FORWARD
16:10
"MADRE DE DIOS. SOMETHING'S DOWN THERE.
"IS IT EATING--?"
19:36
THE-- HELL WA-- THAT DRAGGED-- TRUCK--
"DAD..."
19:37

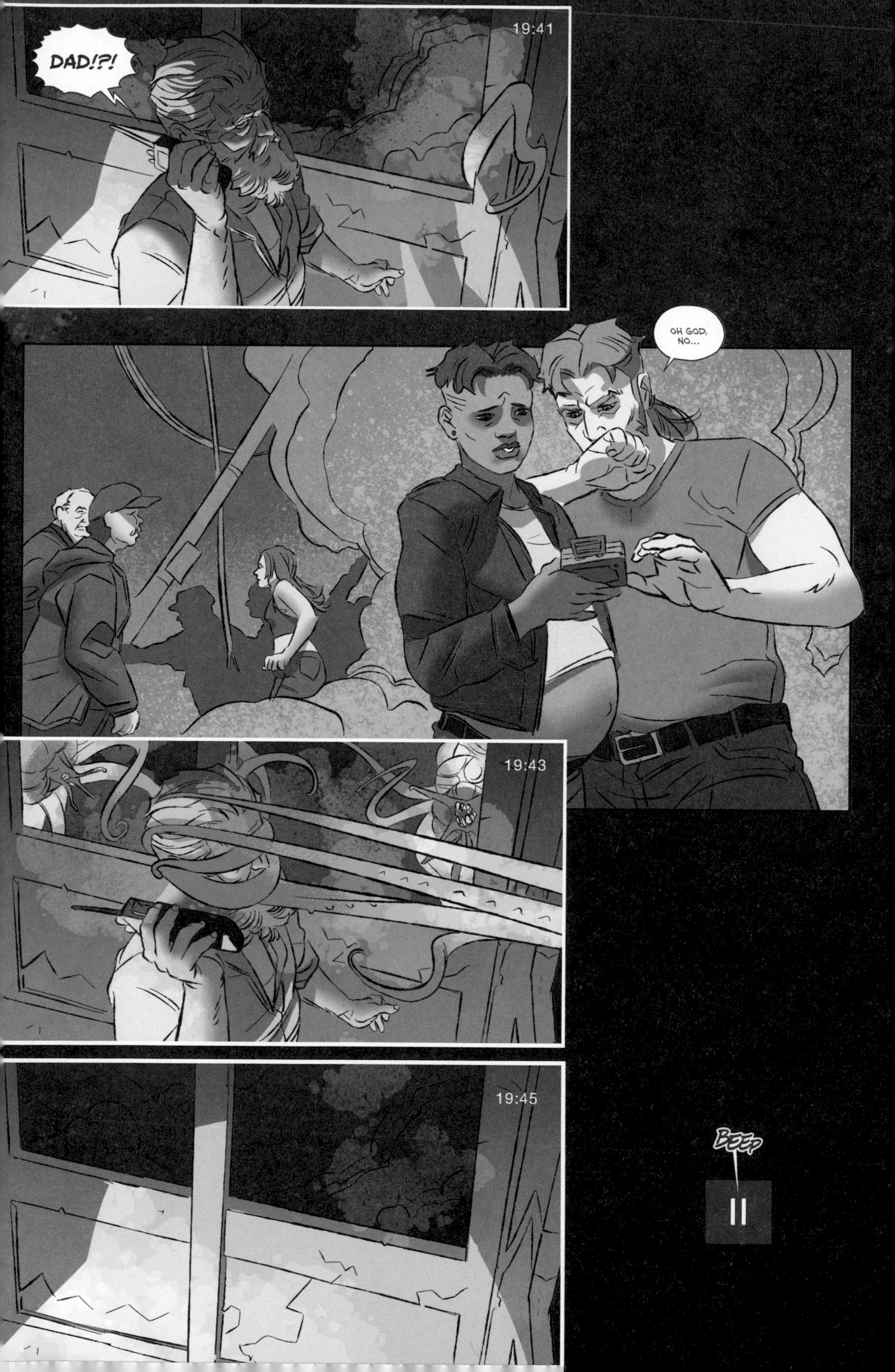
19:41
DAD!?!
OH GOD, NO...
19:43
19:45
BEEP
II

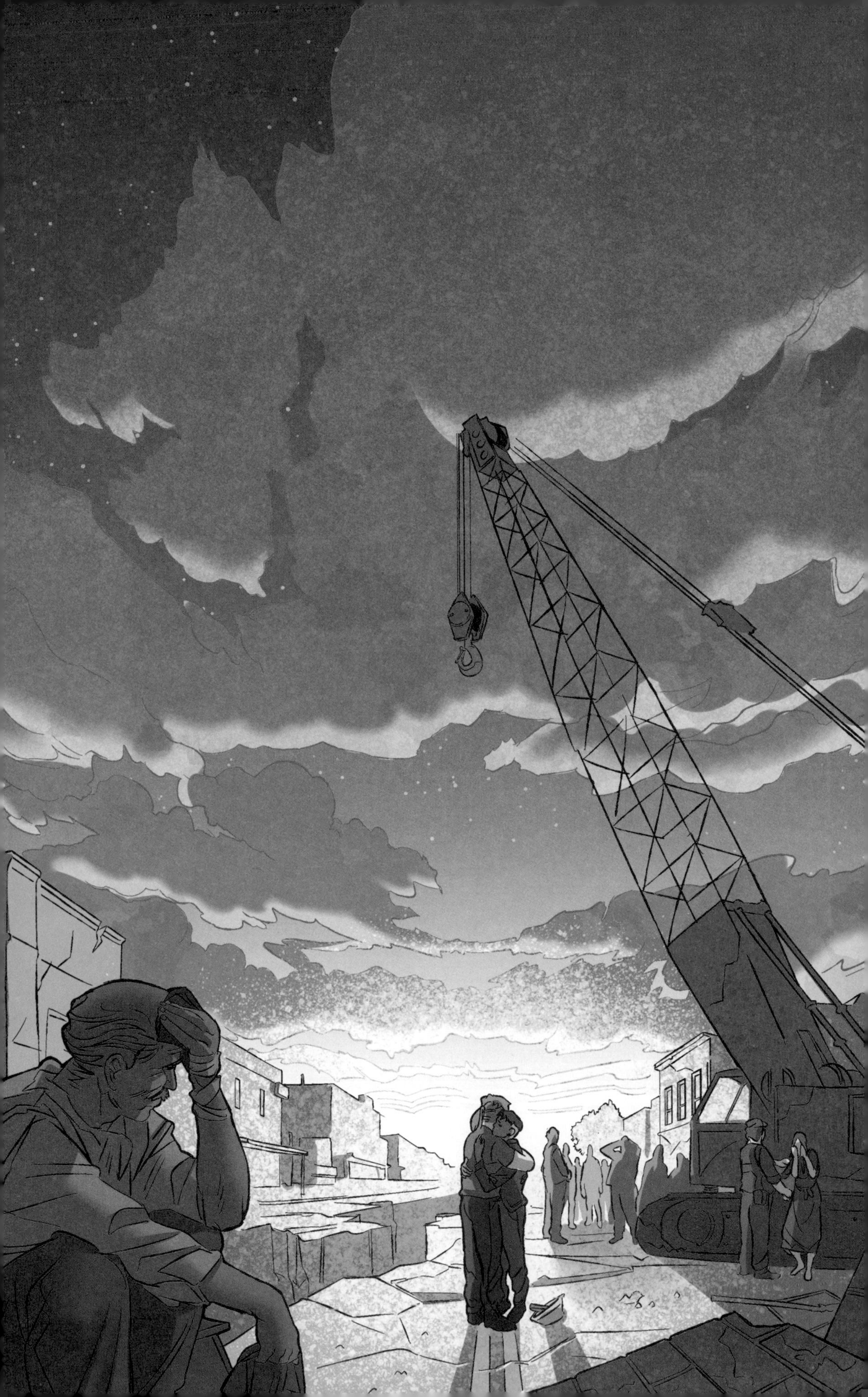

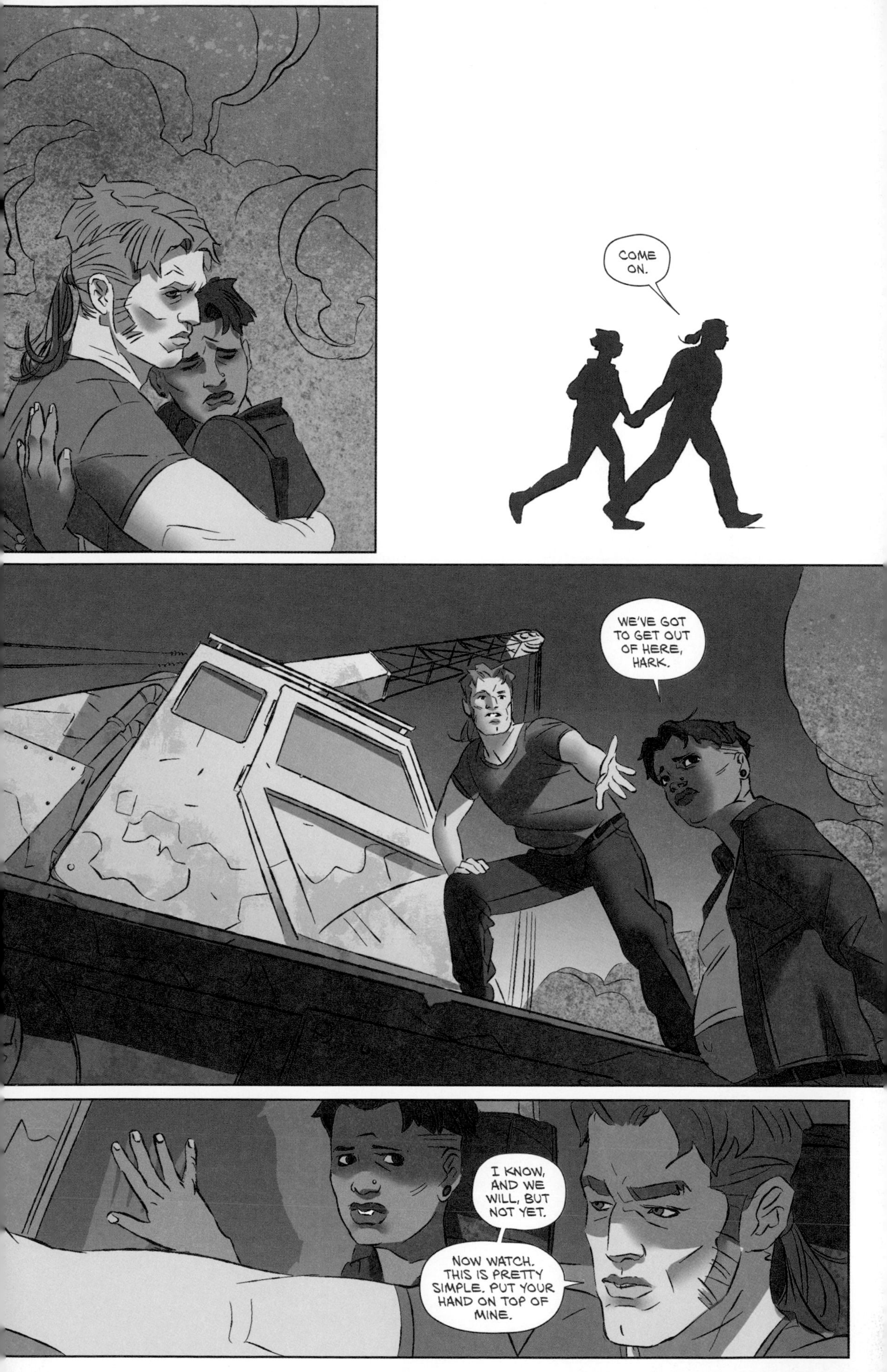
COME ON.
WE'VE GOT TO GET OUT OF HERE, HARK.
I KNOW, AND WE WILL, BUT NOT YET.
NOW WATCH. THIS IS PRETTY SIMPLE. PUT YOUR HAND ON TOP OF MINE.

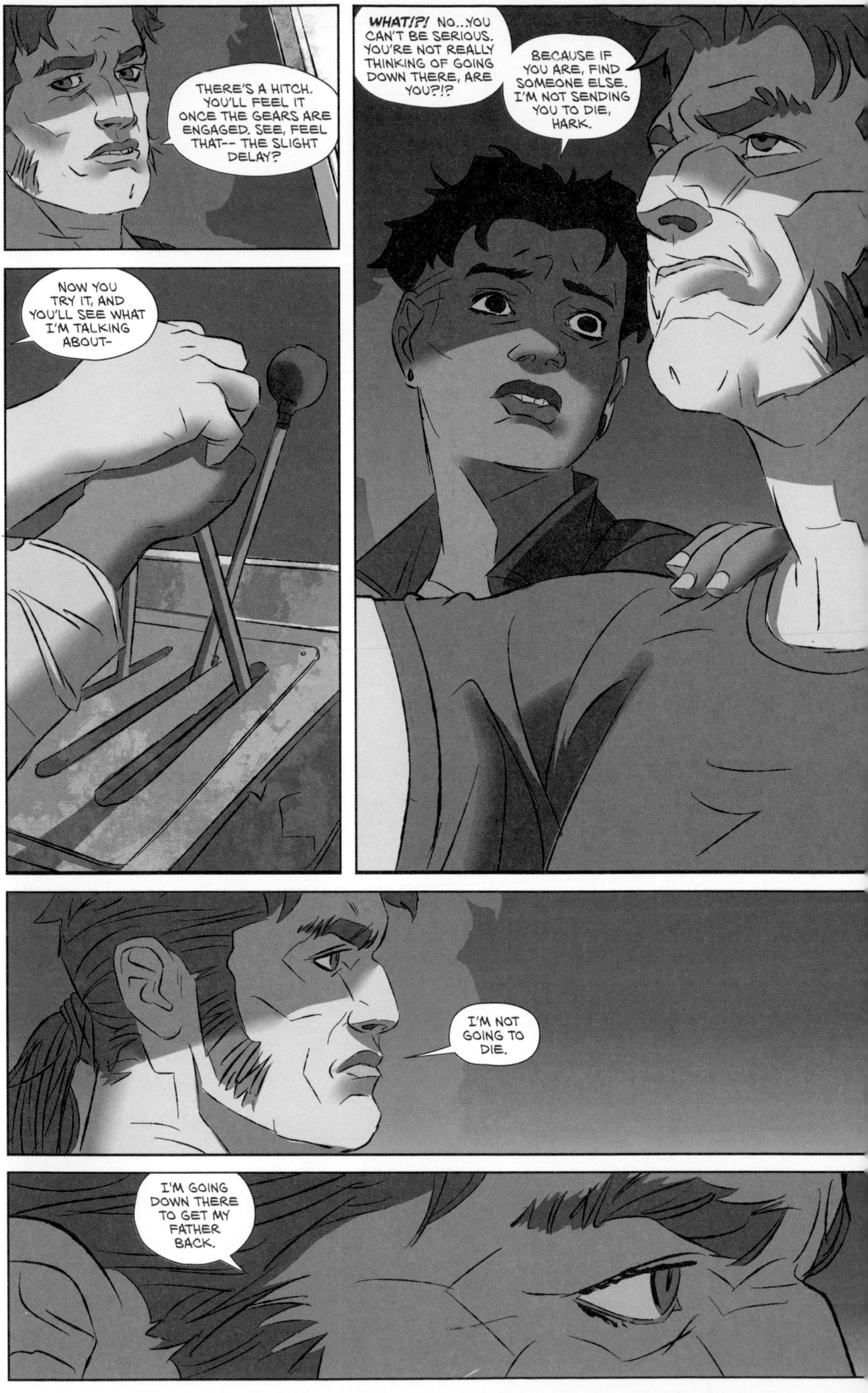

THERE'S A HITCH. YOU'LL FEEL IT ONCE THE GEARS ARE ENGAGED. SEE, FEEL THAT-- THE SLIGHT DELAY?
NOW YOU TRY IT, AND YOU'LL SEE WHAT I'M TALKING ABOUT-
WHAT!?! NO...YOU CAN'T BE SERIOUS. YOU'RE NOT REALLY THINKING OF GOING DOWN THERE, ARE YOU?!?
BECAUSE IF YOU ARE, FIND SOMEONE ELSE. I'M NOT SENDING YOU TO DIE, HARK.
I'M NOT GOING TO DIE.
I'M GOING DOWN THERE TO GET MY FATHER BACK.

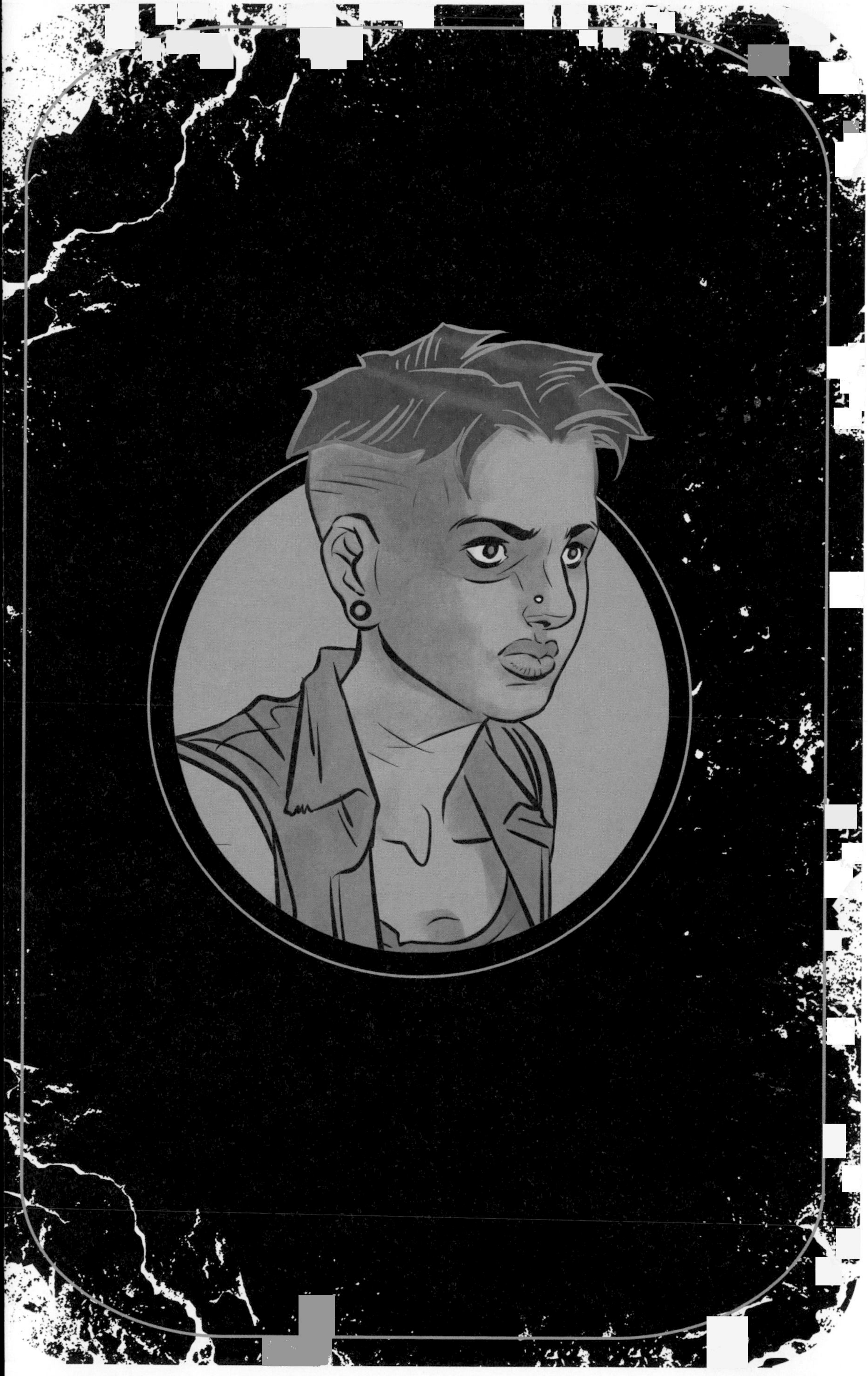

CHAPTER THREE

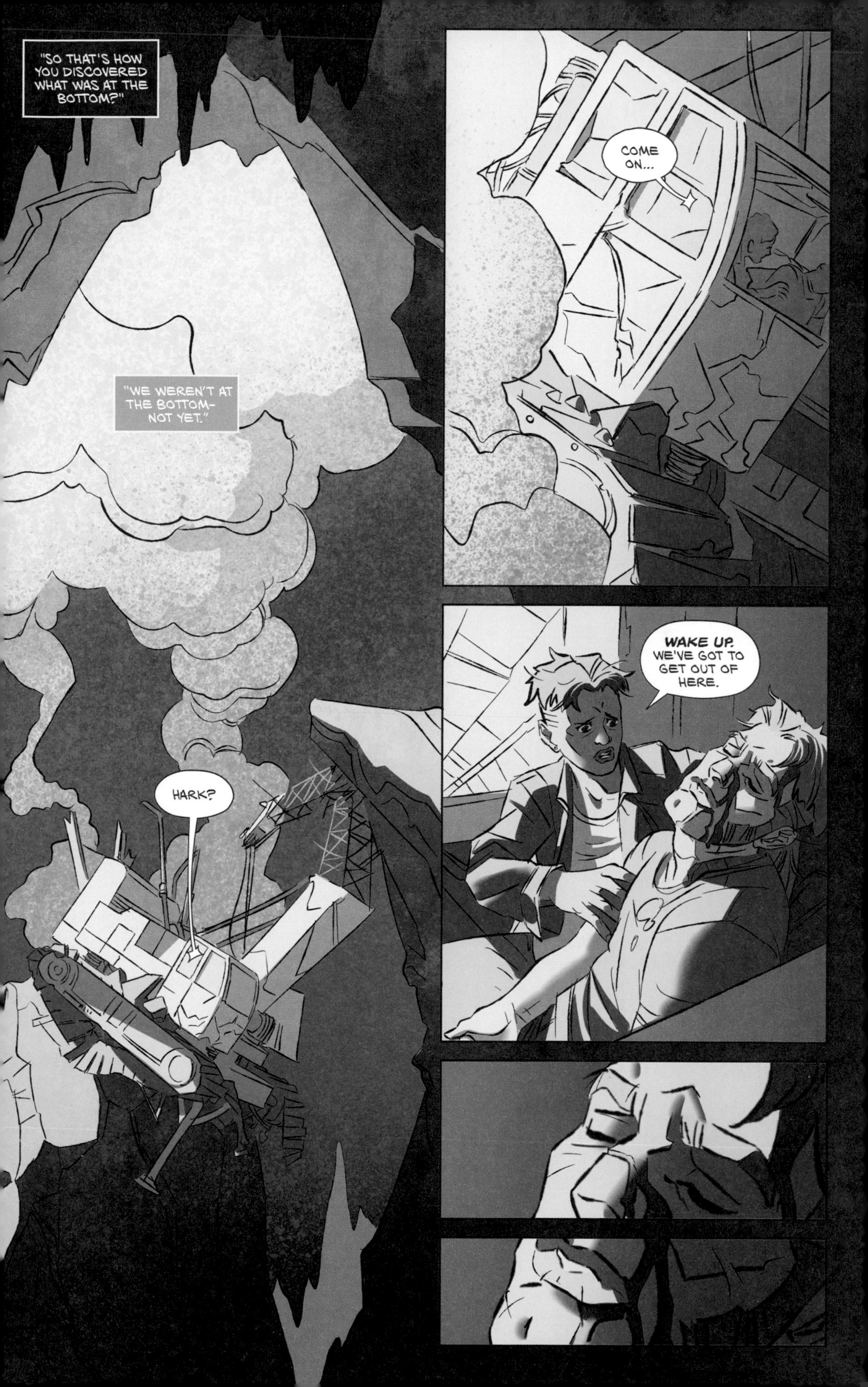
"SO THAT'S HOW YOU DISCOVERED WHAT WAS AT THE BOTTOM?"
"WE WEREN'T AT THE BOTTOM-NOT YET."
HARK?
COME ON...
WAKE UP. WE'VE GOT TO GET OUT OF HERE.

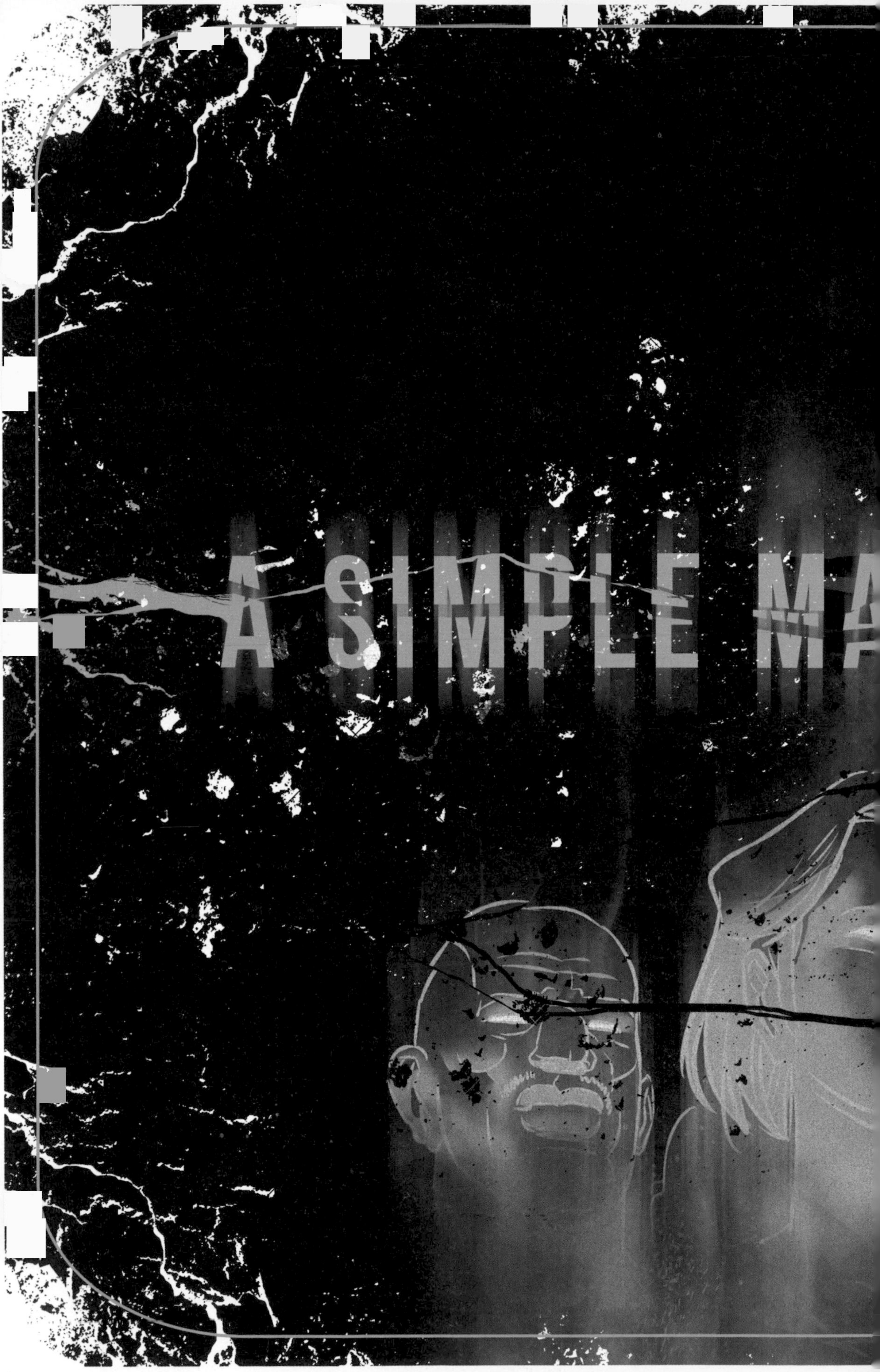
A SIMPLE MA

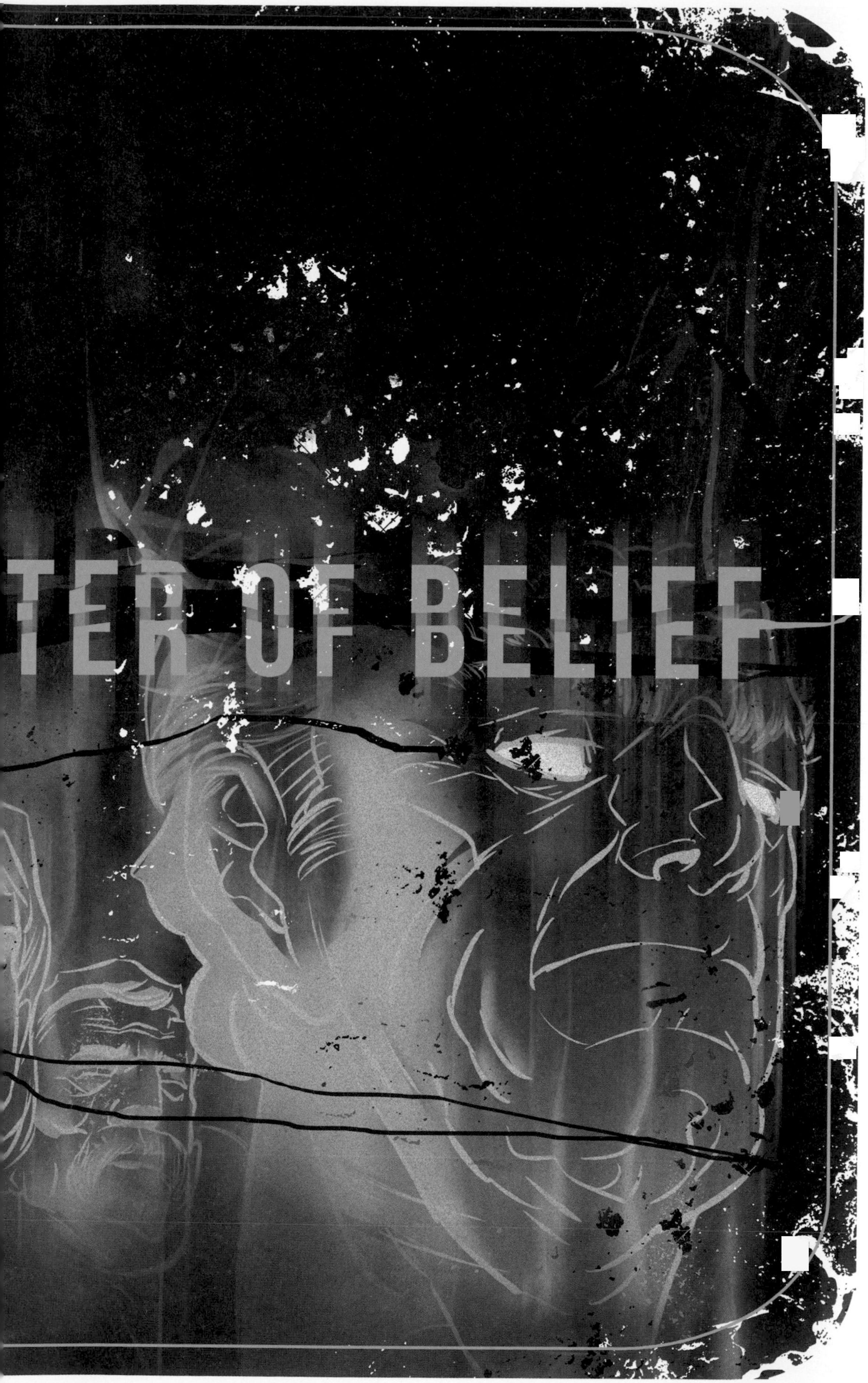
TER OF BELIEF

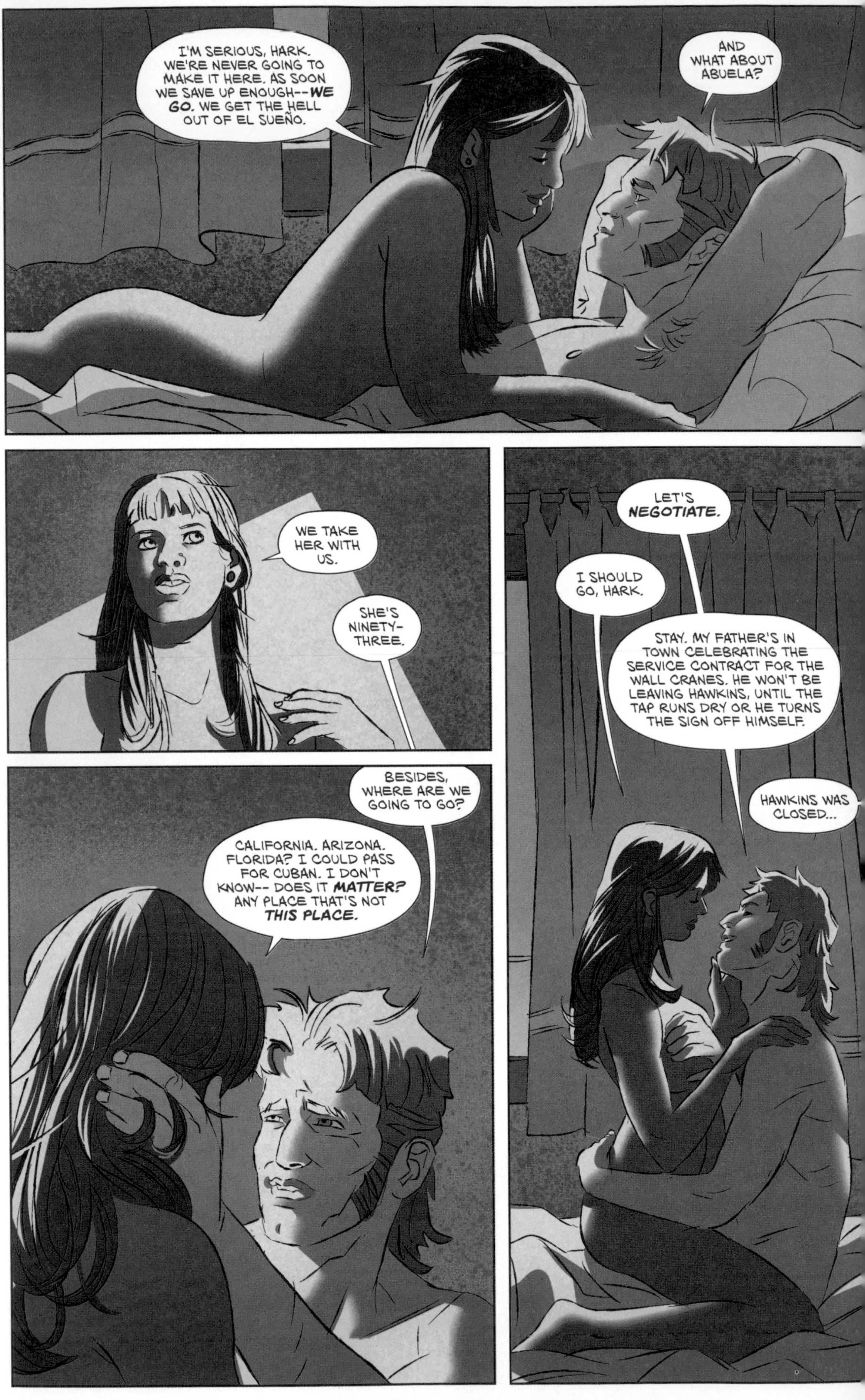
I'M SERIOUS, HARK. WE'RE NEVER GOING TO MAKE IT HERE. AS SOON WE SAVE UP ENOUGH--**WE GO.** WE GET THE HELL OUT OF EL SUEÑO.
AND WHAT ABOUT ABUELA?
WE TAKE HER WITH US.
SHE'S NINETY-THREE.
BESIDES, WHERE ARE WE GOING TO GO?
CALIFORNIA. ARIZONA. FLORIDA? I COULD PASS FOR CUBAN. I DON'T KNOW-- DOES IT **MATTER?** ANY PLACE THAT'S NOT **THIS PLACE.**
LET'S **NEGOTIATE.**
I SHOULD GO, HARK.
STAY. MY FATHER'S IN TOWN CELEBRATING THE SERVICE CONTRACT FOR THE WALL CRANES. HE WON'T BE LEAVING HAWKINS, UNTIL THE TAP RUNS DRY OR HE TURNS THE SIGN OFF HIMSELF.
HAWKINS WAS CLOSED...

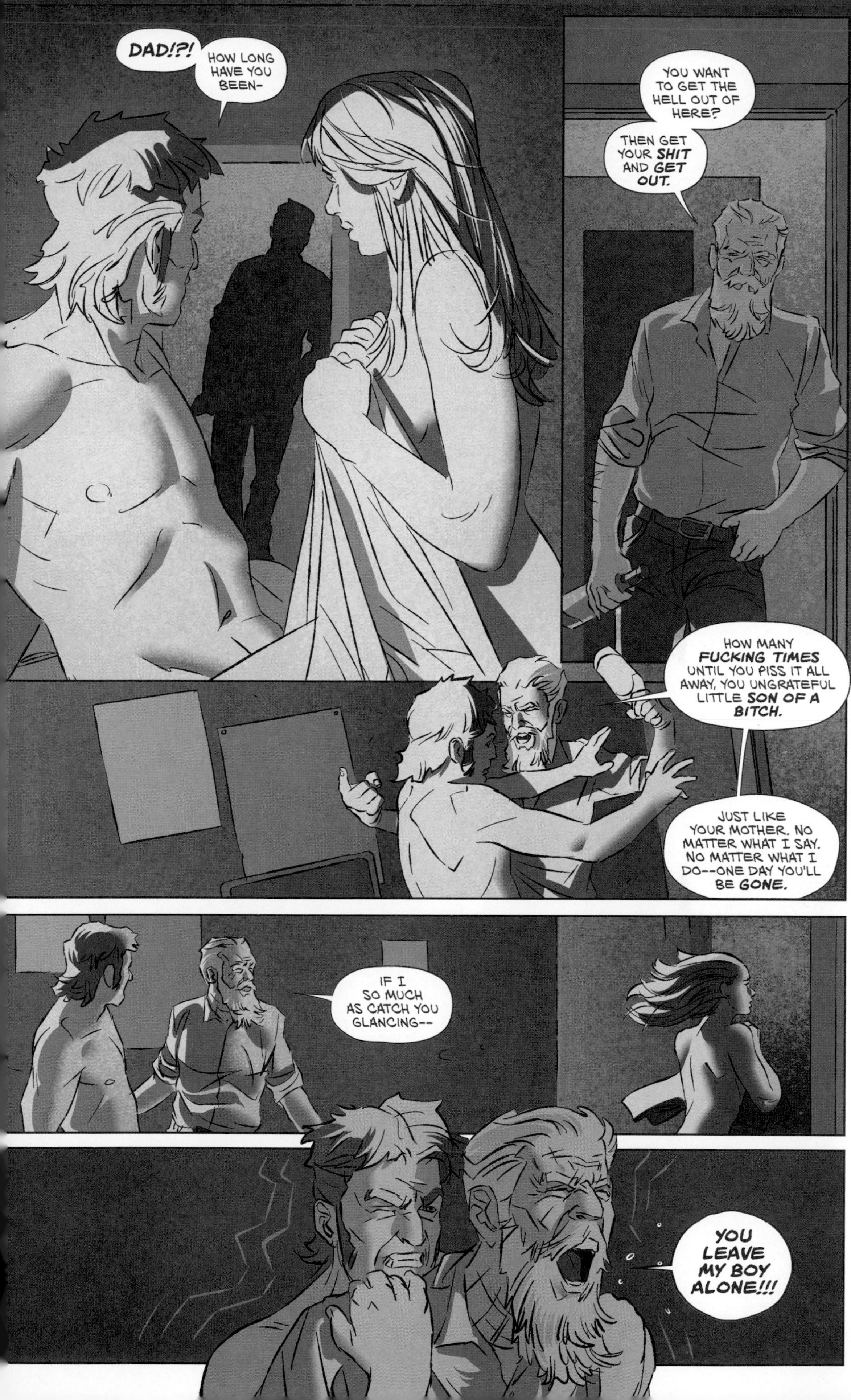
DAD!?!
HOW LONG HAVE YOU BEEN-
YOU WANT TO GET THE HELL OUT OF HERE?
THEN GET YOUR SHIT AND GET OUT.
HOW MANY FUCKING TIMES UNTIL YOU PISS IT ALL AWAY, YOU UNGRATEFUL LITTLE SON OF A BITCH.
JUST LIKE YOUR MOTHER. NO MATTER WHAT I SAY. NO MATTER WHAT I DO--ONE DAY YOU'LL BE GONE.
IF I SO MUCH AS CATCH YOU GLANCING--
YOU LEAVE MY BOY ALONE!!!

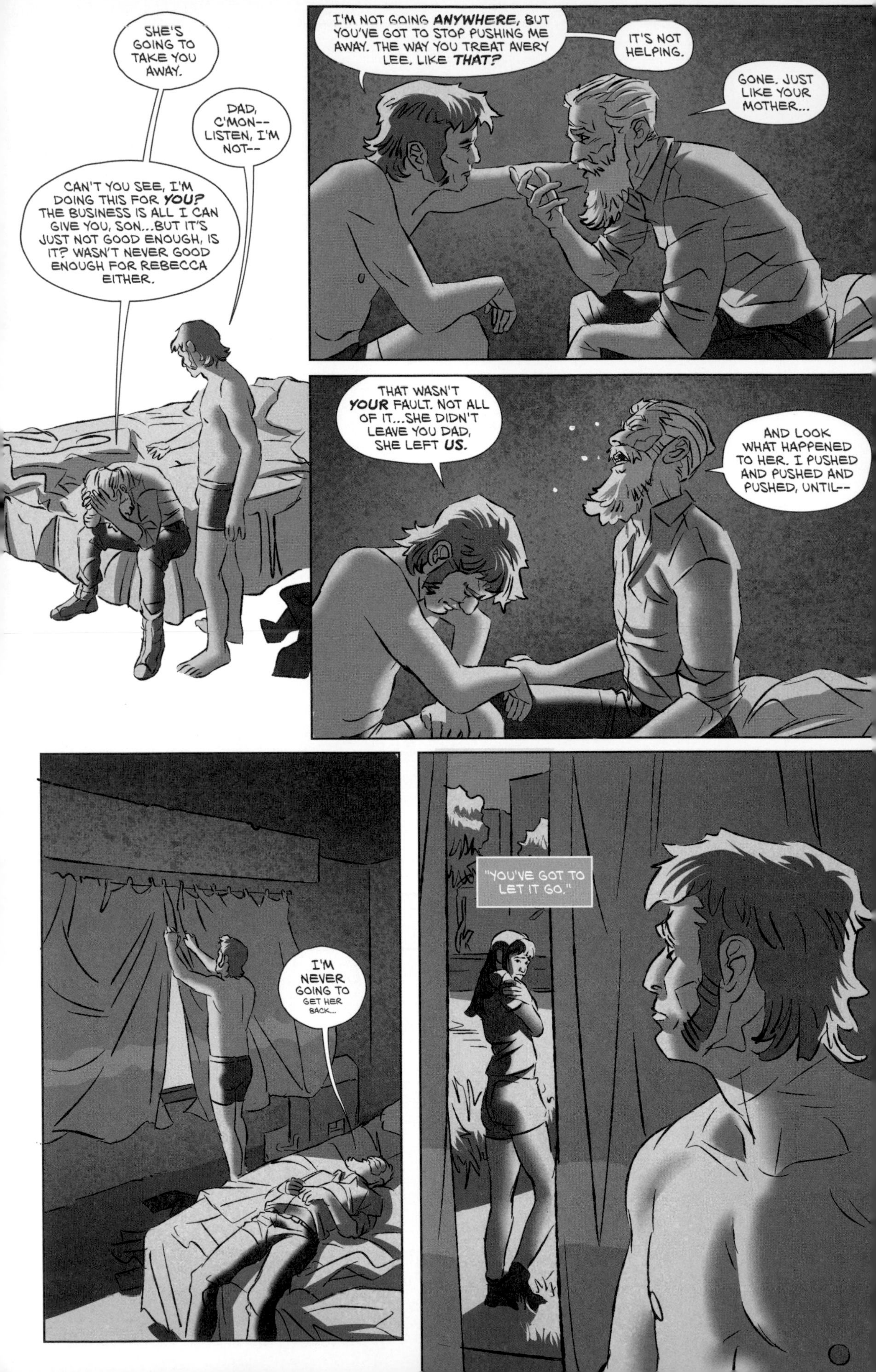
SHE'S GOING TO TAKE YOU AWAY.
DAD, C'MON-- LISTEN, I'M NOT--
CAN'T YOU SEE, I'M DOING THIS FOR YOU? THE BUSINESS IS ALL I CAN GIVE YOU, SON...BUT IT'S JUST NOT GOOD ENOUGH, IS IT? WASN'T NEVER GOOD ENOUGH FOR REBECCA EITHER.
I'M NOT GOING ANYWHERE, BUT YOU'VE GOT TO STOP PUSHING ME AWAY. THE WAY YOU TREAT AVERY LEE. LIKE THAT?
IT'S NOT HELPING.
GONE. JUST LIKE YOUR MOTHER...
THAT WASN'T YOUR FAULT. NOT ALL OF IT...SHE DIDN'T LEAVE YOU DAD, SHE LEFT US.
AND LOOK WHAT HAPPENED TO HER. I PUSHED AND PUSHED AND PUSHED, UNTIL--
I'M NEVER GOING TO GET HER BACK...
"YOU'VE GOT TO LET IT GO."

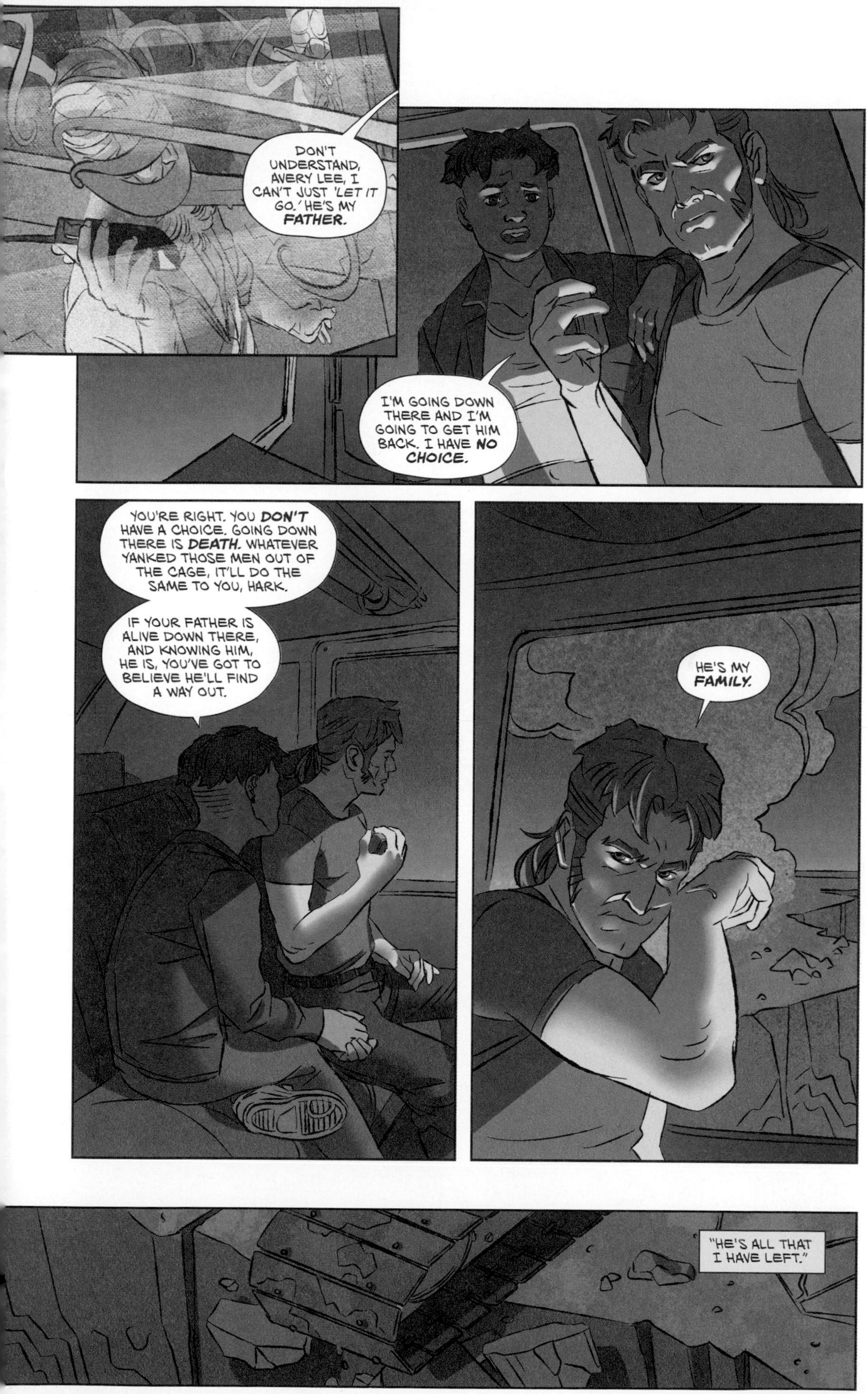
DON'T UNDERSTAND, AVERY LEE, I CAN'T JUST 'LET IT GO.' HE'S MY FATHER.
I'M GOING DOWN THERE AND I'M GOING TO GET HIM BACK. I HAVE NO CHOICE.
YOU'RE RIGHT. YOU DON'T HAVE A CHOICE. GOING DOWN THERE IS DEATH. WHATEVER YANKED THOSE MEN OUT OF THE CAGE, IT'LL DO THE SAME TO YOU, HARK.
IF YOUR FATHER IS ALIVE DOWN THERE, AND KNOWING HIM, HE IS, YOU'VE GOT TO BELIEVE HE'LL FIND A WAY OUT.
HE'S MY FAMILY.
"HE'S ALL THAT I HAVE LEFT."

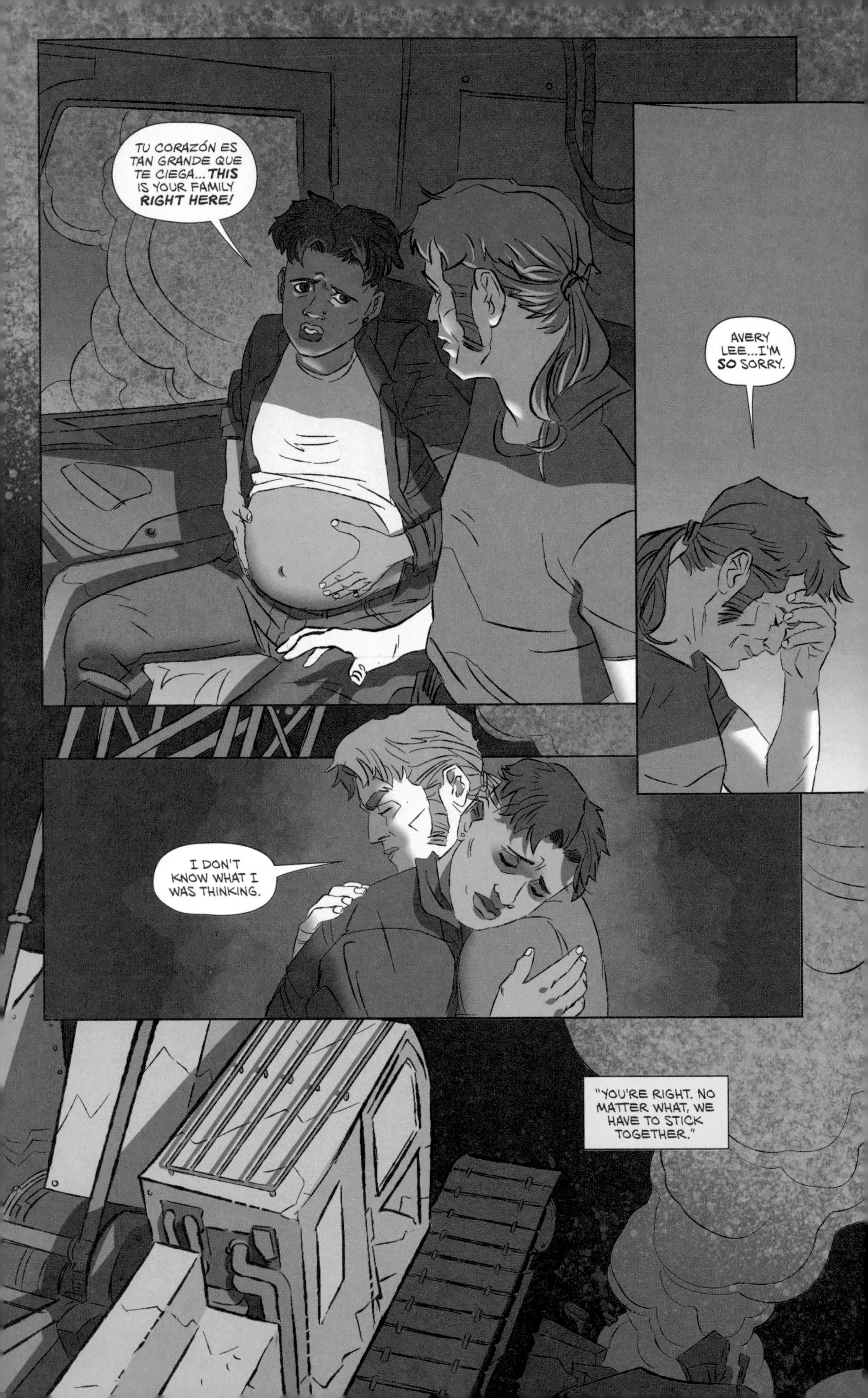
TU CORAZÓN ES TAN GRANDE QUE TE CIEGA... **THIS** IS YOUR FAMILY **RIGHT HERE!**
AVERY LEE...I'M **SO** SORRY.
I DON'T KNOW WHAT I WAS THINKING.
"YOU'RE RIGHT. NO MATTER WHAT, WE HAVE TO STICK TOGETHER."

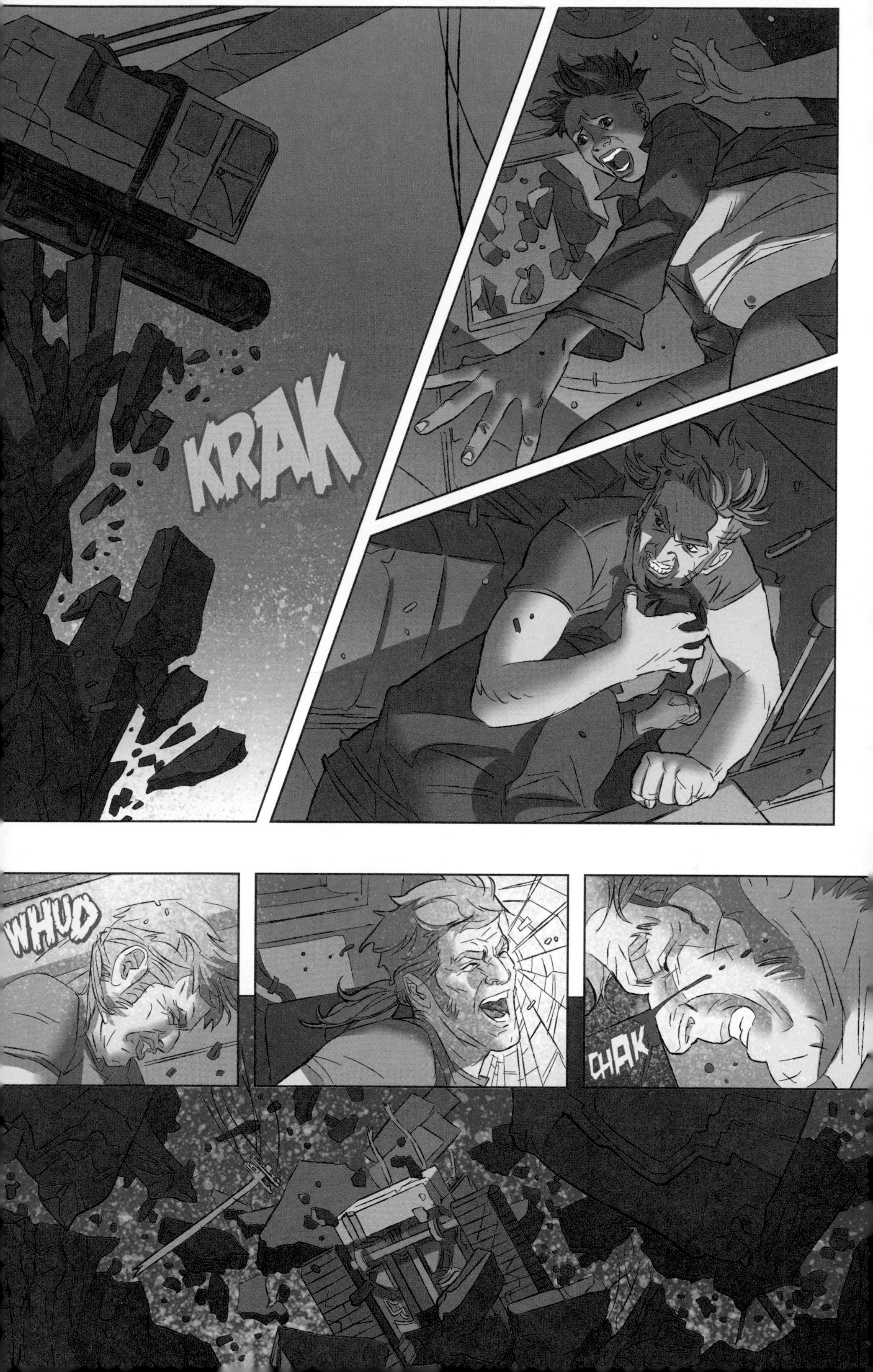
KRAK
WHUD
CHAK

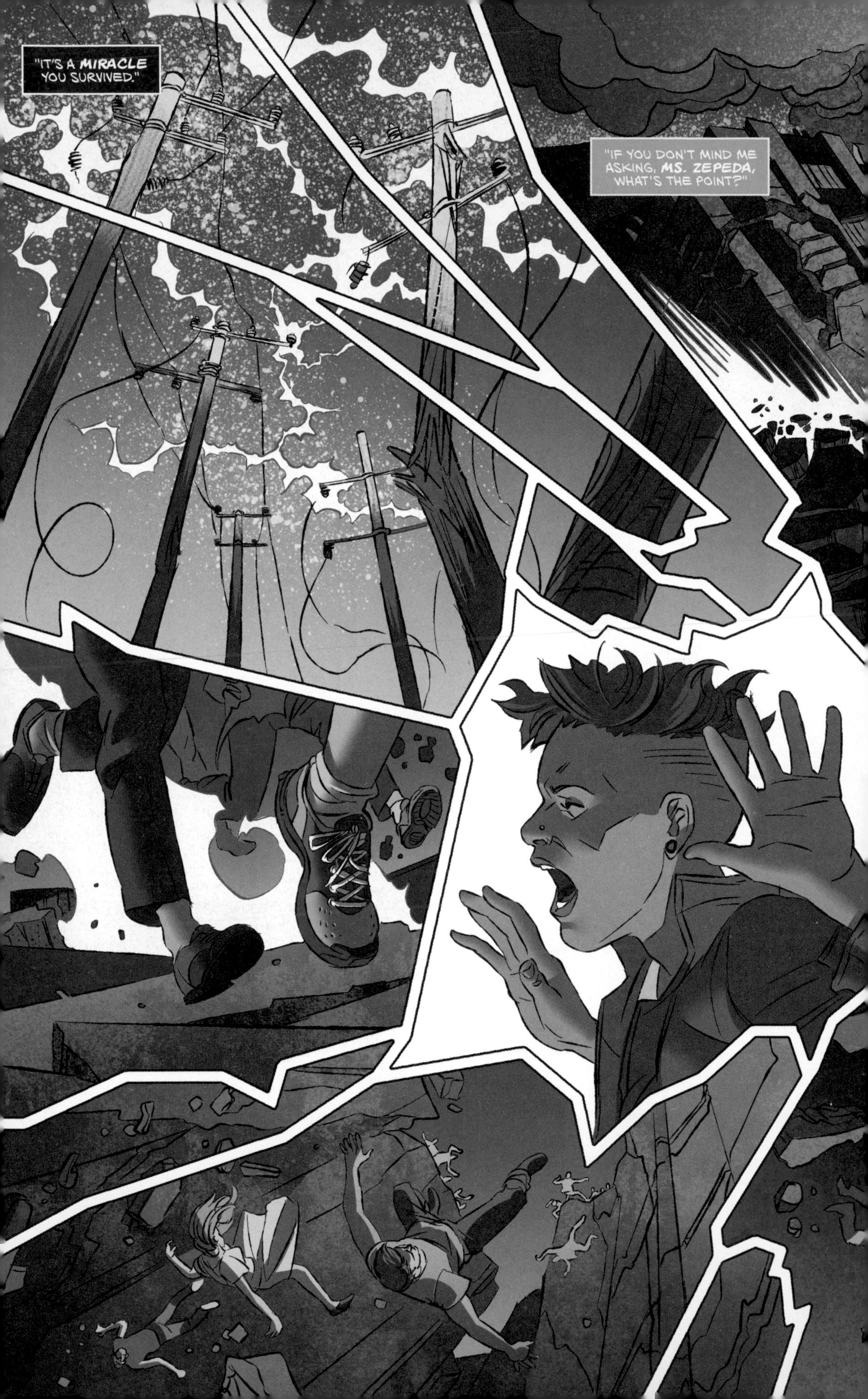
"IT'S A MIRACLE YOU SURVIVED."
"IF YOU DON'T MIND ME ASKING, MS. ZEPEDA, WHAT'S THE POINT?"

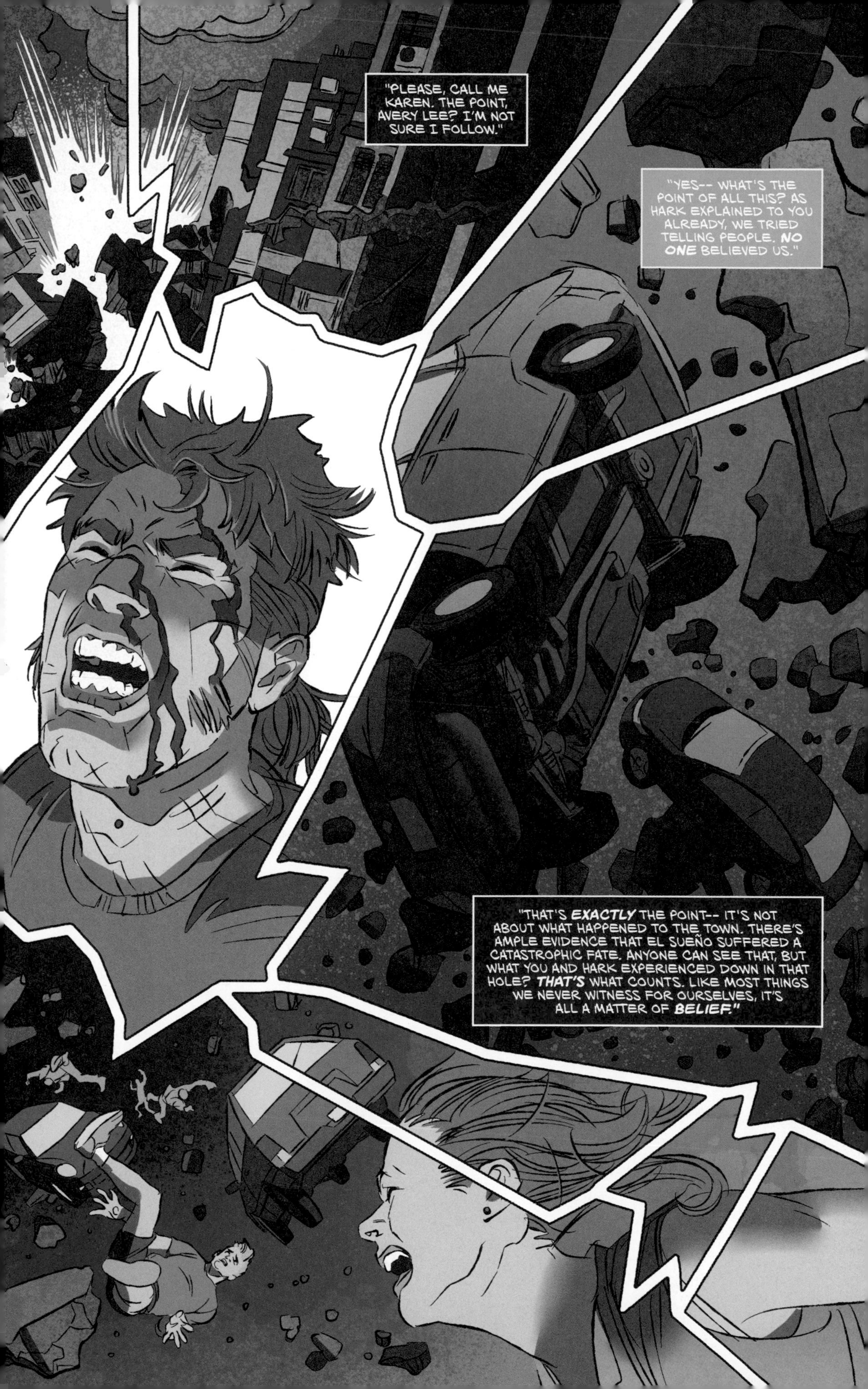
"PLEASE, CALL ME KAREN. THE POINT, AVERY LEE? I'M NOT SURE I FOLLOW."
"YES-- WHAT'S THE POINT OF ALL THIS? AS HARK EXPLAINED TO YOU ALREADY, WE TRIED TELLING PEOPLE. NO ONE BELIEVED US."
"THAT'S EXACTLY THE POINT-- IT'S NOT ABOUT WHAT HAPPENED TO THE TOWN. THERE'S AMPLE EVIDENCE THAT EL SUEÑO SUFFERED A CATASTROPHIC FATE. ANYONE CAN SEE THAT, BUT WHAT YOU AND HARK EXPERIENCED DOWN IN THAT HOLE? THAT'S WHAT COUNTS. LIKE MOST THINGS WE NEVER WITNESS FOR OURSELVES, IT'S ALL A MATTER OF BELIEF."

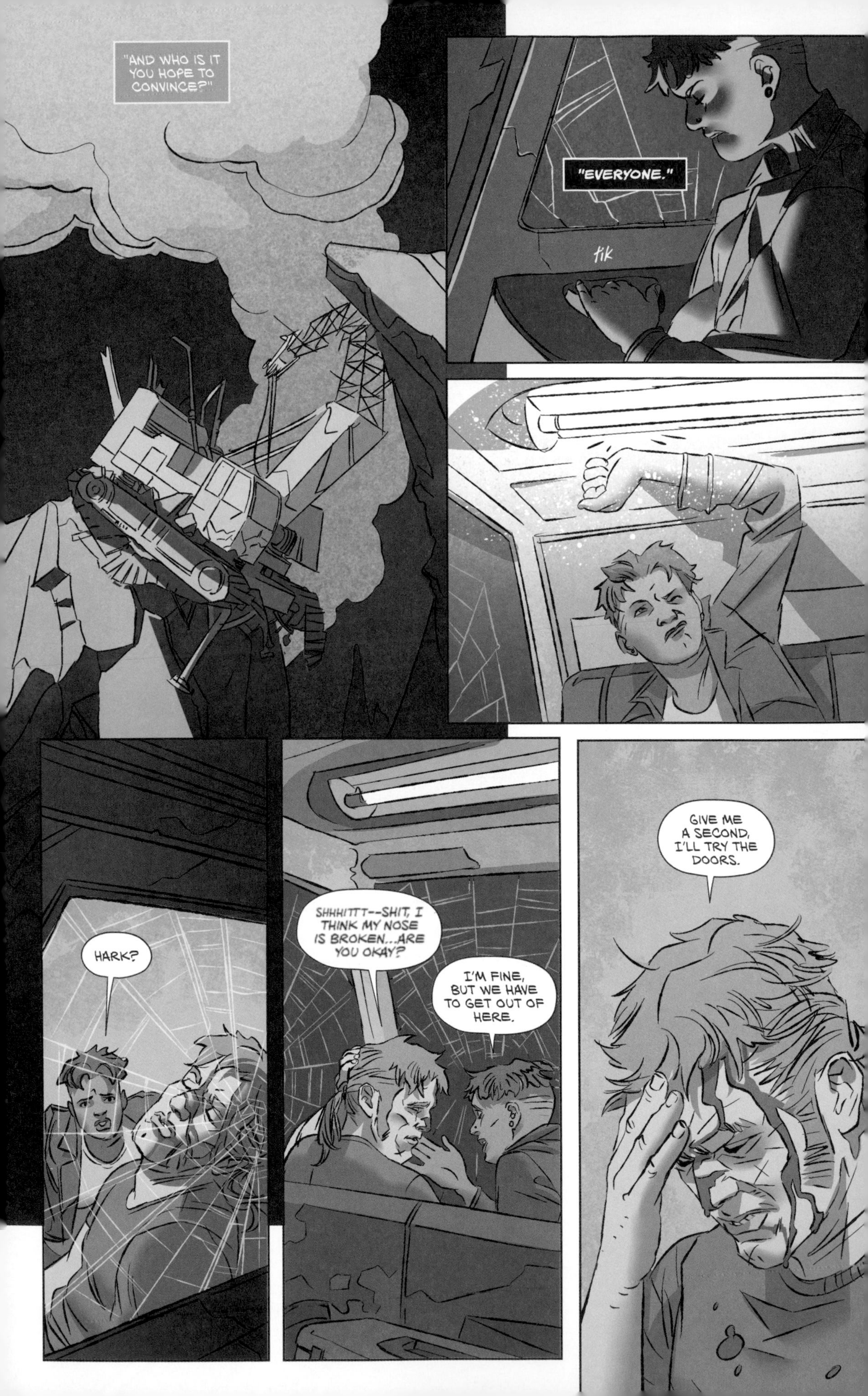

"AND WHO IS IT YOU HOPE TO CONVINCE?"
"EVERYONE."
tik
HARK?
SHHHITTT--SHIT, I THINK MY NOSE IS BROKEN...ARE YOU OKAY?
I'M FINE, BUT WE HAVE TO GET OUT OF HERE.
GIVE ME A SECOND, I'LL TRY THE DOORS.

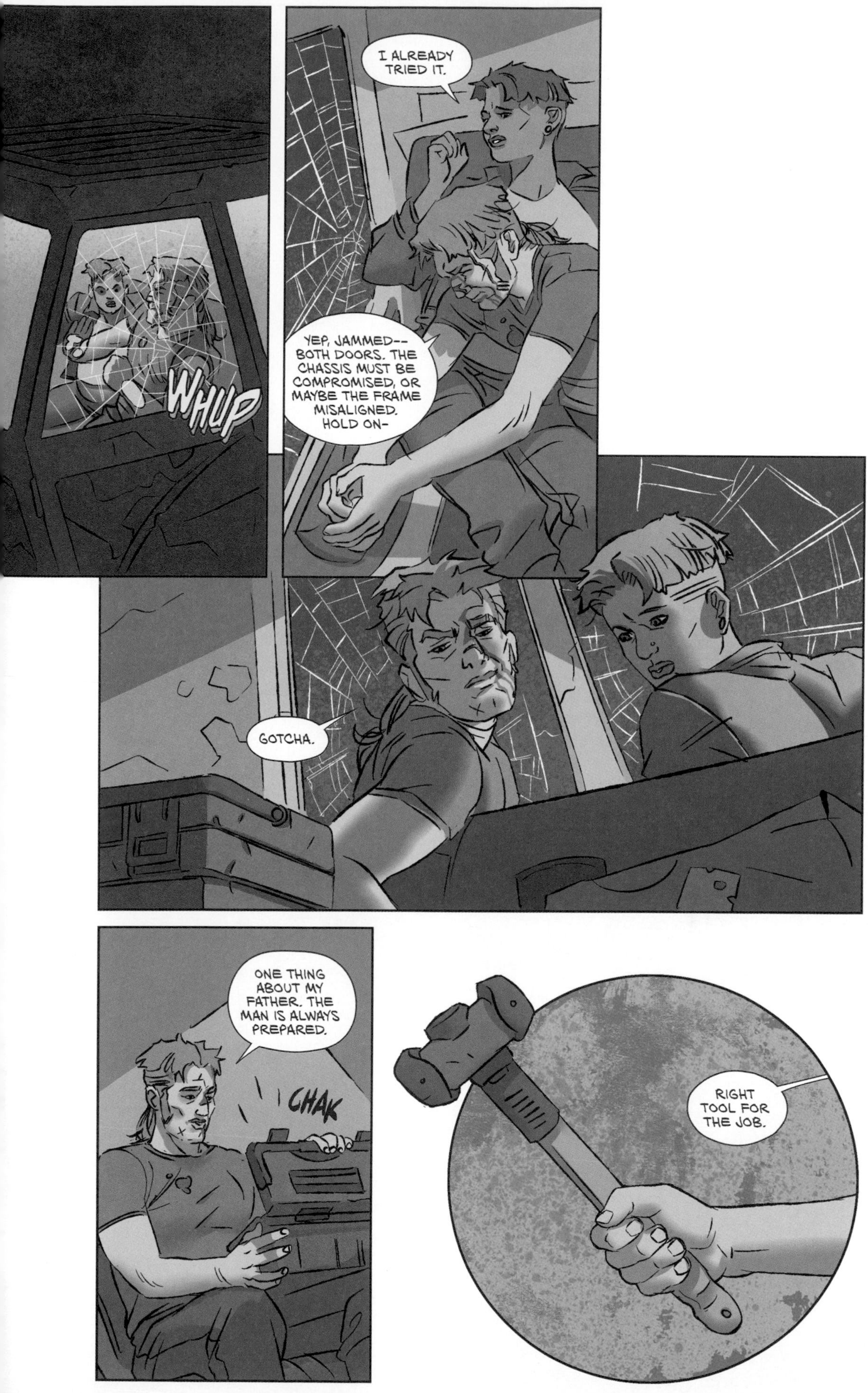
WHUP
I ALREADY TRIED IT.
YEP, JAMMED-- BOTH DOORS. THE CHASSIS MUST BE COMPROMISED, OR MAYBE THE FRAME MISALIGNED. HOLD ON-
GOTCHA.
ONE THING ABOUT MY FATHER. THE MAN IS ALWAYS PREPARED.
CHAK
RIGHT TOOL FOR THE JOB.

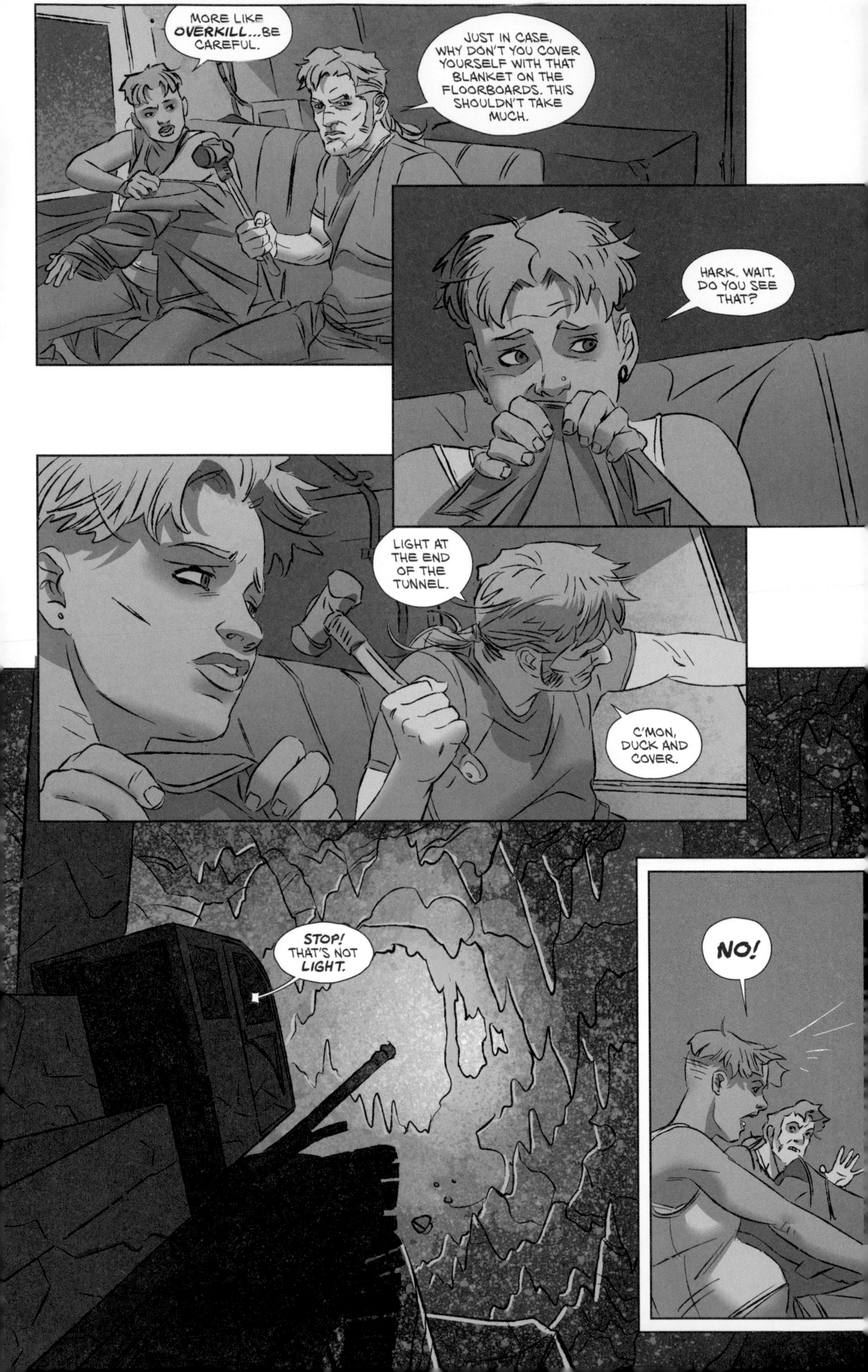
MORE LIKE OVERKILL...BE CAREFUL.
JUST IN CASE, WHY DON'T YOU COVER YOURSELF WITH THAT BLANKET ON THE FLOORBOARDS. THIS SHOULDN'T TAKE MUCH.
HARK, WAIT. DO YOU SEE THAT?
LIGHT AT THE END OF THE TUNNEL.
C'MON, DUCK AND COVER.
STOP! THAT'S NOT LIGHT.
NO!

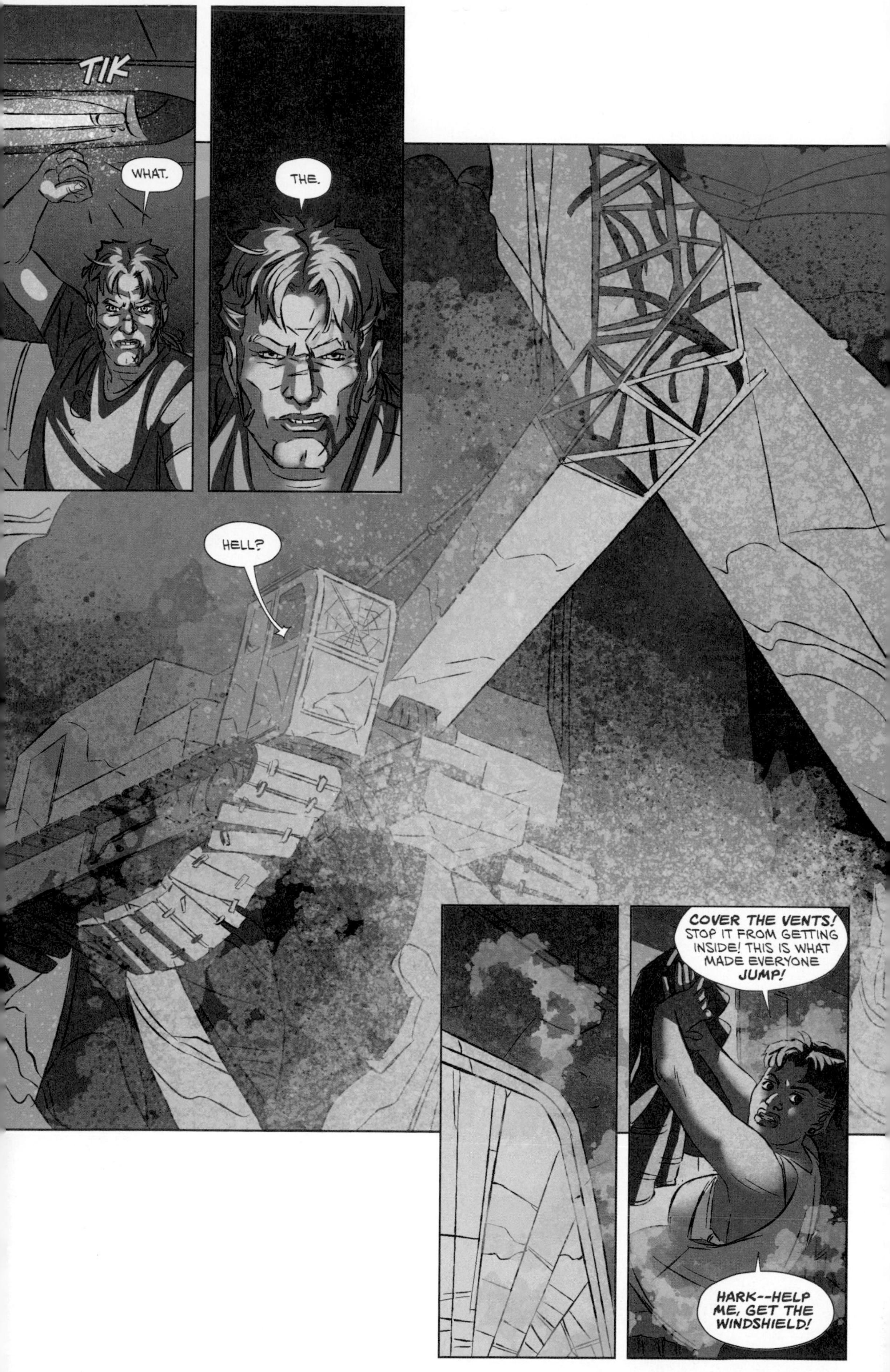
TIK
WHAT.
THE.
HELL?
COVER THE VENTS! STOP IT FROM GETTING INSIDE! THIS IS WHAT MADE EVERYONE JUMP!
HARK--HELP ME, GET THE WINDSHIELD!

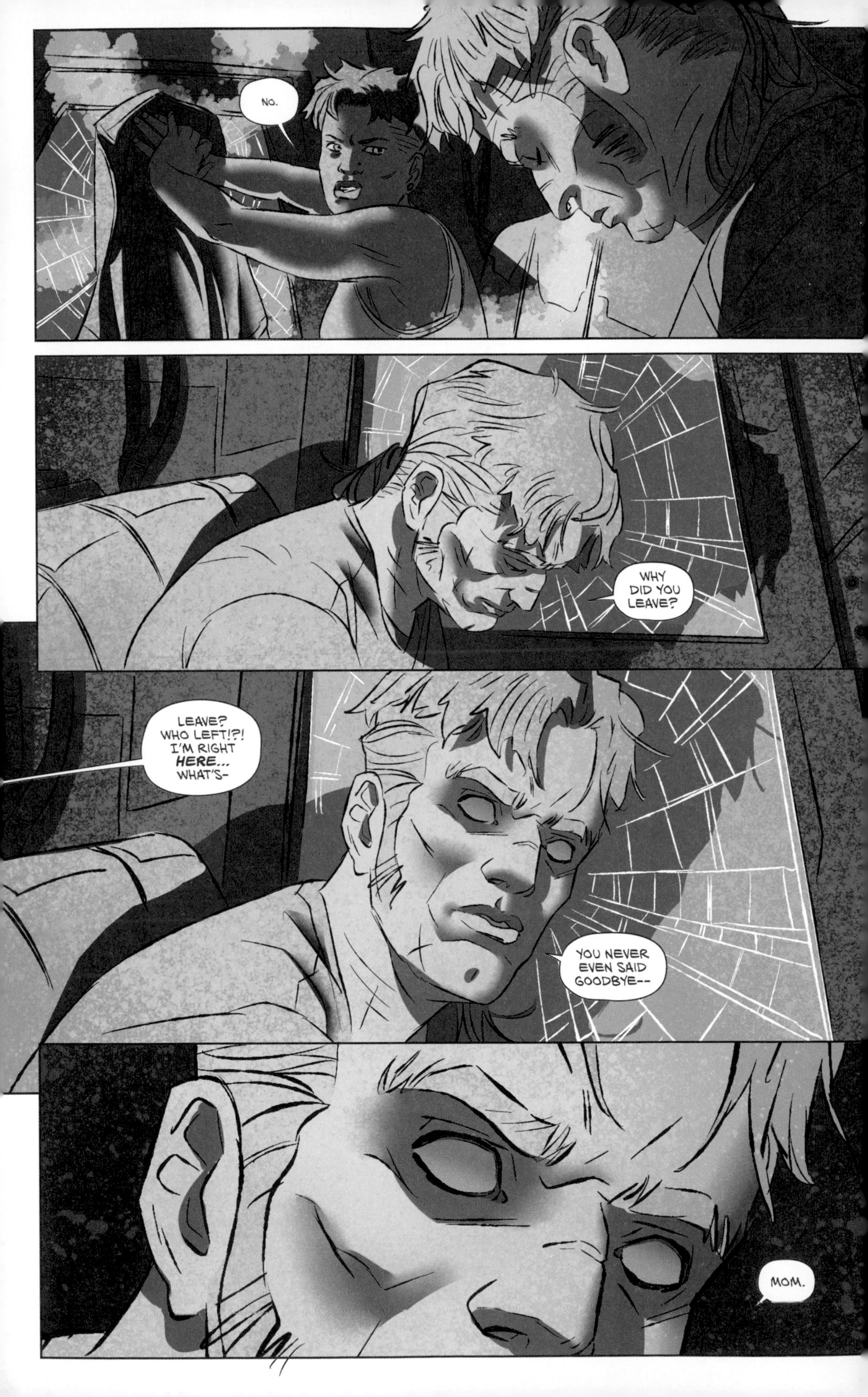
NO.
WHY DID YOU LEAVE?
LEAVE? WHO LEFT!?! I'M RIGHT *HERE...* WHAT'S-
YOU NEVER EVEN SAID GOODBYE--
MOM.

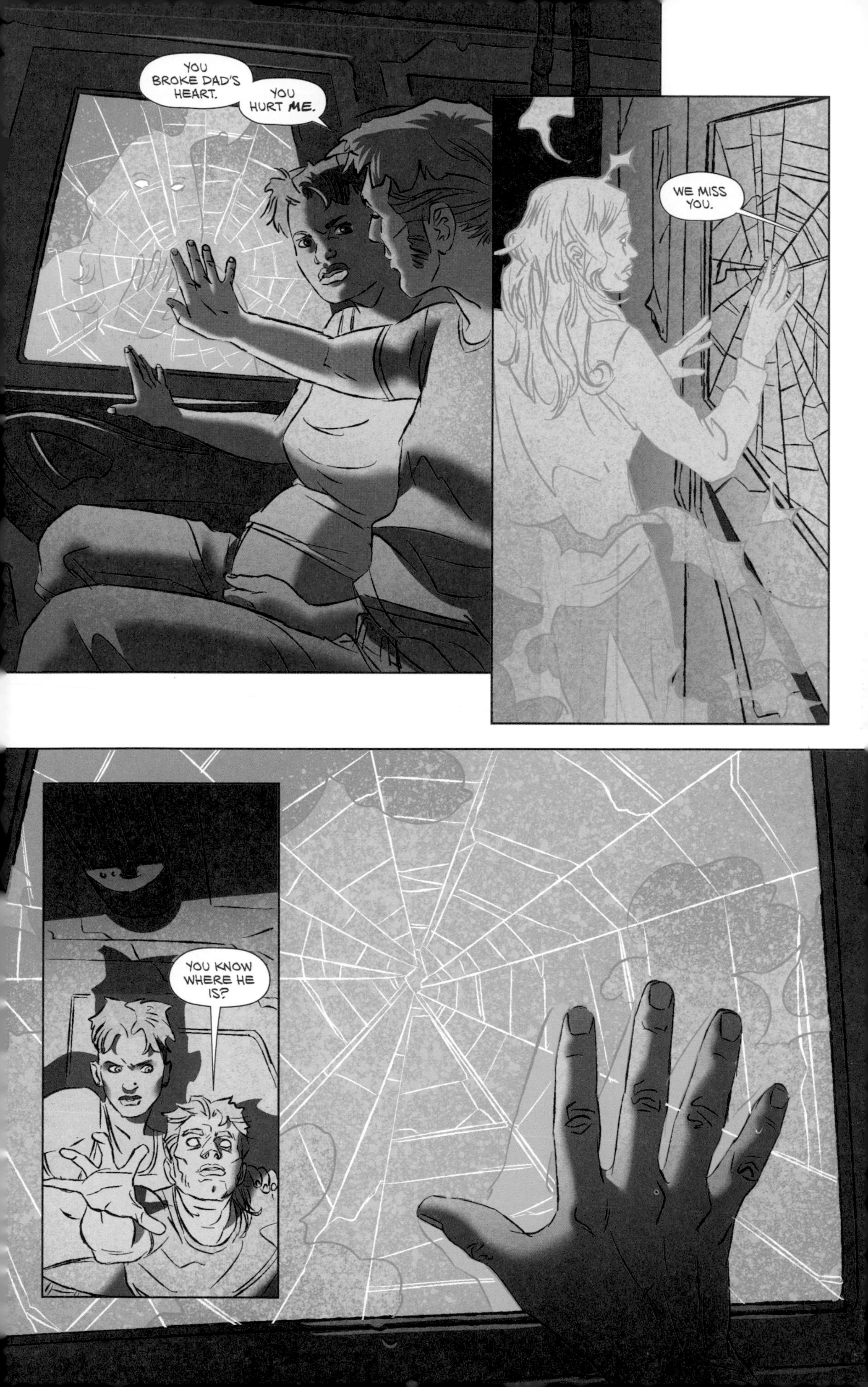
YOU BROKE DAD'S HEART.
YOU HURT ME.
WE MISS YOU.
YOU KNOW WHERE HE IS?

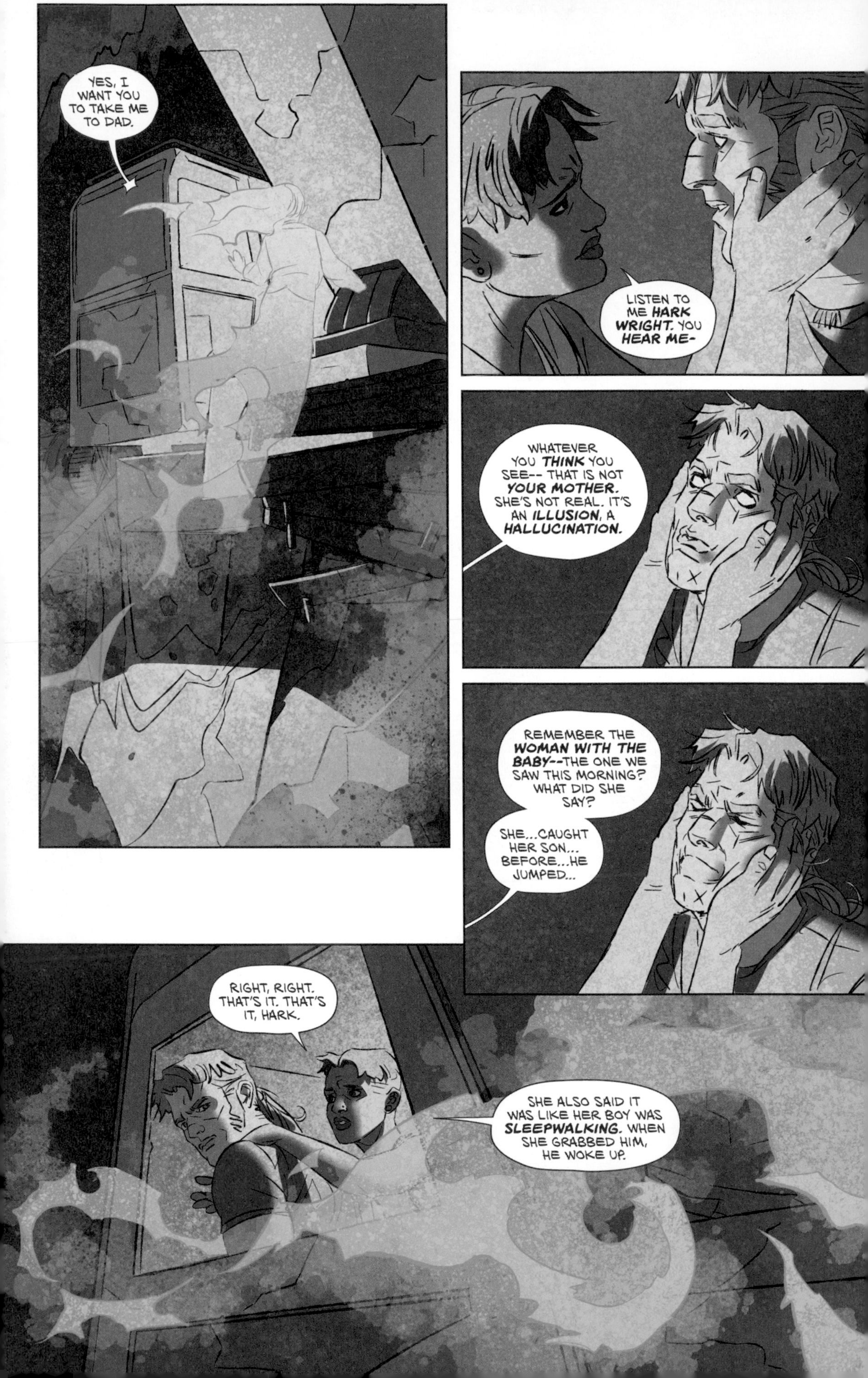

YES, I WANT YOU TO TAKE ME TO DAD.
LISTEN TO ME **HARK WRIGHT.** YOU **HEAR ME-**
WHATEVER YOU **THINK** YOU SEE-- THAT IS NOT **YOUR MOTHER.** SHE'S NOT REAL. IT'S AN **ILLUSION**, A **HALLUCINATION.**
REMEMBER THE **WOMAN WITH THE BABY**--THE ONE WE SAW THIS MORNING? WHAT DID SHE SAY?
SHE...CAUGHT HER SON... BEFORE...HE JUMPED...
RIGHT, RIGHT. THAT'S IT. THAT'S IT, HARK.
SHE ALSO SAID IT WAS LIKE HER BOY WAS **SLEEPWALKING.** WHEN SHE GRABBED HIM, HE WOKE UP.

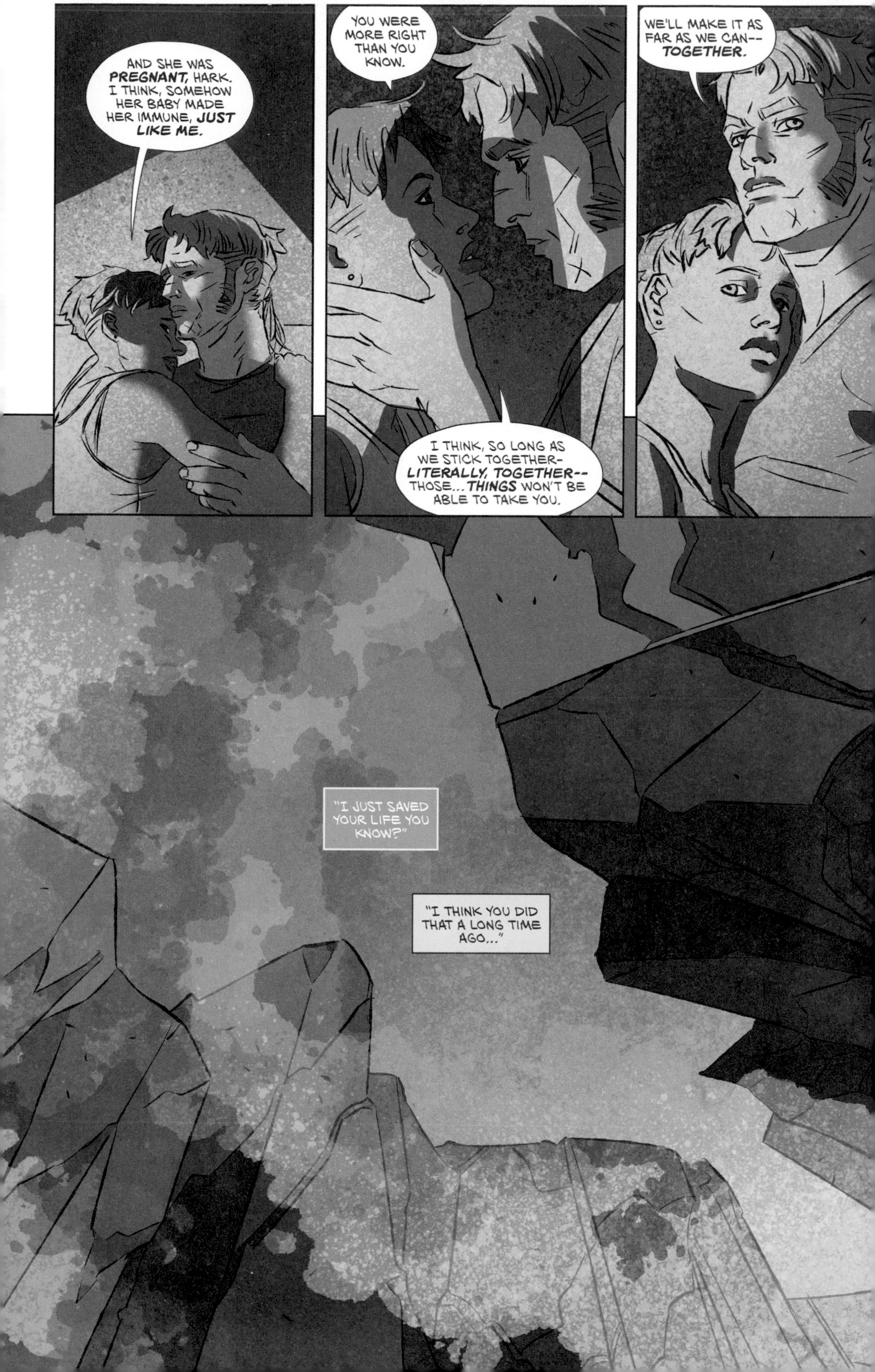
AND SHE WAS PREGNANT, HARK. I THINK, SOMEHOW HER BABY MADE HER IMMUNE, JUST LIKE ME.
YOU WERE MORE RIGHT THAN YOU KNOW.
I THINK, SO LONG AS WE STICK TOGETHER- LITERALLY, TOGETHER-- THOSE... THINGS WON'T BE ABLE TO TAKE YOU.
WE'LL MAKE IT AS FAR AS WE CAN-- TOGETHER.
"I JUST SAVED YOUR LIFE YOU KNOW?"
"I THINK YOU DID THAT A LONG TIME AGO..."

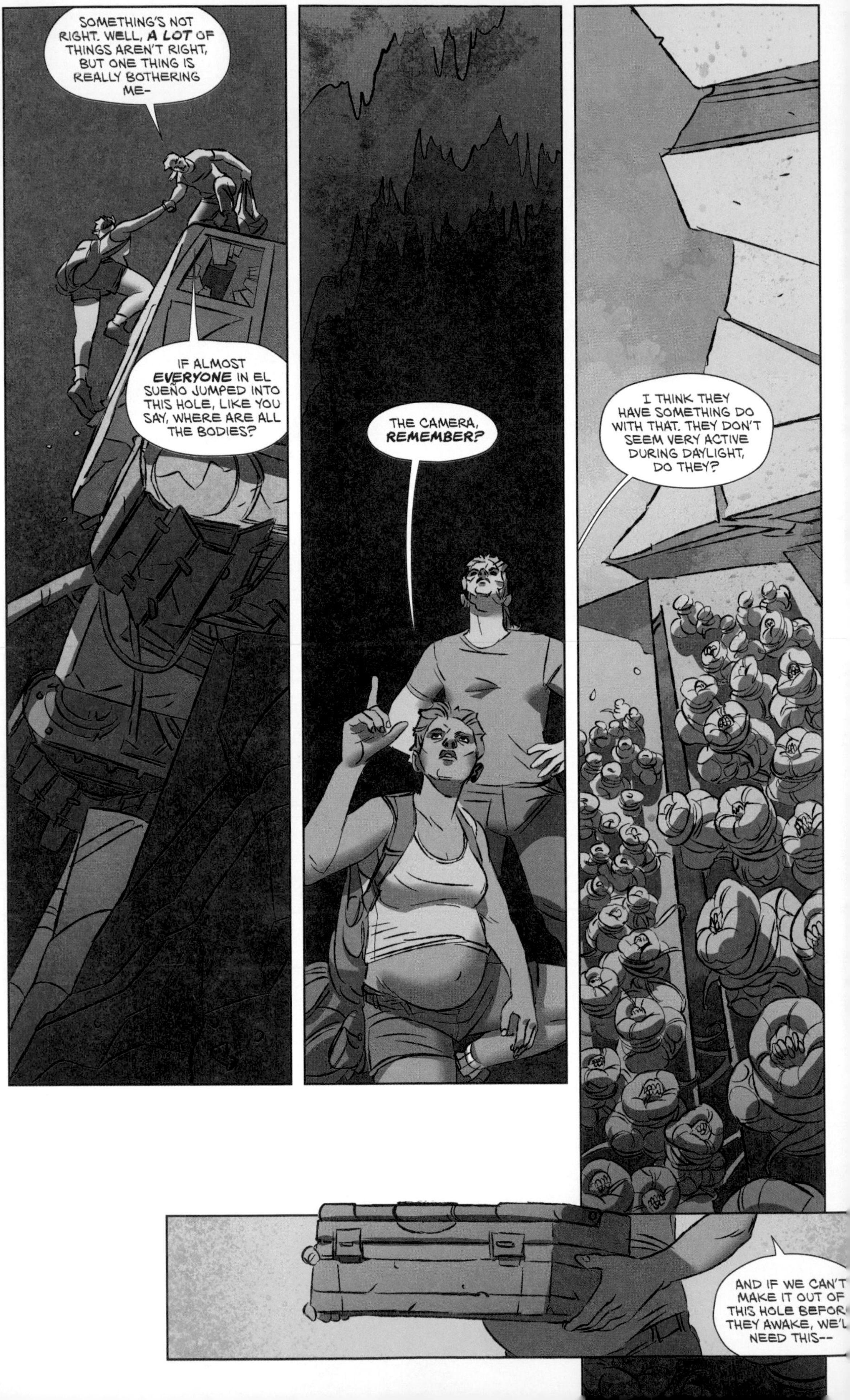
SOMETHING'S NOT RIGHT. WELL, A LOT OF THINGS AREN'T RIGHT, BUT ONE THING IS REALLY BOTHERING ME-
IF ALMOST EVERYONE IN EL SUEÑO JUMPED INTO THIS HOLE, LIKE YOU SAY, WHERE ARE ALL THE BODIES?
THE CAMERA, REMEMBER?
I THINK THEY HAVE SOMETHING DO WITH THAT. THEY DON'T SEEM VERY ACTIVE DURING DAYLIGHT, DO THEY?
AND IF WE CAN'T MAKE IT OUT OF THIS HOLE BEFOR THEY AWAKE, WE'L NEED THIS--

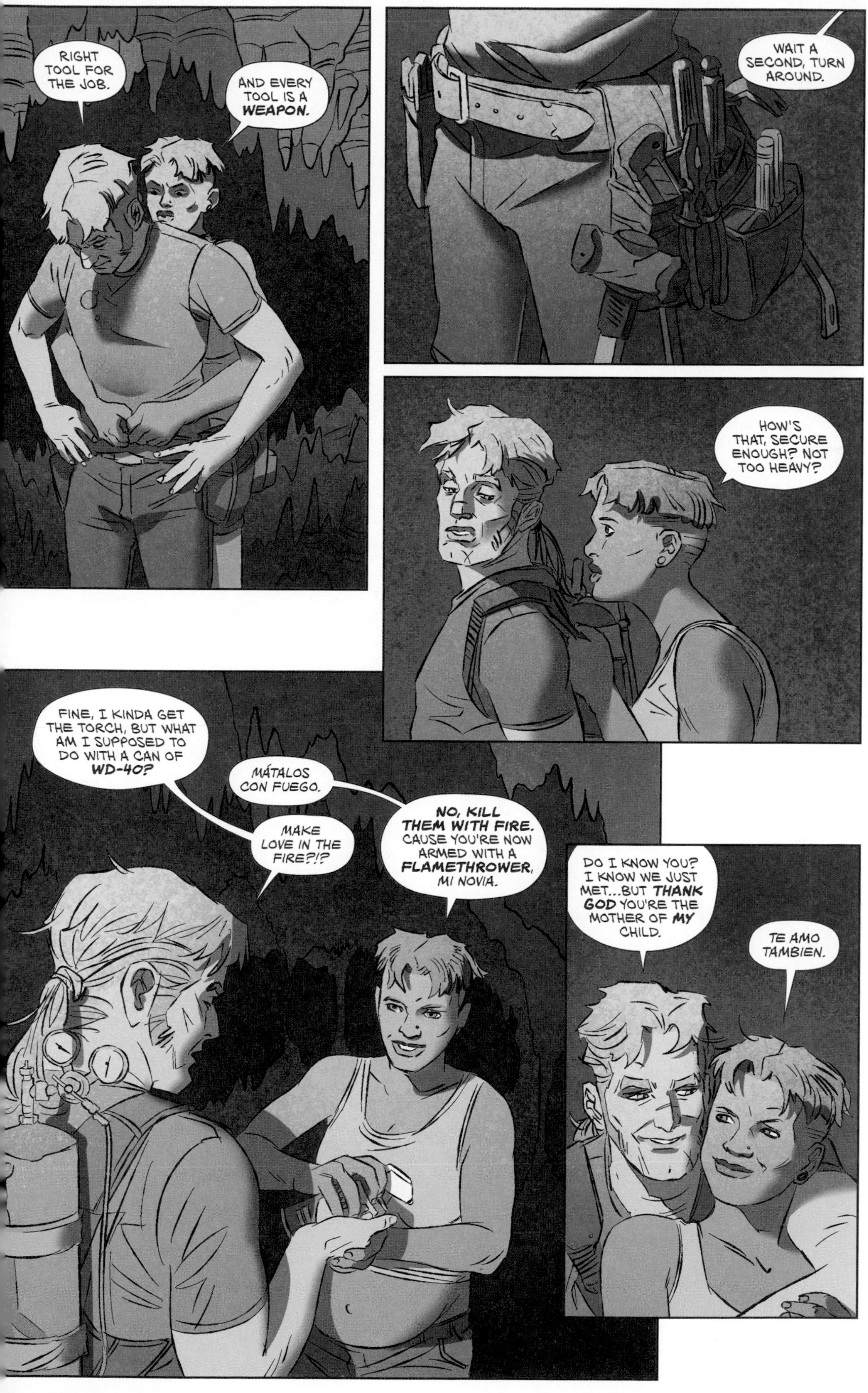

RIGHT TOOL FOR THE JOB.
AND EVERY TOOL IS A **WEAPON.**
WAIT A SECOND, TURN AROUND.
HOW'S THAT, SECURE ENOUGH? NOT TOO HEAVY?
FINE, I KINDA GET THE TORCH, BUT WHAT AM I SUPPOSED TO DO WITH A CAN OF **WD-40?**
MÁTALOS CON FUEGO.
MAKE LOVE IN THE FIRE?!?
NO, KILL THEM WITH FIRE. CAUSE YOU'RE NOW ARMED WITH A **FLAMETHROWER**, *MI NOVIA.*
DO I KNOW YOU? I KNOW WE JUST MET...BUT **THANK GOD** YOU'RE THE MOTHER OF **MY** CHILD.
TE AMO TAMBIEN.

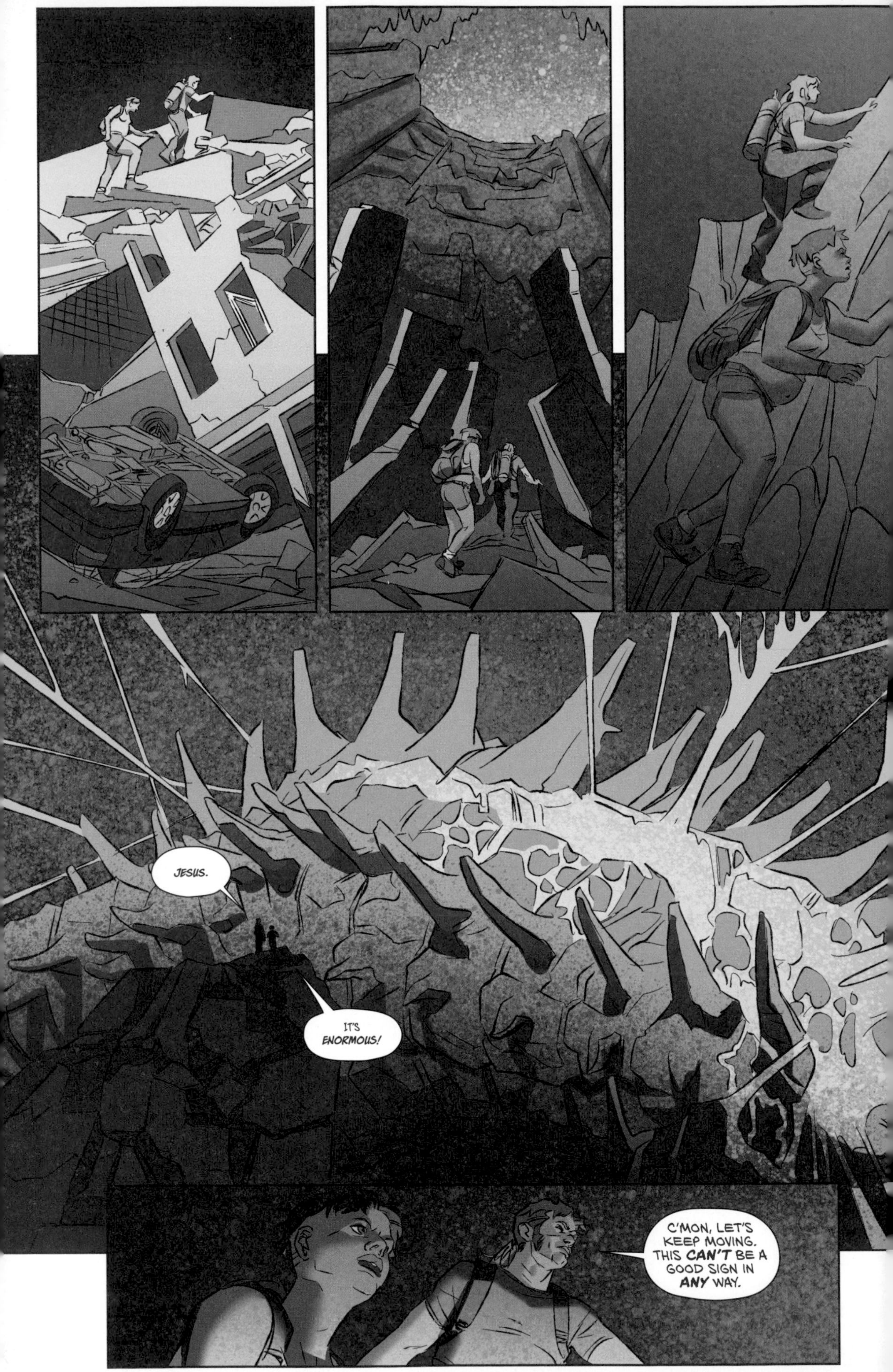
JESUS.
IT'S ENORMOUS!
C'MON, LET'S KEEP MOVING. THIS CAN'T BE A GOOD SIGN IN ANY WAY.

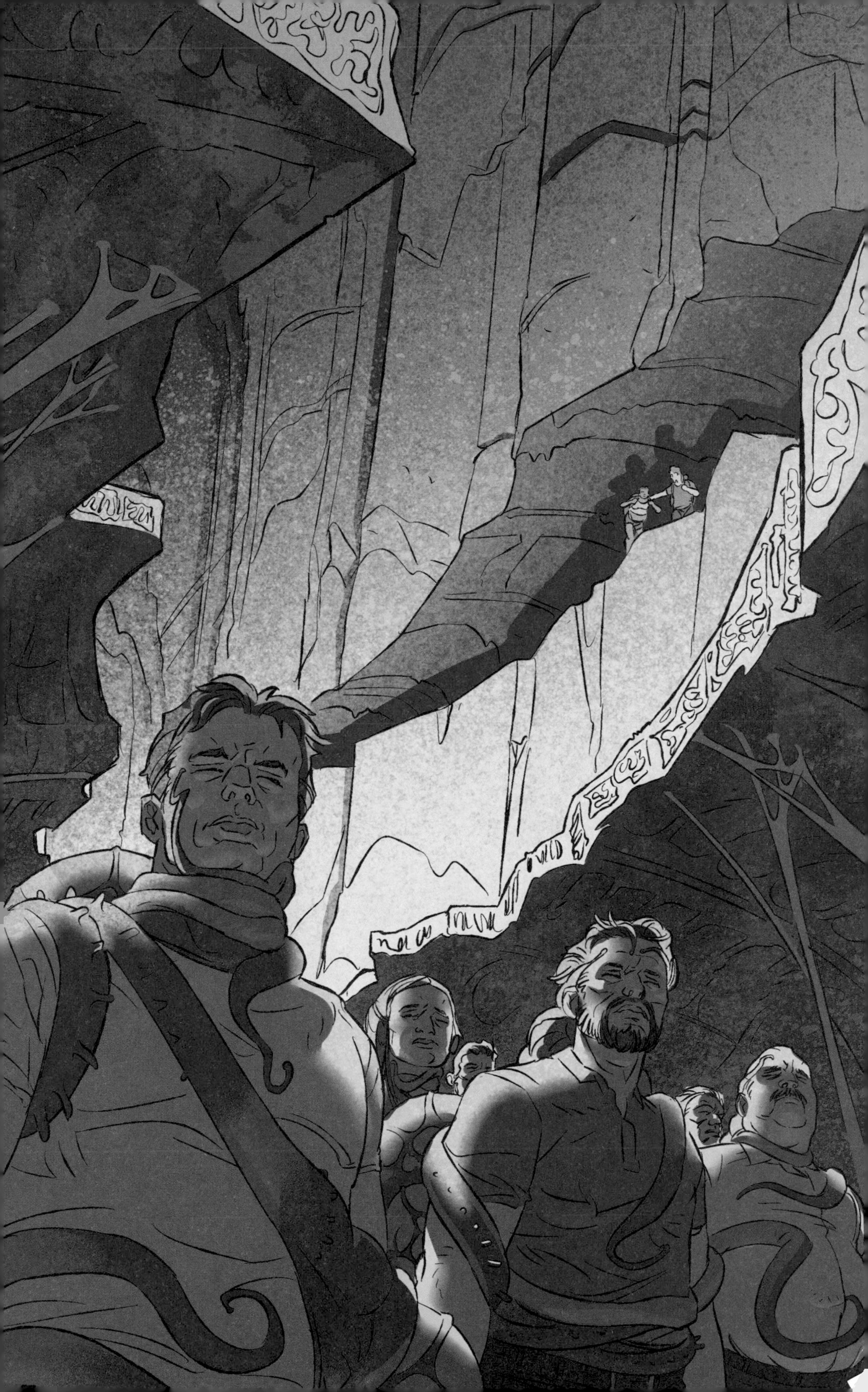

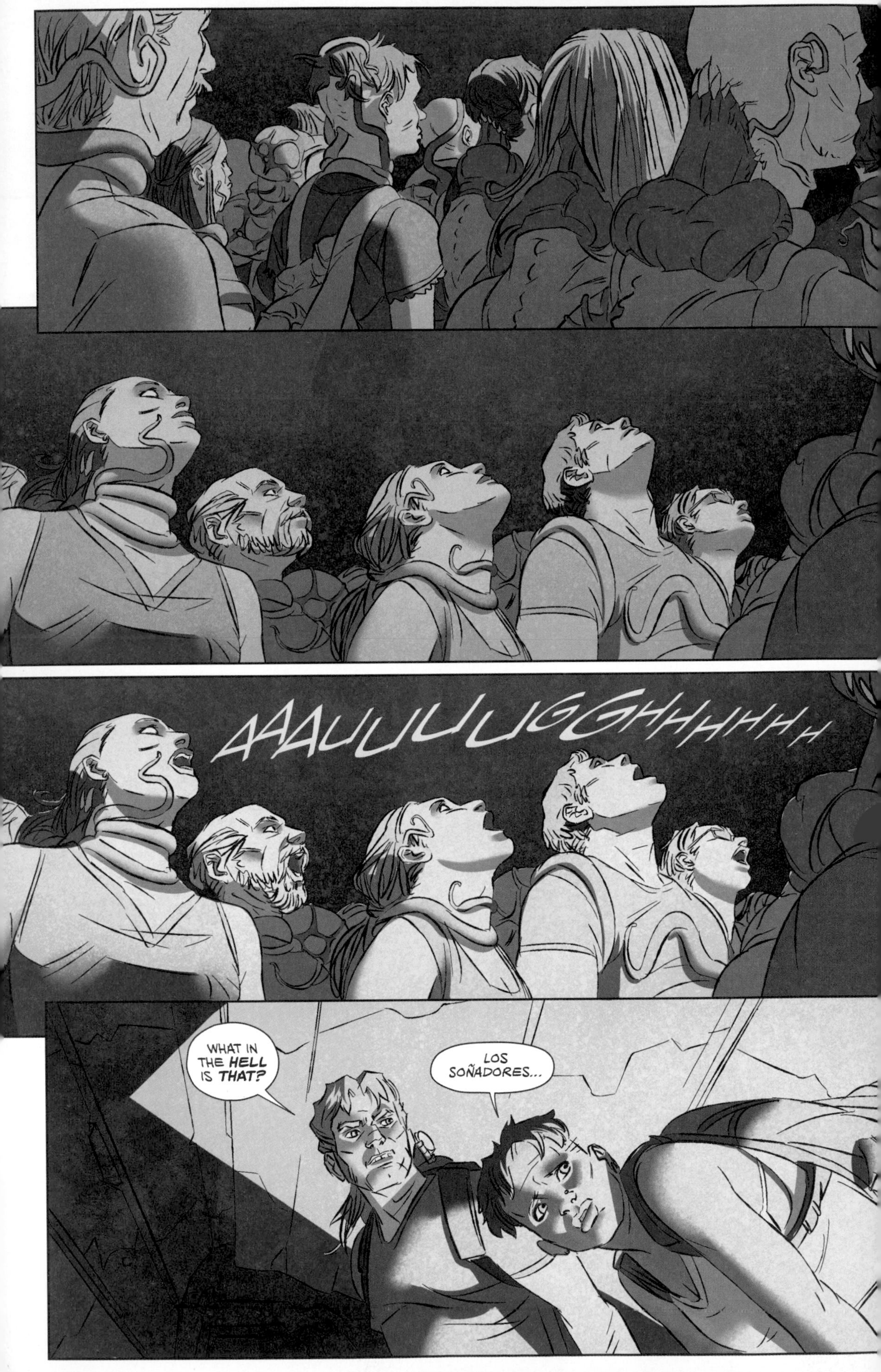
AAAUUUUGGHHHHHH
WHAT IN THE HELL IS THAT?
LOS SOÑADORES...

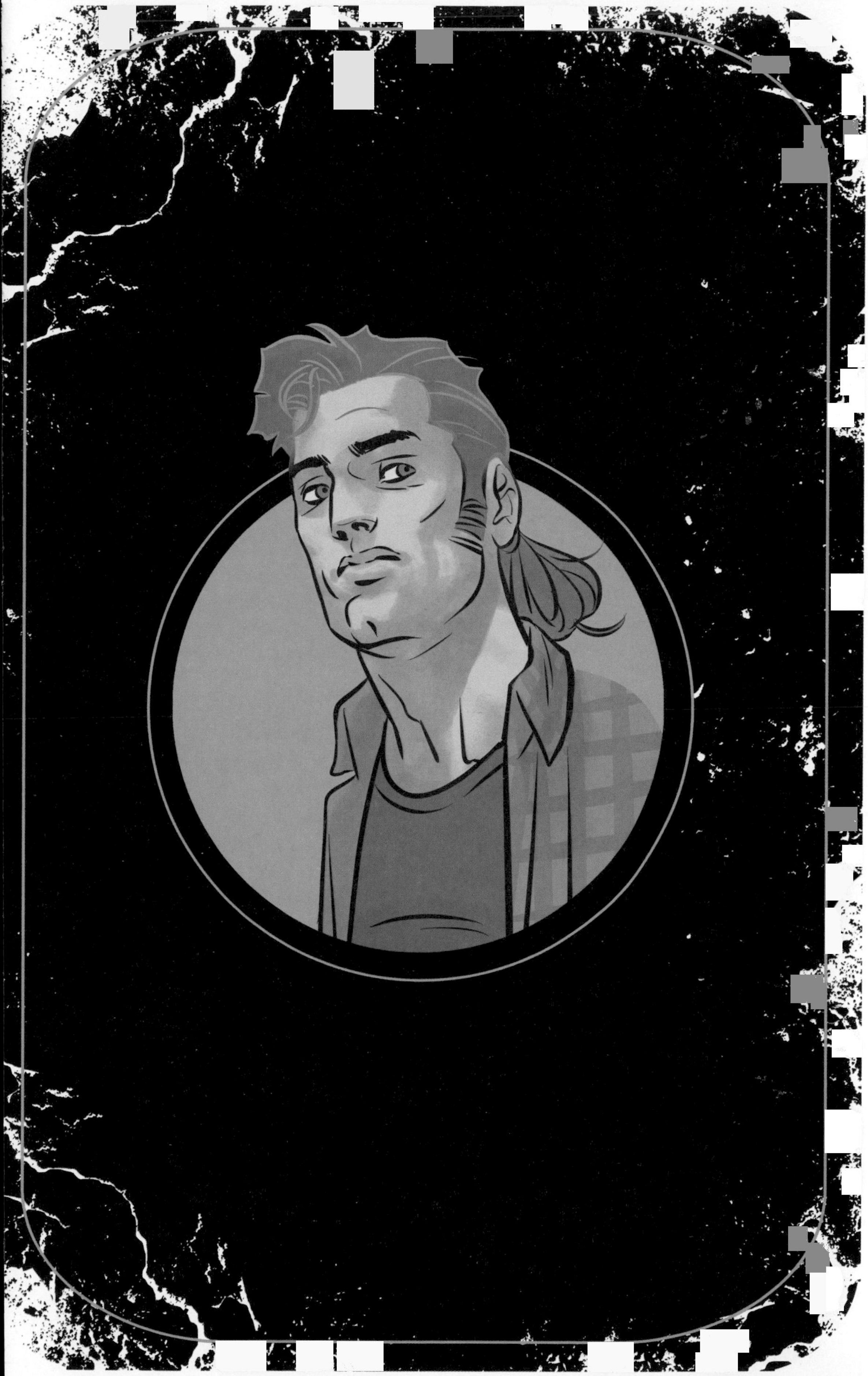

CHAPTER FOUR

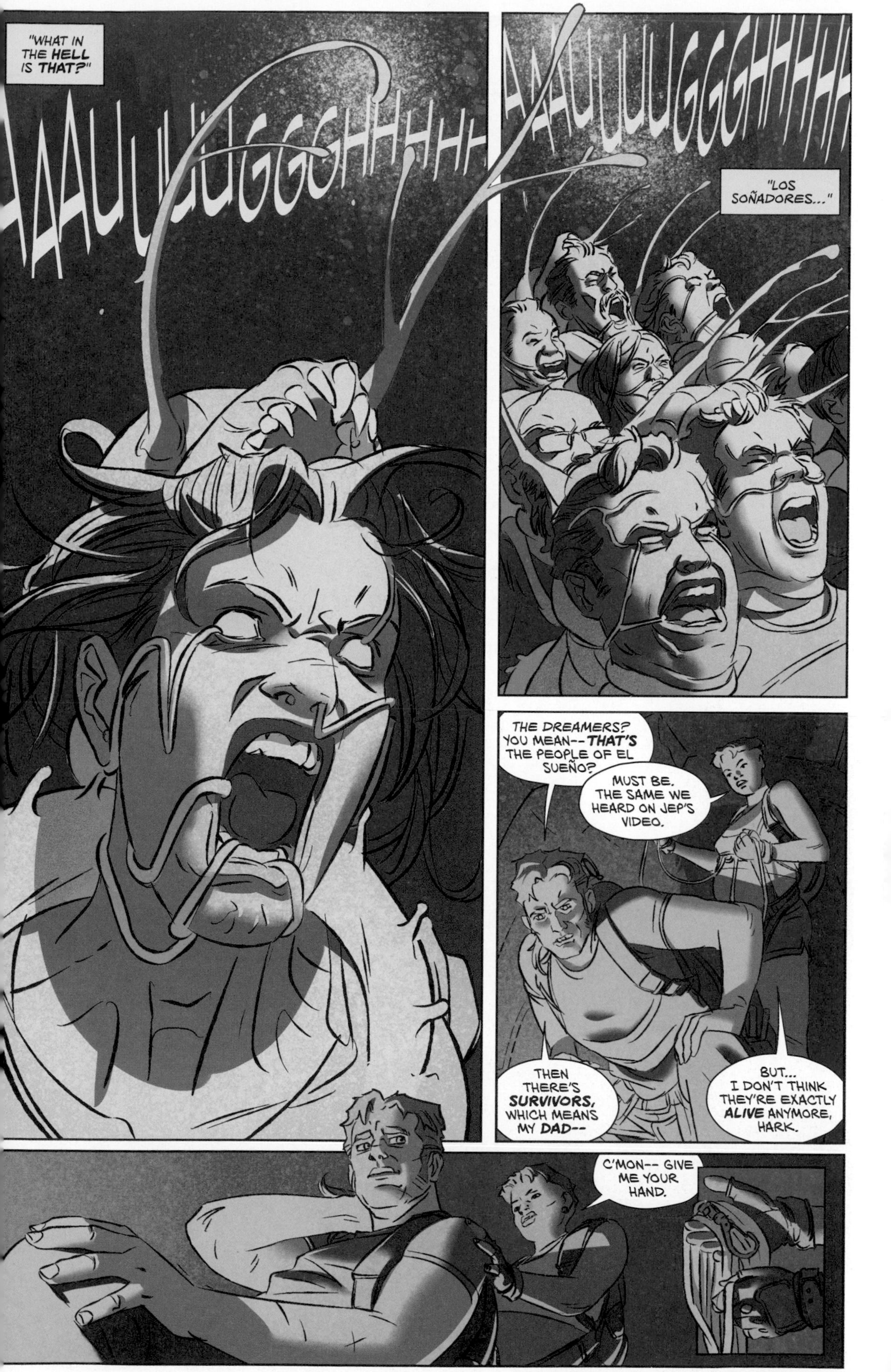
"WHAT IN THE **HELL** IS **THAT?**"
AAAUUUUGGGHHHHH
AAAUUUUGGGHHHH
"LOS SOÑADORES..."
THE DREAMERS? YOU MEAN--**THAT'S** THE PEOPLE OF EL SUEÑO?
MUST BE. THE SAME WE HEARD ON JEP'S VIDEO.
THEN THERE'S **SURVIVORS,** WHICH MEANS MY **DAD--**
BUT... I DON'T THINK THEY'RE EXACTLY **ALIVE** ANYMORE, HARK.
C'MON-- GIVE ME YOUR HAND.

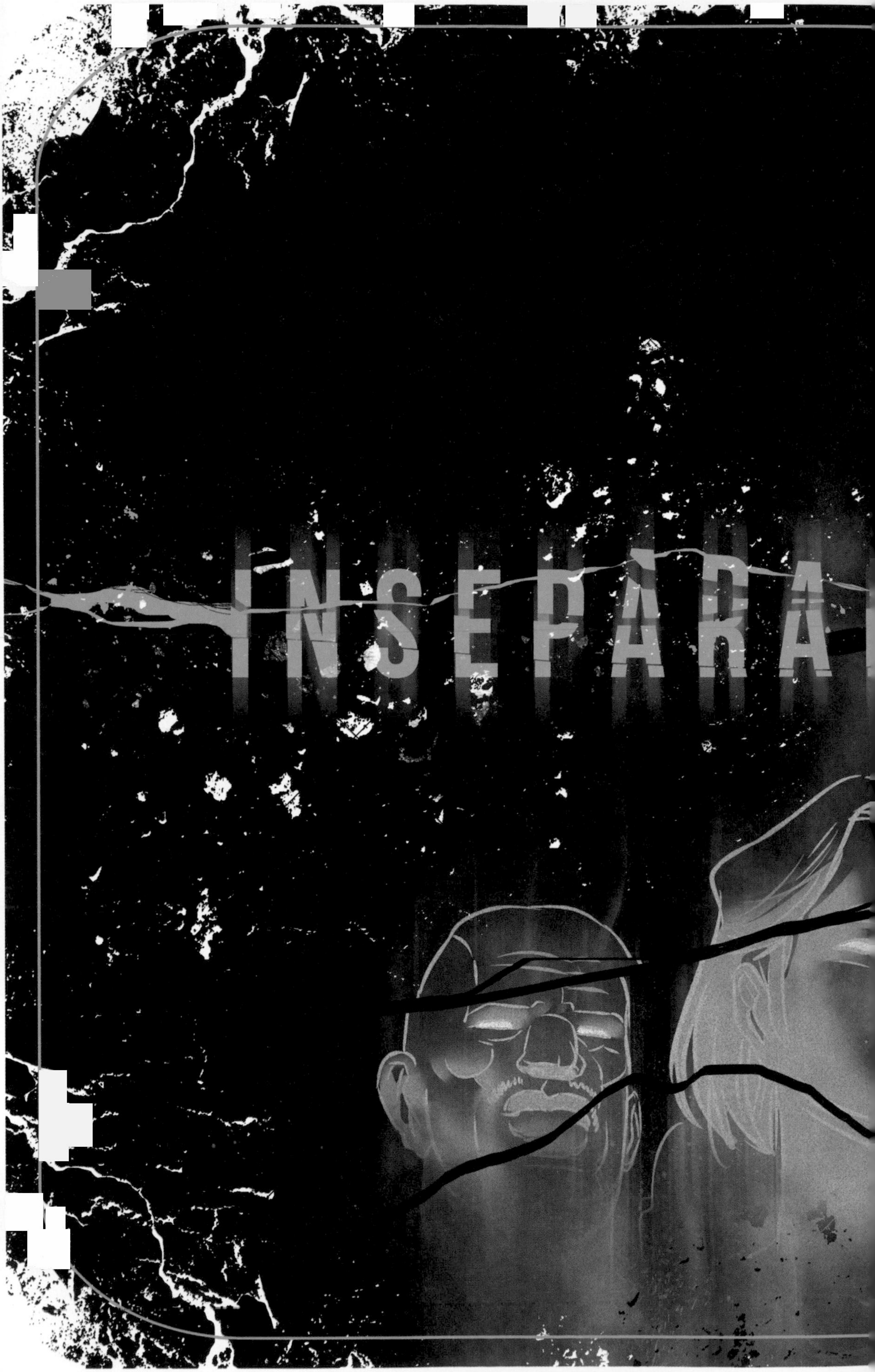
INSEPARA

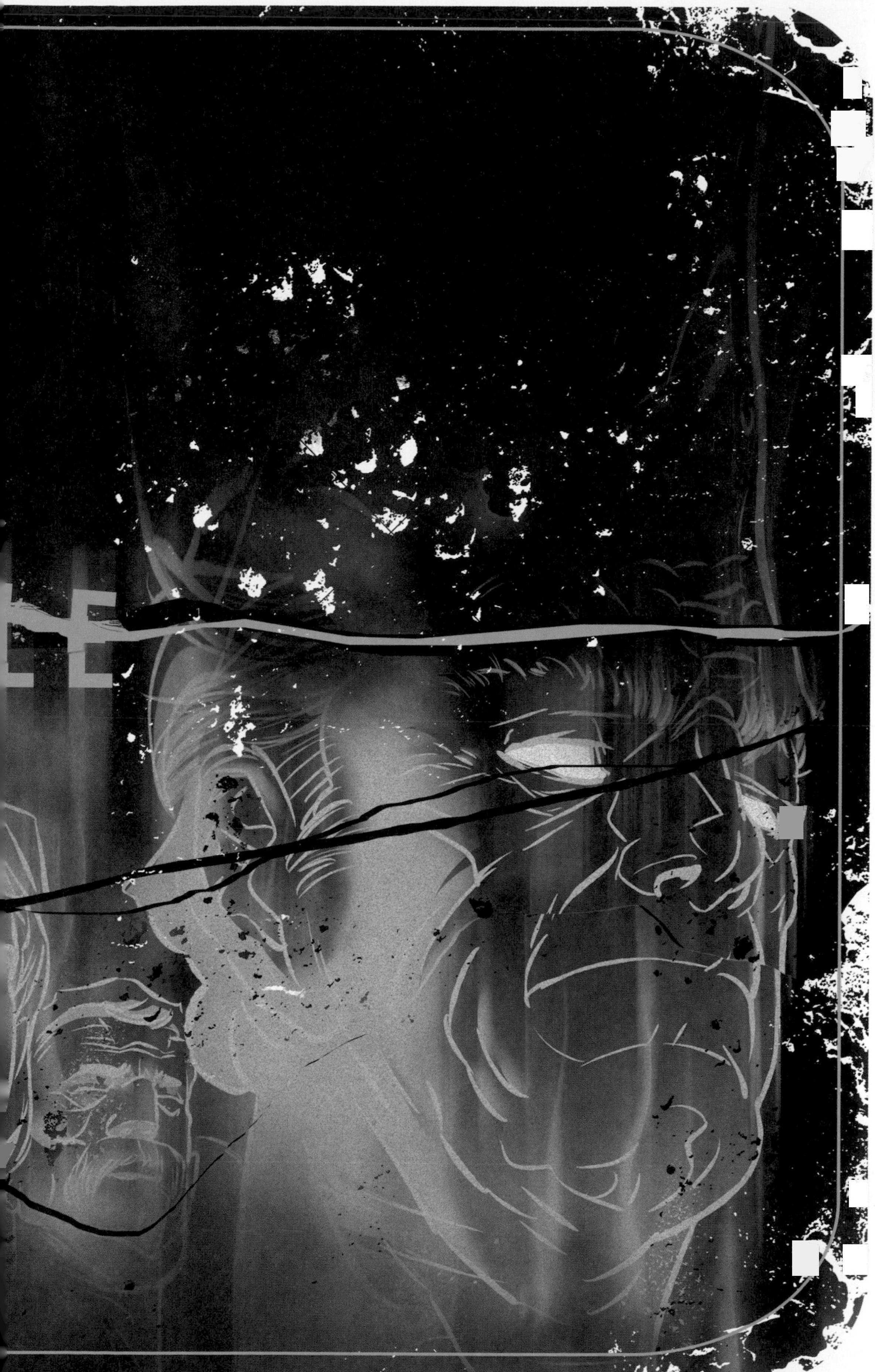

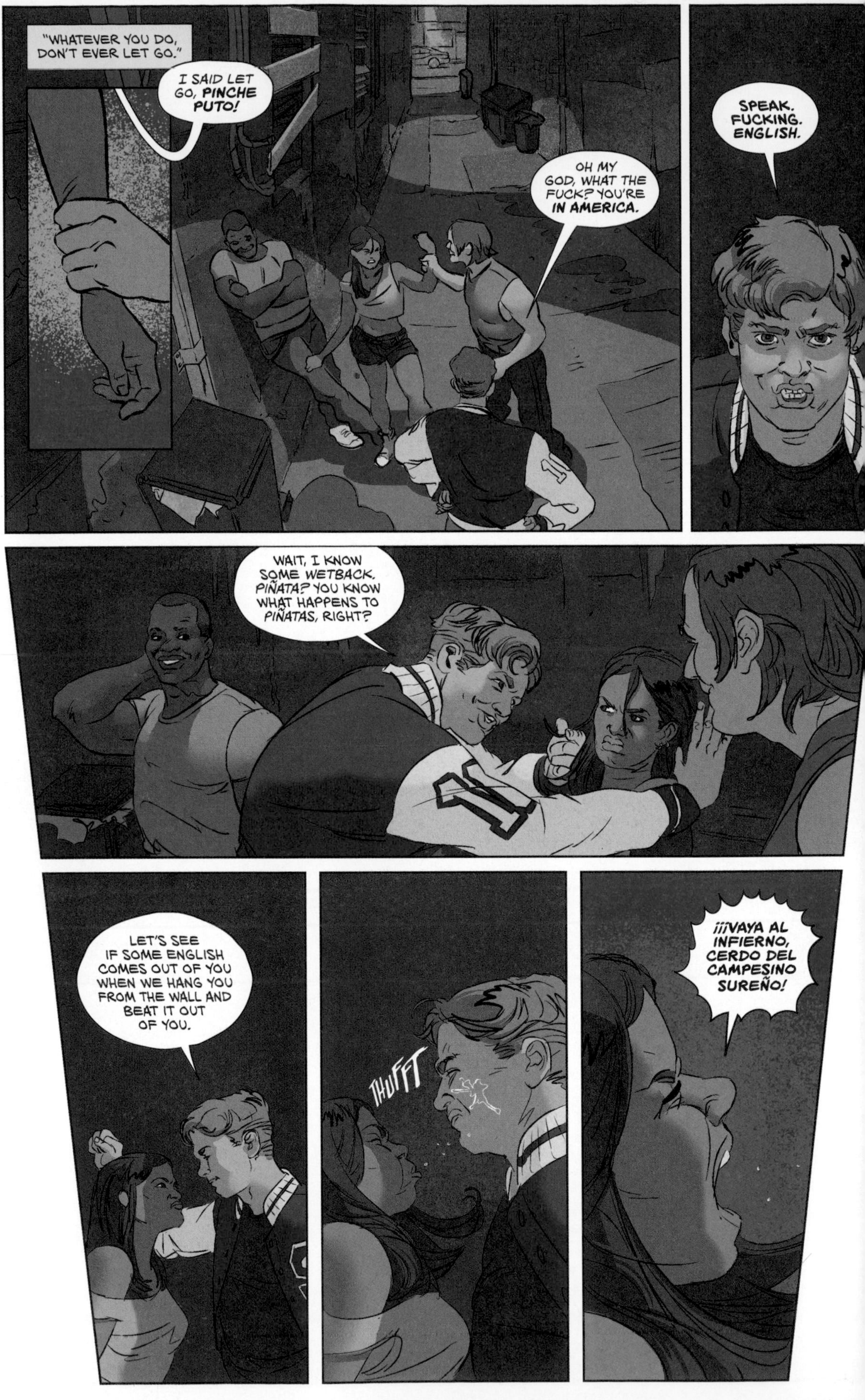

"WHATEVER YOU DO, DON'T EVER LET GO."
I SAID LET GO, **PINCHE PUTO!**
OH MY GOD, WHAT THE FUCK? YOU'RE **IN AMERICA.**
SPEAK. FUCKING. ENGLISH.
WAIT, I KNOW SOME *WETBACK. PIÑATA?* YOU KNOW WHAT HAPPENS TO *PIÑATAS*, RIGHT?
LET'S SEE IF SOME ENGLISH COMES OUT OF YOU WHEN WE HANG YOU FROM THE WALL AND BEAT IT OUT OF YOU.
THUFFT
¡¡¡VAYA AL INFIERNO, CERDO DEL CAMPESINO SUREÑO!

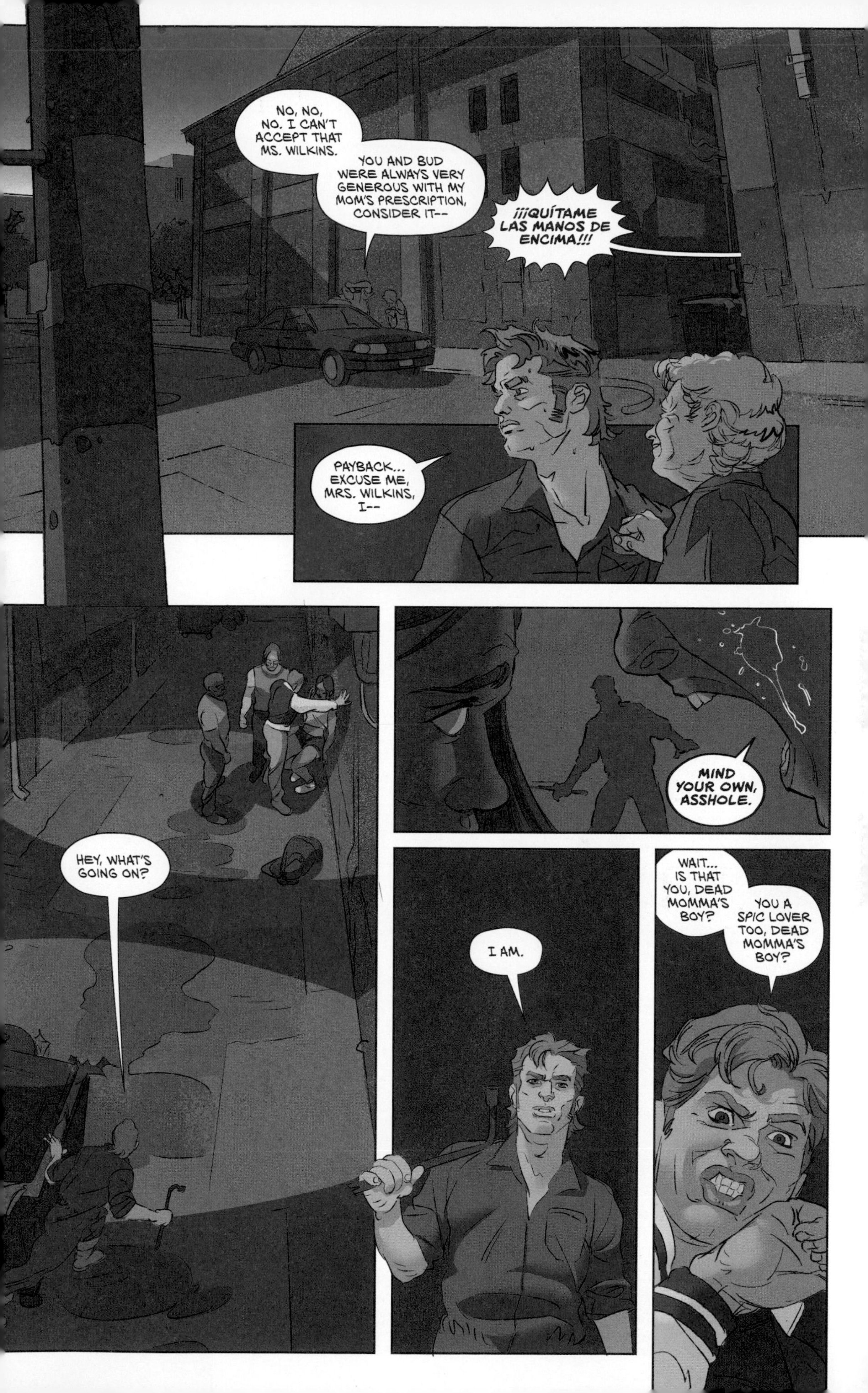
NO, NO, NO. I CAN'T ACCEPT THAT MS. WILKINS.
YOU AND BUD WERE ALWAYS VERY GENEROUS WITH MY MOM'S PRESCRIPTION, CONSIDER IT--
¡¡¡QUÍTAME LAS MANOS DE ENCIMA!!!
PAYBACK... EXCUSE ME, MRS. WILKINS, I--
HEY, WHAT'S GOING ON?
MIND YOUR OWN, ASSHOLE.
I AM.
WAIT... IS THAT YOU, DEAD MOMMA'S BOY?
YOU A SPIC LOVER TOO, DEAD MOMMA'S BOY?

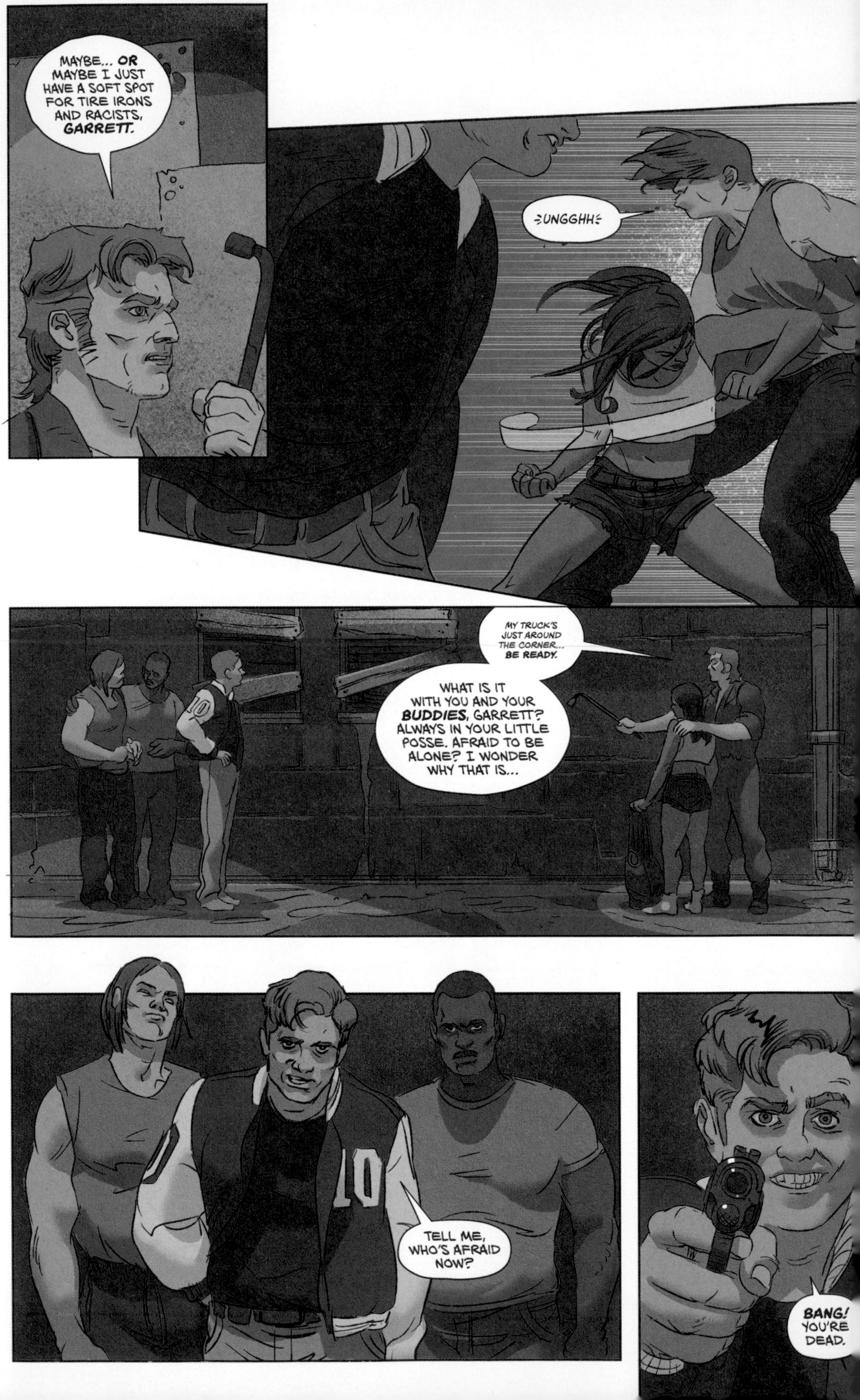
MAYBE... OR MAYBE I JUST HAVE A SOFT SPOT FOR TIRE IRONS AND RACISTS, GARRETT.
UNGGHH
MY TRUCK'S JUST AROUND THE CORNER... BE READY.
WHAT IS IT WITH YOU AND YOUR BUDDIES, GARRETT? ALWAYS IN YOUR LITTLE POSSE. AFRAID TO BE ALONE? I WONDER WHY THAT IS...
10
10
TELL ME, WHO'S AFRAID NOW?
BANG! YOU'RE DEAD.

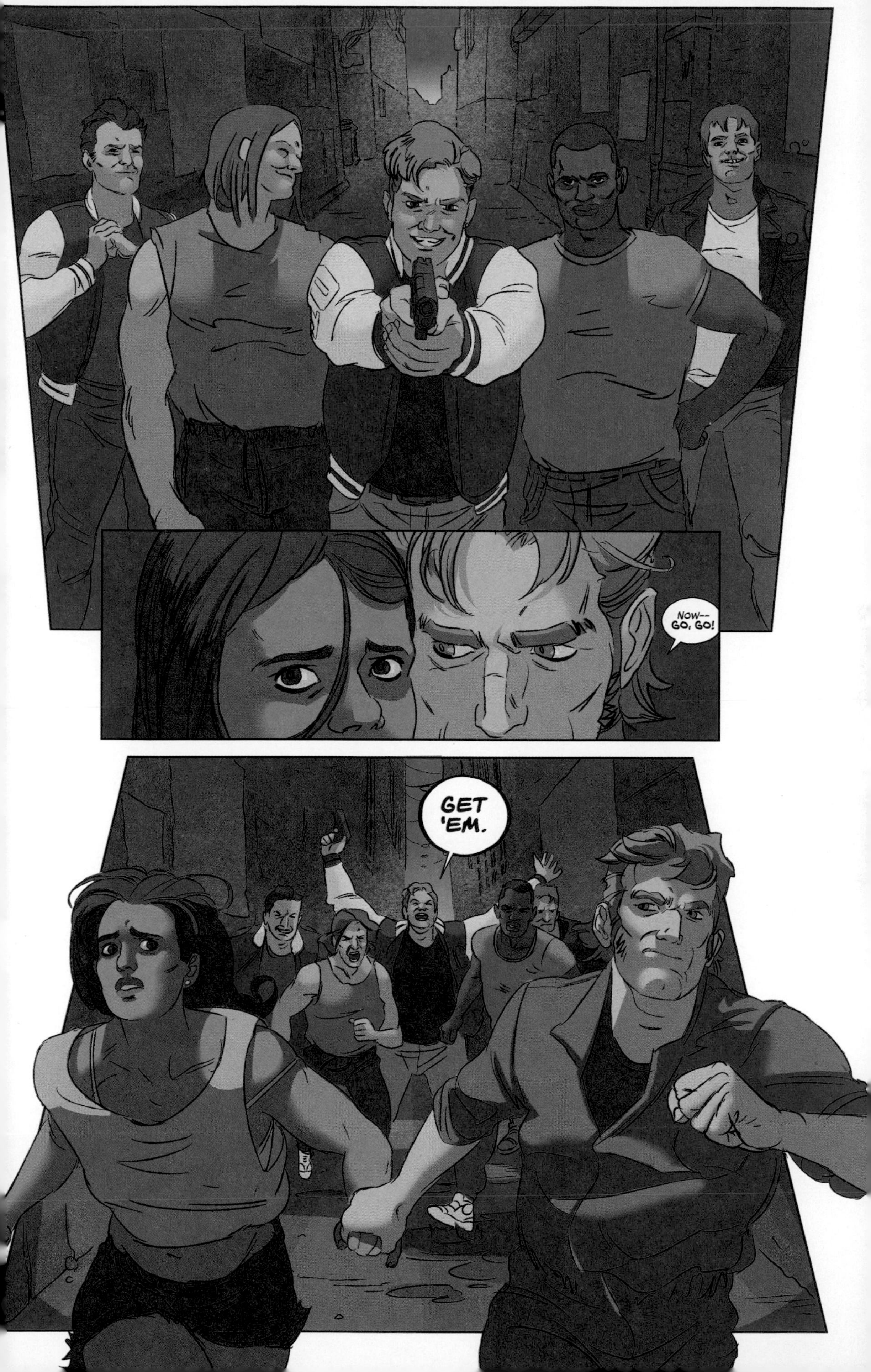
NOW--
GO, GO!
GET 'EM.

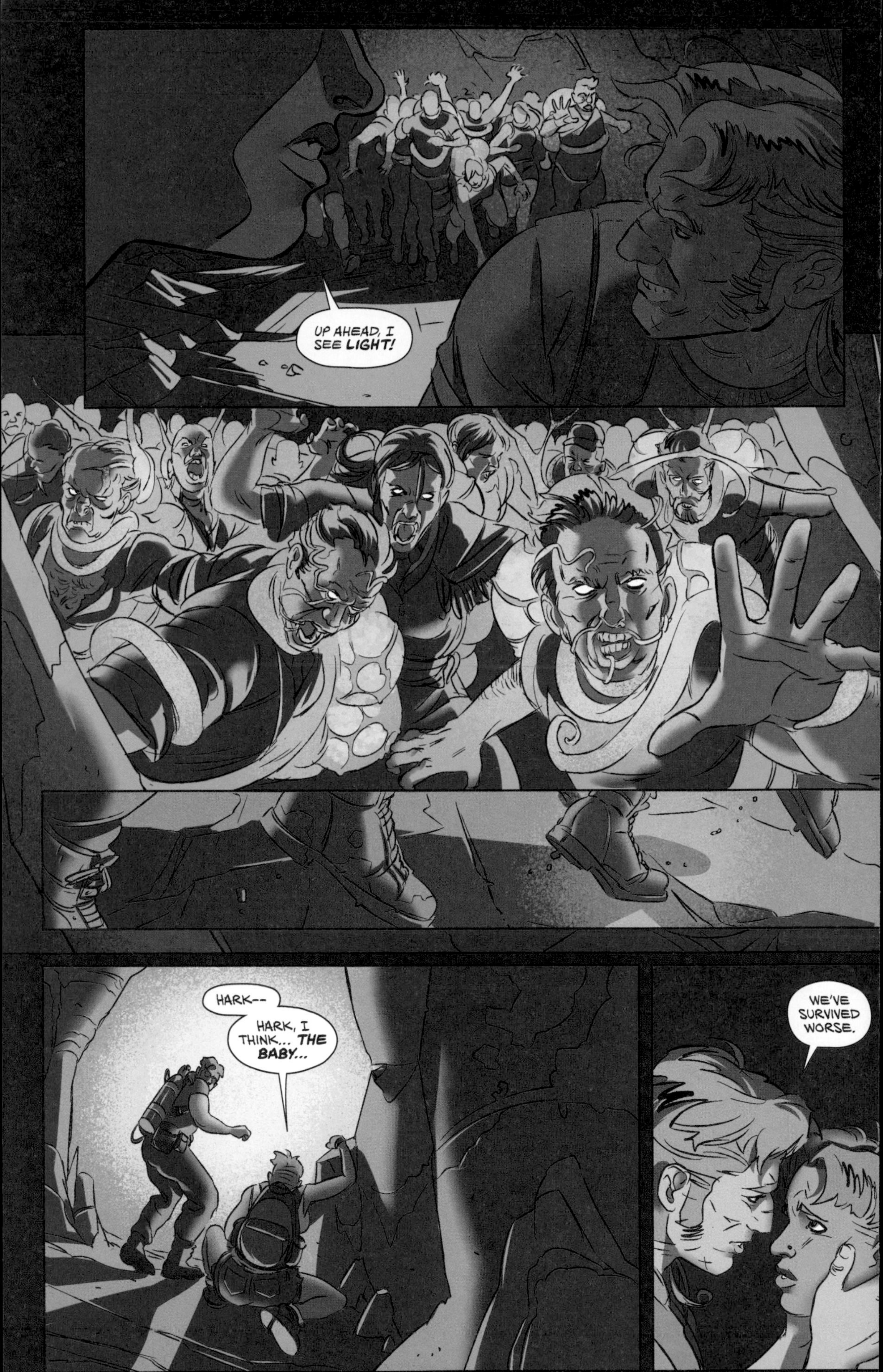
UP AHEAD, I SEE LIGHT!
HARK--
HARK, I THINK... THE BABY...
WE'VE SURVIVED WORSE.

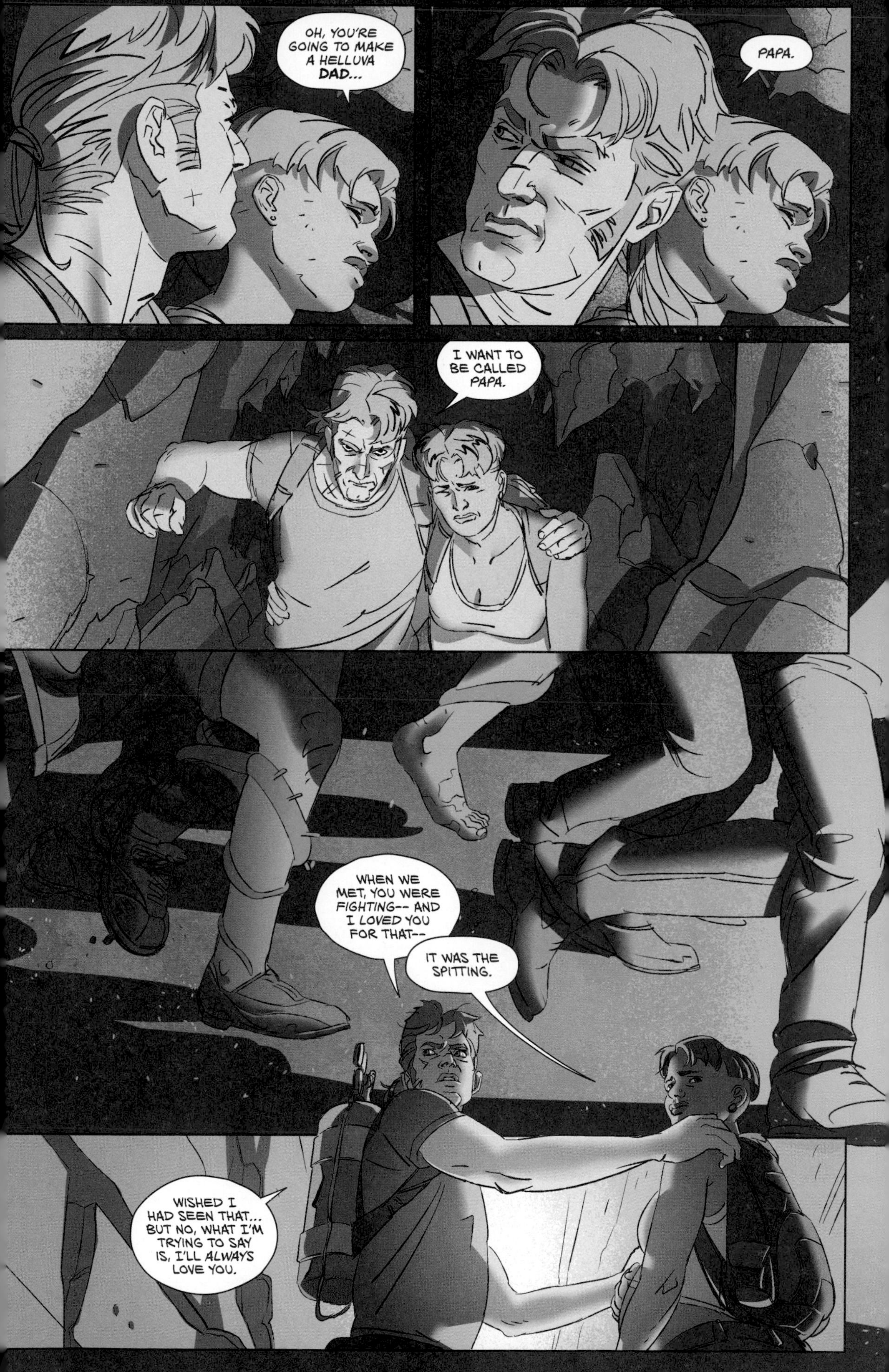
OH, YOU'RE GOING TO MAKE A HELLUVA DAD...
PAPA.
I WANT TO BE CALLED PAPA.
WHEN WE MET, YOU WERE FIGHTING-- AND I LOVED YOU FOR THAT--
IT WAS THE SPITTING.
WISHED I HAD SEEN THAT... BUT NO, WHAT I'M TRYING TO SAY IS, I'LL ALWAYS LOVE YOU.

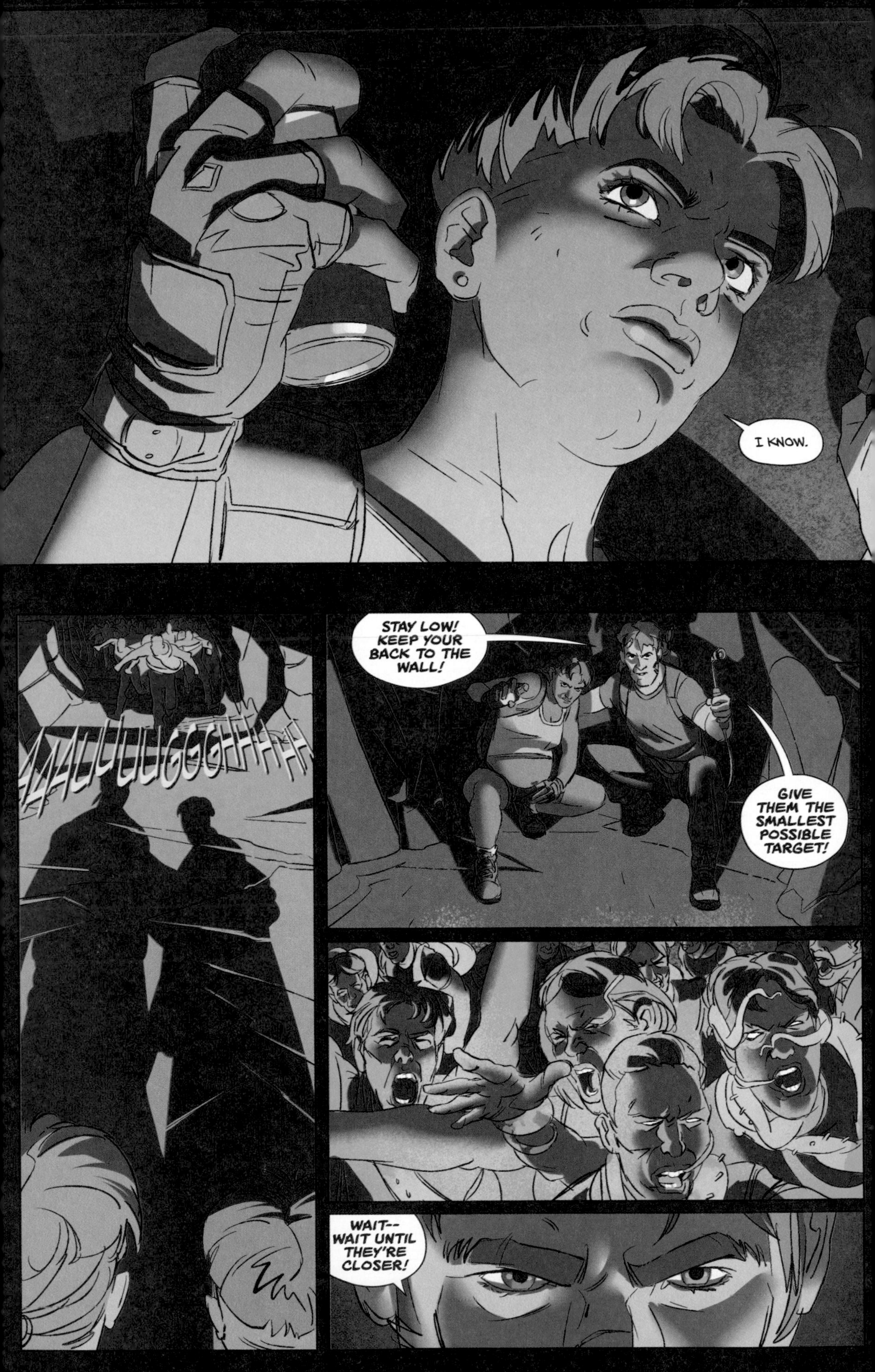
I KNOW.
AAAUUUUGGGHHHH
STAY LOW! KEEP YOUR BACK TO THE WALL!
GIVE THEM THE SMALLEST POSSIBLE TARGET!
WAIT-- WAIT UNTIL THEY'RE CLOSER!

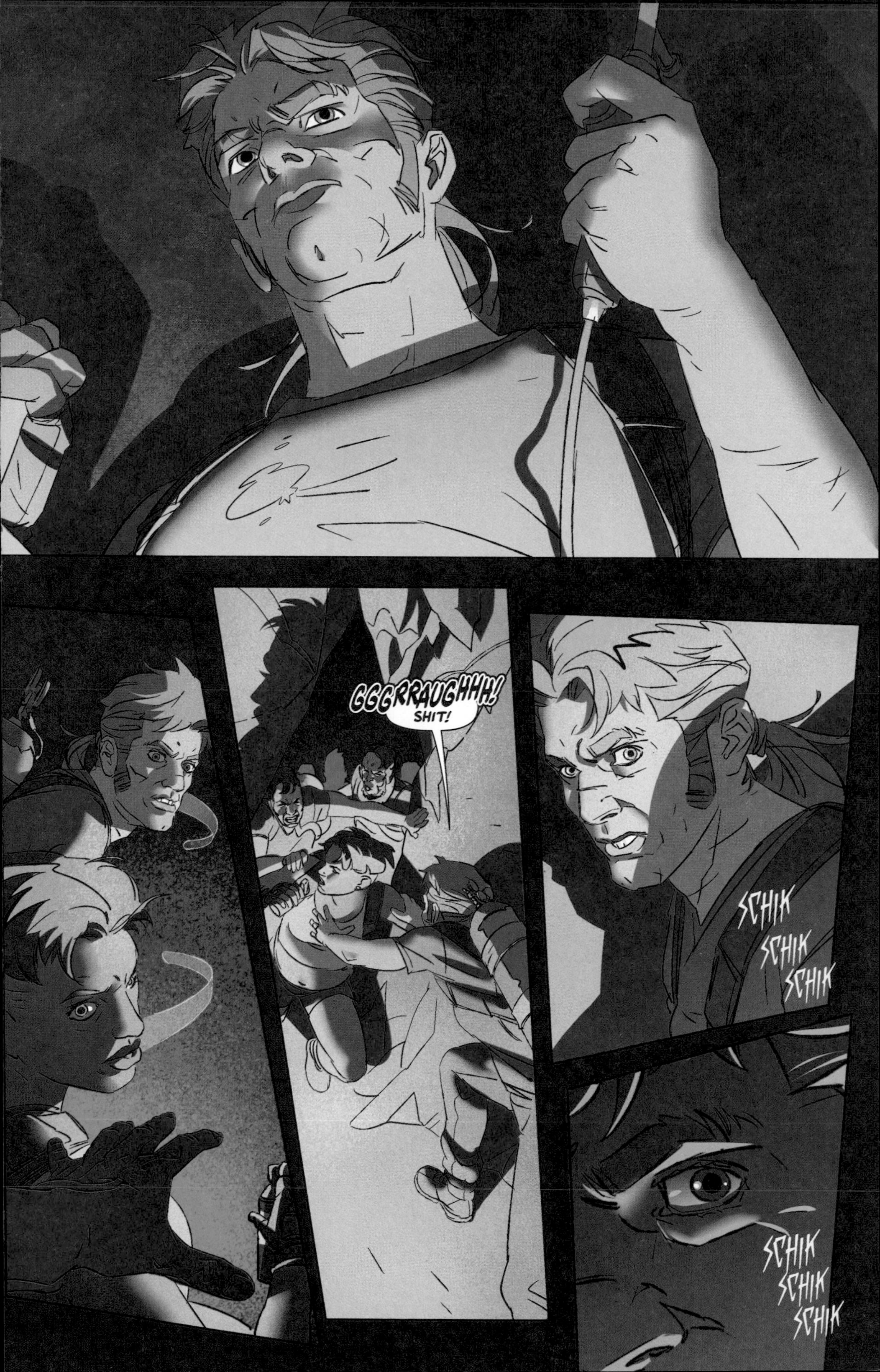
GGGRRAUGHHH!
SHIT!
SCHIK
SCHIK
SCHIK
SCHIK
SCHIK
SCHIK

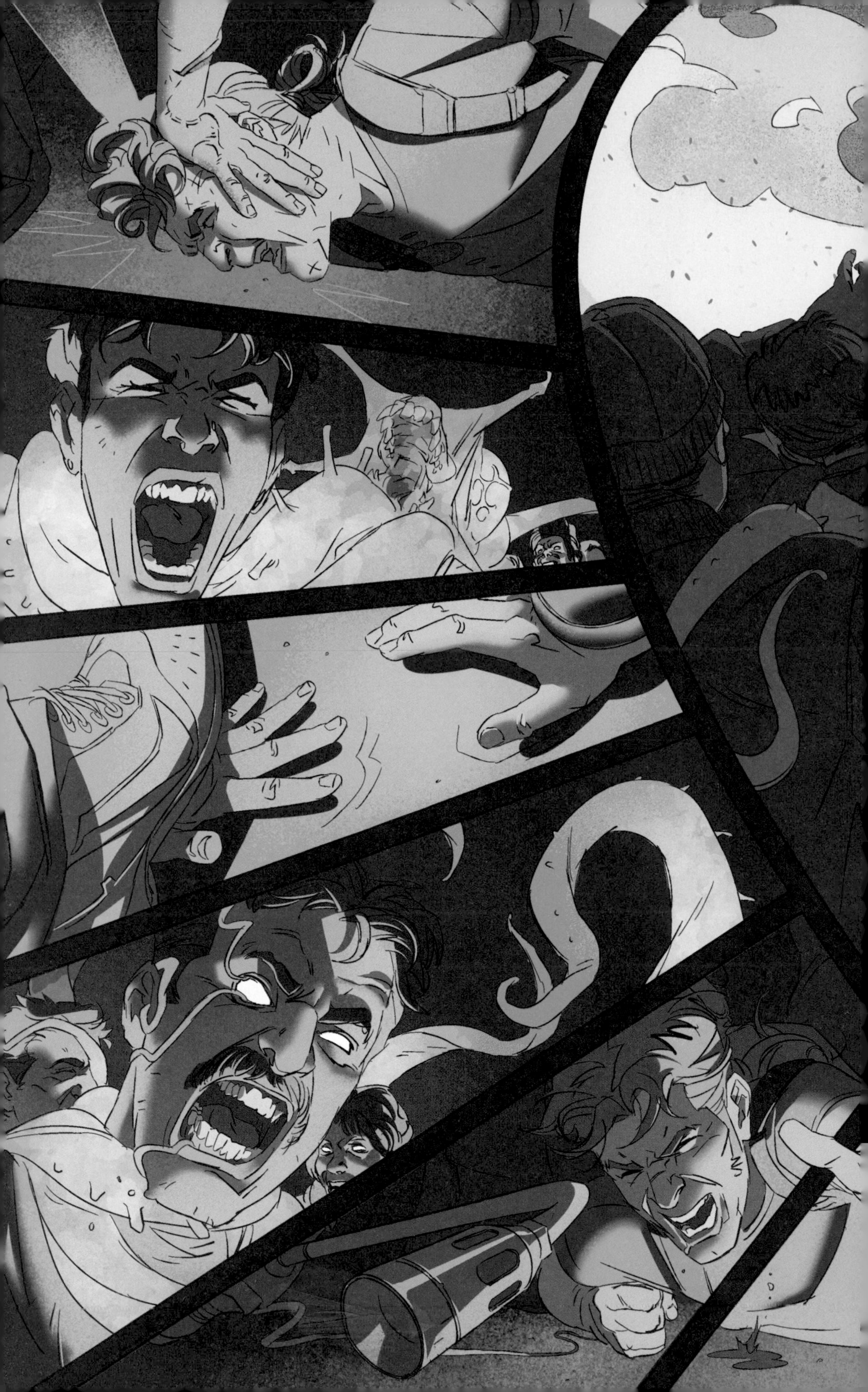

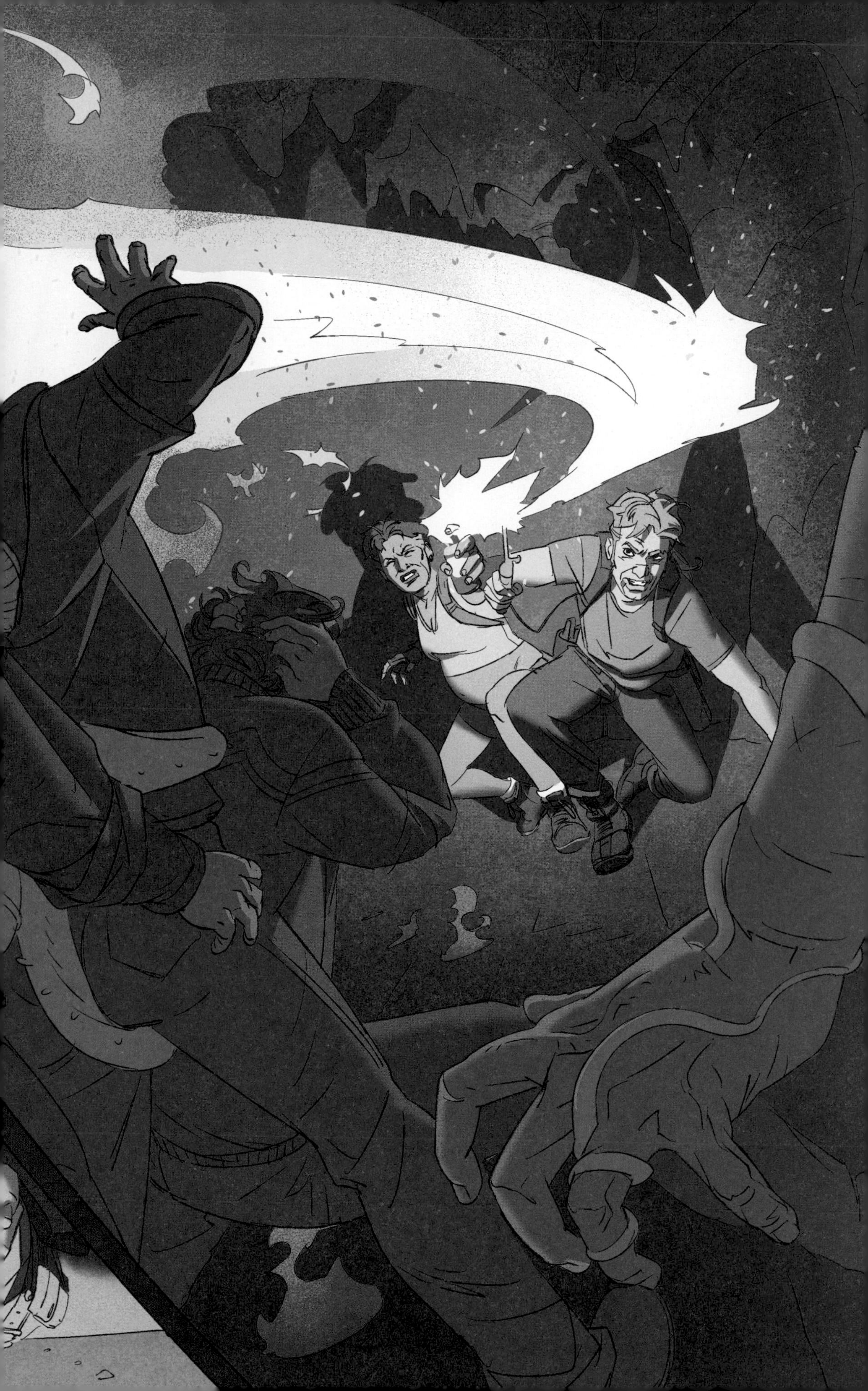

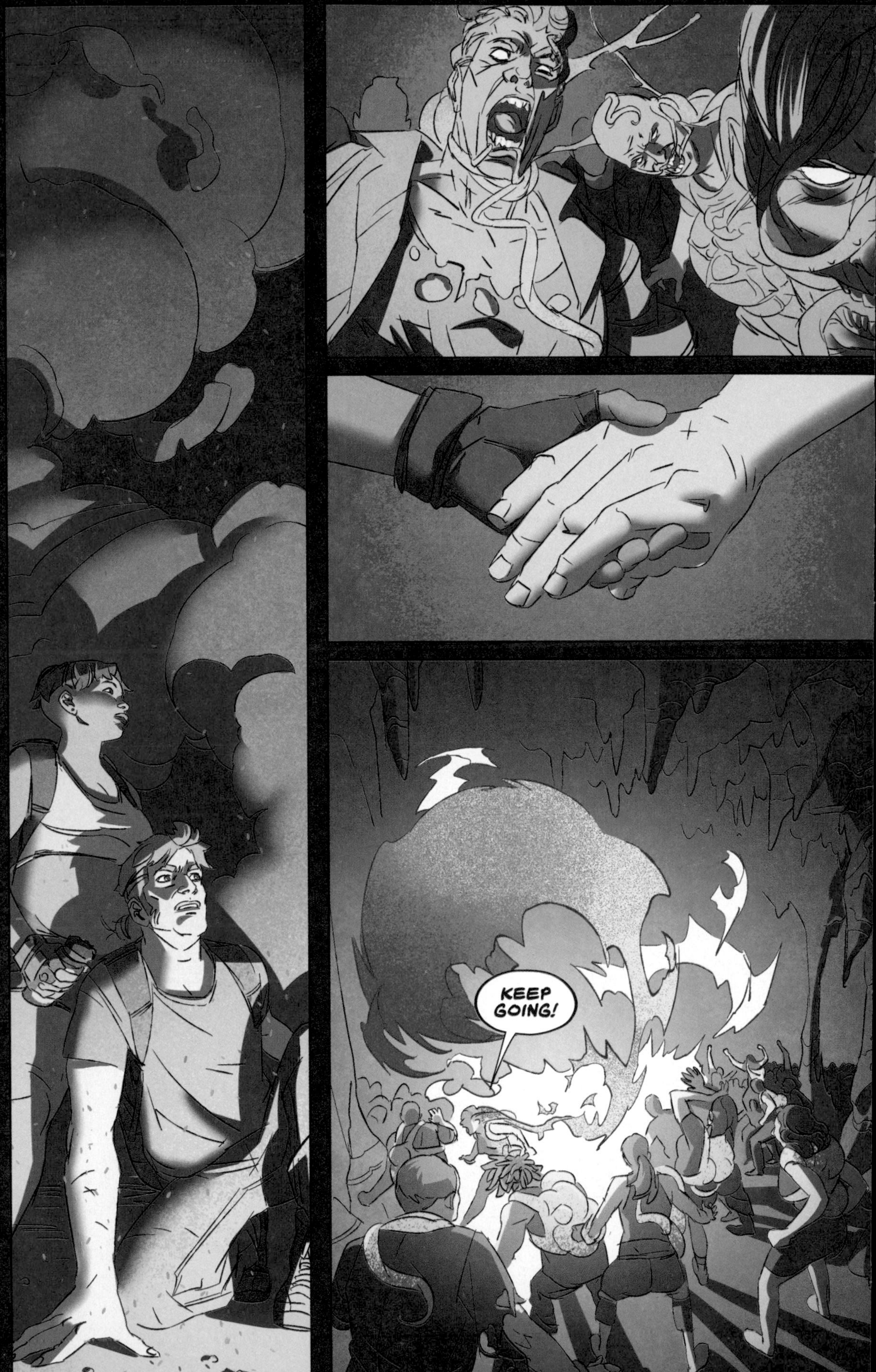
KEEP GOING!

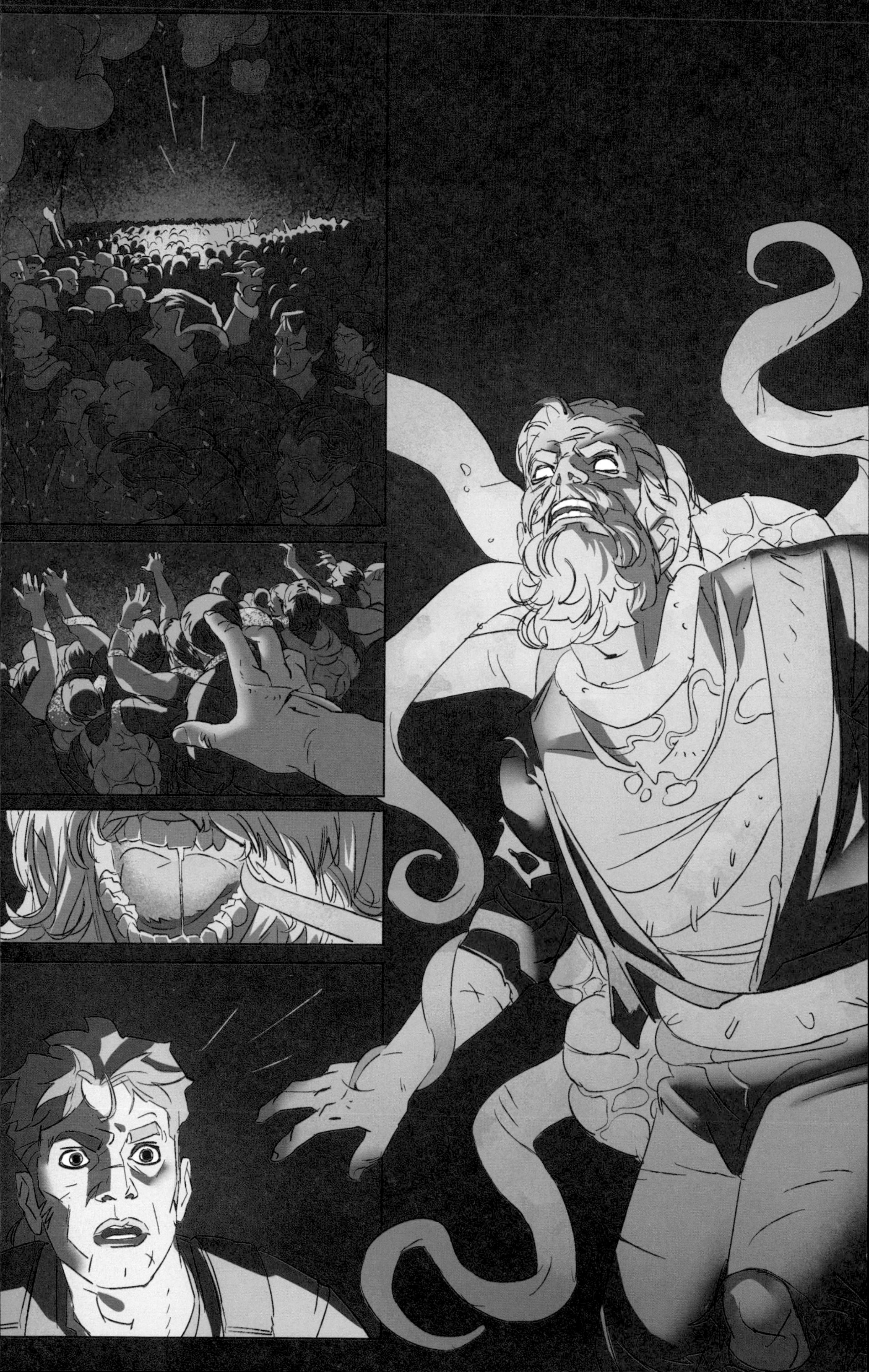

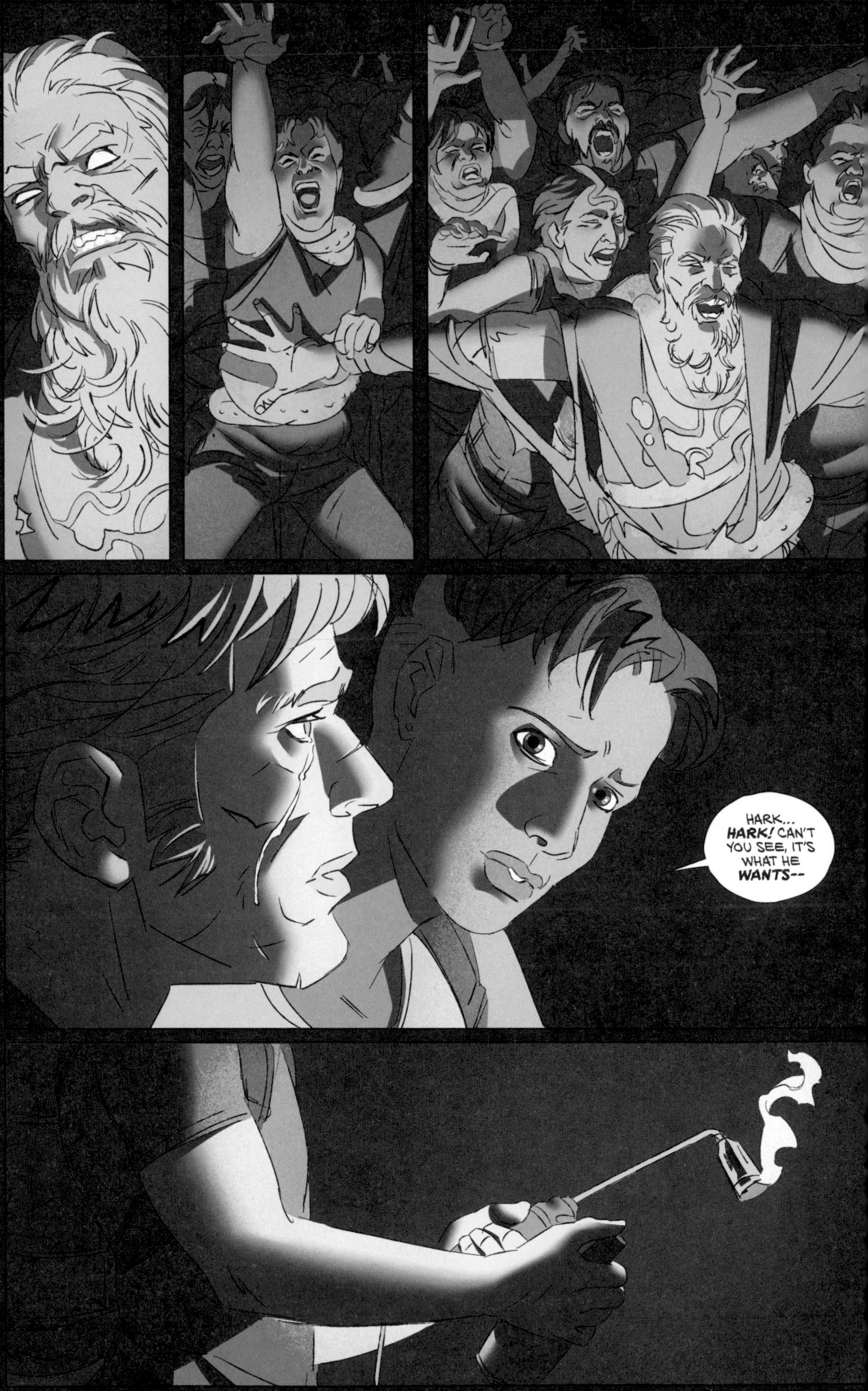
HARK... **HARK!** CAN'T YOU SEE, IT'S WHAT HE **WANTS--**

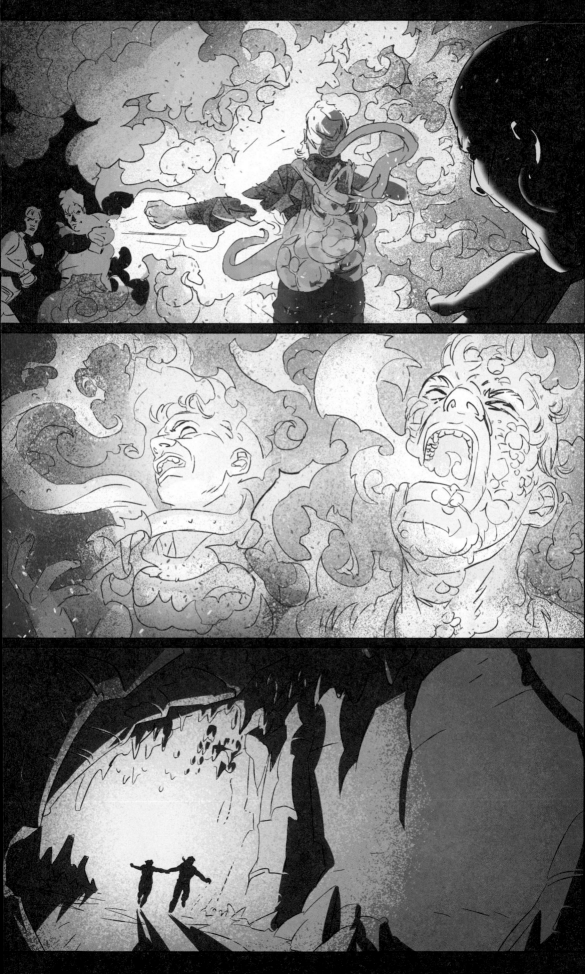

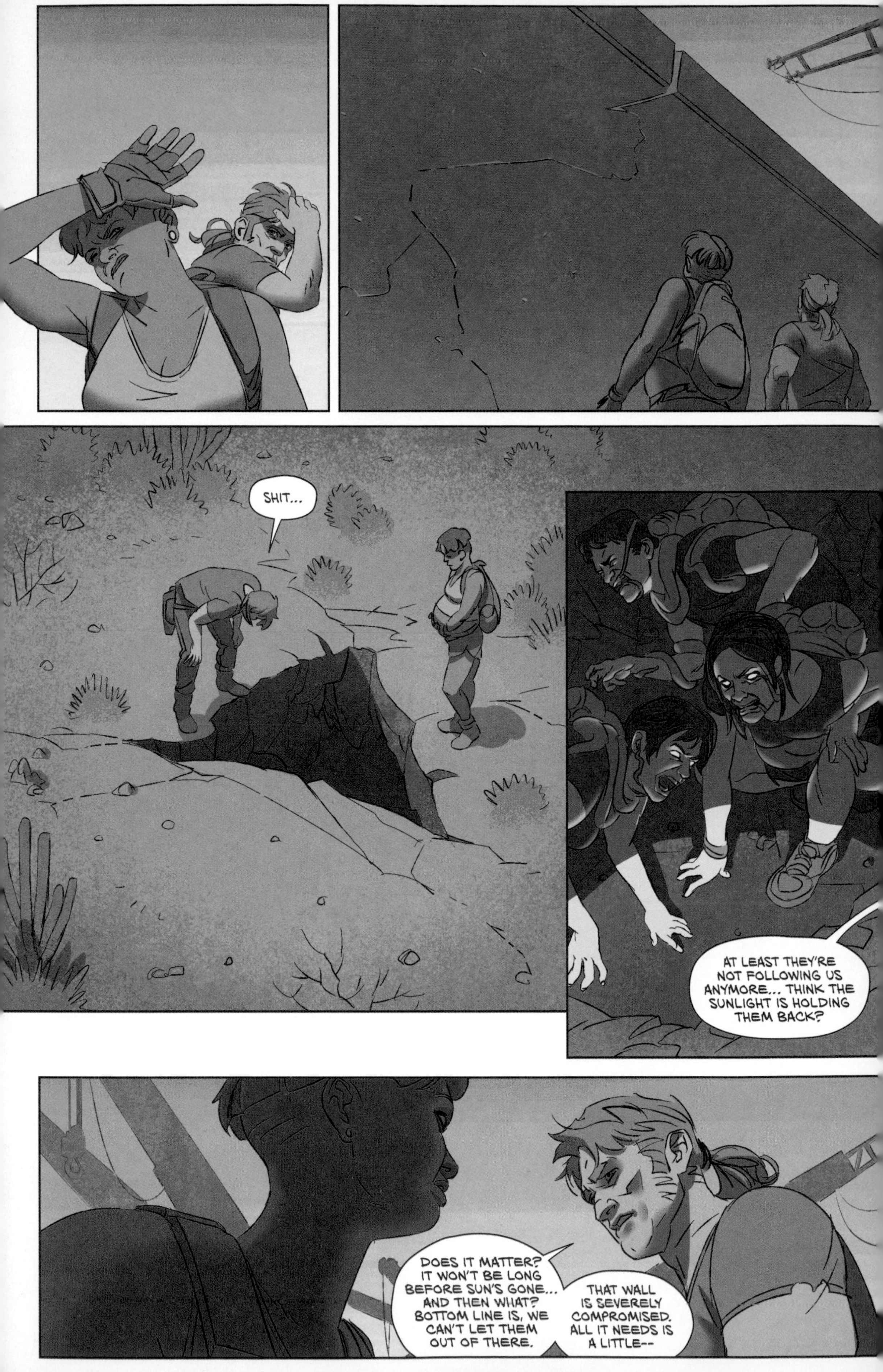
SHIT...
AT LEAST THEY'RE NOT FOLLOWING US ANYMORE... THINK THE SUNLIGHT IS HOLDING THEM BACK?
DOES IT MATTER? IT WON'T BE LONG BEFORE SUN'S GONE... AND THEN WHAT? BOTTOM LINE IS, WE CAN'T LET THEM OUT OF THERE.
THAT WALL IS SEVERELY COMPROMISED. ALL IT NEEDS IS A LITTLE--

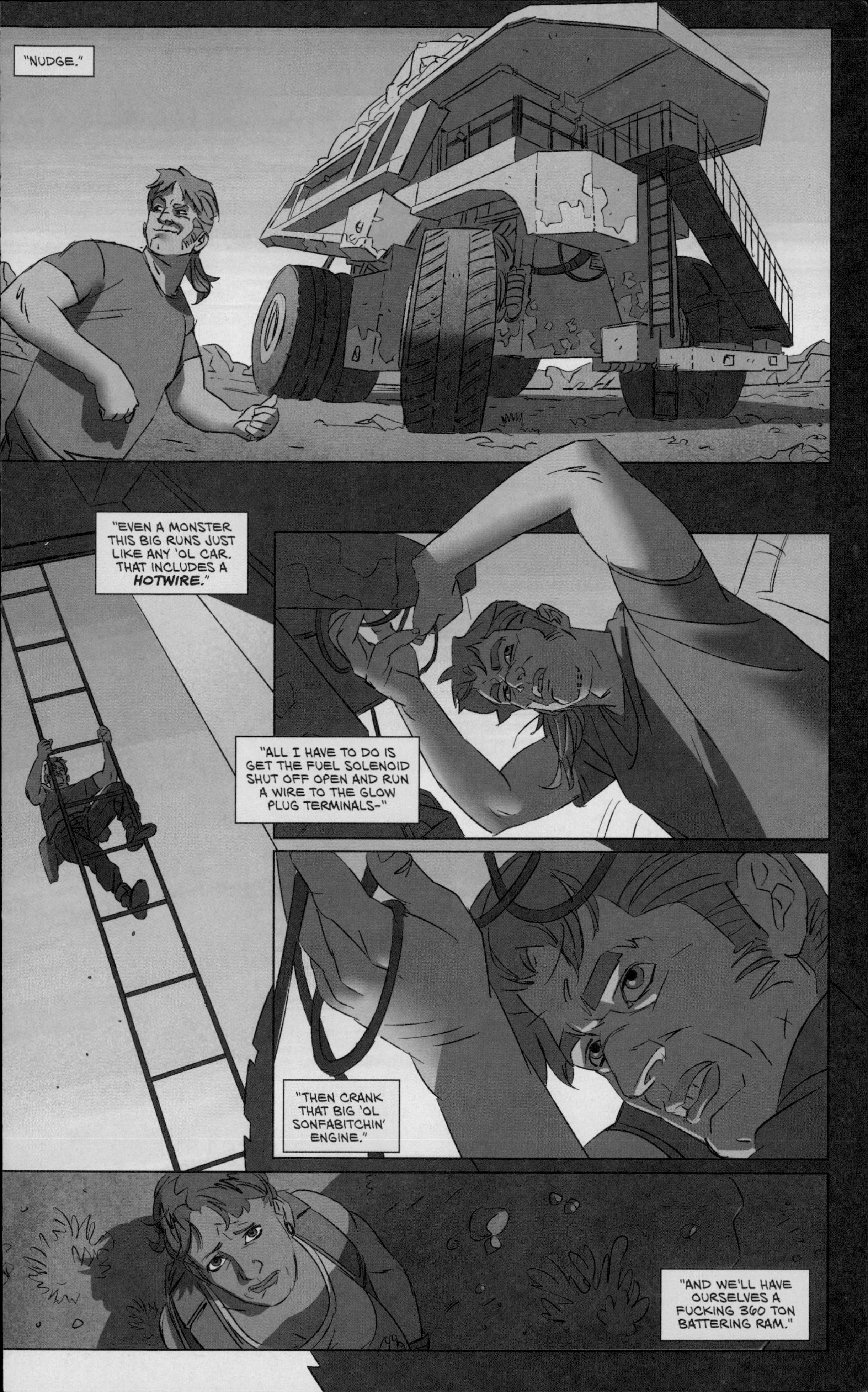
"NUDGE."
"EVEN A MONSTER THIS BIG RUNS JUST LIKE ANY 'OL CAR. THAT INCLUDES A HOTWIRE."
"ALL I HAVE TO DO IS GET THE FUEL SOLENOID SHUT OFF OPEN AND RUN A WIRE TO THE GLOW PLUG TERMINALS-"
"THEN CRANK THAT BIG 'OL SONFABITCHIN' ENGINE."
"AND WE'LL HAVE OURSELVES A FUCKING 360 TON BATTERING RAM."

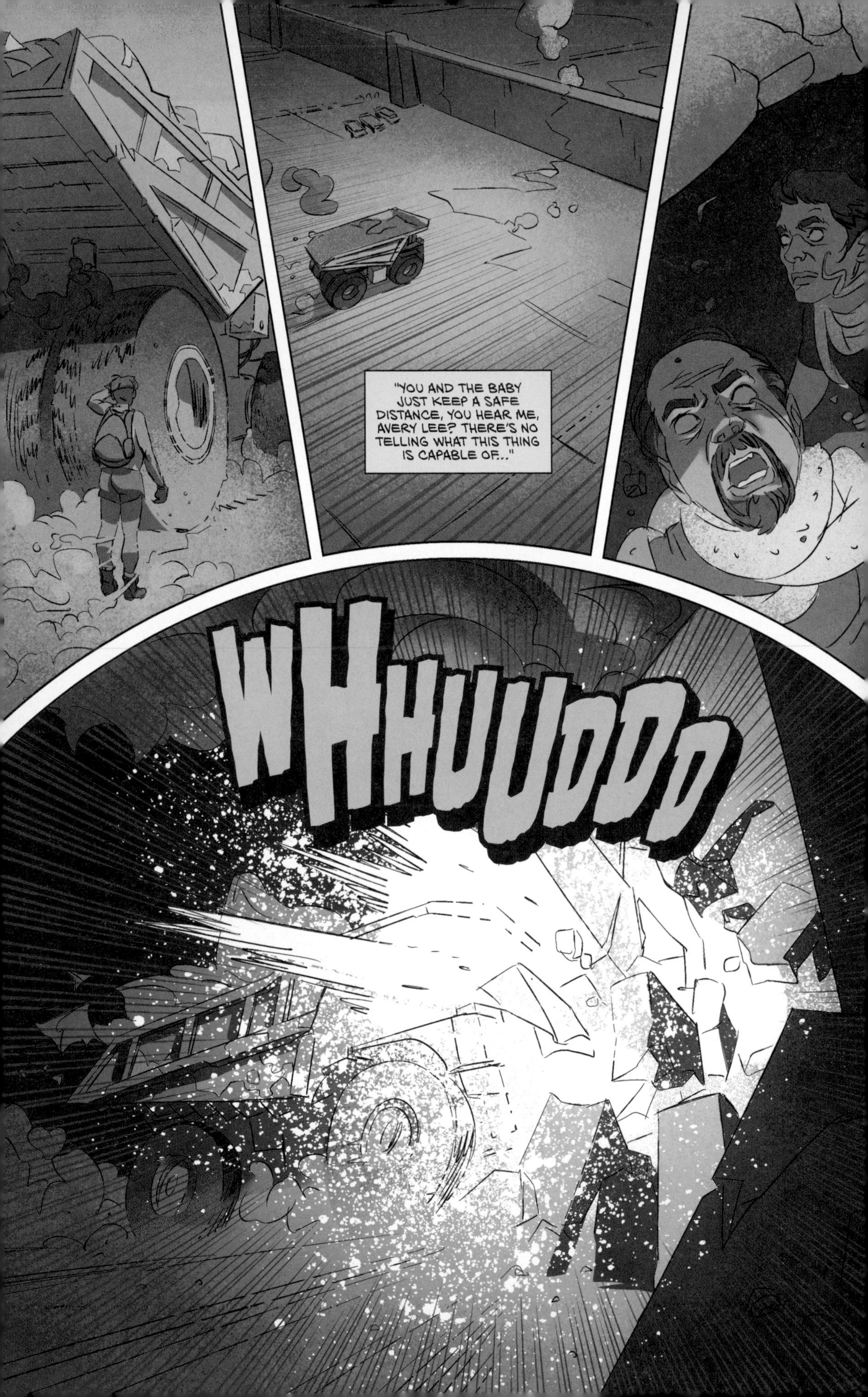
"YOU AND THE BABY JUST KEEP A SAFE DISTANCE, YOU HEAR ME, AVERY LEE? THERE'S NO TELLING WHAT THIS THING IS CAPABLE OF..."
WHHUUDDD

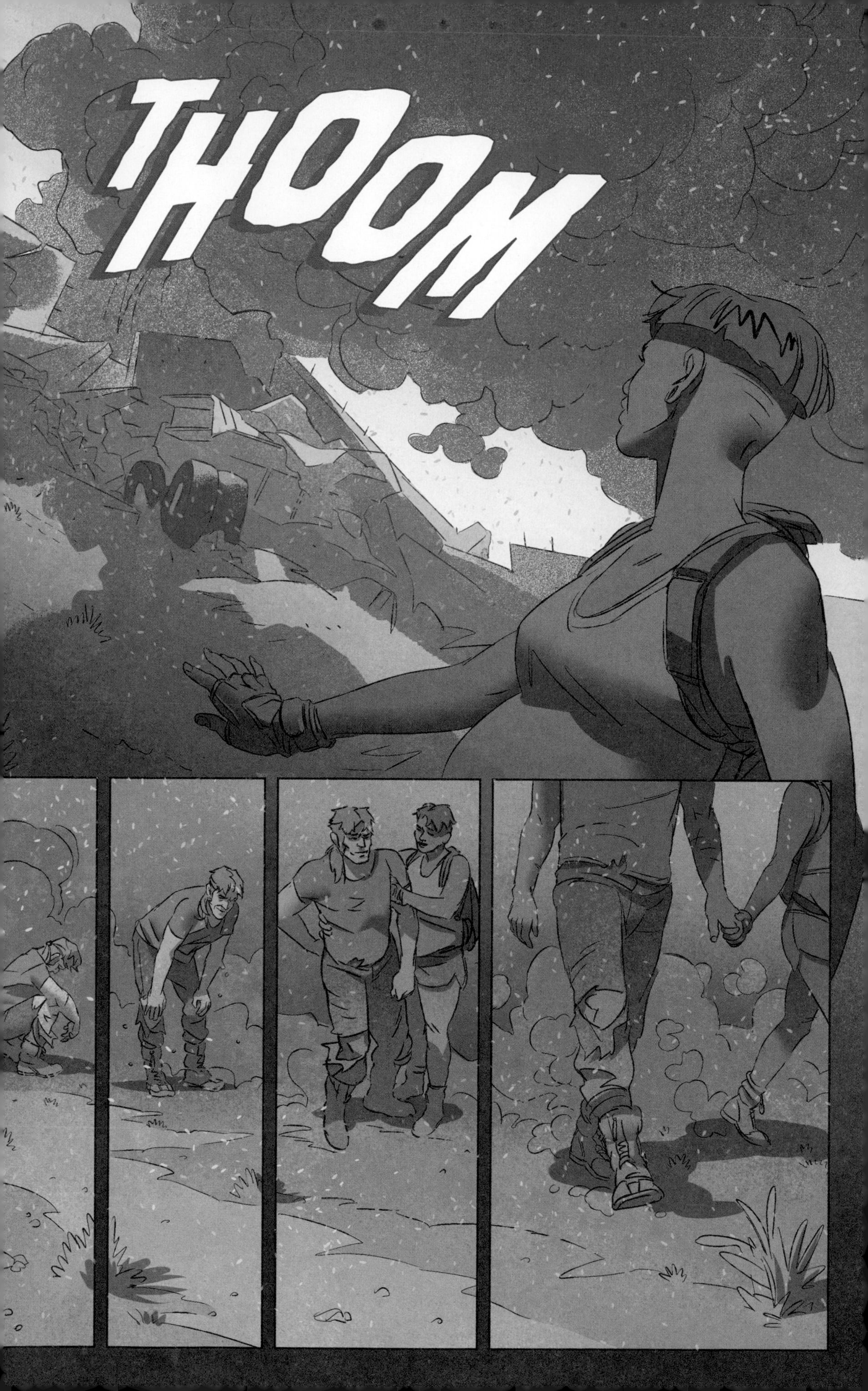
THOOM

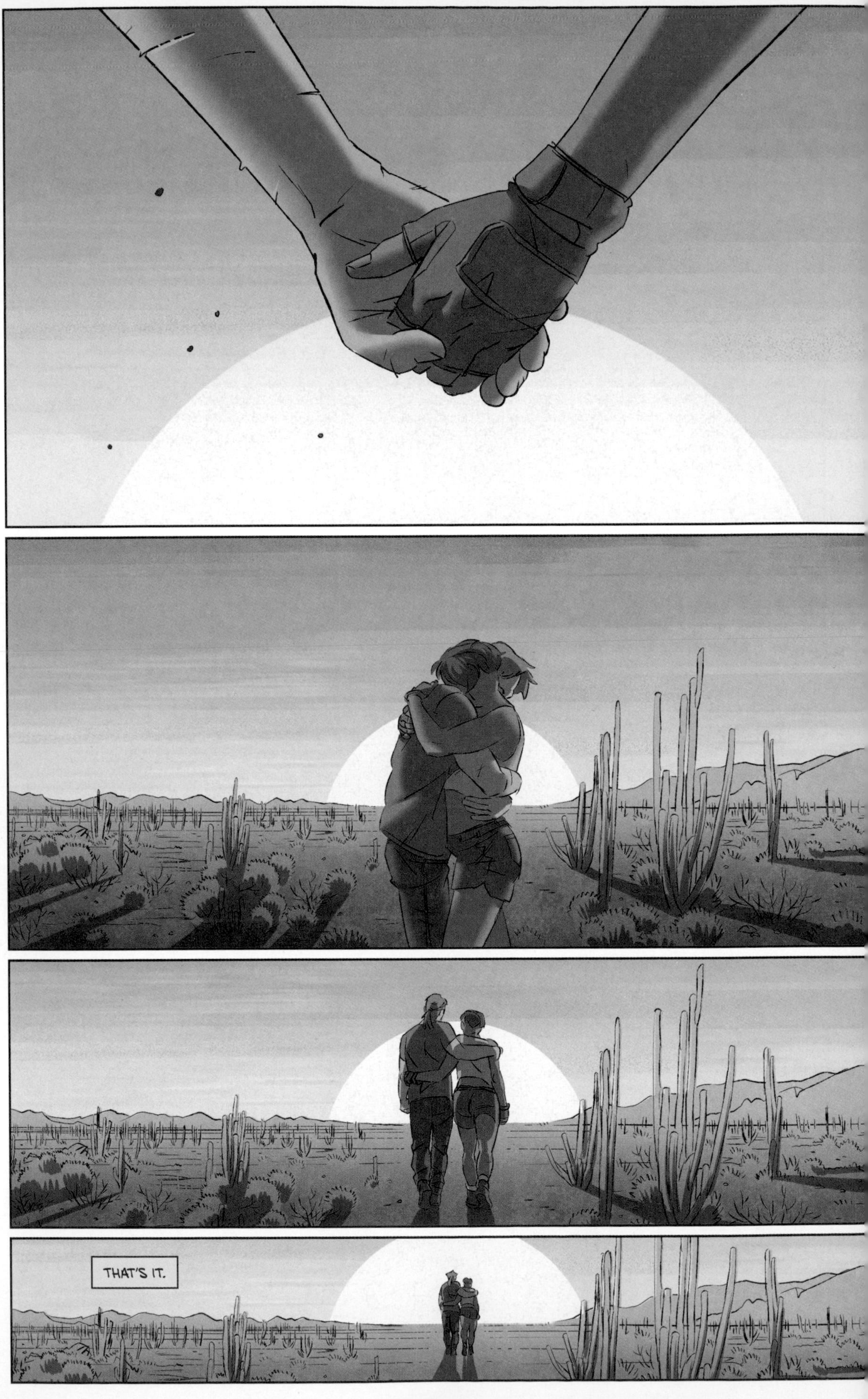
THAT'S IT.

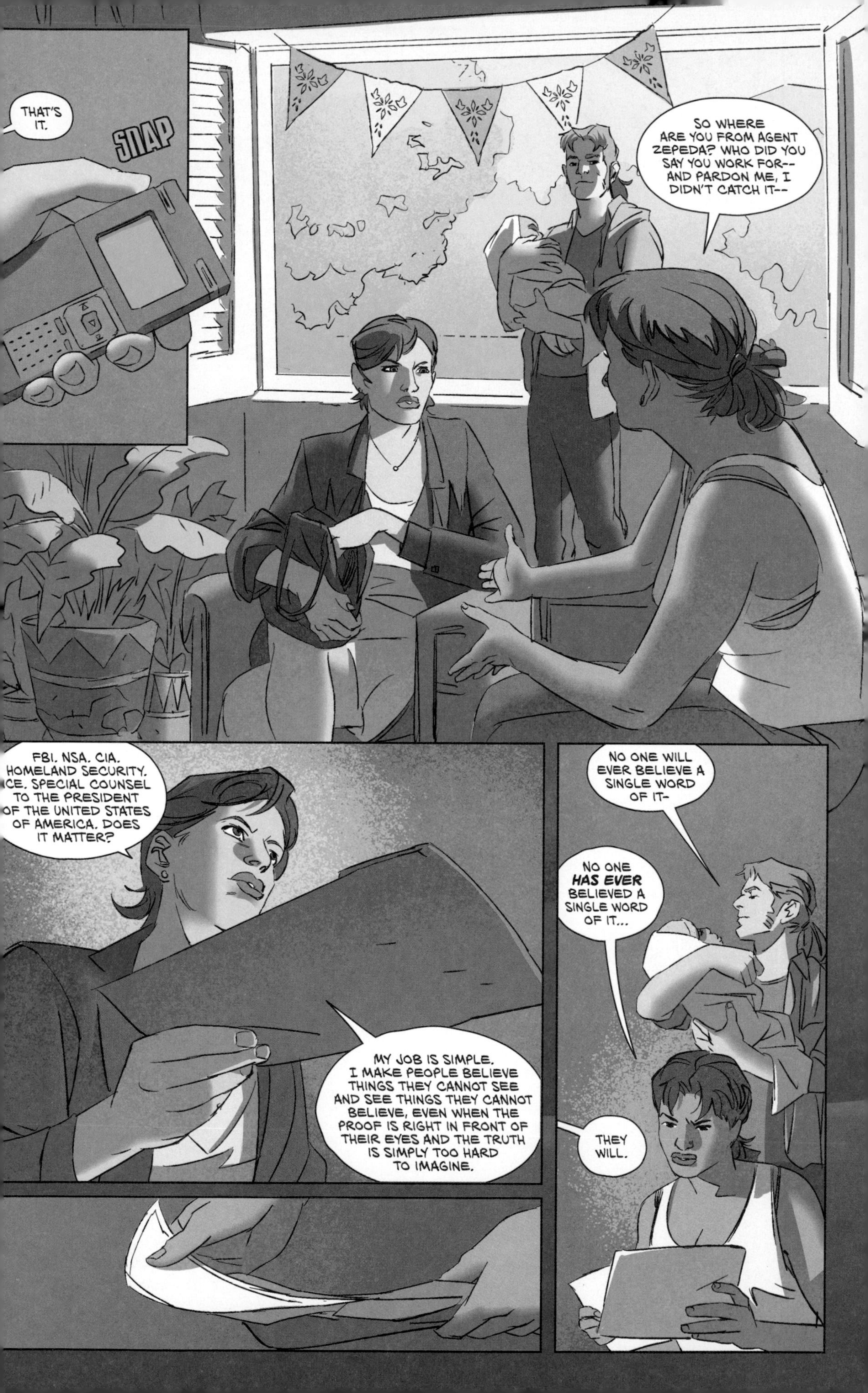
THAT'S IT.
SNAP
SO WHERE ARE YOU FROM AGENT ZEPEDA? WHO DID YOU SAY YOU WORK FOR-- AND PARDON ME, I DIDN'T CATCH IT--
FBI. NSA. CIA. HOMELAND SECURITY. ICE. SPECIAL COUNSEL TO THE PRESIDENT OF THE UNITED STATES OF AMERICA. DOES IT MATTER?
MY JOB IS SIMPLE. I MAKE PEOPLE BELIEVE THINGS THEY CANNOT SEE AND SEE THINGS THEY CANNOT BELIEVE, EVEN WHEN THE PROOF IS RIGHT IN FRONT OF THEIR EYES AND THE TRUTH IS SIMPLY TOO HARD TO IMAGINE.
NO ONE WILL EVER BELIEVE A SINGLE WORD OF IT-
NO ONE **HAS EVER** BELIEVED A SINGLE WORD OF IT...
THEY WILL.

THEY MUST.

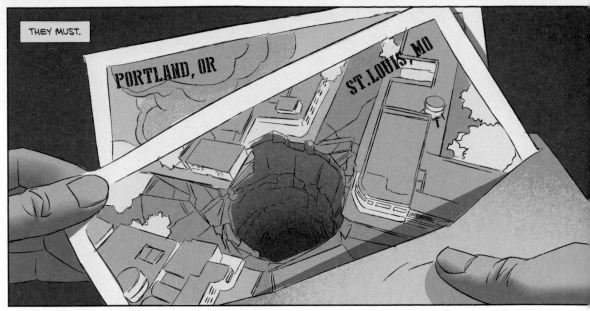

PORTLAND, OR

ST. LOUIS, MO

WE ALLOW SOMETHING LIKE *THIS* TO CONTINUE AND BEFORE YOU KNOW IT, THE GROUND GIVES WAY BENEATH OUR FEET--

SAN FRANCISCO, CA

DALLAS, TX

SEATTLE, WA

AND WE'RE ALL CONSUMED. SWALLOWED INTO THE BELLY OF THE BEAST.

NOPE, YOU TWO ARE ALL THE PROOF I NEED. THE ONLY WAY WE SURVIVE THIS IS TO STICK TOGETHER.

COVER GALLERY
FEATURING THE ART OF

PATRICIO DELPECHE
AND
RICARDO DRUMOND

ISSUE ONE COVER: PATRICIO DELPECHE

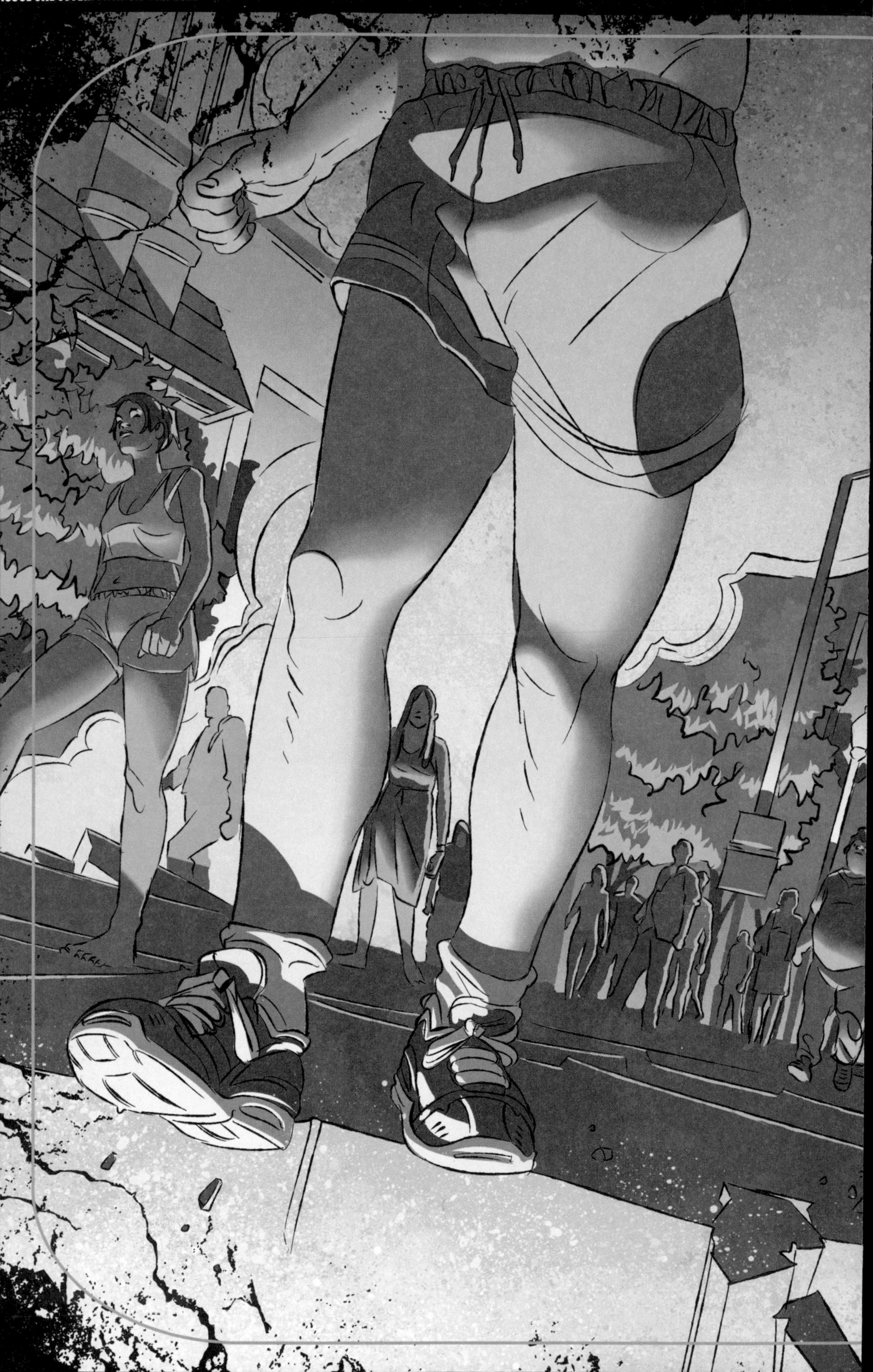

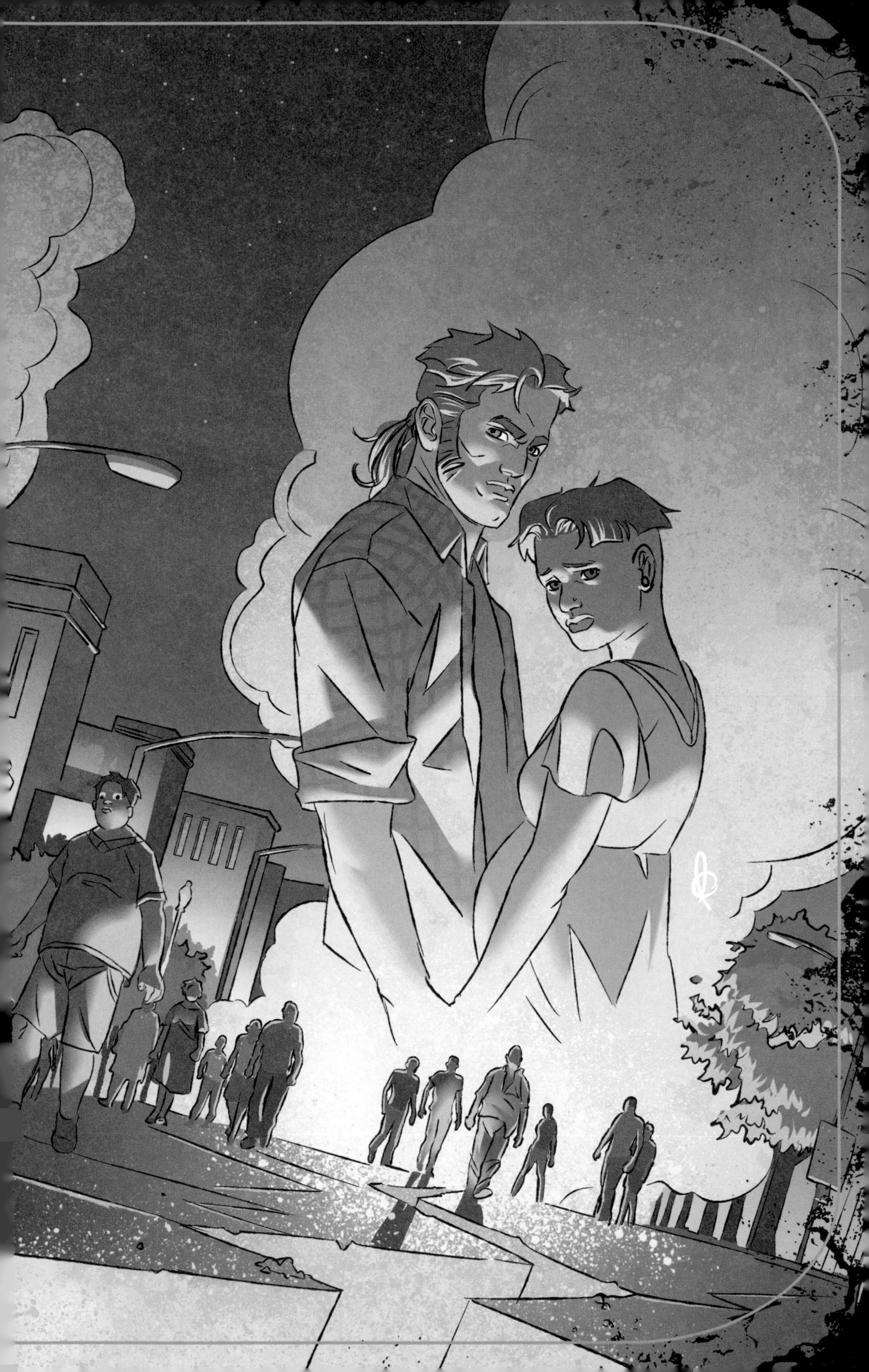

ISSUE TWO COVER: PATRICIO DELPECHE

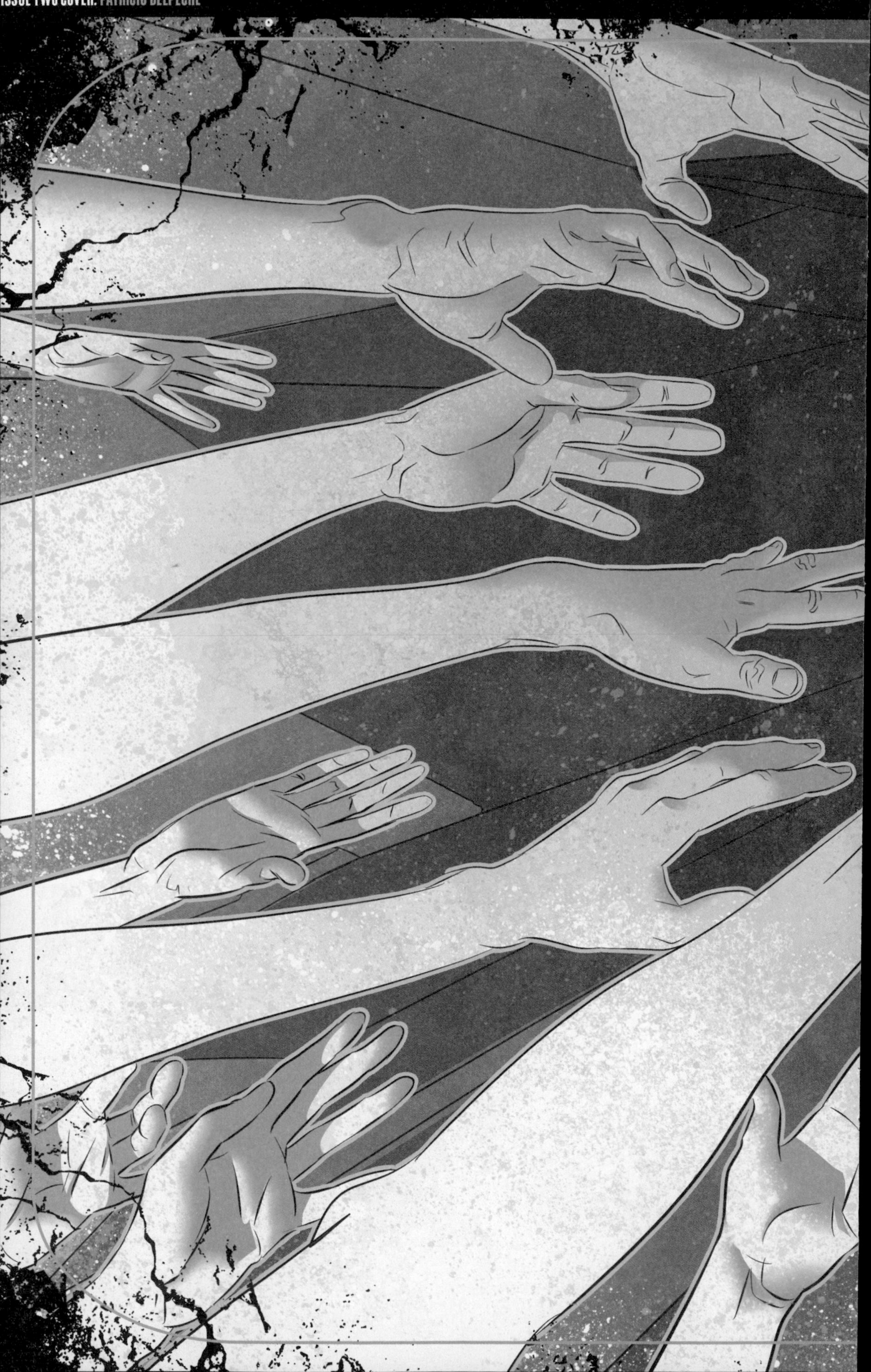

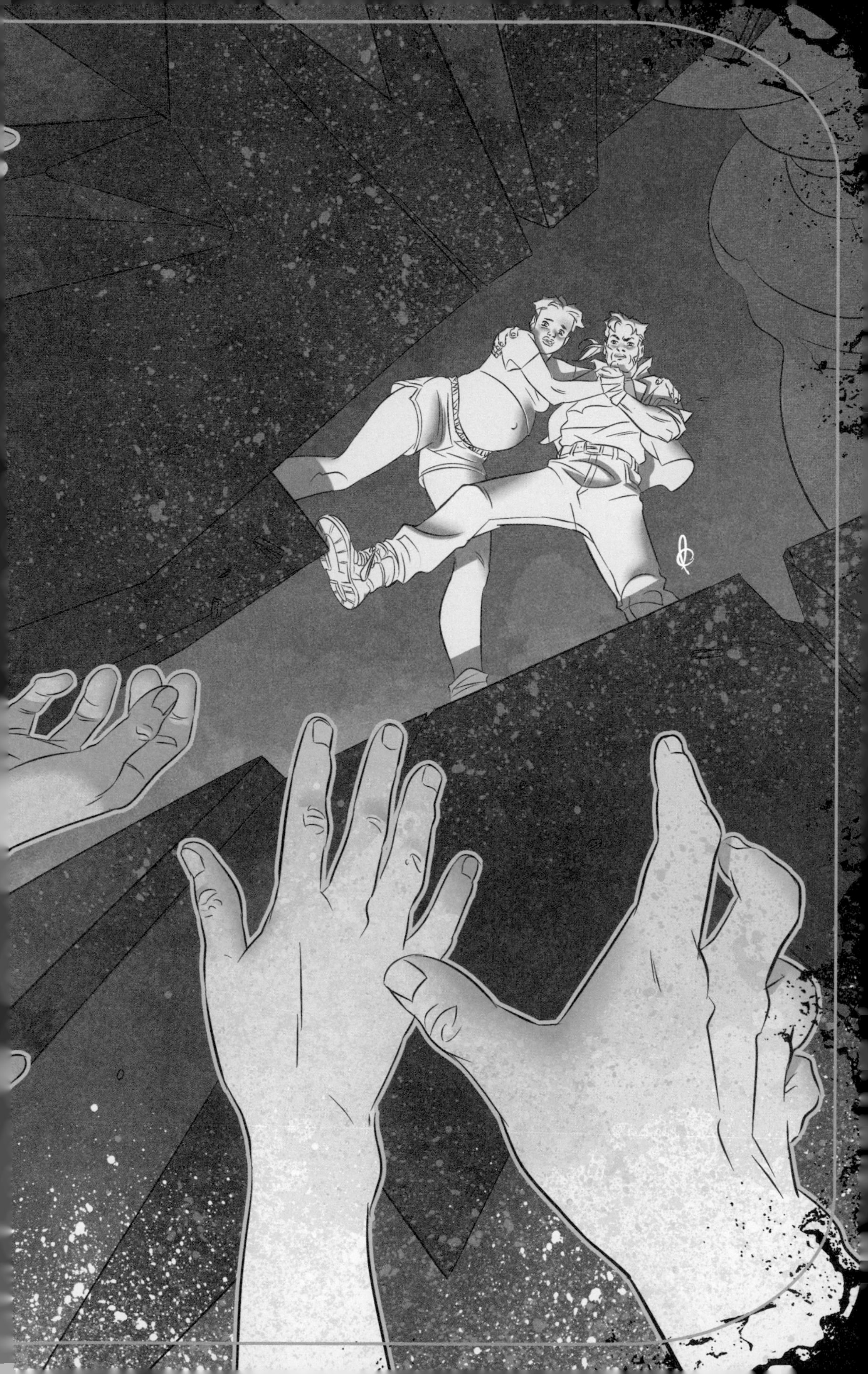

ISSUE THREE COVER: PATRICIO DELPECHE

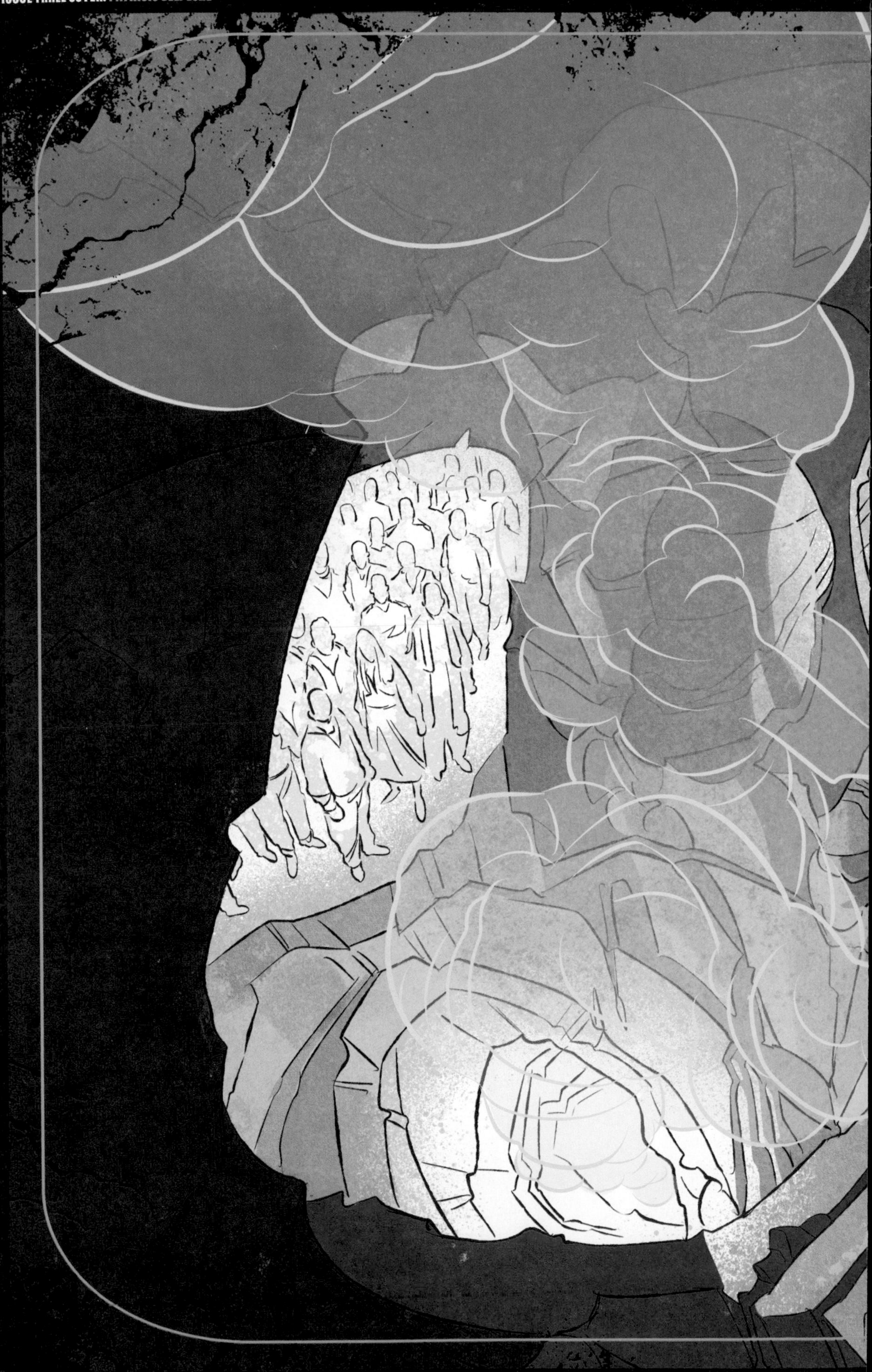

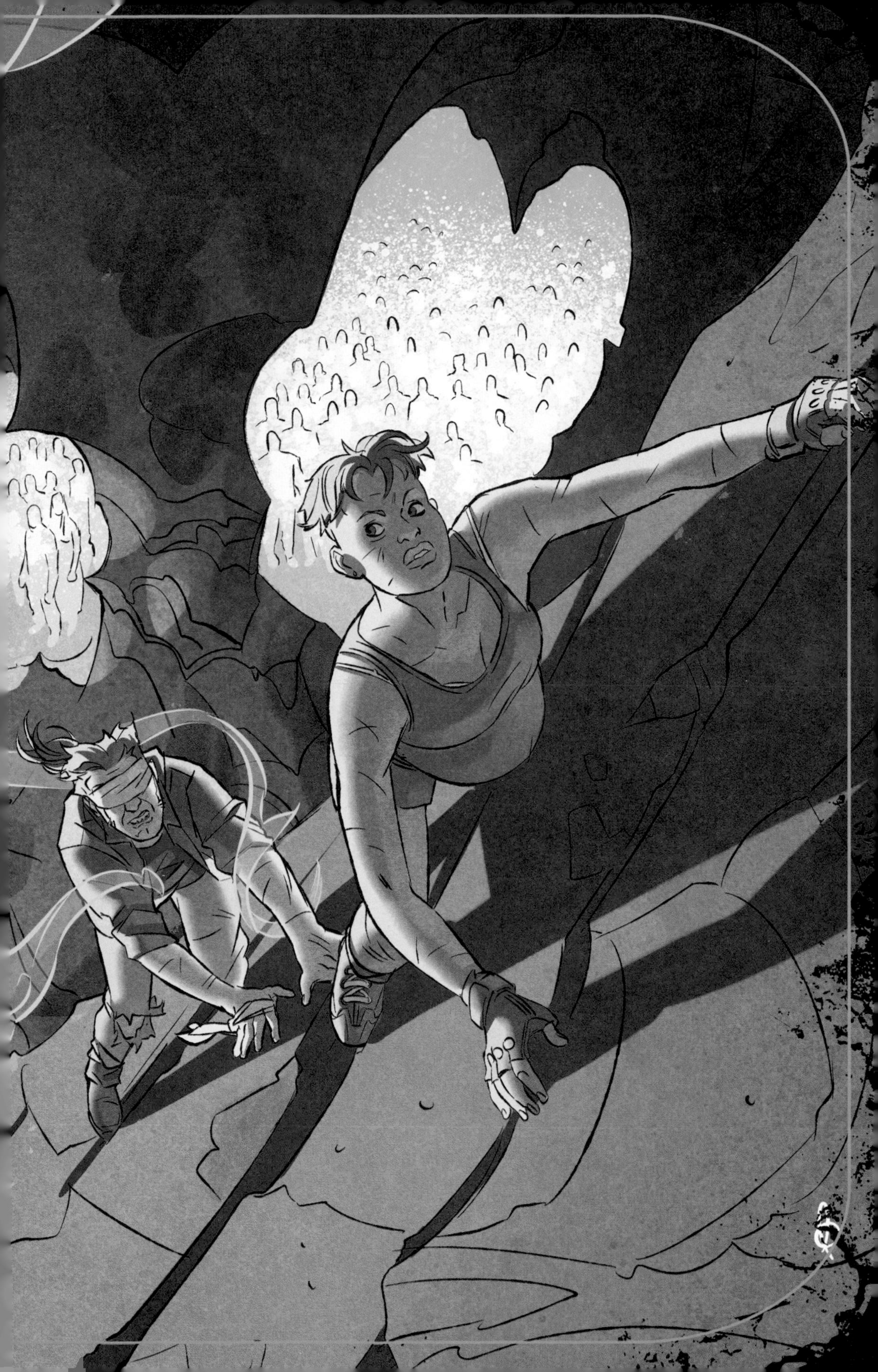

ISSUE FOUR COVER: PATRICIO DELPECHE

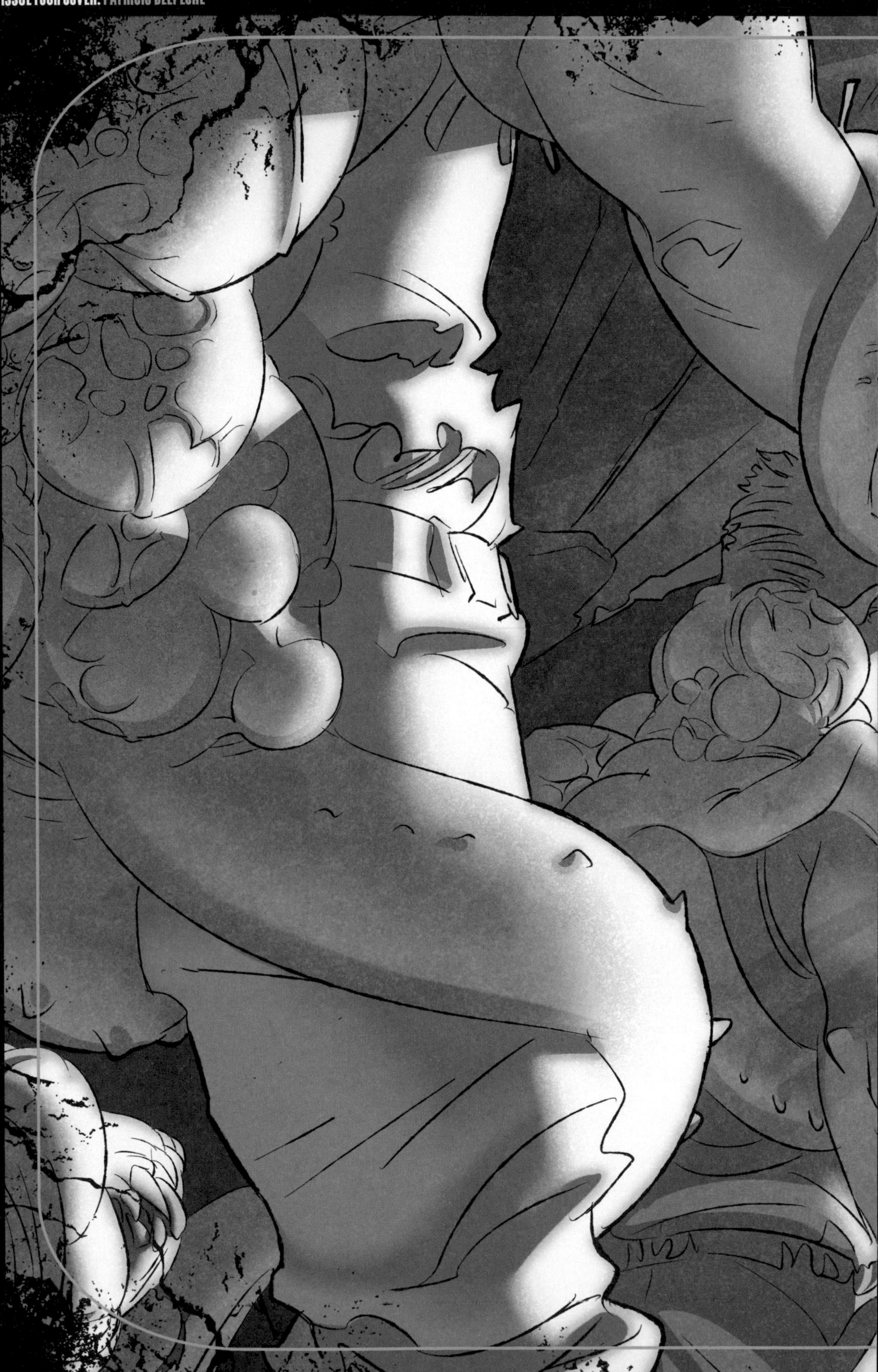

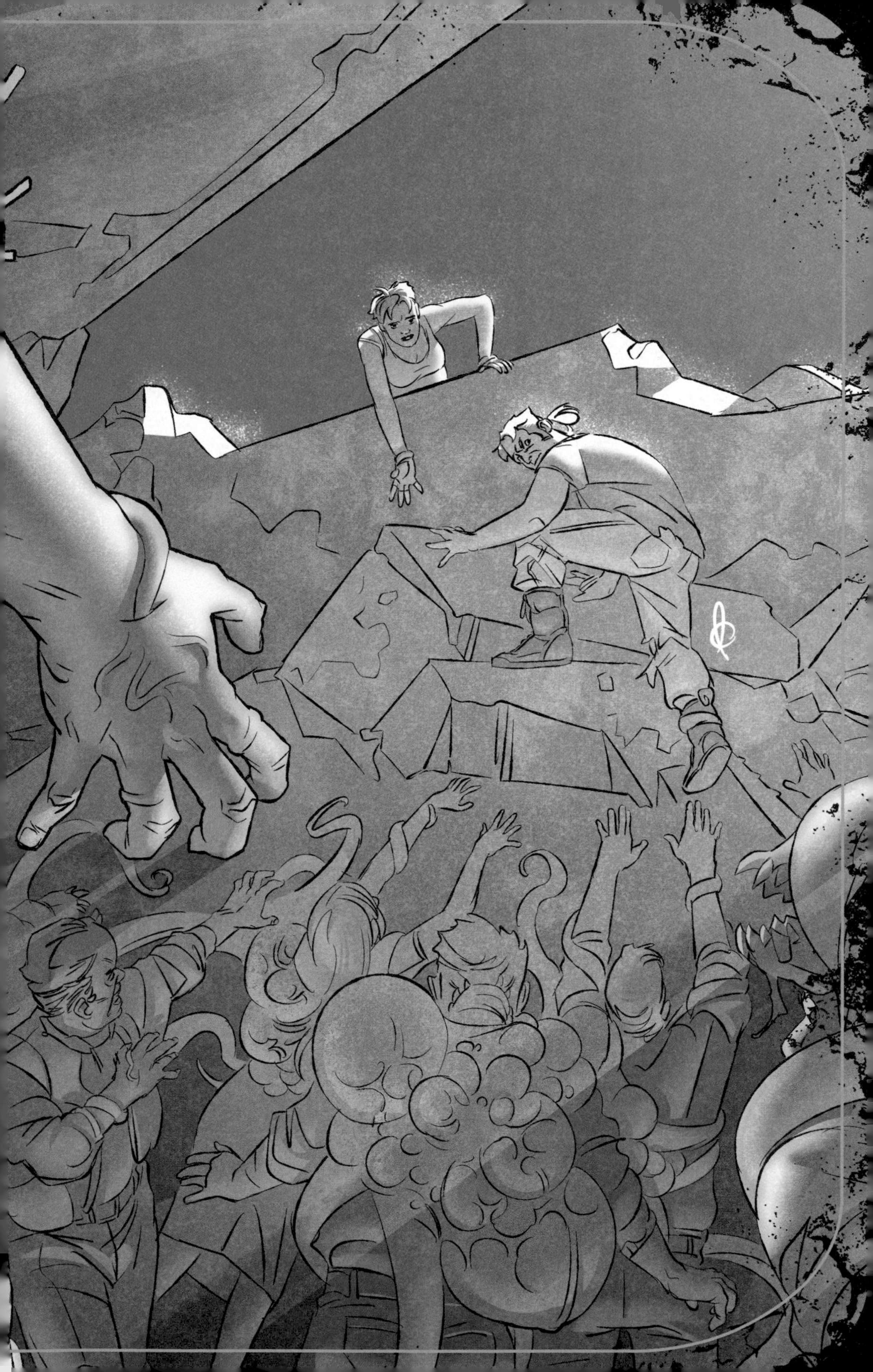

ISSUE ONE ALTERNATE COVER: RICARDO DRUMOND

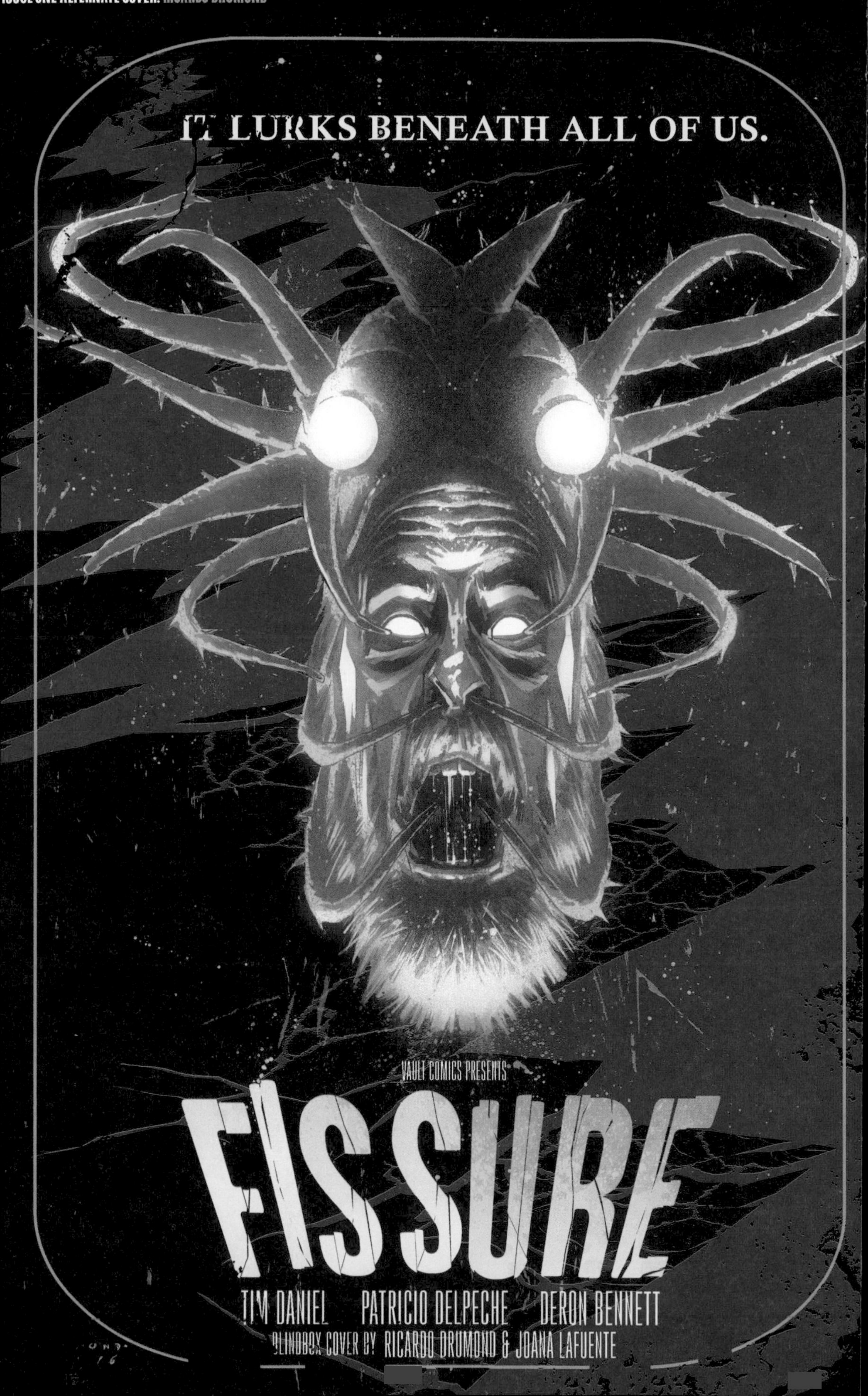
IT LURKS BENEATH ALL OF US.
VAULT COMICS PRESENTS
FISSURE
TIM DANIEL PATRICIO DELPECHE DERON BENNETT
BLINDBOX COVER BY RICARDO DRUMOND & JOANA LAFUENTE

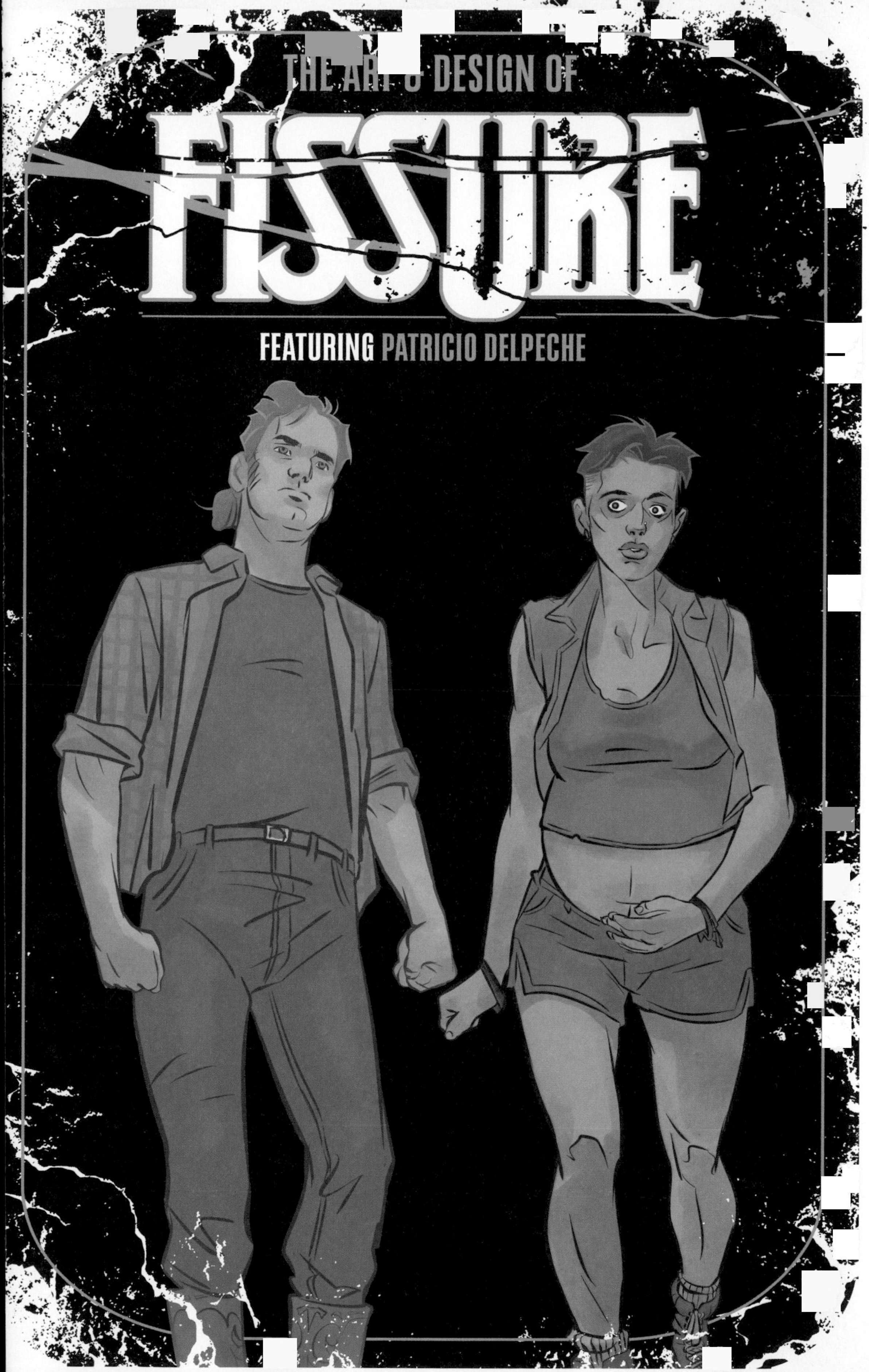
THE ART & DESIGN OF
FISSURE
FEATURING PATRICIO DELPECHE

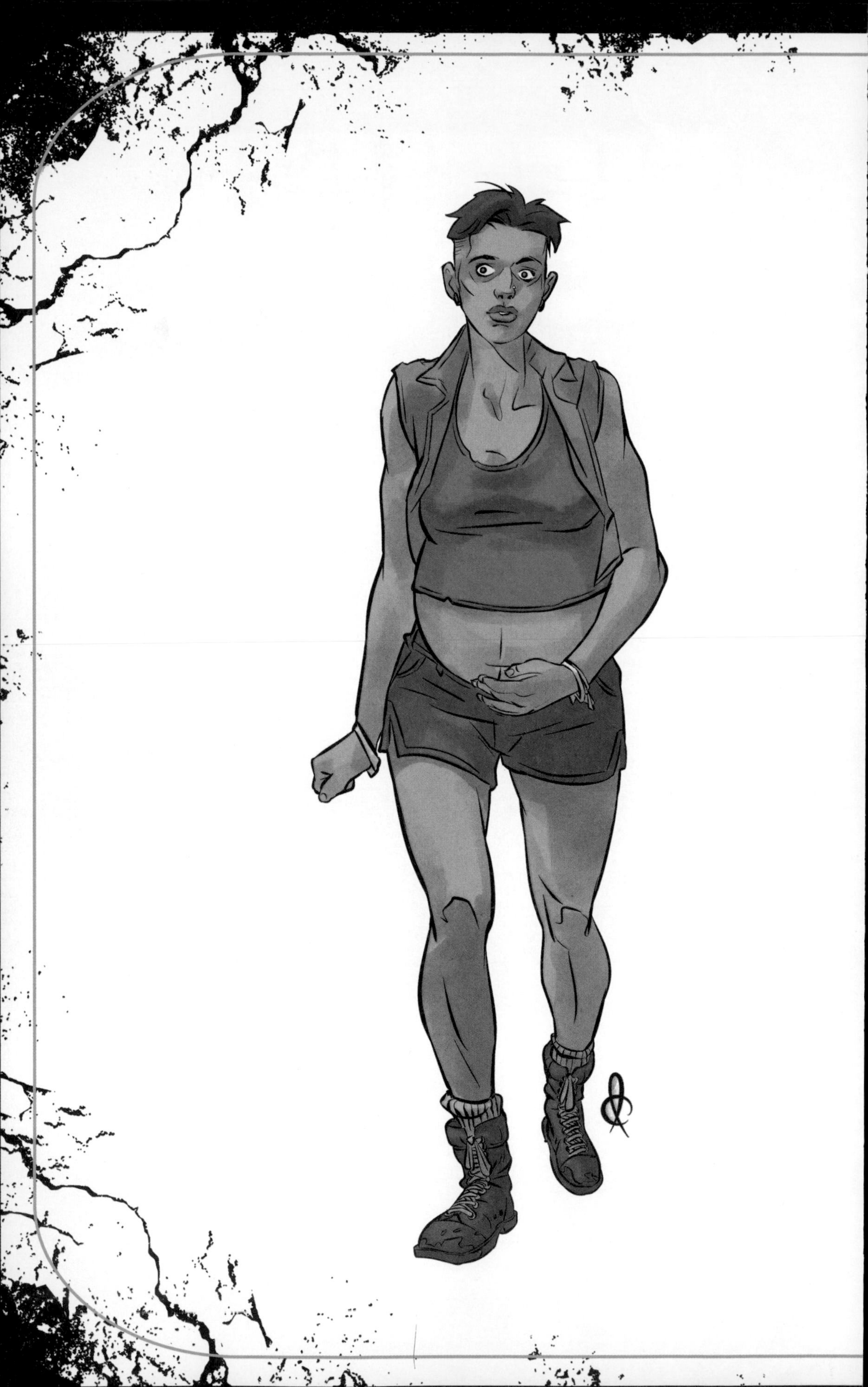

AVERY LEE OLMOS

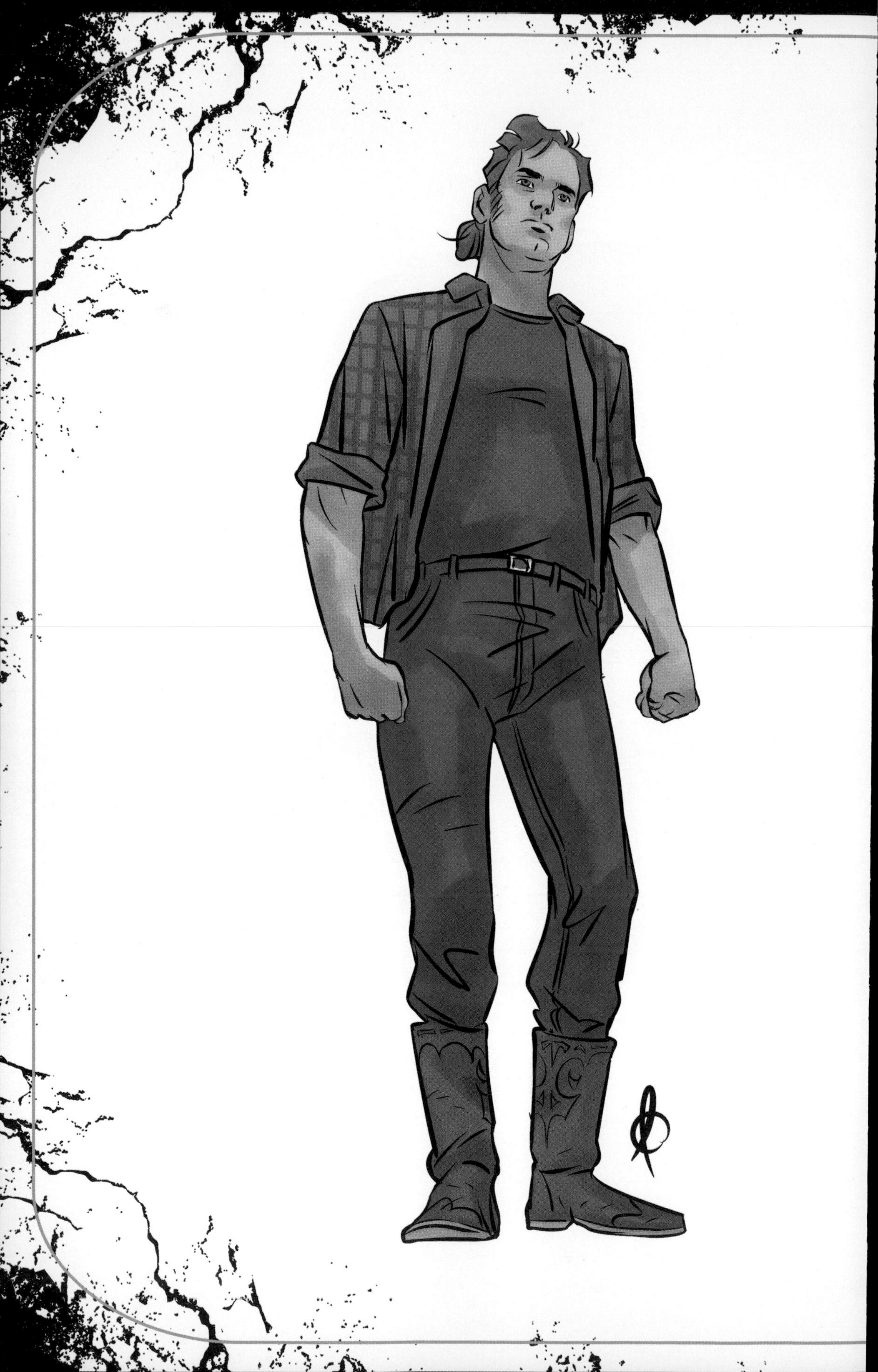

HARK WRIGHT

THE PARASITE

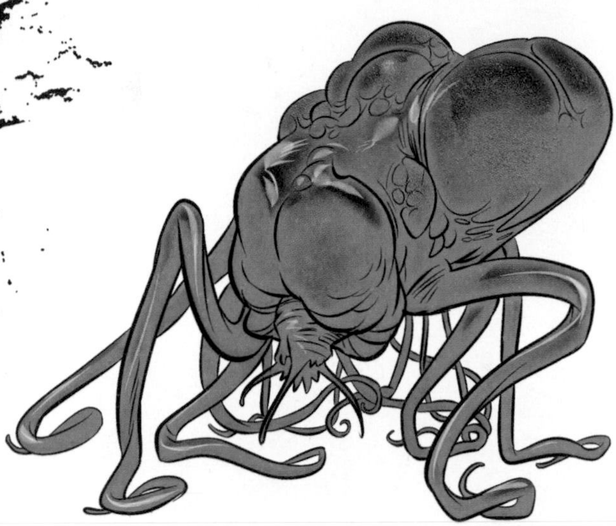

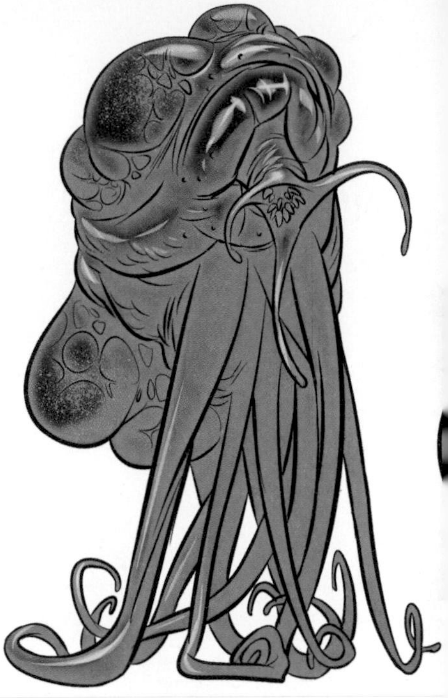

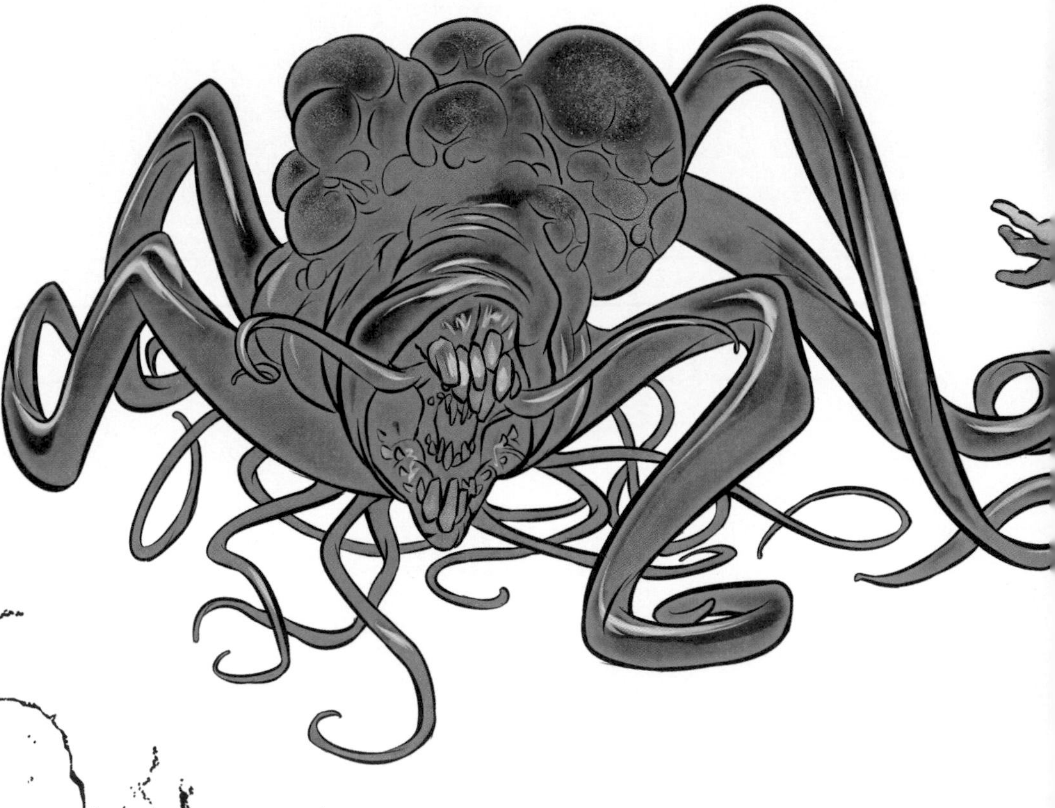

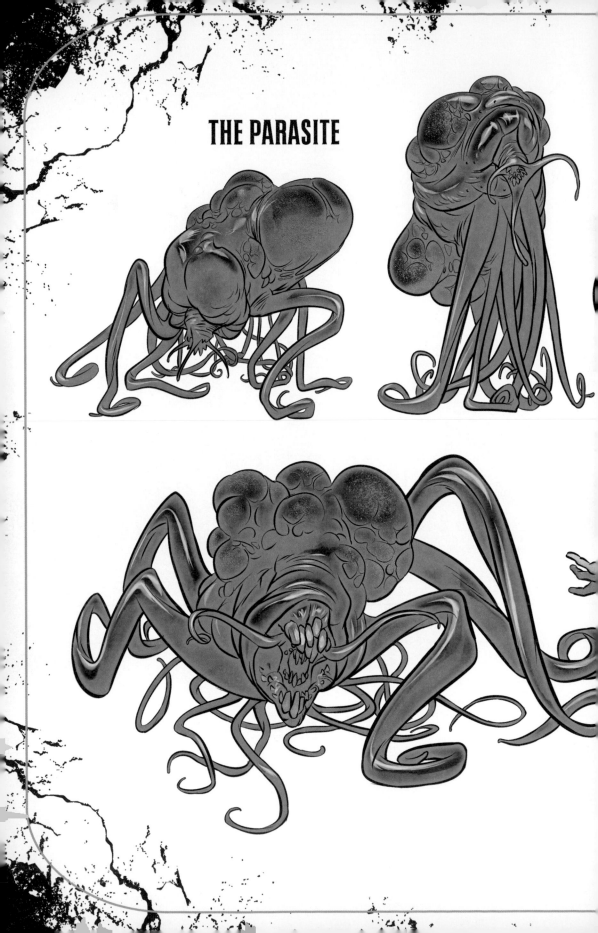

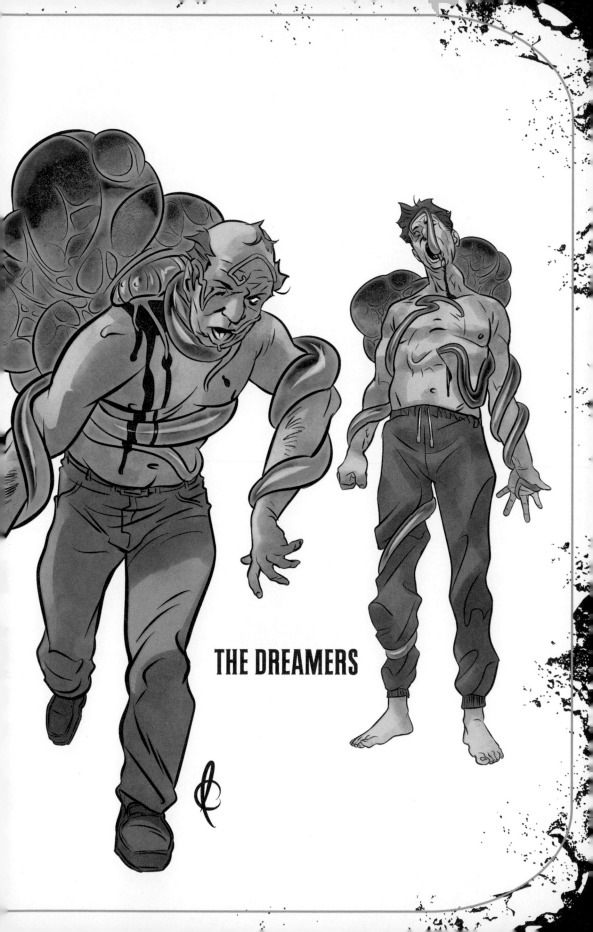

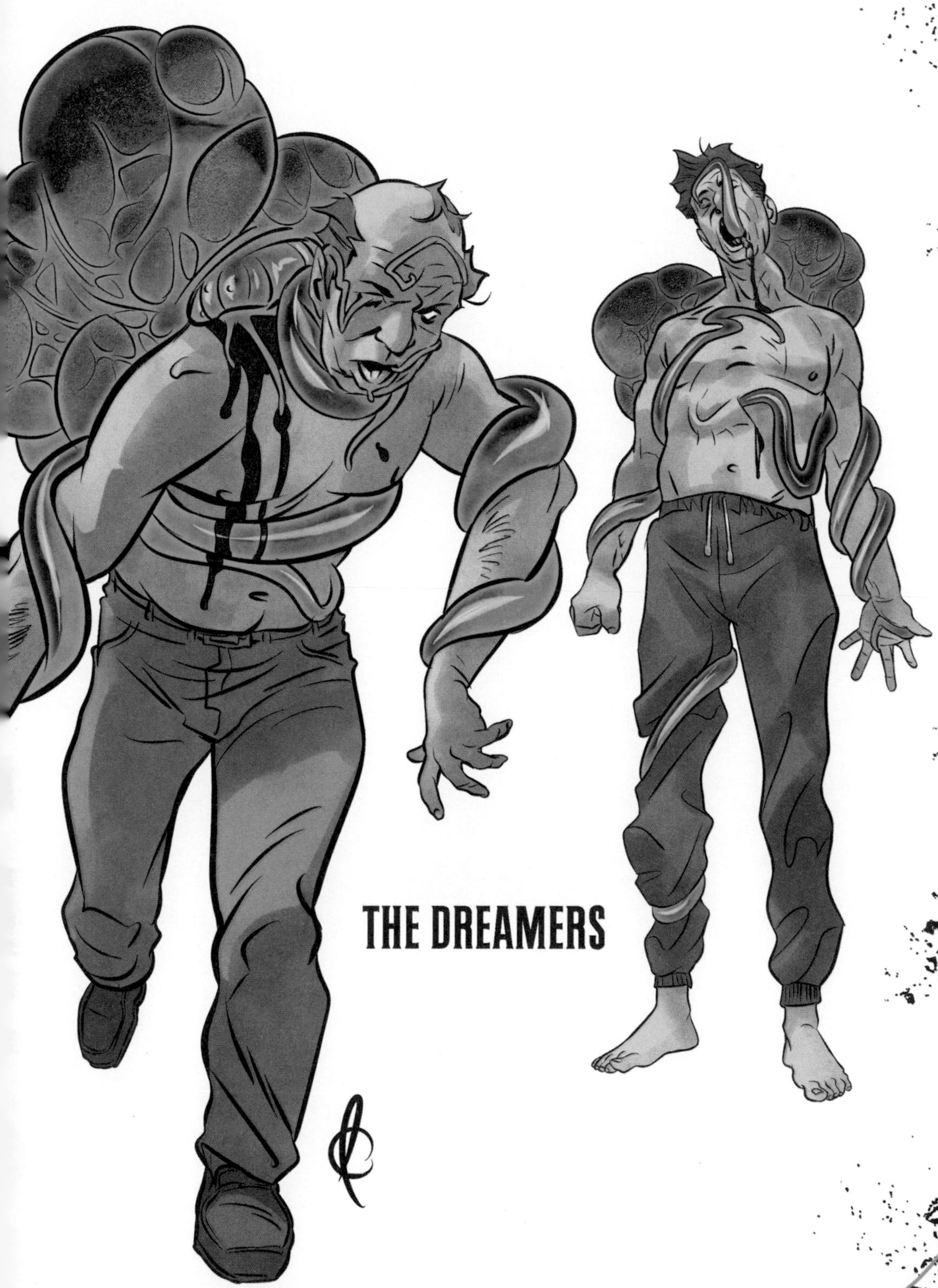
THE DREAMERS

FROM THE SKETCHBOOK

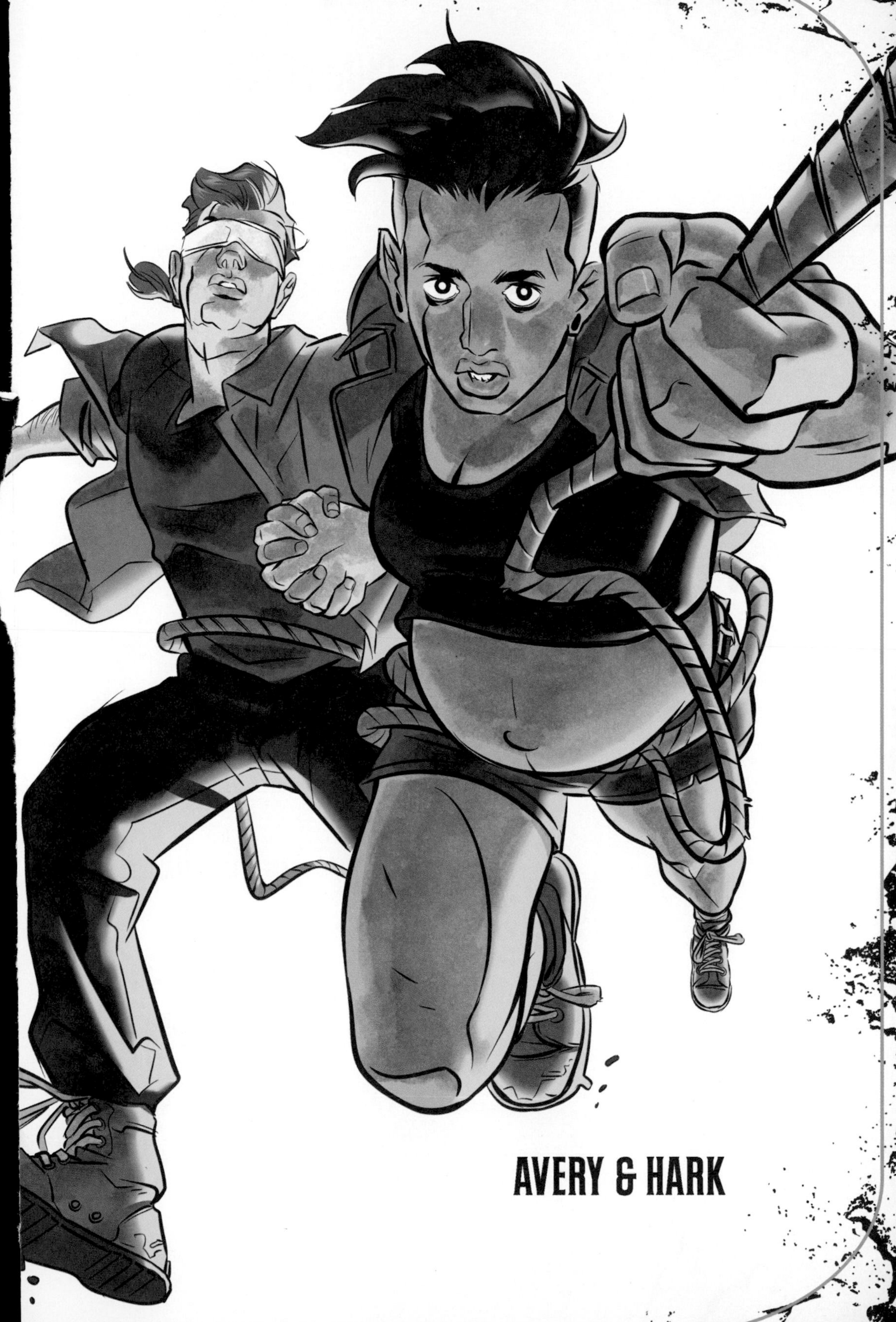
AVERY & HARK

CHARACTER DESIGNS

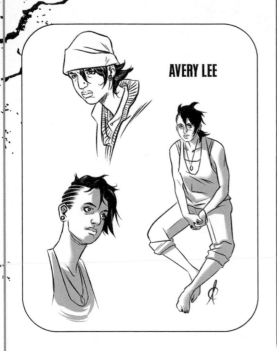

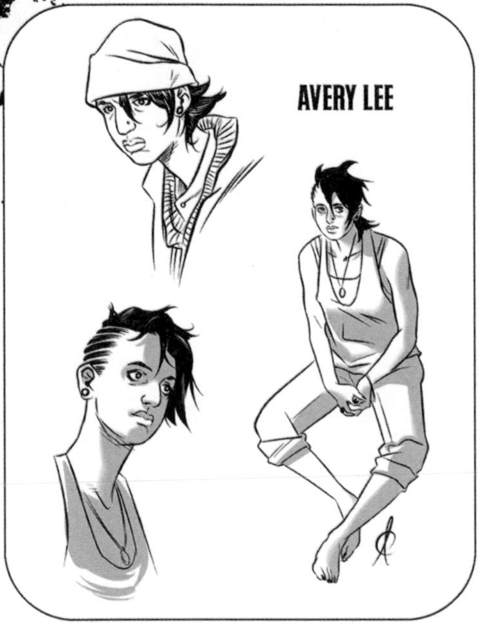
AVERY LEE

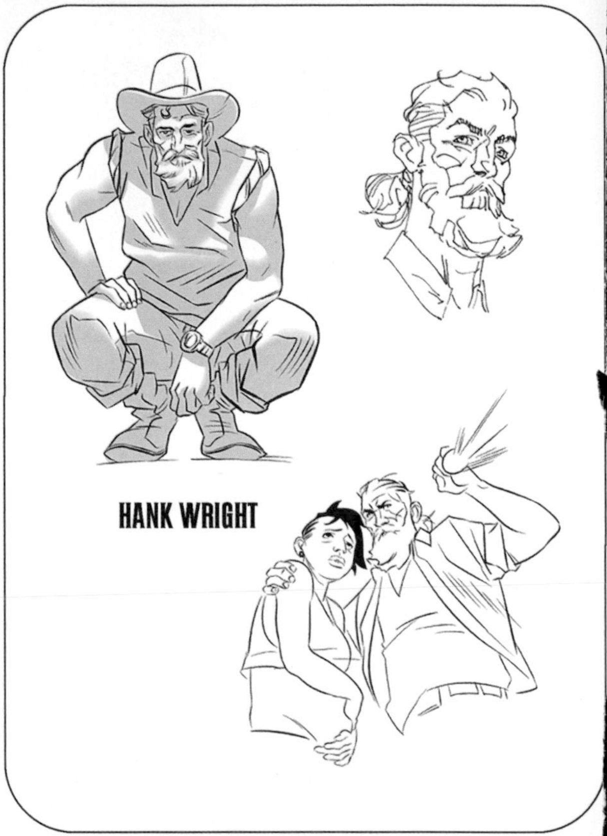
HANK WRIGHT

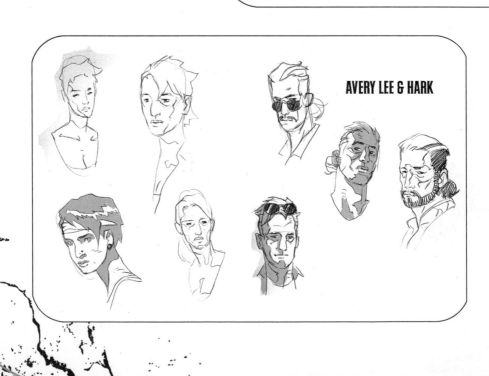

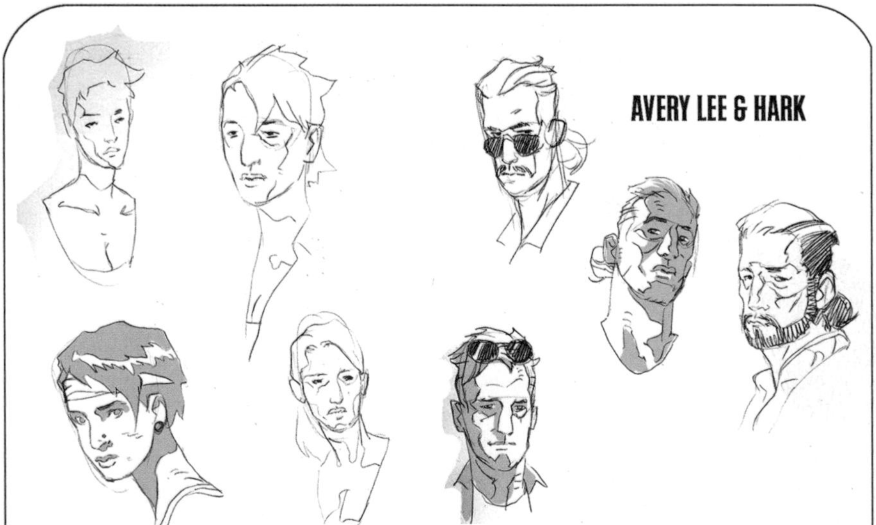
AVERY LEE & HARK

FIRST ITERATION OF SAN DIEGO COMIC CON PREVIEW

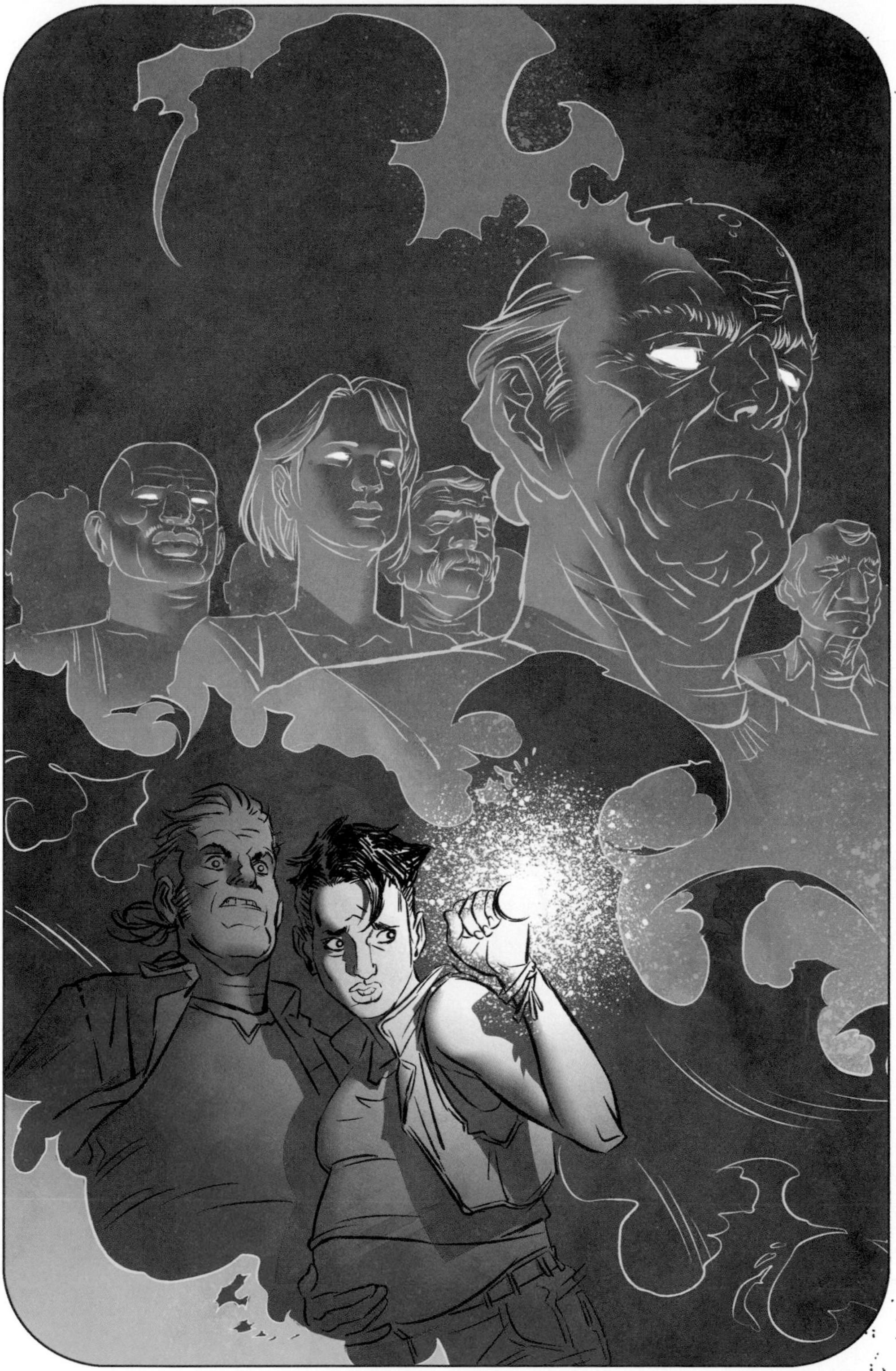

DESIGN:
EVOLUTION OF A LOGO

FISSURE

2014
INITIAL DESIGN

FISSURE

2015
ITERATION TWO

2016
SINGLE ISSUE PRINT

FISSURE

FISSURE

2016
SINGLE ISSUE VARIANT

2018
TRADE PAPERBACK

FISSURE